Bloody Oath

An Apocalyptic LitRPG

The System Apocalypse:// Australia / Book 3

By

Tao Wong & KT Hanna

License Notes

This is a work of fiction. Names, characters, businesses, places, events, and incidents are either the products of the author's imagination or used in a fictitious manner. Any resemblance to actual persons, living or dead, or actual events is purely coincidental.

This book is licensed for your personal enjoyment only. This book may not be re-sold or given away to other people. If you would like to share this book with another person, please purchase an additional copy for each recipient. If you're reading this book and did not purchase it, or it was not purchased for your use only, then please return to your favorite book retailer and purchase your own copy. Thank you for respecting the hard work of this author.

Bloody Oath

Published by Starlit Publishing
PO Box 30035
High Park PO
Toronto, ON
M6P 3K0
Canada

www.starlitpublishing.com

Ebook ISBN: 9781778550362
Paperback ISBN: 9781778550355
Hardcover ISBN: 9781778550379

Books in the System Apocalypse Universe

System Apocalypse: Australia

Town Under

Flat Out

Bloody Oath

Main Storyline

(Completed series with 12 books)

Life in the North

System Apocalypse: Relentless

A Fist Full of Credits

Dungeon World Drifters

Anthologies and Short stories

System Apocalypse Short Story Anthology Volume 1

System Apocalypse Short Story Anthology Volume 2

Valentines in an Apocalypse

A New Script

Daily Jobs, Coffee and an Awfully Big Adventure

Adventures in Clothing

Questing for Titles

Blue Screens of Death

My Grandmother's Tea Club

The Great Black Sea

A Game of Koopash (Newsletter exclusive)

Lana's story (Newsletter exclusive)

Debts and Dances (Newsletter exclusive)

A Tense Meeting (Newsletter exclusive)

Comic Series

The System Apocalypse Comics (7 Issues)

Contents

To Lars

For having my back when I panic attack

Thank you

Previously in Flat Out:

Kira learns to manage her Mana Sense ability by enhancing her sight with ocular implants all while juggling Jackson and Wisp's newfangled educations and helping to run the settlement she owns.

With System placed quests encouraging the growth of their settlement residents, and an Intergalactic Rare Species Hunter's Alliance (IRSHA) breathing down her neck, Kira and the other leaders battle to keep the constantly spawning mutations from encroaching on their safe zone.

When the Crafting Cartel moves in, and run ins with IRSHA begin to get heated, Kira thinks maybe the worst has come to pass. But another species of mercenaries moves into the area upping the danger factor for the human survivors and in the end Kira and co must decide just which is the greater danger to them.

Chapter One:
Combat Wombat

13 Weeks Post System Onset

11pm

Wombat armor plating hurts like buggery when you slide down it. I knew this well from experience and picked myself up off the ground after yet another tumble from her back. The burning sensation from the cheek abrasion slowly dulled as I look at the massive creature.

Even though the walls behind her stood around fifteen feet tall as they helped secure the perimeter of the settlement, her sheer size made them appear smaller. The expression on her face seemed contrite, like she hadn't wanted to hurt me. I patted her flank and murmured "It's okay. The good old System already took the pain away."

Some of the tension leaked out of Mumma's body. I didn't lie; my own pain was already receding, and I knew in ten minutes the injury would be but a memory.

Still . . . if I wasn't careful, there was a distinct possibility that I could fall and break my neck next time, and if I severed my spinal cord—well, there was no coming back from that sort of injury. System or no System.

Damn it. Maybe riding her into battle was just a pipe dream.

Congratulations! You have completed the quest:

A Habitable Safe Zone

Part Three: Staying Power

You need to make it three months into System Onset as a Township.

Goals:

1 - Gather 3,000 total inhabitants. This may include visiting species. Current population 3,272/3,000

2 - Build up your defenses and successfully survive and remain in your growing township for three months from System Onset. Current staying power 13 weeks/13 weeks

Reward: 45,000 Credits for your city Treasury, Expansion Perimeters increased, Defense Bolster amended to Level 1A

Time Limit Remaining: 0 days 0 hours and 00 minutes

Well Done! You jumped through yet another hoop. Don't spend it all at once!

Fantastic. I played with the fur on Mumma Wombutt's flank as I waited for the next popup I knew was coming.

Congratulations! You have been granted a follow up quest.

A Habitable Safe Zone

Part Four: Humans, Aliens, and Survivors, Oh My!

3 months is nothing. How about we try for 12 months? But wait, there's more than one thing you need to do for this specific quest.

Goals:

1 - Gather 10,000 total inhabitants. This may include visiting species. Current population 3,272/10,000

2 - Build up your defenses and expand your settlement to a Level-2 township at the minimum

3 - Expand the Crafting Cartel's reach to intergalactic (the explanation for which can be found in the Shop)

4 - Become self-sufficient as far as food, water, and education goes 42/100% achieved.

5 - Survive until the first year has passed.

Reward: 250,000 Credits for your city Treasury, [unknown] reward.

Time Limit Remaining: 39 Weeks.

Good luck with that.

Congratulations! You have been granted a follow-up bonus quest!

A Habitable Safe Zone

Part Four B: Just a few more!

To tide you over while you desperately attempt to survive, here is a midway quest you can work on.

Keep up the good work

Goals:

1 - Gather 5,000 total inhabitants. This may include visiting species. Current population 3,272/5,000

2 - Expand your Township to the first extension point

3 - Utilize the Town's quest-giving system more efficiently. Or. Use it at all!

4 - Survive 6 months as a township.

Reward: 25,000 Credits for your city Treasury.

That's it. Nothing else. It is just a bonus quest.

I pushed my black hair out of my eyes and glanced up at Mumma, who regarded me with one massive and solemn brown eye as the gate loomed up behind her. Maybe she could see the damned quests too. I didn't have the head space for this right now.

"Yeah, girl. I know. It's late."

She gently puffed out a breath at me, making it cloud up in the cool night air. Crickets chirped somewhere close enough for us to hear, and for a moment I wondered how big they were now. If I hadn't been standing next to a giant mutated wombat trying to train her to be my combat partner, it

11

might have been a regular night pre-apocalypse.

"Kira?" Evelyn's voice surprised me. Had I just not been paying enough attention, or was she using one of her stealth abilities?

Still, she made me smile and I petted my wombutt Mumma once more before heading inside the center. Just this side of midnight and my body was starting to feel bone weary. System or not, I definitely felt my age right now.

Looping arms with the Ranger, I squeezed in a feeble imitation of a hug. "Everything sorted?"

She raised an eyebrow, even if she wasn't looking directly at me. "Sort of. Alliances are all well and good, but this one is causing me more of a headache than I think it's worth. You could cut the tension with a damned . . ."

"Arrow?" I inserted, glad when it made her lips quirk up in a smile.

"Yeah. We'll say it was arrow."

I chuckled, the ache in my body exacerbated by the cool night air. She was right about the tension. Even from here, being able to see the camps set up in the parking lot that belonged to our tentative allies IRSHA, the Hakarta, and the Zarrie, I could feel this wave of taut Mana, as if it was just waiting to burst free and devour everything in its path.

Not like the Mana that suffused everything around us, no, this particular blue wave of power was all of our allies, and I truly use that term loosely. Allies waiting on tenterhooks to see who was going to be the first to break the uneasy truce. You know, either that, or the evolving mutations to overrun us all and eat us. Whichever came first.

I sighed and Evelyn squeezed my arm this time. "Maybe they'll take their aggression out on the rampant mutations instead—you know, the whole reason for the alliance."

This time I laughed. It still seemed a surreal bloody oath for them to have taken. "Yeah. We can hope, right?"

"Wisp is asleep, but I have to tell you." She paused and looked at me. "We need a house or something larger than that tiny shop because the damned baby wombat isn't so baby sized anymore."

She wasn't wrong.

"Guess that means we need a pretty big house." I glanced at her. Was it a mistake to just want to keep her with me? Maybe? But I was going to be a bit selfish for once.

"I could get used to this lull," she said as we walked into the center.

It made me cringe. "Did you have to say that? You know how jinxes work, right?"

"You're superstitious." She laughed and the sound echoed through the entryway and down the massive corridor. Most of the time she was as sunny as the freckles across her nose suggested and because of how often we were out patrolling, the sun bleaching in her hair continued right down to the roots.

"I'd rather be superstitious and still here tomorrow than not and dead," I grumbled. The center itself felt quiet and I wasn't sure if quiet was a good thing. When she said lull, it was all relative. There hadn't actually been a lull in patrols, fighting, or our groups trying to level.

What had happened was that, at least for now, we didn't have any massive mutations trying to break down our town walls.

Approaching midnight meant that most of our communal areas were empty, the bulk of our people in bed. Only night patrols and guard duty were really still on shift. Raybucks was the only one of our little eating or crafting places that pulled an all-nighter. Even now there were about a dozen people milling around and inside it.

As if we hadn't lost over sixty percent of the population when the world ended.

❖

Pulling my reinforced jacket on as I rushed out of our little apartment, I realized it had a massive hole in one sleeve and that a Shop trip was well on the cards. No time for that right now. Dolores didn't call and wake me up for trivial things.

Wisp drifted with me, riding on Wombie's trotting little back. Of course, she could now since he was definitely the size of a Welsh pony. Just a lot plumper. People got out of the way quickly, making it easier to rush and pick up my coffee on the way to the library.

Bonus of your daughter having a mutated wombat as a pet. Not to mention Dog, who was only marginally smaller, bringing up the rear.

Red didn't even pause as he held out my kipatchya while taking someone else's order. He flicked the longer side of his red hair out of his face and grinned in my direction briefly. All the acknowledgement I needed.

He'd taken to stocking a hefty load of kipatchya once I'd taken a liking to the beverage our resident Pharyleri, Ginali, had suggested. It made me wonder if maybe he'd waved a magic fantasy gnome-like wand and made me love the stuff. I'd have to have a chat with the crafter at some stage. I swear the stuff was more addictive than coffee, and tasted so, so much better. There had to be something he wasn't telling me.

Finally, in almost record time, I made it to the library doors.

"Mum. Wait." Wisp slid off her not-horse and proceeded to throw her arms around my waist. "Love you. Don't let them push you around."

And then, just as fast as she got off her mount, she was back on him and halfway back to the commons.

We were going to have to have a talk about that. Closing in on nine and

I could barely keep a handle on her.

Six in the morning was not my favorite time of any day.

The library was crowded. We were going to need somewhere bigger for council meetings, but for that we first needed to expand the city and push people into actual housing so that this could be interim housing and administration, crafting, and the Shop.

That, however, was a discussion for another day.

I'd never in my life imagined that we would be entertaining beings that were nine feet tall in here. But there was Mon'swkinon in all his glory. Hulking, grey stony-skinned humanoid sapient. We'd started out on the wrong foot, and I was damned glad we were sort of allies now. He stood off to the side, and I think he was frowning.

Hirish, my almost-sort-of friend Hakarta commander was, however, death glaring the Zarrie talking to him. Piola, the interim leader of the Finite Zarrie clan, was returning that glare for all she was worth. Ah, that was why Dolores called me out early.

I glanced to the side to see the older woman rocking back slightly in her office chair with her forefinger and thumb pinching the bridge of her nose. Though it was possible she had a headache, I was fairly certain it was all she could do to avoid blowing her temper at them.

Especially at six in the morning. I couldn't get the time out of my head. It was really ruining my mood.

Neither Kyle nor Mike were here yet; neither was Dale.

Just Dor, myself, and our allies. Did they not sleep or something?

"Morning all," I said, much cheerier than I felt, adjusting my ocular implants almost involuntarily to seek for trace amount of subtle Mana subterfuge. Our little alliance wasn't that bad, but it was fresh and new, and I couldn't be too careful.

"Kira." Hirish nodded in my direction, crossing his arms. His demeanor only softened ever so slightly as he removed his gaze from Piola. "Does this mean we can get started?"

I blinked at him, trying to wrack my brain for something I'd forgotten. Combat Wombat training attempts—check. Make sure my kids were still alive and kicking and cleaned my teeth—check. Practice my Mana Sensing abilities and see if I could make out more of the messages, I knew were encased in the power but couldn't crack yet—check.

Nothing in my head had marked a full-on alliance meeting early in the morning.

"You'll have to refresh my memory. Get started on what, Commander?"

I could practically feel Piola grinning from ear to ear, like I'd just proven her right in some odd way. Great, now I was siding with people unknowingly.

Hirish cleared his throat. "Not a meeting, precisely. More coordinating. While there is this pause in the severity of the attacks on us, we should take this opportunity to eradicate some of the stronger mutation strands. There should be efficiency. No wasting of time."

I mulled it over, because he was right, but I was fairly certain we'd already been doing this even before we signed that bloody oath contract thing they did a week or so ago. No harm to the humans or their deemed allies as long as the mutual mutation threat hung over all our heads. I hadn't been about to tell them that I didn't see these huge mutations ever stopping.

Morning Kira sipped on her kipatchya attempting to ignore the fact that in previous times this might have been an email. To be honest, I was just sour at how my training with Mumma Wombutt was not progressing.

Mon'swkinon stepped forward, clearing his throat. It sounded like a rockfall waiting to happen as a low-grade earthquake passed through the region. "We've located a nest of Emugators. At least, we're fairly certain we've found them."

I raised an eyebrow, pulling my coffee cup from my lips, my interest aroused despite my fatigue. "Wait, the mutations are breeding now?" Because you know an alligator in an egg was bad enough, as was an emu. Combine them and I didn't even want to think what sort of nightmare babies that entailed. Hell, we'd met them all grown up.

"Guessing we don't want anyone coming across those cute chicks and being mauled to death by them. Sure, we can go kill them." Still though, there was more. No way there couldn't be. "Now, come on, Hirish. You know me better than this. And you know better than to wake me up at six in the morning and then beat around the bush. Out with it."

Lousesh, Hirish's lieutenant, chuckled and quickly turned it into a cough, but I could tell. I motioned with my fingers, pointing at him from my eyes. I'm watching you, mate. Yeah. He got the message. My implants adjusted slightly, gathering his heat signature. Yep. Don't fuck with pre-kipatchya Kira.

Hirish took a deep breath, and it was then I realized that everyone had probably lumped this on his shoulders because I got on well with him. "We want to send more of our people out with each of your patrols. It will make our containment of the surrounding threats more effective."

I pondered that for a moment, because, and call me silly, but I didn't see what the problem . . . ah, except I did. "Experience?"

Hirish nodded.

"My—" And he glanced to either side of himself and then sighed. "*Our* concern is that we need to be smarter. Fewer injuries will mean that we can proceed faster. If we send out larger groups with more chaperones, we will take care of more of the threats with less danger to all, and also provide good combat training and experience." He raised his hands in a shrug. "The downside is that, even with the increased experience allocated to Australia with its Class-7 inhospitable ZFQ rating by the System, you're all going to level a lot slower than you have been.

"In our professional assessment, that might just be the price you have to pay for survival."

Blunt. I could do blunt. Wish I had one, but that was beside the point right now. My brain was aching.

"No. Yeah. You're right, mate," I muttered under my breath. Because he was, and there wasn't any way I was getting around that. "Let's err on the side of making it through these mutant attacks alive."

Dolores sighed, but it wasn't one of those resigned ones, just pure relief.

Mon'swkinon stepped forward. "Piola and I will make a list of our best people to go along on these hunts with you. Until this threat is controlled, we will work with you instead of separately."

"Good to know." Frankly, it was just a relief that giant rock man was still on my side. Being enemies with someone who could probably lift a car up and throw it at you . . . not my cup of anything.

It was closing in on seven and my damned drink had gotten cold. Screw that. I was going to get another one before the day actually started. "Hirish. You're buying me another drink because we all know this could have waited another hour."

He inclined his head and followed me, catching up in no time. "Forgot that you humans have a woeful constitution."

"Fucker," I muttered but couldn't help the smile that crossed my face. Of all the alien-invaded countries in the galaxy, the sassy aliens had to walk into mine.

Chapter Two:
New Patrols

Hirish wasn't kidding when he mentioned that we'd organize new patrols. It took mere hours for them to set up this new form of torture for the rest of us. Them being Kyle, Mike, and Dale along with our alien tormentor-allies. They were both synonymous in my mind right about now.

Training our skills in the field with more members to prevent unnecessary death or injury. Sounded like a plan, but I had a distinct feeling this was going to suck. Leveling and coordination-wise.

Hefting my Warhammer in my right hand, I glanced back at my updated group.

There was Dannin, the lithe elf like figure who apparently thought mimicking popular franchises was the way to go when traversing a Dungeon World. His blond hair was always getting in the way, but I had to admit he was good with his bow. Sange, the amazingly stoic healer who I listened to when they spoke. They might not speak much, but when they did, it was worth hearing.

Molly, as always, fought side by side with her healer. Her tanking showed true strength and expertise as she wielded the tower shield almost her size with practiced skill. Not that it was difficult to be her size, she was tiny. Today, however, we had a new tank with us, learning the ropes.

Declan Jones
Deflection Weaver
Level 39

He was a newcomer to the settlement, and from what I could tell, an avoidance tank. His specialty was not getting hit. Which, to be honest, I kind of loved. Molly took him under her wing, even though their styles were in complete juxtaposition to one another.

Kyle, my twin, stood in discussion with several newcomers I swore to try and learn their names, but I wasn't promising anything. His short black hair moved with the faint breeze, and I still envied the few inches of greater height he had on me.

We had twelve humans in total, two Hakarta, one Zarrie, and one IRSHA member. Right now, Kyle was instructing the lower levels we'd taken with us to help learn how our groups fought in combat. The idea was to give everyone more experience fighting with varied people. Except right now, while Kyle was instructing them, it took away five of our fighters and reduced our attack power substantially while he went over their powers and best uses for them.

This wasn't ideal when there was a nest of angry mutated cane toads just begging to be cleared out. Not that we'd made them angry, just that toads in general weren't serene creatures. Okay, I wasn't completely sure about their mood, but if I were them, I know I'd be a bundle of angry.

Turning around, I eyed Kyle, who gave me a brief nod, also obviously picked up by Hirish. It seemed we had the go ahead move out of our prep area and into the nest to clear the buggers out.

Molly moved out in front, planting her feet defensively as she brought her shield down into the ground in front of her. Sange, close behind. Clearing nests happened to be one of the best changes the Hakarta had made to how we dealt with mutated monsters. More efficient, quicker, and it was going to give our new group formations much more leniency in teaching newcomers the ropes.

I dodged yet another strike by the angry Caneglobulous. Damn it, I despised toads and their warty skin, and toxic spit. Especially when they'd grown to be the size of small cars and decided to hang around in packs and take on some elements of the alien globules. Globules which I also hated fighting.

You know what? I hated fighting.

Following the faint blue wave of power exuding from its skin, I knew another spit attack was about to happen. The more I focused on my Mana Sense, the easier it was becoming to preempt the magical system powered moves of whatever crossed my path. At least, so long as they were using Mana in their abilities anyway.

I was itching to test it out on other humans too. Just to see what it was I could interpret. How much could I really warn us about—how far could I push this?

Just as the main target began to spit, I launched myself to the side. Once I landed, I darted in as fast as I could, swinging my hammer up into the side of the creature. At the same time, I activated Water Siphon to weaken the creature. There was a crunch as my hammer impacted, fueled by my speed, its strength, and the push of Mana behind it.

Skin crashed inward, and the creature's mouth opened wide, almost as if in surprise. Exploding air from its mouth ruffled my hair, along with a stink best not described outside of the way it churned my stomach.

Yanking the hammer back, barely keeping a handle on it, I shoved my weight back into my heels. I refused to get bowled over by my own momentum. Trying to copy the movements Hirish showed me about a week ago.

I was going to take that momentum and swing it around so I could land another resounding crunch. Pushing along with the energy I'd already gathered with ambient Mana that lingered all around us, I clenched my jaw as the force almost made my hands slip. The attack worked. Maybe not as efficiently as Hirish would have done it, or as well as anyone who'd ever used weapons before could have, but it was good for me. It was progress.

As the hammerhead sank into the flesh of the creature again, this time with enough force that it ripped through layers of skin, I had a moment to regret that I didn't have better balance yet.

The momentum yanked me forward, causing me to stumble, and I only narrowly missed being spat on by one of the other three of the creatures around us.

"Nice, Kira."

Hirish's words hit home, and it was all I could do not to blush like a kid getting praise from a teacher. Still. At my age, I never thought I'd be learning hand-to-hand combat. Well. Hammer-to-toad combat, maybe? I checked my Mana and cast another Mana Transfer to each of the other toads, keeping my own well filled, just in case.

Soon I'd be able to regenerate Mana for the group. *Come on experience, tip me over.*

Even though the canopy was still full and leafy, it let in nice shafts of light. So, when that light suddenly disappeared, we all crouched low instinctively. I shielded my eyes from too much sunlight and looked up, knowing instinctually what it was anyway.

From above us, far up in the air, there echoed a keening sound, mournful in its own way as the Magon passed overhead. Hell, even the Caneglobulous stopped moving for a moment. Like maybe if the Magon didn't see us, it wouldn't dive down and devour us.

After a few seconds that felt like a lifetime, the pass over was done, and Molly didn't lose another second reinforcing the upper hand. I shook myself, bringing me back to the rotation I needed to maintain.

Implantation in place so I could contribute damage and some regeneration while I fought, I threw myself back into the battle. Best form of therapy I'd found yet. And bet your arse that when the apocalypse hit, there was all sorts of shit you had to work out. Fighting was therapeutic and used my time wisely. Win-win.

Evelyn's arrows whizzed past my head in quick succession, and I was proud of the fact that I didn't even flinch. That had to mean she'd already worked with Dannin to dispatch the Caneglobulous Molly and Sange had focused on. Ray's ice bolts shot past my other side, landing with a sickening thud into the flesh of the next quickly fading opponent. He'd grown up in the last couple of weeks, channeling his anger into the actual fights instead of lashing out in bursts.

Wasn't sure how long that'd last.

Tasha and her Spellsword casting dance would be here shortly with me to work on taking this one down, and then I'd change to another, bash it up, set it up, and then mow it down again. Even as Kyle and his little group of lower Level 30s worked through their own spell lineups methodically, I moved onto the next toad on the list so I could tap it and replenish my own Mana base, weaken it with Water Siphon so everyone's hits did more damage, and cast Implantation to inflict some damage and a little extra splash of healing. Everything helped.

Then of course was the fun of bashing the crap out of it, and helping my team knock it down. All the while monitoring the feel of their Mana— the signature, if you will. The more I could recognize, the more I'd understand about my abilities.

This is what we were doing now. Find a nest, wipe it out. Move onto the next. Take more people so we don't get reckless, level those with lower Levels and live to fight another day.

Experience gain had slowed. Like slug speed going up an incline during a torrential downpour. Still, I had to admit that I much preferred this way of fighting, this slow crawl of skills to losing people who were coming to matter to me.

Finally, the last Caneglobulous in this nest was taken care of. Four, maybe five? I think I'd lost count. It took a couple of moments for me to realize I was the one gasping, the one who was out of breath. Evelyn handed me a bottle of water and I gulped it down like I hadn't seen the substance in a year.

"Nice work, everyone," Hirish said approvingly. It was probably the first time since we'd signed the treaty that I didn't regret the extra fighting instruction. He was taking this keeping-us-alive shit seriously.

It had taken him days to talk me into combat training. I kept skirting the fact that I needed it. There were my Mana skills, I said. How about all my earth-based spells, I'd asked him. But when it came down to it, he was right.

Combat was my weak point, and I had kids and now a settlement to survive for.

Safety first, strength would come. All of this helped us work together better as units. As much as I wanted to tease Kyle about the people he'd brought with us, it was the right thing to do. Spread out the potential damage we could take and compound the damage we delivered.

A couple of the newcomers looked familiar, but to be honest, I couldn't keep all the names straight anymore, and these guys appeared to be relatively new additions. Additions who'd managed to hit Level 30 by themselves needed to be given more credit.

Tasha flopped down next to me with a tired smile. "That damn Magon never fails to scare the shit out of me."

I laughed and glanced back up at the sky. "Right there with you. I'm glad it seems to scare all of the creatures, too."

"One of these days we're all going to be too busy watching the magpie dragon that we'll get creamed by what we were fighting." She chuckled a little and then pushed herself back up. "Gotta go hobnob with Hirish. He said he wanted to talk."

I watched her go, glad that she could laugh now. She'd lost her partner months ago when we were scouting near that Rigoll we fought. We'd never found his body. Talk about lack of closure.

Evelyn reached forward from next to me and rubbed my upper arm. "You know that Warhammer is dangerous. Or maybe I should say you're sort of scary with that thing."

I smiled. "Damn right I am."

She laughed, yet maybe there was some nervousness in there too. After all, she remembered what I'd been like when we fought that first Mollecupai almost three months ago. I hadn't been strong enough for this weapon back then and it took me over, reducing me to something I wasn't proud of and didn't want to be.

So that's why I'd come out here and kill shit and let my experience gain claw itself up to the next level. When all was said and done, I needed the strength to know I wasn't going to become a danger to the people I cared about when I decided to dive in and smash shit.

It was only two in the afternoon when we got back to Garbo. Almost six hours of clearing out nests and checking down multiple different streets on the way home, just in case we could find someone new, some survivor we'd missed.

These days it was more likely that we found no one. Torn and shredded corpses, bleached bones and the occasional missing limbs were all the more common. Enough time had passed that even the smell of decay was no longer as prominent. I tried not to look at the smaller bodies, the ones that reminded me all too much of my own kids.

Apocalypses weren't picky as far as casualties went.

It was a grim task, but one that was necessary. We still added to our population on a daily basis, and the shopping center was becoming fucking crowded. Way too many people crammed into such a tiny bloody space.

Jolting me from my morose thoughts, a notification appeared, flashing from the corner of my vision. Hmm.

Oh, I'd leveled. Fucking-finally. I was really starting to see how much I needed my damned Mana Stone spell, and now I'd finally hit the tier I needed to get the Skill.

I popped my attribute skills in too and rounded up my overall Strength, Constitution, Intelligence, Perception, and Willpower.

Status Screen			
Name	Kira Kent	Class	Ecological Chain Specialist
Race	Human (Female)	Level	40 (16,259 XP to next Level)
Titles			
Diviner			
Health	530	Stamina	530
Mana	1200	Mana Regeneration	15.2ps*
Attributes			
Strength	35	Agility	30
Constitution	53	Perception	82

Intelligence	120	Willpower	75
Charisma	25	Luck	20
Class Skills			
Shield of Power		Leadership	3
Analyze	5	Mana Sense*	17
Diviner*	2	Mana Purification	1
Blunt Weapons	6	Mana Cloak	4
Combat Skills			
Mana Attunement	2	Water Siphon	2
Earth Barricade	2	Blood Transfer	1
Rock Slide	1	Mana Transfer	2
Implantation	3	Treesong	2
Top Soil	2	Mud Slide	1
Planted in Place	1	Blood Dispersion	1
Stone's Throw	1	Vine Defense Mana Stone	1
Mana Stone	1		

Mana Stone (Level One)

Effect: Taps into the Mana field of your opponent, sapping their Mana stores and distributing heightened Mana Regeneration to your entire target group. Level 1 redistribution equals 1mps for up to 8 people. 0.5mps if more to a maximum of 15. Mana Cost: 135 per cast - 5-minute duration

Not as strong as I would have liked, but powerful enough. Better than a hit in the head with a sack of cement, at any rate. Sixty Mana per minute was a lot if I thought about it; thirty wasn't bad either. It was more than anyone had right now, and I hoped that it leveled up with each point put in the Skill, but damn was it expensive to cast.

I desperately needed to stop buying every Skill, but the top-tier ones I was coming into were worth it. Thankfully, Basic Class builds were supposedly unimportant once you became a Master Class or something like that. If only the grind weren't so damned long.

Time to stop dawdling in the entrance hall.

Pushing my screens out of my sight, I walked in farther. Past the old news agency, I didn't even spare a glance back toward the library. I was looking for Jackson, not having seen him this morning after I left our little apartment. The kid was always busy, and I could feel the need to keep him close just that much longer. Granted, that wasn't anything apocalypse induced. That was my little boy growing up and me being a mother.

No. Don't go! Come back and give me hugs.

Yep. I knew it, and yet it was like a biological urge to keep him safe. Stupid human brains.

He was nowhere in sight as I made my way slowly through the center, not even in our little shop.

Wisp on the other hand was already sitting at my usual table at Raybucks waiting for me as I returned from the showers. Damn, did I just want my own place with my own damn bathroom. I had maybe thirty minutes to catch up with her, scarf my food down, and get to the library for our daily planning meeting.

"Ordered your food, Mum," she said without looking up. Wisp always sat to the outside of the coffee shop because Wombie and Dog took up so much room. She held a book she was reading, and I realized she'd nabbed some of her favorite series from the kids' section in the library. Good. Let's give the kids a bit of escapism while we still could.

"Thanks, love. You eating?" Two in the afternoon was pretty late for lunch, but most of the patrols took about six hours. Starting at eight in the morning meant having a late lunch. Sometimes they took less time, occasionally even more, but as a general rule we were back just after the afternoon patrols headed out.

Some of the destinations involved driving for thirty minutes to get to where we needed to be, always on the lookout for monsters or more people along the way.

"Mm-hm," she mumbled, obviously engrossed in the book.

I smiled as Red plopped a steaming cup of kipatchya down in front of me, and what I think might have been some sort of sliced meat on a toasted sandwich. He gave Wisp what seemed to be mac 'n' cheese and some fruit that appeared to be apple like. I didn't really ask what the food I ate here was, just took it on good authority that Red wasn't trying to kill me. As long as it was tasty, I wasn't going to argue.

For all the problems we had, at least the damn System had made most monsters edible. We'd found that juicy bit out from the aliens, which helped with the entire food stock problem. Still didn't want to think about what I was eating too much, though. All I knew was that our resident head chef, Paul, who Red dug up, could work magic with anything.

"You looked like you could do with a double shot, so that's what you've got. Want you to try my new mix of kipatchya coffee one of these days when I get the mixture just right." Red winked, but there was still a lingering sadness beneath his eyes. He'd lost his brother not even two weeks into this shitstorm. Now he helped Ray out with the rationing for the coffee shop as well as the rest of the settlement's food supplies.

"Thanks, mate. I'll be your guinea pig any day." I gave him a wink in return as he turned and left and drew in the aroma of the beverage warming my hands. Today the cold felt like it was seeping into my bones. Cold and I never got on.

"Mum," Wisp said, swallowing a mouth full of food. She'd left a tiny bit of cheese sauce at the corner of her mouth that had me itching to wipe it off for her.

"Yes?" I responded, physically having to restrain myself as my eyes fixated on the food.

She eyed me and licked her lips nervously, which thankfully dislodged the sauce and made me not obsess about it. "Can I take Wombie out to Mumma Wombutt on my own?"

I paused, fighting back the urge to just react with a no and really thought about it. She'd be nine years old soon. Not old by any extent, but not a little kid. She was strong and hadn't stopped her gymnastics exercises, and Dog and Wombie doted on her, guarded her even. "I'd prefer it if you had at least someone with you. An adult, your brother, some friends?"

I saw her face fall a bit, but she nodded, and I realized just how confusing this must be for a kid like her. How was she even dealing? Her best friends were mutated animals.

"You know what. Jackson has been working on that long-range communicator. The tech team should be done with it soon. As long as you message me or call me to let me know what you're doing so I can alert the people on guard duty to be aware of you—only because if we get attacked, I want them to get you inside," I added quickly when I saw her face. She'd thought I meant she was being baby-sat, which maybe it would be a bit like that, but it's not what I intended. "No longer than thirty minutes for now, and only once we get the communicator figured out, okay?"

Her face lit up and she practically preened. Pride shone in her eyes, and it made my heart ache just that little bit at how easy it had been to make her smile. Impulsively, I leaned around the table and gave her an awkwardly angled hug.

For a few moments I felt like she was clinging extra hard, and then we pulled away.

"Thanks, Mum." She smiled. "I won't let you down."

Reaching forward, I ruffled the top of her tidy black hair. She'd been putting it up in a ponytail for months now, keeping it out of the way. "You never do. No matter what happens, I will always love you. I hope you know that."

Her grin widened, and then I saw a moment of hesitance. "Do you think . . .there might be a way for us to contact Dad?"

I could feel her ache as it echoed my own. Keeping Mason from his kids had never been a part of our divorce. Right now, the apocalypse didn't give us a choice. "When we have the technology to communicate with the settlements farther than Carindale, or if we can mount a search team down there—we'll contact Dad as soon as we can, okay?"

"Awesome." A wave of relief washed over her face, and she leaned in closer. "You better eat that before you're late for your meeting."

Damn it.

Kids.

Chapter Three:

Expansion

Today's meeting had nothing to do with training, nothing to do with incoming new residents and their abilities, surprisingly nothing to do with the Cartel even though Ginali would be present. And nothing to do with leveling.

No, today was all about how to expand our borders without stretching ourselves too thin while still emptying the complex of a few thousand people.

The thing about the System and the way it worked made expansion sound like the best possible thing ever, except that the reality was anything but. We couldn't just buy a few houses and extend the boundaries. We had to go through explicitly chosen possibilities.

They made sense, even if we didn't like that fact that it did. So just pushing out to Tryon Street, for example, didn't make sense because that was a relatively small street and not a main thoroughfare. Which meant that out of the room for about eighteen hundred people, we needed eighty percent of that to be purchased outright from individuals or families before we could extend the borders and claim that area as part of our city.

Hirish and Lousesh, Mon'swkinon and Dequasha, Zyrilian and Piola all squashed into our tiny library with us as well as Ginali and several of his crafters. Then we had Mike, the head of our security in all his burly gruffness.

Frankly, I didn't envy him his position, considering I was pretty sure he'd been the one for organizing the patrols to clear corpses out of the houses in the surrounding areas. There were so many little things you just didn't think about until the actual apocalypse hit. I liked Mike. He was a good sort.

Dale and my brother Kyle sat together. They'd formed a bond only two medical professionals stuck with medical Class abilities could. Between them and their gathered brood of healing types, we had enough dedicated medical personal to send at least two of them out with each group that patrolled. And in the last couple of weeks, they'd really pulled their shit together.

No one wanted to lose people. It might be inevitable, but we'd be damned if we let it happen easily.

Evelyn sat next to me, munching on some sort of bar she'd probably got rationed out to her from Coles or something. With this many people to feed and no new delivery trucks, the supplies we'd inherited from the supermarkets in the center were dwindling.

There'd be no more Tim Tams soon.

Dolores and Sienna mumbled amongst one another. Dor was like the grandmother I'd left behind in the States when we moved to Australia in my teens. I had a real soft spot for her, and I'd fight to keep her just the way she was.

Sienna had learned to clamp down on her damned high Charisma since I'd first met her. Or else I'd grown used to it. No matter how hard she tried, she still oozed a portion of it everywhere. I could see it with my Mana Sense. Constantly in motion, in perpetual use. Maybe it resembled the slime some politicians seemed to thrive on. But in her case, with her adorable kid Rolo, I got the feeling she'd chosen what she did to keep them both safe.

I could cut her some slack.

I nudged Dor. "We are supposed to give out settlement quests?"

She glanced at me and requested to share her settlement interface. Once I accepted, she spoke in that succinct way she had. "Here. You can give them too. When you go out to fight each nest, make sure the group is working on a clearing quest. As the settlement owner, or organizer like I am, we can set which monsters to include in those quests. Or what items to fetch. Ginali probably has some crafting quests for the settlement too."

Guilt seeped into me. I should have been exploring the whole interface more. "We can give some experience?" My interest perked up at that.

Dor eyed me critically. "Yes, but it's limited by what type of quest, and how many undertake it. Still, it's better than giving our precious treasury money as a reward."

I nodded, and, while waiting for the rest of the council to gather, began to create a few quests for general monster clearing around the area—from the close ones with lower Levels, to the higher ones my patrols took out. A few hundred extra experience would add up eventually, and then we all won.

Molly and Sange always appeared at these things too. Their expertise in fighting as a tank and healer was often a part of the discussion considering how well they did it. Even if we weren't talking patrol tactics right now, they were an integral part of the operations around the settlement. After the meeting, I had no doubt they'd be training some of the lower-level tanks and healers in their ability to work as a team.

Yep. Everything changed when we made the alliance. To be honest, everything had changed for the better. Except maybe Hirish and Piola's moods.

The door burst open, and Chris ran in, her blond hair bouncing as she did. It had grown longer now, and the shorn side really needed a trim, but she was full of smiles, Sarah hot on her heels. Chris's partner's hair was like a sheet of hellfire. I was pretty sure Sarah had raided all the stores in the center for their hair color the moment she set foot in Garbo. Which was a good thing because the color suited her bubbly personality.

Another person I didn't recall followed them into the room, their eyes focused on the floor. Their brown hair was pulled back into a sharp ponytail and they walked hunched in on themselves as if they lacked the confidence that Sarah exuded.

"Sorry we're late!" Sarah smiled, waving around what looked like a pretty bulky watch in the air. "Rin will help us explain our news after we talk about expansion."

Sarah's expression changed to sheepish as she realized just how excited she sounded. It was a breath of fresh air. Rin was the new techy, then. Nice roundabout introduction there.

Dor smiled at her, cleared her throat, and spoke in that gravely endearing way of hers. "Right. Getting down to it then."

At that moment, Gemma slunk into the room, appearing in the middle of it. Her eyes were sunken and her skin pale, making her sun-kissed freckles stand out even more than usual. "Sorry I'm late. Scouted out the potential new borders."

Hirish nodded at her. "Clear?"

"Yeah. A couple of minor nests, but nothing that a group of twenties can't take care of." She plopped down on the other side of me, and I could practically feel the weariness radiating from her.

"Mike? You got the list of who can even potentially afford a damned house?" Dor was impatient. While these meetings were generally productive, I always got the feeling she'd prefer to be doing anything else.

Mike stood, grabbing a clipboard and paper. We were resilient buggers here in Australia. It wasn't that the Shop didn't have all sorts of tech we could have bought. But we had a plentiful supply of paper from all the retailers around us. Enough for the kids' arts and crafts, for them to use school supplies, and enough for us to do a lot of our inventories and important recording on. If we could avoid spending money in the Shop— we did.

Once we got our borders extended and could breathe a bit more, we'd look at figuring out all the alien tech we could get our hands on.

"We have about seven groups of people who want to pool their money and purchase one of the several apartment blocks around here. Which should get about five hundred people taken care of. I get the feeling they like the thought of safety in numbers. Can't blame them."

I heaved a sigh of relief. A couple of those buildings had like thirty units. The other few would easily house fifty people each. We could work with that.

"But then we also need to take care of the commercial spaces." Ginali spoke up, his voice nice and clear as it rang through the room. "We will purchase several of those spaces, bringing the Crafting Cartel's provisions closer to people who live farther away from Garden City."

Kyle spoke up before anyone could respond to the Pharyleri. "Look. Are we sure going up Newnham and crossing back down Mt. Gravatt Capalaba Road is the way we should be looking to expand?"

Gemma responded before anyone else could. "I would have agreed before my earlier patrol. But this area has fewer nests, and no damned Dungeon. For the most part there are plenty of single-family homes, but also communities like the retirement village and several apartment blocks. It's going to be the easiest way for us to expand. And the smallest we need to spread ourselves."

There it was. We couldn't afford to spread ourselves too thin. Not yet at least.

Kyle let out a heavy sigh. I knew he'd wanted to expand out the back, past the MacGregor Dungeon and out that way. But it was a lot of space, and I didn't think we could guarantee getting eighty percent of that paid for and recognized by the System as owned by the residents.

"What about families?" I asked, suppressing a sudden yawn attack.

Mike shrugged. "Surprisingly, a lot of them have been scrimping and saving. Most of us contribute to the food supplies and thus our food doesn't cost money. So gear and savings are what most adventurers have managed.

And a lot of those are family members, or friends with groups they want to split a house with."

"Especially considering this first expansion will be a close distance to the hub, we will probably fill up the eighty percent we need pretty fast," Sienna mused as she popped in numbers and adjusted the street locations. All of our council had access to the System information on our settlement. "It's a bit cramped in here for most of us right now."

"I hate to be the realist," Evelyn piped up. "But how are we going to do this? Walk around in a big group for safety reasons and let people claim the buildings or houses they want?"

I could hear the sarcasm, but probably because I knew her better than most.

Instead of choking down their laughter, Mon'swkinon grumbled an assent, and Hirish nodded emphatically followed by verbal reinforcement that he thought this was a good idea. "That actually sounds doable."

Then the Hakarta turned to Mike. "Can we allow people access to see the map and mark off potential living quarters they'll consider? Might make it quicker for all of them to be claimed."

Mike glanced at Dor who gave him an almost imperceptible nod. "Sure. We can work with that." I could practically see the cogs of his brain turning as he ran possibilities through his mind. He took his position as head of security very seriously.

"If we can figure out who wants what first. Perhaps the best bet would be to split up while they're claimed." Piola's tones carried. The jackal's interesting colorings always fascinated me. I kept wanting to boop her snoot, but I was quite certain she'd flay me where I stood.

"Still." Dolores frowned, changing a few of the parameters as she fiddled with the figures, and I pulled up the interface to watch what she was doing. "Even with all these volunteers, this might end up being tight. I would advise against people moving into their domiciles straight away since we'll have to get them all checked off first, and only once the System has verified that we've met its requirements will we be able to activate the new defenses. That'll take a few days."

A murmuring spread round the room. We were all getting restless. I knew I wasn't the only one who just wanted our own goddamned space. Three months in a cramped place full of way too many bodies had me gnashing at the bit.

But I could see Dor's point. There were so many prerequisites that we had to fill up. For example, when checking things off in the interface, those commercially designated areas were easier to leave as such. It appeared there were a whole other set of rules for potential commercial locations that we changed into living space. Best to just stick with what had been categorized.

"Time frame?" Gemma blurted out; her final vestiges of patience frayed. She never did well in meetings, but she was our resident stealth expert, and her reconnaissance was second to none.

Mike shrugged. "Day or two? Maybe three? I'd ideally like to have our status set with the System so the defenses can start rebuilding by the end of this week, start of the next."

"The settlement will be vulnerable for a little bit while they catch back up to what we have now. And we'll increase patrols while we wait and have to expand patrols afterward." Hirish paused, like he was gathering thoughts. "Yes. More land to cover. More vigilance required."

"That's the plan, then." Dolores clapped her hands like she was dismissing the meeting. "Mike, you'll have people begin checking off their preferred locations, right? So we'll be ready to go soon."

"Already on it, chief. Grabbing the council first. Need to make sure we'll all be in a place where we can get back here as soon as possible."

"Which brings me to our newly extended communications array!" Sarah had been holding that in since she'd stepped foot into the room, and I couldn't help smiling at her sheer enthusiasm. Granted, I was also plain excited that we might get to be a little more connected to one another. Safety issues. I didn't need any Angry Birds or game-type things.

Sarah pulled out the bulky watch she'd had when she initially entered and began going over its range and purpose. I could tell she'd visited the Shop for some of the gadgets that went into creating it.

But we had to be able to communicate more readily. The twins, Talia and Tarin, were only two people. Their unique ability to communicate with each other over almost any distance was unparalleled, and something we couldn't replicate. Our engineers were working on having enough ways for the council members to communicate freely, especially in time for the community to expand. I could deal with that.

Rin cleared her throat, eyes still downcast. "We are working at producing five for each patrol and should have them in a few days. However, there are components we can't source naturally and must purchase from the shop, so any contributions, donation-wise, would be greatly appreciated."

"Noted." Dor flashed a rare smile at the shy techy. "Is that all?"

Sarah gave Rin an encouraging nudge, and I felt like the redhead was trying to build her friend's confidence.

Rin rolled her eyes and squared her shoulders. "To start, we'll have to make sure patrols hand the watches onto the next group to go out. We won't have enough for a while. That's all."

Great. That settled that. Now I just needed to understand how the settlement interface worked with a bit more detail and my day would be going pretty well.

The Shop connection Rin mentioned, however, only reminded me that my jacket needed a replacement and Jackson was in need of new outer armor too. Getting some for Wisp wouldn't hurt either. And hell, if we were going to be getting our own houses, I wondered if the Shop had something like a cleaning spell, or I don't know, doing-the-housework spell. Because I didn't know about anyone else, but helping to run a settlement in the middle of the apocalypse wasn't conducive to my wanting to fold laundry.

Yep. I just used the apocalypse as a laundry excuse. And I wasn't even the least bit sorry.

❖

Mike cornered me immediately after Sarah and Chris finished going over the communication information. What lot did I want? Which house did I think was best suited for me?

And I had no fucking clue.

I glanced at the detailed overview contained in my settlement interface now that we'd chosen the potential expansion route. Damn, it was detailed. Each street, house number, potential floorplan, approximate costs to purchase, and taxation amount that would be dedicated to the settlement treasury.

Then it also listed the upkeep costs, remodeling costs which were all dependent on exactly what you wanted to do with the place. Connected hot water and electricity were extras, not to mention restoring the previous state of the dwelling. There were security options, and the ability to list who would live in the domicile.

Delving deeper into the interface, I realized that the settlement was in charge of road maintenance through the System, as in the cost came out of our treasury. Just like a regular old city council. The upside? The System could basically perform all of the tasks we'd otherwise need teams of people for—as long as we were willing to pay.

"Kira?" There was concern in Mike's voice and I realized he'd been waiting for me to respond. Here I was diving into the settlement management portion of the expansion instead of trying to find a house for my family.

Sure, there were a few houses just over the road and down a ways. But they didn't seem bright or airy. I wanted somewhere with enough of a yard to pop the wombutts in, and enough sunlight that Wisp wouldn't feel too enclosed when at home.

For all intents and purposes, I wanted somewhere we could hide and forget about the fact that the world around us had completely changed. Just for a little bit. Just every now and again. Just to hold onto those threads of sanity that still clung desperately to me despite our circumstances.

"I . . . "It was difficult to enunciate. How did I say that I wanted to be close enough that I could be here within sixty seconds, but that I didn't want to be anywhere close to here because it reminded me of so much? "Hey, some of these places are totally devastated?"

Go Kira. Change the topic for the win.

Mike smiled. "Hirish assures me the fix-up options or the restore options are remarkable."

I raised an eyebrow, thinking of the costs involved. "True. Not like the System will hire construction crews when it could do it all itself."

Mike glanced around at the mostly empty library. "Look. I'm giving you first choice. There are a couple I'd suggest, if you like?"

"Please?" Because too many choices always left me unsure of what option to pick.

"Okay, so there's this nice little brick place down here directly opposite the park on Tryon. It's a bit of a hike, but you can get one of the cars, or else the scooters. You know? Cut through the retirement village paths and shoot across to Garbo. You'd literally be here inside of two to three minutes."

I looked at the lot he was talking about. Right there on the corner of Mascar and Tryon. It was hidden by trees. Had a yard Mumma would likely squeeze into . . .but also a park she could roll in if needed. Hmmm. Wasn't too pricey, nor were the upgrades going to break the bank. "I like that. Got any others?"

"Yeah. Just up the road on Tryon. Directly opposite the retirement place—so an even straighter shot. Close to a lot of other people. Safe for the kids." He waited, expectantly.

He was right. They were both good choices. Within budget, doable. Though there was one more there that seemed to have a nice big yard. Would be great for Mumma. It was just up the road from the park so a little in between both locations. "Can we hold this one too? Let me run it by my kids and check to see it in person. We have to be able to fit the wombutts in there. And while I love the one across from the retirement village, it's got a lot of concrete and she's had enough of that in the carpark."

Mike chuckled. "You're a good egg, Kira. Fine. I'll hold these three. Not everyone is going to want a yard."

"Thanks, mate." I smiled, closed off the settlement interface, and headed outside to Mumma. Late afternoon meant that Wisp was with Jana doing one of the art extracurriculars. I never understood how that woman had so much kid energy. But then again, she had Avery helping now. I'd helped Avery's son, discovered my ability to trace sickened Mana, and helped Kyle heal shit he wouldn't have been able to find otherwise. She'd been eternally grateful, and I felt guilty as fuck for it. It wasn't like I wouldn't have done it for anyone—especially someone with a kid close to Jackson's age.

Then I was out of the center and found Mumma Wombutt sunning herself near the gates.

Or at least that was my first impression. Upon closer inspection, however, she was sunning herself in the precisely strategic spot that allowed her access to treats thrown from the guards as they patrolled the walls.

"Glutton," I mumbled at her, loving the feel of the strong afternoon sun on my face. Spring couldn't come soon enough for me. It'd be August shortly. And then things would start to warm up again. Her fur was warm to the touch, and I reached up to scratch around her chin as she lowered her face to me a bit.

Something about her presence always calmed me. The way she'd sought us out to help her protect her baby, the way she'd never forgotten it and done everything she could to repay us. And the way petting a mutated giant wombat under the chin just felt right.

I could go to the Shop tomorrow after training. I'd take Jackson with me too. Right now, though. For right now I was going to appreciate my newfound mutant friend and the fact that we'd all managed to survive the first three months of an apocalypse.

For better or for worse.

Chapter Four:

Shop Shenanigans

I ushered Jackson in front of me, his sullen expression such a delight to my heart. What thirteen-year-old ever wanted to go shopping with his mum? Especially when she came and got you in front of all your friends for the entire world to see?

Yeah. Not even one of them. Not even my boy. Not even when you were buying cool magical and tech shit from an intergalactic Shop.

Teenagers.

Still. He was growing and he needed new clothes. Preferably things that would increase his armor rating, up a few of his stats, and—my personal preference—boost his regeneration. I knew we were about to drop way too many Credits onto all of this stuff. But we needed it because we survived by getting stronger and having more abilities at our disposal.

Transitioning to the Shop was always instantaneous. One hand on the Shop orb, the next, we were in a whole different dimension.

Shi'enah glanced up as we came in. My inventory was full to exploding, and I knew Jackson had a lot on him too. After all, despite my misgivings, he was still venturing out with groups. Fairly close to the settlement mind you. I'd gotten that much of a concession out of him at least.

Considering he'd almost died during one of the sieges a couple of weeks ago, he just needed to put up with me extending my mum bubble of concern to include him for once.

"Can I really keep this, Mum?" Jackson asked as Shi'enah tallied up all of the items my son was selling. If there was anything for the Crafting Cartel, he'd long since sold it to Ginali, just as I had. But for the most part, there was always what I called grey trash that was simply that. Easily sold to the Shop to line our pockets.

"Of course. If you ever come out with me to fight the more dangerous creatures, we'll have to negotiate a bit, but you've killed everything you looted without any of my help. Whatever you get that we can't immediately use or craft with, it should be yours." Sort of like having a part-time job, but I didn't add that bit. Technically, with Australian labor laws, he was still too young to work.

The smile lit his face up like the sun, and I guess it was worth it. Maybe it told him that I was trying to give him his independence even if I might want to lock him somewhere and throw away the key just to keep him safe. Here I was being grown-up and all that shit.

"There is one condition. You can keep the cash on the proviso you spend a bit of it on like . . . self-preservation, okay? A new staff, a new armored jacket. Something. Okay?"

He grinned. "Read my mind, Mum."

Good, at least that interjection didn't backfire.

Finally, it was my turn.

"Caneglobulous toxin mold?" Shi'enah raised their exquisite foxlike eyes to meet my own. "You have been busy."

I laughed, but it was sadly lacking in humor. There wasn't much of it to go around when I was this exhausted. One of these days I was going to sleep. Not when I died, though. That song had been fun in my teens, but not so much now there were frequent opportunities for me to actually expire.

Mortality. It liked laughing in my face.

Finally, Shi'enah finished their tally. "121,928 Credits. I'll make it 122,000 if you promise to stop bringing in a week's worth at a time."

There was faint disapproval in their tone.

"Kira, you have to understand that even though your inventory preserves the items somewhat, depending on the type of items you're selling, good is not good enough. The fresher the better. The fresher, the more Credits." They paused, like they were trying to figure out if they'd screwed up the last part of that sentence. Then Shi'enah shrugged. "Promise?"

I laughed. "Fine. I will try harder, does that suffice?"

The fox narrowed their eyes. "Very well. But only because your son is much better about it than you are."

Ouch. That barb stuck.

Credits ticked over making the balance just that much healthier. Though I knew I was going to be draining the bank as soon as we moved house. I'd finally recovered from the damage buying my ocular implants caused.

"Anything in particular today?"

"That obvious?" I asked.

"You look like a being with a mission," was all the answer Shi'enah gave me? I'd take it. They weren't wrong.

"Are there . . ." I paused a moment, trying to figure out how best to phrase my utter laziness and unwillingness to take care of an actual house without coming right out and saying it. In the end, I decided it didn't matter. "Are there cleaning spells? That will take care of say, laundry, or mopping and vacuuming tiled floors in a house?"

Shi'enah's nose crinkled while they thought. "It'll be in with all of the Skill books and Chjaveen. But you'll need to specify you are looking for magic skills. There may actually be a pre-requisite, but I'm unsure, as I don't undertake that side myself. Still, one-off scrolls shouldn't be too expensive either. Or you could just get a cleaning drone, if you don't mind the tech roaming your house."

"Thanks." I sighed and headed toward the room I dreaded. Cleaning drone might be the best option because anytime I walked into that damned Skill bookshop, I walked out a hell of a lot poorer than intended.

House, Kira. You've got to save for the house. You can't live in the shopping center a moment longer than you have to. Perfect little mantra for convincing myself to only look for exactly what I needed.

As long as I didn't end up having to spell a mop and bucket in order to clean my house and end up flooding it like a certain mouse once did, I'd be fine. And I'd keep telling myself that until I proved it.

First things first. I pushed Jackson in front of me in the direction of Chjaveen's domain. He shot me a glare, obviously no longer mollified by my permission to keep his gains. Fun.

Chjaveen's shop, as usual, reminded me of those meticulously organized secondhand bookshops I'd encountered as a child. Precious wares, delicate subject matter in some of them. My child's expression of complete and utter boredom only slightly lessened my joy at entering it again.

Chjaveen blinked like a chameleon as I outlined my need for a cleaning spell scroll, or something. "There are ssscrollsss for thisss, but I do think you would be better ssserved with a cleaning drone. They have senssssors built in and can navigate your living areas. Wouldn't that be more sssuitable?"

I nodded, cringing inwardly at what I was sure this would cost. "Where do I have to go to purchase a drone?"

The Shopkeep shrugged. "I can order you one easssily. For delivery?"

And that stopped me. Damn it. I didn't have a house to deliver it to yet. "Can I put a hold on the delivery until I have the address?"

"Of coursssse"

I swear, nothing rattled Chjaveen.

"Mum. Can we go now? I have items I need to get." Jackson's impatience found me counting to ten under my breath.

To his credit, Chjaveen waited patiently as I shot my son a glare. "Wait. I want to make sure you're getting what you said you would."

Jackson scowled. "I'm not a kid. I can get my own stuff, Mum."

"Jackson Kent." I snapped out his name before taking the breath I really should have. "Stop being impatient and let me finish."

I could practically feel my son reaching his boiling point, but seriously, we'd only been in the shop a few minutes. He could wait. So I turned my attention back to Chjaveen, who was studiously examining his sharp nails.

"I'll order one and update the address for delivery in a few days." I amazed myself with the ability to keep my voice somewhat even and squash the need to shake with irritation.

"Done. I will put in the order now."

That taken care of, I turned back to my simmering teen and escorted him out to the armor shop. This definitely wasn't either of our ideas of fun. But I was going to make sure he armored himself well. Like it or not, I was still responsible for keeping him alive, even if all the rules had changed.

The armor shop contained so many options and so many variations of each option, it often gave me a headache. Thank the System, I guess, for the ability to search for what you wanted, and to narrow down the choices. If it wasn't for that, neither of us would have found anything.

My own choices on the backburner for a moment, I looked over what my son had chosen.

"Turn around."

Jackson reluctantly did so, and I had to admit, he'd made his choice wisely. The jacket he'd picked was about mid-calf length on him, solid black, and frankly made him look like he should have been staring in a blockbuster action movie about a kickass deadly mage.

The stats he shared with me weren't anything to sniff at either. More Constitution, extremely minor regeneration for both Mana and Health, and a slight Mana boost. He'd spent well, and probably a lot.

I nodded. "Damn fine choice, that one."

"Do you think you'll be okay with me going out on patrols more?" The grin he offered was tentative, and it was all I could do not to snap a *no* at him.

When he'd been injured those couple of weeks ago, I'd thought I was about to lose him. There's nothing that compares to how that feels. Everything in me screamed to hold him tighter, but my brain, what tiny bit of it wasn't reacting maternally, didn't want to completely ruin my relationship with my son.

The harder you grip children, the more vigorously they fight and the less they'll listen to you when it really matters.

Unfortunately, in the apocalypse, it seems like everything matters, all the damn time.

Sighing, I brushed my hand through my hair, forgetting that it was in a tight bun today. Instead, I snagged enough out of it that I'd have to redo it. "Okay. But not with the deepest patrols, okay? Second level you can do. You're high Level enough, but just not to the big nests yet. Promise?"

His smile was enough to blind me, and he grabbed my hands, radiating excitement. "Of course! You put the groups together anyway. Not like I can sneak into one of them. Is it okay if I go like every second day, maybe? If not every morning?"

I eyed him, critically this time. He was almost as tall as me now. Though he hadn't grown in a while. Probably waiting on that late-teen growth spurt to shoot up to his uncle's towering six feet. Although, come to think of it, thanks to my genome treatments, I was almost five ten now. And Kyle was a little taller too.

"How about we aim for every second day to start with? As long as you don't come back half dead inside of two weeks, we'll revisit then?" Shit, that hurt to say. It felt like my heart was trying to break into two pieces.

The gratefulness on his face was almost enough to reassure me I'd done the right thing. "Thanks, Mum."

He leaned forward and gave me a bear hug. Probably lasted about ten seconds, which was the longest one I'd had from him in a while.

Pulling back, he grinned. "Just wait until you see some of the stuff Chris and Sarah have us cooking up now. With the Shop and the Cartel, there's no limit to the things we can come up with. I'll make you proud."

The last he said after a moment's hesitation, and I wondered what had ever made him think I wouldn't be proud. "Always proud of you, son. I hope you know that."

"Yeah. Just sometimes, I want to do better things. Bigger things." He smiled, but this time there was sadness in it, like maybe he thought he was losing at something. "Have stuff to do. See you at dinner?"

"Definitely." I was about to let him go as he began to open the door to the corridor of the Shop. "Hey. You *will* do great things."

The look he shot me made it all worth it. Gratitude, outlined with confidence. "Thanks, Mum. You do too."

I watched him go and took a couple of slow and steadying deep breaths. Well, I'd promised him he could go out on patrols more often, so I needed to contact Kyle, Dale, and Mike. They'd have to start slotting him in. Besides, maybe he'd find some crafting materials he could use. New and improved gear for him and us all. Ways in which he could help keep himself safe . . .

Focus.

Now I could turn my attention to what I'd picked out for myself.

I ran my fingers down my new jacket, feeling the material to ground myself. It sat well on me, coming down to the top of my thighs. The material felt strange to the touch, almost iridescent to the eye, unless of course you had my eyesight which was almost like Superman X-ray vision. I wondered if I could get a laser zapper upgrade and beam death unto my foes. That would be pretty cool, although I was fairly sure that wouldn't adapt well to human anatomy.

Jacket decided on, I reckoned I may as well get the matching pants. I wasn't a fan of leather; squeezing into it was always annoying, and while likely synthesized, this stuff looked like it'd be worse.

Jeans—I was so much more comfortable in good old jeans. Thus began my search for perfectly reinforced jeans that probably didn't exist. Except I found them. It looked like jeans, felt like very soft jeans, and yet also somehow impenetrable with my feeble attempts to pull at it.

Close enough, I guessed. Black leather-like jacket, three pair of dark blue armored jeans, new reinforced boots, several new shirts that would up my survivability, and a belt made out of this armored material that would hook my Warhammer in better with an easy release clasp.

Fighting with a weapon in close proximity still onset that bit of panic, but I had to get used to this. I was stronger than my fears. And if I kept telling myself that, I'd believe it.

The hundred thirty-five thousand Credit price tag it cost me didn't feel very good. But there was that part of my brain now certain I might survive the next few weeks. Couldn't put a price on survival, right?

Jacket of Reinforced Confidence

+ 5 Constitution

+ 20 Mana

Activate: Stealth Spelled

You must remain still for this stealth spell to work. Any movement other than breathing will reveal your location.

Duration: 30 seconds

Recharge: 90 minutes

Yeah. That was over half of my bloody cost right there. But maybe even worth it in a pinch. You know, if we ever got overpowered and I wanted to insure I made it back to my kids by hiding like a coward. More likely, I'd use it if I needed to observe some of the scary mutations we came across so we could get a better understanding.

My eyesight let me zoom in, so to speak, and stealth would keep me safe while I concentrated on observation. All of it hypothetical, but thirty seconds could sometimes feel like a lifetime.

The other items were only reinforced material. No special skills or anything attached. Just upping that whole survivability rate.

Because ultimately, our aim here wasn't just existing; we needed the human race to thrive so we could shove that damned dangerous continent assessment down the fucking System's throat.

If it didn't have a throat, I was all for making one.

And now I had to venture into the Cartel Courtyard and see a gnome about supplies and ingredients.

❖

Ginali shook his head at me, his usually twinkling eyes not flashing at all. It was almost like he was disappointed in me, and that bothered me more than I liked to admit. "That's not how it works, and you know it."

I didn't want to point out that that's how it *should* work, considering I was trying to get him to cut me a deal, but at the same time, I really wanted to.

"Look. When we get the crafting items that you're interested in, I have no problem with bringing them to you to trade, but as we're growing and developing our own alchemists, and our own crafters, we're going to need less of a trade and more of a bartering system. We are going to need gear that will make us stronger, keep us safer, and frankly, help the entire settlement including your Cartel." I tried to keep my voice nice and even, but I could tell some of my irritation shone through.

Ginali eyed me like he was trying to weigh my words and my seriousness, with the potential benefits that he might be able to wrangle from them.

My patience pretty much snapped. "Gear. The best of it. First right of refusal to purchase any advanced items you craft from the items we have provided in trade. I don't mind you making money off what we bring you, but as we grow, the exact terms of our arrangement will have to grow with it. And you know *that.*"

He sighed. "You are right. The contract and terms do make room for this. Things have been moving along rapidly, and your continent's increased experience percentage has made adapting more difficult as you encounter higher-Leveled creatures at every turn. Their strength directly reflects on the items you retrieve from their corpses. Fine. I will draw up a contract adjustment addressing the current changes to our agreements under the applicable clauses of settlement growth."

"Perfect. Have you had anyone working on housing items?" It was worth a shot, even if I didn't think it was going to be a yes. Most of the houses we were moving into would be empty, half torn down, probably torn up, but mostly furnished.

The Pharyleri frowned and I could practically see the cogs turning in his brain. "Some things. Do you think people will prefer to buy items from us? The Shop can have items placed in your houses directly if needed. It's a lot more generic than what we would make and more expensive—what with teleporting it across the vastness of space—but also much more convenient."

Convenience. Something we'd lost about three months ago. He was right. People would definitely choose it over unique items. With the apocalypse smacking us in the face, I was certain we'd choose easy wherever we could. "Might just be worth having some stuff hanging around. There'll always be the more eccentric among us."

"Of course." Ginali nodded. "Some of our artisans will be happy to look into side projects like that."

I gave him a thumbs up in return.

"Now, can you get me a list of the sorts of armor, weapons, and other gear you're thinking would be best created?"

I raised an eyebrow. "That's not my area of expertise and you know it. What I need to know is what *can* be made from the items we frequently bring you, and if we trade in things that we haven't been seen before, it would be helpful to know what sort of items you discover through using those, too."

Ginali let out a low sigh but nodded. I could practically sense the businessman in him cringing.

"I'll have a list of things I believe would be most beneficial for you by tomorrow. It'll be a long list. The differentiations and the sizes of your mutated creatures has allowed us to expand our lineups." He hesitated. "You realize there'll be a markup, right? We do have a business to run."

I scoffed. "Of course, there will be. I'm greedy, not stupid."

Ginali laughed, a genuine and almost magical sound as I turned on my heel and headed out. Tomorrow was going to be a long day. Patrol followed by the first of our housing runs. And tonight, I was determined to get some actual sleep.

Chapter Five:

Housing

13 Weeks, 6 Days Post-System Onset

Wisp clung to my hand while Dog walked on her right and Wombie was relegated to my left. In order to claim the housing, we had to go to the actual house, step into it, and purchase it from the System.

Right now, we had three groups on patrol taking care of nests, while the rest of us were establishing the first wave of house owners.

Oddly enough, there were about fifteen people or families I guess who had previously owned a domicile in the area we'd cordoned off for our expansion. As far as I understood it from the research Sienna did, they'd end up with a decent discount on the purchase price for reclaiming their house.

A part of me couldn't believe we were going to buy houses in one of the more expensive districts around here. I was fairly certain we wouldn't be paying five hundred thousand Credits for these places, and that made me feel like in some ways, maybe the apocalypse resetting our shitty housing economy had been worth it.

Only to feel horribly guilty for that thought five seconds after I first formed it. How could anything that killed so many people be anything but a fucking tragedy? Way to go, Kira.

"Nervous?" Evelyn smiled at me. I'd asked her to move in with us. It would feel weird without her there. But I got the feeling she might go grab one of the apartments at some stage, so that she at least had somewhere to call her own.

We needed our house to have five rooms . . . so that automatically ruled out the one across from the park. "Not nervous, just have a lot on my mind."

She nudged me with her elbow and reached down to squeeze my left hand. It was amazing what a little bit of physical reassurance could do. "We'll make the most of this dang apocalypse, if it's the last thing we do."

Evelyn shook her free fist, holding it up into the air in mock ferociousness.

I caved and laughed. Yeah. Might have lost my work colleagues, had yet to see any of my friends, had no idea if Mason was actually doing well, and was pretty sure my parents were dead . . . but I'd also found some damn good people. And my kids. Together, it would have to be enough.

"Mum. I'll get my own room, right?" Wisp's eyes shone as she waited impatiently for the groups to gather so we could all head out.

"That's the plan," I said, dropping her hand so I could ruffle her hair.

The grin on her face was reward enough.

We were taking this in groups. The retirement village had an entire set of couples and singles who wanted smaller homes that were still theirs. Because each home in the village wasn't more than two bedrooms, a living space, kitchen, and bathroom, it was best suited to a couple, a couple of friends, or even singles with the one-bedroom option.

Then there were the apartment block groups. The people today were going to set theirs up in four of the taller apartment blocks. They were one group and would all stick together until everything had been claimed.

Our group would claim houses along Tryon and onto Mascar. Another group would head out along the front section on Marada, Mirimar, and Kelburn. Those who were patrolling today would get to pick tomorrow. Mike had been meticulous. Most of the actual decisions were already made. We just had to chaperone everyone and make sure no surprises popped up.

After all, it wasn't secured territory just yet. No Safe Zone meant potential danger.

We began to head out, down to where the traffic lights used to matter, where Mike's crew had already removed a section of the fence into the retirement village because we'd be using those streets in there as a shortcut to get to the center from now on. It wasn't only restricted to residents of the village.

"What's our house like?" Wisp asked, and I could tell she was barely containing the bouncing.

I really hoped the one I'd chosen would be big enough for what we needed. "It's two stories, has four beds upstairs with two bathrooms. Downstairs there's a couple of rooms and a living area with a bathroom and a little kitchenette. From what I could tell about it. So, it'll work for Uncle Kyle."

"I really get my own room!" Then she scrunched her face like she was trying to do some difficult calculations. "And you, and Evelyn, and Jackson! We can all have our own space."

Then she paused again. "Wait. Where will Wombie and his mum go?"

"There's a garage." I grinned when relief flooded her face.

Even as we began walking through the retirement village to get to the homes directly on Tryon Street, I started receiving pop up notifications.

Settlement Expansion Initiated

Current Progress 2%, 78% remaining.

Well, at least Sienna and Dor had managed to activate the correct portion of the settlement maintenance controls. Getting a running total would help. Though I didn't think we'd get passed sixty percent today, I was hopeful anyway. I knew Ginali and the other potential shopkeepers weren't claiming the commercial areas until tomorrow. They were still preparing.

We moved through the small village quickly and groups started breaking off to begin the apartment block possession. The percentages rose rapidly as we moved along the street, finally coming to the nice brick house I thought would be best for us. We splintered off from the main group, and for a few moments I just stood on the little footpath looking up at this nice dark brick house.

Brown bricks, with a two-car garage, trees out the front, and a really nice little veranda up on the second level. It'd definitely do. Invisible weight I hadn't even realized was there lifted off my shoulders, making me feel lighter than I had in months.

Residence Available

Do you wish to purchase 34 Tryon Street, Upper Mt Gravatt?
Cost: 224,000 Credits
Yes or No?

I glanced at the Credit cost and hoped that the apartments were cheaper and smaller houses were too, because this could be prohibitive to the more non-adventuring types. Though most groups had several. Even now we had wealth equality discrimination.

I only hesitated a moment before indicating that yes, I did want to buy this house.

Congratulations

You are the proud owner of 34 Tryon Street.
Note: This property has substantial interior damage due to several nests spawning in this specific domicile—none of which are currently active.
Would you like to reinforce structural integrity and make interior repairs so that the property is habitable, including plumbing and electrical grid adaption?
Cost: 45,000 Credits
Yes or No?

It was a good thing I'd been saving was all I could say. There went more money. Of *course* we wanted to be able to use the house and hook it into the power systems the city was getting going.

You have been granted access to the homeowner's tab. Please list those people who will be residing in this domicile and have access to their own limited version of the house interface.

I frowned; my name and Wisp and Jackson were already there. I added in Kyle and Evelyn. It blinked at me for a moment before prompting another popup.

Be advised that there are optional improvements for your newly acquired place of residence. To perform these at any time, just access this menu and choose your options.

I waited a moment, but there was nothing else, so I closed everything out and finally looked up at our house. Wombie and Dog were actually rolling in the grass, and I thought, once the System had accepted our eighty percent expansion, that putting up a fence might be one of my first choices.

Evelyn and Wisp had already run ahead of me and were impatiently waiting at the front door. Typical security screen set up, I placed my hand on the handle and felt a brief tingle. I wasn't sure if that was System initiated or if it was just my own excitement at finally having a space to call our own after all these months. Either way, the door swung open, and cool air wafted out.

The place was all tile. Not a surprise in the least, considering where we were. It didn't snow in Brisbane. You wanted everything as cool as possible as much of the time as you could. The house had been in the middle of upgrades with a newly appointed kitchen, and the rest of the house a mix and match of mid-eighties decor and ultra-modern.

I liked it. It had character.

"Mom! Mom!" Wisp squealed from somewhere above me.

It was a good thing I knew her excited squeal from her panicked one. I walked up the staircase to find her at the end of the hall jumping up and down half in a doorway and half in the room it led to.

"Guessing this is your room?" I crossed my arms.

Evelyn laughed. "I told her the master was yours, but she could pick anything else. Hope that's okay."

"Perfectly fine." I barely restrained the need to run into the master and double check that we had a master shower and bath and actual civilization.

"When can we stay here?" Wisp whined in typical eight-year-old fashion. "Why can't we stay here now?"

I laughed and wrapped her in a hug. "Because it's not technically a part of the settlement yet, and we're not protected here."

She quieted and nodded, returning the hug with fierce strength. "I will be ready to move in as soon as we can, Mum."

Kids were precious. So, so precious.

Another popup flashed in my eyes.

Settlement Expansion Initiated
Current Progress 42%, 38% remaining.

Things seemed to be moving along nicely. But right now, I didn't want to get too attached, just in case some weird phenomenon made all the Koalzillas in existence converge on this location overnight and take out the house that had cost me almost three hundred thousand Credits before we could even use it.

"Let's get back to the center and let Mumma Wombutt know she has a nice patch of grass now."

Wisp brightened up immediately. "Wombie!" she called out before proceeding to run down the stairs and out into the yard.

Evelyn sighed. "It'd be nice to feel that way again, even just for a bit."

I nodded, completely understanding. "Growing up is hard. Doing it in this situation? I don't think you could pay me enough."

❖

Back at the center, I settled into my chair, kipatchya in hand, and surveyed some of the information filtering through the expansion section of the settlement interface. Being the settlement owner gave me some perks, nothing overpowering, but perhaps just more convenient.

I could access the settlement interface anywhere within the settlement, and in a limited capacity outside of it. There was also the token bit of experience I got. As our settlement continued to thrive, I managed to amass a couple of thousand experience per week. Sure, nothing that was going to catapult me through the leveling ceiling, but enough that if I had to miss the occasional patrol for parental or settlement-owner duties, it helped cushion the blow.

No falling behind for me.

The seat next to me got pulled out and sat upon before I could register who it was.

Gemma flopped down on the seat next to me, her sun-kissed hair pulled back in braids, and put her head down on her arms sighing theatrically.

Shoving down a laugh in response, I waited a moment for our head stealth expert to speak first, and when she didn't, I dove in myself. "You trying to pretend you're invisible, or just waiting to see if I'll order food for you?"

She sat up and eyed me thoughtfully. "Neither. Just. How do you do this? When people approach you? How do you not just tell them to suck it up, we're in an apocalypse, get out there and kill shit or die?"

I shrugged. "Might be the mum in me, could be the fact that I understand. If I wasn't responsible for the lives of two small people, I don't think I'd be pushing on like this. There are people who are all 'when the end of the world comes, you just put up or shut up.'" I opened my arms, indicating the late time of the day and how many people were still milling around the center.

"But that's like the parents who say they'll never let their kid have screen time before they actually have kids. Trust me. Screen time was sanity saving." I'd veered off on a tangent a little, but Gemma was still listening, so I got myself back on track. "When everything changes in such drastic fashion, when you've lost people you love, or have to change the way you do everything . . . it's not just about sucking it up.

"Everyone works differently, and for some, toughing it out might be their best coping mechanism. But for others? For neurodivergent people who work best with a routine, for those people who need to fixate on aspects of life who are left floundering without those same fixations—it's just not that easy. We are human, and we value being human. Survival is an instinct yes, but for some of us . . . we need to build coping mechanisms, we need to build new routines in which to flourish, and we need to find a new way to give a fuck when everything feels like it's lost.

"I guess you could say I just try to be compassionate. To give everyone that benefit of the doubt, because without my kids, I think I'd be one of the lost ones."

Wow, I'd just given a speech. Gemma's gaze was still focused on mine.

Intense and thoughtful at the same time.

"I tend to have difficulty putting myself in other people's shoes. I've always just thought it's best to get stuff done so that it's done." Gemma rubbed her nose. "But Jules, you know, she was more like that. Routines and fixations, and yet when this all started, at the very beginning—she was amazing. When she died, I stopped caring."

Impulsively I reached across and squeezed her hands. "That's a perfectly natural way to react to grief, on top of monumental life changes in the same first two weeks."

She nodded. "I'm realizing this now. Thanks. I'll try to be less . . . abrasive." Pushing her chair away, she stopped and looked down at me. "You should try to actually get some rest. After patrol tomorrow, I think we'll have the eighty percent we need. Go get some bloody rest for once. Your body can't keep on if your mind doesn't calm down."

Even the smile she shot me as she walked away didn't dull the reality behind what she said.

I checked to see where we were with the settlement expansion.

Settlement Expansion Initiated
Current Progress 61%, 19% remaining.

Perfect. With any luck, by the time we got back from morning patrol tomorrow, we'd have the entire eighty percent we needed, and we could trigger the expansion and the reinforcements extension.

Gemma had been right. . . . If I didn't get some actual and decent sleep, I'd die during the patrol before I ever got to move into my bloody house, and then where would I be?

Dead and haunted by Wisp and Mumma Wombutt, I bet.

Chapter Six:

Upgrades

13 Weeks 7 Days Post-System Onset
11 a.m.

Emugators and their damned elastic necks were going to be the death of us all one day if we weren't careful. Agile and stretchy like Gumby, you'd think they were made out of Play-Dough. Their beaks held a toxin that hurt like all buggery.

When I got hit by that what seemed like a lifetime ago, I'd thought I was going to die, I thought I'd orphaned my kids. But the great thing about the System was, that regardless of how bad your injuries were, as long as they weren't mortal, you were pretty much going to survive anything.

And with Kyle's help, even to the point of regrowing limbs.

Out in the bush again, I just wished the sun could break through the canopy and give me some much-needed warmth. Emugator nests tended to be in areas close to water, with an abundance of underbrush. Bulimba Creek ran way too close to the settlement for us to let these nests go unattended for long.

Clearing them out had become something I dreaded. They were fast, smart, and difficult to pin down. We couldn't even rely on Dannin and Evelyn's kiting to keep the extra Emugators at bay.

Hirish grunted as he fired his pulse rifle at the Emugator Molly was currently occupying. The thing was . . . humans weren't the only things the System regenerated. Not only were we fighting mutated creatures who wanted to kill us, we had to battle the innate System regeneration in those creatures.

Although, I guess they had to do the same with us. Fair is fair, right?

Still, Hirish's pulse rifle was mega useful as a deterrent from the mutation plunging its beak into multiple body parts.

I let out a frustrated roar as I brought my hammer whirling around with all the centrifugal force I could muster to plunge into the weirdly scaled side of the damned bird. There was a subdued thud as it dug deep into whatever made that hide tougher than nature.

Groaning with exertion, I managed to pull it free and only just avoided being stabbed in my torso thanks to Molly's impeccable timing with her shield. She shield rushed the damn creature, blocking its thrusting head and the clang of beak on metal reverberated through the bush.

"Still need more practice with that damned hammer before you use it on these guys, Kira." Her words were hurried and low, as if she didn't want to embarrass me.

Sweet kid. "Yeah. Thanks."

So instead of making her job even more difficult, I backed up to work with the ranged damage dealers. Back here with Ray, Evelyn, Dannin, and Eritia, I couldn't help feeling useless.

Sure, Implantation was an awesome spell with the ability to heal people after it exploded, even if the amount was a minuscule percentage of the damage. I had my Blood Dispersion active too, and now I was Level 40, I could tap each mob with Mana Stone and help replenish certain members of my group's Mana levels too. Let's not talk about how long it took me to get to 40.

My abilities helped assist everyone else, bolster our power and reinforce our defenses. But to be honest, I wish I had something a little more volatile, a bit surprising. More powerful. Sue me. Mums could want to be superheroes too.

Mana Sense chose that moment to kick in with an alert. Although I shouldn't call them that. The thing was, it felt more like a sensation of foreboding, or a forewarning. "Spit balls incoming."

They knew what I meant. There wasn't any actual way to tell what the skills were that the creature used, but we'd all devised names for them ourselves. Spit balls went everywhere, so we hunkered down behind Molly while she extended and reinforced her shield.

Wherever she'd gotten this new one from was amazing. It was massive and strong and acid didn't even appear to harm it in the least.

"Thanks Kira." Sange smiled at me, their expression reaching their eyes. "We'd be dead ten times over without those warnings."

Which made me feel marginally better, but I still wanted to get stronger, and if it wasn't going to be with my Warhammer in melee situations, I needed to figure out a way to make me more useful for the rest of the teams. I'd talk to Hirish later about it. After all, he'd worked marvels with me since the alliance formed.

Ray and Eritia, our Ice and Fire Mages, worked amazingly well together. Ray froze things, and Eritia exploded them with fire, the sudden temperature change more than effective almost every time they did it.

Dannin and Evelyn were beginning to work so well together that they sometimes appeared to fire their arrows at the exact same target with no previous communication. Hirish and Piola, despite their differences in the council room, worked beautifully in tandem. Piola with her assassin style meshed perfectly in tune with Gemma. Their ability to phase in and out of places, disappearing and reappearing inside of a split second, wielding their blades with deadly precision, looked almost like a dance of daggers to me.

Morton wasn't with our group today, so we were missing our sharpshooter. Instead, we had Declan with us, but he wasn't tanking much today. He was learning to work with Piola and Gemma on melee rotations.

Hirish and his guns helped round out our main fighters. Even though I would have assumed a pulse rifle could one shot most things, at least his damage chipped away expertly at the tough hides of our opponents.

Even Kyle's little project of four newbies were beginning to grow stronger and learning to work well as a team. He had two mages with him, Allen and Glen, I think? Both blond, one tall and one short . . . and that was about all I could tell. From what I could see, their powers appeared to just . . . be magical. They didn't seem to be affiliated with any type of element like fire or earth, but instead shot out what looked like magic missiles with varying levels of accuracy.

Kyle was always very careful to direct them to aim higher than lower. Too low and it was possible to hit the melee fighters that ran into the fray. Getting injured and healed was par for the course, but getting injured by friendly fire was mostly insulting.

The other two newbies my twin had with him were close contact fighters, and while maintaining heals on the group, Kyle instructed them how to run in and out of the fight, how to shadow Gemma and Piola and basically learn not to get smooshed. Smooshing was a true and inherent danger.

Not that they hadn't. The time when a Koalzilla had squished the younger rogue by sitting on him was quite funny, especially when they complained—endlessly—afterwards about the lingering smell. Not that we let them stand next to us, of course.

Funny in hindsight. In the moment, it had been terrifying.

Now, training them while we fought Emugators? That wouldn't have been my choice, but it did make sense. Learn not to die while fighting harder monsters and you should manage to avoid dying with easier ones. Train hard and fast for survival. Then we could swap them out and bring in more, effectively upping our attack power throughout groups as people graduated out of ours.

We weren't the only group doing this. Our best five patrol groups were training in the same way. Survival would only be possible once we got stronger, and we weren't going to get stronger if we kept letting groups out-level everyone else.

Working together as a team, and teaching others the ropes of how to do it, only helped our ability to fight. Hopefully, we'd all be stronger as parts of a team than individually.

The sucking sound when I engaged Water Siphon always made my skin crawl. It sucked the moisture out of the bodies, and weakened our opponents so our attacks held more ground, did more damage. Debuffs is what they called them, and I could see how effective they were, but I wished I had more to contribute.

More power. More abilities. I wanted to be dangerous.

But you are . . .

I paused the thoughts in my head for a bit to concentrate on getting through this nest. I threw out Water Siphon, made sure Implantation was in constant rotation, activated Planted in Place to make sure the creatures we weren't ready for were completely immobilized.

Meanwhile, Evelyn and Dannin kited one of the Emugators together. These creatures weren't the best at focusing their aggro, and Molly already worked super hard to keep what she could. The Archer and Ranger did their best to occupy at least one of them. It took concerted effort to keep it focused on their attacks and not to look at all the other shiny people it could attack.

They were very focused on each other and acted more like a flock of birds in the way they approached life than an alligator lying in wait.

We whittled down the health of the one Molly tanked, little by little. It was all about consistent damage, pacing yourself to preserve Mana. That was something the lower Levels working with us had to experience first-hand.

These higher-leveled creatures took a lot more work to get down.

Slowly, Kyle's proteges slotted in with smoother movements. The melee fighters blended in well with Gemma and Piola, not to mention Drake, moving in with fluid movements in a timing sequence I didn't understand. But it almost looked like they were all locked into a deadly melee dance.

The ranged newbies were learning that it was better to aim high and miss the creature, should it duck, than to hit the members of your own group. One glower from Gemma being hit by an errant Arcane Shot was enough to drive that lesson home.

The apocalypse was nothing like a game, even if sometimes the terminology felt right. Any spell, or weapon, could hit anyone—friend or foe. It wasn't picky. I dreaded having to use bigger groups to fight harder monsters. Shit was going to go haywire.

We continued to work through the Emugators' nests, and it was truly starting to warm up out here. Even without the direct sunlight, the mugginess was beginning to hit in full force. Summer would be hell when it arrived, considering we had to wear armor for our safety.

Evelyn called out to Molly. "This one is getting wily. You done yet?"

Molly grunted under her breath, and I was fairly certain whatever it was wasn't complimentary. Suppressing a chuckle, I watched Molly chuck out a Taunt in the direction of Evelyn's mob—our last creature to kill for now.

While our current target wasn't dead yet, it was close to it. Which meant Molly was building up aggro to nab that final target from Evelyn. The Ranger's shoulders lost some of the tension. Luckily. It had been a long day, with several nests. We all wanted to get home.

And as Molly finally pulled in the last creature, I let my mind go back to its previous thoughts.

Hearing voices that weren't mine sent waves of cold running through me. What the hell did the Mana mean that I was dangerous?

I might want the creatures to fear me, but the tone of that whisper left me questioning just who or what was in danger from me.

❖

The thought plagued me for the rest of the day. No matter how hard I tried to reach out to the Mana around us and ask it what the hell it meant, I received no hint in return. Just as we passed through the gates the popup in my face distracted me from my irritable thoughts.

Settlement Expansion Initiated
Current Progress 82%, 0% remaining.
Expansion Permitted
New Control Panel Access Granted
Settlement has been Upgraded to Level 1.

I cringed. Did that mean we'd been Level 0 before this? I'd never really paid attention to it. At least we'd exceeded the eighty percent required.

Guess I was going straight to the library. The good thing was that most of us council members had been out fighting in patrols this morning and thus all of us would stink. I wouldn't be alone in my stench for lack of time to take a shower.

"What's got you smiling?" Kyle nudged my elbow, and I was glad I had my jacket on. He'd fought without one and his lower arm was crusted in greenish black blood that I really didn't want to feel the texture of.

"We all stink.

He laughed. "Yes. We do. I've finally gotten used to not having to sterilize before performing healing magic."

My twin winked at me, and I hoped that meant he was feeling more confident in his powers. For a while there, I'd been worried they'd stress him into anxiety attacks. He didn't deal well with change; none of our family did.

Well, unless it was forced on you in the form of an alien takeover, I guess?

"We're expanding, then," he added as we walked into the library, his tone more somber now.

"Looks like."

It also looked like one of the beanbag chairs was vacant, and I thanked our lucky stars for cleaning spells that would allow my bloody and dirty body crumbs to vanish after I'd used it for the comfort my aging bones needed.

Fine, the System made me physically feel like a spring chicken, but I still liked to be comfortable.

Dolores watched as I collapsed into the cushy chair, eyebrow rising underneath grey hair. "Tough out there?"

I shrugged. "No more than usual, I guess. Less life and death defying now that we're going out in larger groups."

"Good. That was the point, I believe. Slower progress versus not dying. Pretty much a win-win there." Then she paused and looked at me. "You finally hit 40."

"Yeah. Like yesterday or maybe the day before that; I can't quite remember." I glanced to the side of my vision to check the state of my popups. I was so used to them just being little inconsequential things and being so focused on whether or not the settlement was expanding, I never thought to check them.

Dor grimaced. "I didn't notice, but then I've been a bit preoccupied." She gestured vaguely around.

"Yeah, I think your preoccupation definitely trumps noticing when people level."

While I waited for everyone else to trickle in, I checked my screens. I was so excited about the settlement expanding that my leg was jittering on the ground, sending the little beans in the bag skittering. Not only were we going to have our own house, but the defenses would be reinforced, too.

I flipped through all my skills, pulling up Mana Stone again to study it. The thing was, I wasn't quite used to triggering it yet. I needed to build it into my regular rotation consistently.

What with my damaging spells, my debuff spells, and my buffing of my raiding party spells, there was a lot to manage. This is why computer games had all of those add-ons to manage them. Me? I just had my brain.

Granted, I'd also expanded my brain's capacity so I could utilize the ocular implants I got. Maybe I needed to look into that too. There had to be a better way to keep track of everything I needed to during a fight. Sometimes being in such close proximity with other fighters, or with the creatures themselves, just made me forget things I shouldn't.

I looked up from my inner dialogue and noticed the rest of the gang filtering into the room. Wrinkling my nose at the lingering smell, I watched as Sienna muttered under her breath with each new entrant, effectively giving them a basic cleansing that luckily, served to clear the air a bit.

The System might be a dick, but damn did it come with some handy stuff. Twenty-odd people who'd been fighting for five or so hours was not a stench I wanted to inflict on myself.

Sienna stood and cleared her throat, and I was glad Dor, Sienna, and Mike had taken the lead on this because I was running out of spoons. In fact, they'd reverted to plastic and weren't overly sturdy anymore even when I managed to have spare ones.

"Expansion has cleared; we can start adjusting our walls. Now. Keep in mind the treasury isn't overflowing with riches. With Cartel and Shop percentage contributions, donations by our residents, and the taxes included in upgrading the houses once people bought them . . . we're a little over a million Credits. It's enough to deconstruct the current walls, salvage some of the materials, and put up the extended walls. The bad news is that we will not be able to get the new ones up to the same level these old ones are yet." She paused, glancing at Mike as if giving him permission to continue.

Hmm. Was there something more there? Maybe. They had been working awfully close together lately. Frankly, for the both of them? I think it would be amazing. Mike was great with kids and an all-round good guy. Not sure why my brain was on a Cupid spree, but it took a bit of effort to focus my attention back on the head of security.

". . . we will get the walls back up to this level of security, but it'll take a couple of weeks of raising money. The good thing is each house has a taxation amount that goes toward the funding of defenses. So money will be specifically set aside for them." He frowned down at some notes he'd made. "The walls should be in place soon though. Maybe another couple of days. We'll start moving people into their housing beginning of next week. Now that we've qualified the area as an official Safe Zone, it makes us moving into our new domiciles that much easier. It won't be long until we're more spread out."

He grinned good-naturedly, and Kyle piped up. "Bit sick of feeling like sardines in a can."

"Oh, you have a house?" Evelyn called out, her tone gently ribbing him. "Where will you be living?"

Kyle groaned. "Oh no, has my own twin forsaken me?"

"As long as you pay the rent, we're good," I called out, only half joking. I wasn't made of Credits, after all.

Kyle put on mock shock, placed his hand over his forehead, and sighed theatrically. "Anything for you, dear twin."

Sometimes Kyle knew just how to diffuse a situation. The nervousness in the room had dissipated.

I snuggled farther into my comfortable chair, and I could almost feel the dried blood flaking off my jacket. "Well, if you don't, I can always find room for you in the garage with the wombats."

He laughed. Everyone laughed. I was thankful none of the bookcases laughed, because then we'd have a mimic in the midst of our meeting. Not that I'd seen one yet, but I wouldn't put anything past the System.

Chapter Seven:
Moving Day

14 Weeks, 2 Days Post-System Onset
8 a.m.

I didn't want to forsake patrolling this morning. We'd gotten into such a good groove as we rounded the learning curve, pushing our Classes and abilities, and ourselves. But as I looked down at Wisp with her bags packed sitting on top of Wombie like she'd been born there, and across at Jackson with his backpack, duffel bag, and grim determination, I realized that sometimes, I just needed to take a day off.

Reaching over, I ruffled my son's hair and received a roll of the eyes directed at me. But there was a lift to his lips too, a smile I'd take. He'd been going out every day with the lower thirties and I knew he was getting stronger. That alone was what leant me the strength to keep allowing him to venture out. A few deep breaths and I could even believe I wasn't almost panicked about it.

"Move-in day is here. Moving all my things from this really weird year."

Wisp was singing softly, almost under her breath, making up strange little songs about moving. Just like any girl her age should be doing. Having fun with the most mundane things.

Sienna and Rolo stood close to us, Mike with them, his large hand firmly gripping Rolo's tinier one. Yep. I had been oh, so right. Good for all of them. Finding some solace in this crazy, messed-up apocalypse. Throwing a glance to the other side of Wisp, I looked at Evelyn. She had her bow in her hand and was tightening the backpack cords with her other one. A duffel lay at her feet, typical army green in color.

None of us had much, but we were taking what we could. We were all moving, all adopting this new beginning. Because when life hands you an alien invasion apocalypse, you either went with the flow, or, quite literally, died.

And here I was, laughing at my own comments. Go Kira!

Mana saturation dropping significantly

I had no idea why the Mana spoke into my mind sometimes like that. And nothing I'd read or researched about gave my any clues. It would be nice to just go and buy a book titled *Mana: Why It's Speaking Into My Brain and How I Can Interpret These Signs.*

No such luck. Looked like I was going to have to be the one to write it if I wanted to get it done. Maybe the System gave us profits from that sort of thing . . .

"Kira?" Kyle sounded breathless as he jogged up to me. He had one of those massive hiking and camping backpacks on his back, the sort that went halfway down his thighs.

I raised an eyebrow, gesturing at the monstrosity, and he just shrugged at me. "No sense in leaving any of my stuff behind. Plus, I went to Red and got some of the rations I'd never used. Thought it might be nice to have some old-fashioned snacks in the house."

Blinking at him, I realized I'd not even thought about food. Shit. What about a kettle for drinks? In typical twin fashion, though, Kyle threw his arm over my shoulder, squeezed me, and whispered in my ear.

"Don't worry, sis. I gotchya covered. Red forked over kipatchya and a kettle for you too."

I blinked away sudden tears until I realized that wasn't necessarily a good thing. Apparently, everyone except myself realized I'd replaced my caffeine addiction. Oops? "Thanks."

I still meant it. It'd be downright rude to refuse to accept a gift anyway.

"Mum." Wisp had stopped singing and her tone was one of excitement, mirroring the gleam in her eyes. Wombie could feel it too, and he hopped from one foot to another. Well, sort of. I mean, he had four feet. "I think they're starting to leave."

She was right. We, however, were going to bring up the rear. That whole having a massive wombat traveling with us was going to be a thing. I hadn't had time in the last week to continue our training much, but eventually, I wanted her to be able to patrol the border with me, to help keep the city safe.

And we'd just expanded those borders.

The others began to file out, led by Mike and Sienna, leaving Dor in the library to watch over the settlement. We'd left a token wall and added a couple of gates to the main hub of the settlement. Not so grandiose and not a line of defense, more of a divider from residential to the administration and temporary housing area. We passed through easily, waving to those who stood watch for now.

As soon as we hit Logan Road, we began to splinter off. The bulk of us ventured through the retirement village, but there were others of us going to the left and those streets directly in front of Garden City.

Suddenly a kindly older man stood in front of me, blocking my way for a moment. He had thick almost white hair with glimpses of pepper through it. "Thank you," he said, taking me somewhat by surprise.

"Um, you're welcome?"

"Kurt! Stop it. She has no clue what you're talking about." The woman smacked him lightly with her handbag and peered up at me. "We used to live here. Thank you for making the expansion possible. I'm Rose."

"Well, you're welcome, Rose." I smiled at the old couple as Kurt reached out a hand, his demeanor gruff. I shook it, still smiling.

"Even got our unit. Eighty-six. We'll be up helping Red and Paul with the food sometimes." He stepped back, ushering Rose with him. "Thanks again," he called over his shoulder.

I stood there for a few seconds watching them, until Jackson cleared his throat none too subtly.

"Sorry. Just thinking." And we moved on. It was nice to know that some people were just getting to go back to the homes they'd known. At least it helped make some of the hardships easier to bear.

Many more of our little migration ventured through the retirement village to Tryon and from there out to Newnham and Old Capalaba Roads and all the housing streets in this little expansion.

Groups broke off and moved into their apartment blocks on the way. I knew that not all of the apartments in those blocks had been purchased, but overall, the groups in there had bought the entire thing. So that when it came to people requiring an apartment, they'd end up reimbursing the humans who lived there.

Two apartment blocks were purchased by our allies. The Zarrie and the Hakarta. They were closer to Logan Road. More as waystations for them to use like barracks. If I'd understood Hirish correctly, that is.

And then it was our turn to branch off.

The five of us, Dog, and the two wombats barely fit across the roadside portion of the property. But we did fit.

I knew that inside, this had once been someone else's house. The only person who knew how many dead bodies were amongst the initial debris inside of it was Mike and maybe those he'd allocated to cleaning things up. If the owner had still been among the living, they would have had first right of refusal to it.

Maybe we were lucky. Maybe the owners had not been home. Little lies like that were what helped you survive an apocalypse and stay sane.

As it was . . . there'd be remnants of someone else's life in there. Maybe toys, maybe clothes, perhaps even some food choices in the pantry. Perhaps, if we did our best to honor who'd been there, we could somehow avenge them, somehow let them know that the world continued, and we weren't giving up without a fight.

"Mum. Can we go inside? Can I show Jackson my room?" Wisp's enthusiasm was contagious, and I found myself grinning back at her.

"Of course! Just don't take Wombie yet. I think I'll need to widen the staircase first, and that's not on the cards quite now."

She nodded, sliding off her mount's back with practiced ease and leaned in for a moment before patting him on the head. "This way he can spend time with his own mum!" She yelled the last out as she raced Jackson into the house.

Even my teenager was in good spirits. Wonders would never cease.

Kyle stood, looking up at the house, and I couldn't read the expression on his face until he turned to me. "If we blocked out everything else, this would be a really happy moment, you know?"

Yeah, I got that. Probably more than he realized. I gave his arm a squeeze. "There's like a bachelor pad downstairs for you. Gives you access to the back yard too, so you don't have to tromp through the house at all hours."

He paused before heading in and returned my hand hug. "Thanks, sis. You've always looked out for me."

Then he headed inside, leaving me with Evelyn, the wombats, and thoughts that were turning dark quickly.

"Are you really okay with me staying here?" Evelyn asked suddenly.

"Of course!" How did I tell her that it wouldn't be the same without her here? That I'd gotten so used to her it felt like something was missing if she wasn't with me. "You're part of the family."

She eyed me for a moment, and I wasn't sure if she took it the way I intended or if she was trying to puzzle out some other meaning. But then she nodded and headed in too.

Yeah. Really needed to come clean with myself and her about all of that, but right now I wanted to settle into my home and have a fucking long private shower.

I turned to the wombats who were snuffling the grass. It sounded cute at first, but they were massive and thus, their noses were also huge. Tufts of grass and clouds of dirt flew up every time they breathed into the ground. Still undeniably cute.

Frowning at the two-car garage, I pulled up the house interface, tried very hard not to eye my fast-dwindling savings, and got to work creating a better shelter for them. As it was, it just wouldn't work.

I ripped the two garage doors off, making sure to leave structurally sound aspects present. Falling down on the wombats wouldn't make the best shelter. Then I put doors they'd be able to push through in place, that would spring back and leave them room inside for when they needed to get out of the weather.

I also cleared out most of the flooring because truth be told, they would want to dig, and I didn't want them hurting their claws, though I was fairly certain they'd be able to rip through almost anything. Mutated wildlife—no need to think it through more than that.

Not knowing enough about how wombats did with hot climates, I was fairly sure there'd end up being some burrowing around the neighborhood and my property and tried my best to convey to Mumma Wombutt that I sincerely needed her to not impact the structural integrity of my home if she wanted to burrow.

When I was happy with her understanding that the house would be gone if the ground became unstable beneath it, I stepped back for a few moments to watch them.

They snuffled in through the new doors with ease, their noses seeking out all the different smells that didn't even register for me. Mumma's eyes seemed bright, and I thought it might be with excitement. Her fur shook ever so slightly, and I realized she was trembling happily.

Wombie was, quite literally, bouncing. Sort of like pushing off from all fours and just pushing himself in the air. I don't think I'd ever seen something quite so adorable.

Walking forward, I scratched Mumma under her chin, leaning into her for a few seconds just to soak in that happy feeling I got from her. "Time for me to check out my house."

Her hot breath wuffed at my hair, tickling the scalp as she said her own form of goodbye. Yeah, shitty overall, but the apocalypse had some good things that came from it too.

❖

Hot water never felt so good.

I'd pay that initial forty-five thousand credits every week if it meant keeping this hot water on. Didn't need to let the System know that, though.

Toweling my hair dry, it was already after lunch, and I could smell food cooking downstairs. It smelled like actual food, not newly found monster food. I pulled on clean clothes, including a reinforced white T-shirt and pair of blue jeans and stepped into the kitchen.

Wisp sat at the table, her eyes shining, Dog on her right-hand side. Jackson was laughing at something my brother had said to him, and as I walked in, they all started banging their utensils on the table yelling out "We want food! We want food!" before cackling loudly.

Evelyn smiled and dished out what looked like a fried mac 'n' cheese with broccoli cake. And damn, it smelled divine.

She saw me as she turned to portion some out into Wisp's plate, completely accidentally dropping a little for Dog to wolf down. "Hungry?" she asked.

"Starving." And I hadn't realized just how famished I truly was. Which gave me the idle thought of whether or not the System would allow a being to starve to death.

Sitting there, having a late lunch in my own house after a completely and utterly humanizing shower almost made me forget everything that happened in the last three months or so. Almost.

Time passed too quickly, even though I tried to savor every single mouthful of that delicious macaroni cheese dish. Pushing my plate away, I eyed Kyle and Evelyn.

And then I looked at my kids. Damn it. Jackson would be going back to work with the tech department, and Wisp couldn't be left alone at this age. Maybe it was a good idea to have a live-in nanny or something? Or maybe see if someone in the neighborhood was thinking of doing some childcare? Where Wisp could run around in the park with her pets, having a bit more of that childhood she'd lose in a few years.

Time for that later. Didn't have time for it now.

"Sadly, we're going to have to head back." Then I remembered I'd totally forgotten to bring the scooter with me. I knew we'd all need one of them. Make it just that much faster for us to get back to the shopping center when we were called or needed for our shifts.

Though I guess we could take the wombats and just make everyone think there was an earthquake as they thundered through the streets.

For a moment Wisp looked upset, and then she swallowed her last bite of food and smiled at me. I leaned in to give her a huge hug. She didn't have to go being brave for me, even though I knew she'd deny it if I told her that.

"Can I go shopping for the house, Mum?" she asked when I let go.

"Sure, as long as Jana doesn't have too much school stuff to share with you." I checked my walkie to make sure it was switched on, even though I knew the range wasn't that great yet. It's not like our house was all that far away from Garbo.

I needed to get my brain back on track. "Okay . . . should I take Mumma or let her settle in?" I asked everyone.

Jackson laughed. "Let the poor thing have some fun where there's some grassy surfaces. She's been stuck in a bitumen jungle for months."

Nodding sagely along, Wisp pushed my side and I got up. Back to the daily grind for me, then.

Chapter Eight:

Lull

14 Weeks, 5 Days Post-System Onset
5 p.m.

Gemma let herself fall unceremoniously into the chair opposite me at Raybucks. Again. Don't get me wrong, I loved my house and family time, but there was something about sitting there that just felt right. And kind of like an office so I could ward off too many at-home visits.

Because if I didn't make myself openly available some of the time, I was fairly certain people would find me when I was trying to relax.

"You look beat," I commented, going back over the settlement screens Dor asked me to triple check after I'd gotten back from the house. She and Sienna took care of most of the daily things, but it was always nice to have another set of eyes go over decisions and make sure we hadn't forgotten anything.

Gemma let out a sigh of frustration and leaned back, looking up at the ceiling. Her jacket was ripped over her cybernetic arm, and I could see the gleaming black layer of armor staring back at me. I knew she'd added other, less visible enhancements to herself; I only hoped she stopped while she was still human.

Ha! I could probably bench-press a car these days. A small car, mind you, but a car. The definition of human seemed to be stretching however you looked at it. Old wounds healed, bodies rejuvenated, and our lifespans, for those who survived the initial onset appeared to be extending. What it meant to be human? Yeah . . .

"Took the scouts out today. Tasha is getting so much better, and we have a few newbies who show promise. Drake hates me giving him directions, but he tends to actually do what I say in the end. It's just very same old out there, and it's giving me the shivers." She focused on me, and I realized her genome treatments had made her facial features somewhat sharper than they'd been; even the freckles stood out more in contrast.

Was it rude to ask about Shop-bought body modifications? What even was the etiquette there?

"So. What's giving you the shivers?" I prodded her instead of being what was probably highly invasive with my questions like nosy me really wanted to be.

"Same old nests, constantly respawning with around the same time stamps. The only reason we're beginning to need to branch out is that our settlement is growing, even though it's slowly. The increase in output means we're taking care of the respawns much faster than we were." She finally sat up straight. "We should probably start sending each major group out a little farther, just to keep up with what we have and to prevent new threats from surfacing. Experience gains are dropping too, as we all level. It's just . . ."

Gemma shook her head and stole my glass of water, wolfing it down before she spoke again. "Never mind. I'm probably just being paranoid."

"Paranoia is a large part of why most of us are still alive," I quipped. "Do entertain me with yours."

I watched her as she sorted through all those thoughts in her head and realized that she never seemed this comfortable talking in front of the council. Before this new world dawned, I'd been far less of a people person, but there had been many presentations of research and papers before rooms filled with experts. Not all humans were social creatures, and some of us only by necessity.

"It feels too convenient. And nothing about this Dungeon World shit we've seen so far has even been in the least bit convenient." She glanced around like she was afraid to be seen spouting conspiracy theories. "It all seems too quiet, too nicely laid out. Far too easy."

Now *I* caught the shivers down my spine. She definitely wasn't wrong there. Had we grown complacent in our systematic patrols and training? I didn't doubt for a moment that Hirish knew was he was doing when it came to making all of our people, all of our fighters, just that much stronger. But at the same time . . .

"Thanks, Gemma." I smiled at her, and some of the tension faded from her shoulders. "You know, it'd be nice if we'd get to chat once in a while when it didn't involve scouting reports."

Standing, she laughed. "Yeah, except without those, I never know what to say, to anyone."

Ouch. That hurt, but not in a personal way, just an I-totally-got-where-she-was-coming-from way.

A thought struck me. "Hey. Did you end up moving out into the expanded settlement?"

Gemma shook her head. "Not yet. I mean, I fully intend to, but right now isn't the time. It's easier to lead scouting troops from here and far less hassle to report into. Some of the guards and Mike's security teams are staying here too. But for the most part I know they're converting Garbo into interim housing and operations."

She was about to leave but turned back toward me. "Also, I think they've finally got the fun zone place hooked up. Might be a nice break for the teens and the littles."

I watched as she walked away. Gemma was an odd duck. Come to think of it, most of the people around me here were odd ducks . . .I think I had a thing for them. Even the guys back at Carindale had been very odd ducks. At least I didn't have to have all of them in a row.

Which brought me back to the whole weirdness of the incident with

Carindale and the uneasy feeling it left lurking in my gut.

I'd need to check in with Dolores about their communications. So far, I think we'd been keeping up with them, but the wrongness of that situation never left the back of my mind, and now that we'd finally set our own town up with housing and a hub, I felt like it was safe enough for us to start caring about others.

More than we already did, anyway.

❖

14 Weeks, 7 Days Post-System Onset
3 p.m.

Rushing back from patrol to my house days later so I could shower and grab a bite to eat actually gave me ten minutes less to do everything. But having privacy to get ready? That in itself was priceless.

So it was, I stood on my scooter as I raced along the streets doing all of fifteen kilometers an hour through the retirement village, waving at Rose and Kurt, and the other few people who were out and about, and across to Garbo. It could have been any day in my normal life, except the plant mutations were beginning to alter their appearance so much that they were barely recognizable.

My fingers itched to dig in the soil, to analyze shit in my lab, to study the leaves and growth rates under microscopes. There just wasn't enough time in the day for me to get my hands into everything.

But we are enough. There's enough Mana for you to do anything.

Well, it had a point. Pity it couldn't come out and tell me exactly what all these cryptic messages actually meant.

Or maybe I was selectively listening . . . definitely wouldn't put that past myself.

Enough Mana to do anything, eh? I'd need to ponder that one.

The center was bustling with a new type of energy. Over the last week, we'd taken in several hundred new people due to patrols and scouting missions reaching areas we hadn't yet been to. We'd even begun to have waystations and stops set up, places that people could crash in temporarily and rest.

None of the new residents we'd brought in recently had been below Level 20. They were scrappy and determined, and as I passed them in the carpark on the way inside, it made me excited to think we were surviving this well.

My mood, however, washed away when I walked into the council meeting to find Hirish and Piola staring each other down. Again.

Ever since the bloody oath they'd taken that the system punctuated, they'd been trying to prove that they each knew better than the other. At least when it came to deciding what training regimes to implement.

Mon'swkinon stood to the side, his face typical in its Dash'Kiri impassivity. He glanced at me as if he wanted to say that he wasn't about to step in and stop the children from fighting with each other. Fine. I guess I had to do it, because Dolores looked like she'd dialed out and Sienna wasn't there yet.

It appeared to be difficult to get any of us here exactly on time anymore. We might have to push the meeting out a bit if it kept going like this.

"What is wrong with you?" I had to admit that I sounded more impatient than I intended to. Just because I had my own house now didn't mean I was getting any more sleep.

Hirish turned his glare on me, and I returned it tenfold. Turn that expression on me? I don't think so, even if you're an alien who could probably rip me in half. I didn't stand for that sort of shit from my kids and definitely not from him.

After a moment, he turned his gaze away, his expression somewhat sheepish. "Piola will not listen to reason."

"What reason, Hirish? How am I supposed to know what you're talking about if you only speak in riddles?" I ran a hand through my still-wet hair and plopped on top of one of the tables.

"We need to begin including twice daily drill exercises," he added as if that explained everything I needed to know about the topic.

"Expand on that. Pretend I'm five."

His expression clouded over as he tried to understand what it was I meant, but then he pushed on anyway. "Drills. One in the morning for those who head out in the afternoons. One in the afternoons for those who head out in the mornings. Weapon usage, magic usage, fighters, healers. Variations depending on who is attending on what day. Real training."

He sighed. "Patrols are good for hands on application, but a lot of these people we're sending out have been . . . I think the right human term is 'winging it'? They need to know and understand their abilities on a deeply personal level."

Piola rolled her eyes. "Next time I am not agreeing with you, I will ask you to explain it like I am five. This I do not have a problem with. The Zarrie will also allocate experts in their fields who can instruct others."

I would have heaved a sigh of relief except that I wasn't sure how wise that was and how it would be interpreted. Barely stopped myself from doing so, and instead turned it into stretching my arms above my head. "Great. If we're done with that, can we get it sorted?"

Of course, I was also wondering how well training would go down with some of our residents. The thirty-and-up crowd might not take so kindly overall to being told how and what they should do. Still, I was willing to bet most of the kids who'd grown up playing computer games would be decently excited. I'd call this a draw until I witnessed actual reception.

Hirish nodded and motioned to Mike. Kyle joined them and together with Mon'swkinon and Piola they took over a corner of the library to hash things out.

I pinched the bridge of my nose with my fingers. One of these days I was going to wear that piece of skin out with all the action it'd been getting lately. Mana headaches didn't help.

While I waited for the others to trickle in, I engaged my optical implant, still trying to get a full feel of it. It'd been weeks now, and I still felt I didn't know the full extent of what I could do with this, of how I could interpret data. Ginali seemed to think I'd gotten all of the components I needed in order to use my skill to its full potential, but I wasn't so sure.

There were different amounts of Mana for me to perceive and sort through. Consistently changing colors, differentiating colors. You wouldn't believe how many shades of blue there actually were.

Sometimes the difference in them meant that the Mana was stronger, or gathering, or changing even with a mood. Sometimes it reflected that ambient Mana was building up in the area and making a small hotspot, though usually only outside of the settlement.

A lot of times, I had no fucking clue what it was doing.

Did I need to just take a few days off and work on expanding my abilities? I glanced over at where our alien allies were working with Kyle and Mike and decided that there was no time like the present to grab the bull by its horns and learn to understand my skill fully.

I could feel Dor watching me as I jumped off my perch. She nodded almost imperceptibly, and I wondered how she did that almost mind reading thing she did.

Maybe I was just easy for her to read.

The group looked up when I approached.

"Kira?" Piola asked, crossing her arms at the interruption. "Is everything okay?"

Maybe I was frowning. I did that often when I overthought things. Go wrinkle creation, go! We can and will beat the System somehow! "I was wondering if there's anyone who could help me with . . . my ocular implants and how my Mana Sense skill interprets Mana flows and pooling?"

Hirish blinked at me, a thoughtful look on him and Piola seemed a bit consternated. But it was Mon'swkinon who surprised me.

"Dequasha could likely help. There are a couple of other hunters in IRSHA with Mana and Mind capabilities." His voice still held that gravely tone, and I'm not certain why, but it felt like maybe he was happy he could actually help with something. Like for me . . . he was a literal huge help in other areas.

"I could potentially speak to her and up my skill training too?" I wanted to push it, because I'd gotten the feeling Hirish hadn't been talking about me when he mentioned the training classes. After all, he'd trained me himself, hadn't he? And I had to admit that my melee fighting skills with my hammer had drastically improved. Were still improving.

"Of course." Hirish sounded strange, sort of worried. "I apologize for not previously thinking of this."

He bowed his head for a full second before righting himself.

I took a step back. "That's okay. No one, myself included, seems to understand just how this skill works. I'm just glad to have the opportunity to look into it in more detail."

Relief flashed briefly across his expression. "Excellent."

"I'll let Dequasha know you'd like to speak to her," Mon'swkinon said in that commanding way. I took my leave of the group, getting ready to go over patrols, housing updates, defense fundings, Crafting Cartel implementations, and food developments.

You know, the day-to-day mundane tasks we all needed to take care of for a thriving population of survivor humans.

I checked up on the quest info to see where we were, how close were we to the five thousand people we needed to complete the bonus quest.

A Habitable Safe Zone

Part Four B: Just a few more!

Goals:

1 - Gather 5,000 total inhabitants. This may include visiting species. Current population 3,792/5,000

2 - Completed: Expand your Township to the first extension point

3 - Utilize the Town's quest-giving system more efficiently. Or. Use it at all!

4 - Survive 6 months as a township

Reward: 25,000 Credits for your city Treasury

That's it. Nothing else. It is just a bonus quest.

Well, it was coming along, and we still had a good chunk of time. It was the quest-giving system I didn't totally understand. Heading over, I waved to Dor and Sienna.

"What's up, oh fearless leader?" Dor cracked the moment I got close enough to hear.

I rolled my eyes at her. "Town's quest-giving system?"

She blinked and Sienna let out a groan, making me turn in her direction.

"Totally forgot. I activated it ages ago, and it's set up for minimal beginning quests for reputation with the city, small Credit rewards, small experience award, stuff like that, but it's totally slipped my mind. I'll get on it." She ran flipped a piece that thick, brown curly hair of hers behind an ear and continued. "It'll be great for newly arrived people, and I think I can set it up for the monsters you guys are clearing out even . . ."

"That's so cool." This sounded good. I'd love it if I could maybe train and somehow gain more idle experience.

What? Sometimes I was lazy too.

Maybe I could set up a babysitting quest for someone. Ideas, ideas . . .

I was about to continue when Drake, our erstwhile enemy and now one of our better scouts, came bursting in through the library doors, his eyes wild and panicked.

"Kyle, Kira, Dale! Injured in the emergency bays now."

And then he was gone, leaving us three to scramble after him.

Chapter Nine:

Injuries

14 Weeks, 7 Days Post-System Onset
6 p.m.

There's something about the semblance of peace that makes us all forget how very close to disaster we actually are.

The sight before my eyes wasn't anything new, nothing I hadn't seen twenty times over since this whole thing started. A part of me felt numb, that I could look at this clinically, classifying injuries with my Mana Sense, and categorizing what I'd need to help Kyle with.

Drake continued to speak as we approached, and I had to give him credit where it was due. His voice didn't even shake as he gave us the report. "Magon attacked the three Koalzillas that our patrol was bringing down. We got caught in the crossfire and lost four of our people. Whatever toxins are in the Magon's spit that splashed over onto our survivors are harsh. The wounds aren't healing over properly."

Fuck. And it was only then that I noticed his arm had been slashed and was oozing sickly looking grey sap. "Go get yourself seen to now. We'll deal with the more immediate injuries and be with you shortly."

Using my Mana Sense to look at the patients, I began to give them in-depth scans with the Mana Purification skill. Seriously, System, come up with another word for it, I felt like I said Mana about three thousand times a day.

We left the injured to Dale if they didn't need me to guide Kyle on how to heal them. Sadly, there were four of the patrol with injuries that made my stomach roil so much I could taste bile in the back of my throat. I closed my eyes, touched my twin's shoulder, to guide him through removing the poisoned areas of Mana that were impeding the System's natural healing.

It didn't take as long as it had when the Zarrie besieged us, running out of desperation due to the mutated creature attacks on their own camp. Now, we'd done this several times over and each time we were more in tune. It helped that Kyle no longer fought his Class abilities, but instead found new ways to make it his so that it would do what he chose to do.

Maybe this was our twin ability, just like Talia and Tarin had their telepathic communication ability on top of their others. Even if it wasn't, I made myself believe it gave me that deeper connection to my brother.

One arm saved, one bad torso wound fixed, and two massive thigh wounds later, we stood by Drake, who hadn't sat down as I'd requested, and who definitely didn't take it easy.

"There's too much to do, to organize. I couldn't just not do it." He sounded stressed, and there was a level of tension in his shoulders that I'd never seen on him before.

"Drake?" I spoke softly as I guided Kyle's healing. Damn it, the wound was a nasty one, with something embedded inside it. "What aren't you saying?"

The slinky guy sighed. "Gary didn't come back with us."

The words were so soft, I wasn't sure if he'd really spoken to them. How would I feel if Evelyn, or Ray, or Mike didn't come back from a patrol?

"We didn't see him die," he added hurriedly, but I could still hear the pain underlying the words. "But he wasn't there. I think he might have led the Magon off . . . like tried to distract it. That damned thing made such short work of the Koalzillas we were fighting. Like they were ants it plucked off a leaf. I don't even think it knew we were there."

His observation was probably accurate, too, though I'd never thought Gary would be the self-sacrifice sort of guy. Sometimes people surprised us.

"Do you think he could have escaped?" Drake asked pleadingly. It was like he wanted me to lie no matter what.

Little lies, sweet little lies. Right now, they were more important than ever.

I gave his good forearm a gently squeeze. "Not sure, but if you didn't see a body, maybe he got lucky. We won't know for sure until we scout out the area and double check. Let's not give up hope until then, okay? You can probably pay to find out if he's alive in the Shop, too." That was the best I could do, and at least some of the tension left him as Kyle healed the last vestiges of the wound and I watched it close magically in front of me.

"Thanks," Drake said, his normal facade returning.

"Always," I responded, wondering how many of us were running around with masks on in this desperate situation. "Don't suppose you have the energy to report?"

Drake nodded. "Yeah, I do. Still getting used to the fact that this alien System heals us of pretty much anything. Kept trying to help people, though they didn't need it."

He sounded mad, but the ferocity in his eyes was gone almost as fast as it arrived. We might have to watch him; he seemed a bit more volatile than he'd been several weeks ago. Damn. Maybe we really needed to set up social work or therapy centers. We were going through a lot of trauma, a lot of adjustment, and a hell of a lot of desensitizing. The human psyche wasn't made for this much, this fast.

I beckoned Hirish and Piola over, who'd been attending their own wounded. Their expressions grim, they joined us, both of them scanning the rest of the injured.

Drake cleared his throat and focused on the ground. Maybe it was the easiest way to get through the report. "There was only about a second's warning as the shadow of the Magon fell over us. I guess we don't have the reflexes yet to react that fast. We lost Risesh of Pirra, and Arto of the Zarrie.

The Magon ripped through them like they were nothing, as they'd been two of the closest ones to the Koalzillas. It also managed to rake claws completely through both Greg and Jason, killing them instantly as well."

He took a deep breath. "Gary yelled for us to run, and we did. Bolted through the trees back toward the vehicles, zigzagging until we all met up. A few of us doubled back to help the injured, and when we looked behind us, Gary wasn't there. We piled into the vehicles and sped home. We didn't have time to wait and see if anyone else made it. But the four we knowingly left were definitely already gone."

By the end of the speech, he sounded cold, dispassionate, and his eyes got this glazed over look to them. People being tossed into an intergalactic mutant monster war. Yep. All this killing and death was starting to change us.

I patted him on his good shoulder, proud of my forethought for not exacerbating his injured arm while it healed. "Thanks, Drake. Rest up a bit, right?"

Using Mana Purification tired me out. There was an in-depth connection in the way I had to connect my magic to my twin's, and it left me reeling half the time. Surely there was a better way to get a handle on it.

We left Kyle with the injured as he joined Dale, going over treatments and plans to make the most of the System's innate healing abilities. It was almost seven in the evening and the twilight had already started. Days kept melting into each other, until I couldn't even remember what they were.

"Kira?"

I looked up realizing we'd made it to the entrance again and I had just stopped. "Sorry. Mind elsewhere."

Piola regarded me with what I felt might be sympathy. "Your species is much stronger than we'd been led to believe."

I laughed. "People keep saying that."

Pity the fucking System hadn't given us a decent assessment in the first place.

❖

In the wake of the Magon attack, it seemed the training sessions were more sorely needed than ever. As soon as we announced them, an enthusiastic murmuring went through the center. People wanted to understand how best to fight, how best to use their powers, how best to defend themselves and their loved ones. We were determined not to become victims of the apocalypse, despite what the System had set up for us.

The afternoon following the Magon attack, I found myself nervously eyeing Dequasha as she sat in front of me. It was all I could do not to stare every single time I was near her. Her lithe body and extra two arms weren't even startling because of the ribbon-like way they flowed. She almost felt like a walking, breathing optical illusion.

Her delicate floral transparency was heightened by the summer sun, and everything about her, even the way she spoke, was simply languid. Her hibiscus flower feet gave her great steadiness as she stood with me contemplating the task before us.

We'd chosen the same area I'd sat in back when I was upping my Mana Sense through the book absorption. Nice and quiet, away from people, and above all, it was near greenery. Totally comfortable.

Or that's what I tried to tell myself.

I was secretly terrified of learning more about these skills. There was such an intimate level of concentration involved when I used them that I wasn't sure I wanted an alien to be in such close contact with me. After all, what did I really know about them? What were their true intentions?

It didn't matter that my Diviner skill constantly showed me they were never, in fact lying; there was still that completely different factor about them that made me hesitate. It was difficult not to be suspicious when the world was taken over by a faceless, intergalactic council.

"You are concerned?" she asked me in that delicate way she spoke.

Flashes of her fighting from the ramparts flitted through my head. Of her melting skin from bones, returning bodies to the earth.

I suppressed a shudder. "A little. It's been a while, and I know logically that you're all real, tangible, and exist. But at the same time, it's difficult to reconcile someone less humanoid than the others, and while your appearance is just gorgeous, you seem exotically dangerous."

Best to be upfront, right? If we were going to work together to figure my shit out, it was better to be honest.

Dequasha nodded. "I can see how that might feel. I would like to apologize, though I know it's not in either of our hands. We must make the most of it?" Her smile reminded me of sunshine in the dawning light.

"The most of it it is."

She took a breath, closed her eyes, and placed one of her petal-like fingers against my temples. There was a surge of power, just brief, not even a full second, but I could feel it as if it traveled through all my synapses one by one, down paths of thoughts I didn't even realize I'd had before. All of it in that fraction of a moment.

When she opened her eyes, I realized I'd seen something of her too. She hadn't wanted to come here, but as a part of that specific IRSHA division, she hadn't had a choice. At the same time, she was beginning to love it here and was fascinated by the humans and other creatures she'd encountered, by their resilience, stubbornness, and willingness to learn.

She'd also been hurt by thoughts she'd gleaned about her species, her appearance, and what her motivations were. Though she understood the latter, it wasn't like it didn't wear at her, eating at her confidence.

I was a guilty party there too. Making assumptions about a species I knew nothing about. What a dick. At least, that's how I felt in that moment. Most of all, though, I found myself trusting her. While she might have gotten a glimpse into me and how I worked, she'd realized that as a form of trust she had to show me a side to herself too.

"Thank you," I said, and won another sunlight-filled smile from her.

"Shall we begin?" she asked.

And for the first time since deciding to do this, I knew, without a single doubt, that it was the right call.

15 Weeks 2 Days Post-System Onset
11 a.m.

"Fuck!"

I stood there, in the middle of my work area around the front from the Crafting Cartel Courtyard, trying to get my breath back while I went over what I'd done wrong again.

Dequasha and her endless patience just stood waiting passively, no judgement like always. Well, always being the last two days.

Even though she deliberately altered her Mana intake, output, and energy, it was so fucking difficult trying to understand what she was doing and interpreting what it meant.

I squinted, which gave me a stab of a headache behind my left eye as I tried again. The Mana flowing into her had subtly darkened to a vibrant deep blue instead of the stream of light royal that usually permeated her body.

And then it hit me. "You're targeting me with a debuff."

Dequasha smiled brightly. "Yes! Okay, now I will quick-fire them. As soon as you know, just blurt out the type."

That was how it began.

Deep but brightly so. "Debuff."

Softer, lighter, more like usual. "Buffing or healing."

Deep but dark. "Readying an attack."

Slow flow of lighter royal blue. "Replenishing through ambient."

We did it until I couldn't see straight. Right down to being able to differentiate healing from buffing. Not to mention attacks that were damage over time or else just pure instant damage. Right back to single target and area-of-effect spells, debuffs, healing, buffing . . .

It all swirled in my head, and before I knew it, the sun was setting, and I was famished. We'd missed the council meeting, I hadn't seen my kids all day, nor had I patrolled. But I had accomplished something I'd been convinced I never would. The variations of Mana strands were complicated. Subtle. And yet being able to tell them all apart could give us the edge we needed in combat.

I stumbled to sitting on one of the planters, noticing belatedly that the thing was cracked with the way the vegetation was beginning to burst out of its seams. Nature had indeed begun to reclaim her environment. I absentmindedly soothed it with my own Mana, bleeding some Top Soil manipulation into it to coax it to grow, but not destroy our settlement.

Damn, I loved nature.

Doing this, using my Skills to grow something and not destroy, it felt right. It felt good. I so wished I could do more of it.

"You did it." Dequasha stood next to me. I don't think I'd ever seen her sitting down before. I wondered if she could.

"Thanks to you. I couldn't have done this without your patience." I meant every single word of it. That stubborn part of me that wouldn't take the time to properly learn by myself was extra grateful to having found someone actually able to assist me.

She grinned.

I think that's what it was, although I thought it looked a bit terrifying. In a good way. It was hard to explain.

"This is just the beginning. We will be adding more Classes, more people over the next few days, and I will guide them in using their powers. All so that you can learn the subtle differentiations in other forms of Mana usage."

I groaned but it felt good. More practice meant I'd get better at it, stronger. Perhaps we'd be able to save more lives. I just wished it gave me experience. But we couldn't have everything, could we?

Looks like I had a lot more work ahead of me. To be fair, it looked like we all did.

Chapter Ten:
Waves

15 Weeks, 3 Days Post-System Onset
4 a.m.

There was no forewarning when the proximity alarms went off at four in the morning. I fell out of bed, pushing myself up from my knees as I grabbed clothes to pull on while dashing downstairs.

All of us bleary eyed, I pulled up the perimeter defense portion of the settlement interface and swore.

Proximity alarms were why we'd only been able to get the walls to a certain strength before we ran out of funding, and there was no way for us to afford pushing more defensive capabilities right now. "Meeting points, everyone."

Any alert of an attack or a perimeter warning prior to seven in the morning was part of our emergency plan. Except we'd only implemented it yesterday. I hoped people remembered they had places to be with their allocated patrols.

We hadn't needed an emergency plan when we'd all been crammed into the one spot.

"Jackson, I need you to make sure Wisp and the other twelve kids around here get safely to Garbo. Then you're to help Sienna and Dor in monitoring. I know you know this, and I know you want to be out there fighting, but we need multiple members of the tech team inside our hub for this." My brain was running at nineteen to the dozen, and all I wanted to do was make sure he knew this was important. That he was important.

It hadn't been necessary.

"Got it, Mum," he said as he grabbed his bleary-eyed sister and guided her out to where Wombie was waiting, his little wombutt eyes bright.

Kyle, Evelyn, and I grabbed the coffee Kyle had prepared and headed out to our checkpoint. It'd have to do. My brother didn't like kipatchya for some reason I still hadn't figured out.

Scooters were a godsend, and I watched as people sped from houses and apartment blocks as fast as the small vehicles would carry them. I had to admit I was impressed with the implementation of the emergency plan. Sadly, most of our patrols were called upon for it, because we didn't have the luxury of a large enough force to give anyone time off.

Maybe one day.

But for now, we headed down to where Newnham met Logan Road because that's where the largest blip on the radar was approaching. Taking several deep breaths, I stood there as the others gathered around me. Hirish and Piola, Dequasha and Mon'swkinon, Drake, Gemma, Evelyn, Dannin, Molly, Sange, Tasha, Ray, Eritia, Talia, Morton . . . two full patrol squads were gathering here.

And I was still scared shitless.

We still hadn't found Gary, though Drake did know he was supposedly alive. For now. That was another back burner thing to do. So much we had to do.

Kyle walked over to me, his expression grim. So much frowning in fact that he almost drew his eyebrows together. "It's there, but it's just not approaching us. And there are a lot of them."

"Can we like stealth down or something and check?" I asked. There was a reason I didn't take charge of scouting missions. Mainly because I had no idea how the hell any of that stuff worked.

Gemma materialized next to me. "Exactly what I was thinking, boss." She winked, tapped Drake on the shoulder, and then they weren't there.

While we waited, the rest of our formation moved down Logan Road toward Bulimba Creek and the intersections, moving as quietly as we could. Almost thirty of us, some of the faces only vaguely familiar to me.

Yeah, we weren't that quiet but for a group of untrained civilians—we did pretty damn well if I had to say so myself. Experience teaches, and we'd been schooled in the hardest school of them all. Australia in an apocalypse.

We pulled up in line with the creek and paused to make sure none of us were straggling. Meanwhile, I double checked the defenses' interface. Now that we were outside of our System-designated settlement limits, some of the options were no longer available to me. However, checking on security was something it seemed I could access no matter how far out we were.

At least within about thirty kilometers or so.

From what I could tell from the interface, there were several different types of creatures approaching our boundaries. In fact, they were converging on each other. Which I could only surmise due to the different directions they flowed from. It wasn't like the interface labeled the hostile dots for me.

Were they trying to get to us, or were we in for a clash of the creatures if they were going for each other? So many dots, super close to us, but because of trees, I couldn't see anything definitive.

The clash of dots centered in two places. One close to us, and another over the top of Newnham where it met Creek Road. That one didn't appear to be any immediate threat, and there were notes from Sienna and Dor that we'd sent out scouting troops to keep an eye on the activity there.

Good. I turned my attention to the next set of dots.

Which was right about when Gemma popped up again, practically on top of me, Drake just to the rear of her.

She was frowning but didn't seem particularly worried. "It's completely weird. Like you don't even understand. Koalzillas and Emugators literally fighting each other. About maybe . . . five or six of each. It's like they've ventured out of their nests and are seeking their prey farther afield. But then they ran into each other?"

"So they're not moving to attack us?" I asked, a little incredulously. At least I knew that many little dots did mean there was more than one type of creature.

I guess we'd been ripped out of bed at 4 a.m. for a clash of the titans? Not my idea of fun. But better to be alive and kicking than sorry, I supposed.

Drake shook his head, and from the slump of his shoulders and the sadness in his eyes, I knew he'd been hoping see Gary. "I would be willing to bet that whoever the victor is, they might start coming toward the settlement. For now, we just need to monitor them."

"Just?" I sighed softly. "Probably a good idea."

I turned back to the group, though I was fairly sure all of them heard the information. "Okay, Group Two, head back and see if you can get some more rest. Drake, Gemma, Tasha? Can you backtrack and get us vehicles? May as well start our patrol now that we're all here anyway."

They nodded and dashed off. Hirish stepped up next to me, an approving smile on his grizzled face. "This is to be expected, and we need to remain vigilant. Some of these will survive, and we need to study them to discern why they're fighting now. It could be nothing, but it could also be very telling in its own right."

"What do you mean?" I asked, almost immediately regretting wanting to know.

He smiled, but this time there was a creepy edge to it. "Sometimes they roam because they are beasts, and other times because they are running from something that's more dangerous. Running and moving into another monster group's territory. Sometimes it's a mix of both."

I didn't need to continue my line of questioning to know Hirish liked it when it was the latter. He was a mercenary. I'm not sure why I felt a little disappointed.

While we waited, I leafed through the settlement quests and grabbed one. May as well get a little more bang for my hammer swing.

Quest Accepted

Quest: Clear out two nests in Garden City's direct clearing routes

Reward: 900 Experience.

There we go. Nothing amazing, but since we were going to do it anyway . . .

It didn't take long for the scouts to return with the vehicles. After a moment's pause and check of the wind direction, I realized it was better for us to be where the survivors couldn't smell us and tempt them into coming after us. Then again, we'd want to be where we could monitor them as well.

"Let's head back to the Koala Bushlands and see what nests we can disrupt there. Maybe even push the Dungeon a bit. It hasn't been cleared in several days." And then I sent Dor a message through the admin interface that if the alarms went off, when they did, to alert me as well.

Just in case.

Because we all knew people would die if those surviving beasts made it to our settlement.

❖

The drive to our next nest hunting ground was eerily underpopulated by monsters. It didn't give me a warm fuzzy and victorious feeling. No, it gave me this deep-seated sense of dread.

From the looks Piola and Hirish shared? I was fairly certain I wasn't the only one. We moved closer to the conservation area in Daisy Hill and would likely need to delve out even farther to do any real killing today.

We made it through the forest so easily. Nothing jumped us from the paths, and there were no indications that we were being watched. And yet an eerie, ominous sensation pervaded our journey.

Even the first level of the Dungeon appeared to be empty. Cold sweat trickled down my back when I tried to engage my Mana Sense and saw nothing but cool and calm Mana. There were no darker areas, nothing that told me something had laid a trap and was just waiting for us. The only use of Mana appeared to be the ambient version of it as Mana reinforced walls and gathered in order to set up the next nest.

"I thought no one had cleared this in days?" I asked, suddenly wondering if I'd gotten our information wrong.

Kyle responded, his tone somewhat perplexed. "No one has since four days ago—"

"Then there should be respawn," Hirish interrupted, kneeling and placing his hand against the ground, closing his eyes like he was feeling for something.

It seemed like a sort of tracking thing, and I didn't have the heart to tell him that I already knew what he was going to say. Mana Vision 101—Mana activity reveals everything. Even if you can't understand what that everything is.

"It's cleared, and only in the early stages of respawning." He seemed perturbed by the revelation.

An odd idea occurred to me, and at first, I brushed it off. There was no way that was possible, right?

"I mean." It was difficult to figure out how to phrase what I wanted to say. "Could other monsters have come in here and cleared the Dungeon?"

Even just saying it out loud made me feel sort of nauseated. Surely not.

How could monsters the size of the Koalzillas fit in there? But that was just it. It wasn't only fifteen-foot-tall monsters. The Emugators were much shorter in height, and yet longer in body. They could easily fit down here. Hell, what else could?

"Do we really think they're smart enough for that?" Kyle asked, even though I could tell he just wanted someone else to say it.

Piola stepped up to the crease, like it was her turn to bat. "They are. Especially with the number of mutations your country is producing, there could be several possibilities. Since they mutate, if the mutation combines the intelligence of both species . . . it's just taking the best elements from the splicing that occurs. Science and all." She shrugged like it was no big deal.

I guess for someone who had lived in the intergalactic world their entire life, it wouldn't be such a scary thing. She was an assassin who hunted down people, beings, and retrieved things and property. For us humans, however, this was what the really good horror movies were made of. Experiencing it in real-world time didn't help any of us process things better.

"Great," Evelyn muttered. "This is like *Australia and the Bikini Mutants.* B-grade movie extraordinaire."

I couldn't help the laugh that escaped me, and several other chuckles peppered the break in tension.

"Next stop, then!" Kyle clapped his hands, almost giving me a heart attack from the shock of his loud exclamation and turned on his heel to hoof it back to the vehicles.

The sun had risen by now, and its warm tendrils snaked their way through the trees, flickering on my face through patterns of gum leaves.

At least they used to be gum leaves and were now this slowly mutating form of flora that scared me a little. I'd get my hands on plant samples as soon as I could spare a few days to research them.

I couldn't help but feel disappointed as we clambered back into the vehicles to find somewhere else to kill things. There was also an overlaying sense of wrongness about all of this. The mutations fighting each other, the Dungeon cleared when it hadn't been one of our patrols, and us having to drive farther and farther to make sure we kept the area clear of danger.

Though that could also be seen as a good thing, I guess. That we'd been keeping the area so clear of monsters we had to go farther afield.

Anything? I shot back into the admin chat.

Everything's quiet . . . maybe too quiet

That was Dolores down to a T. Completely and utterly not reassuring. She didn't need to poke the bear and all the foreboding feelings I was already having. Doom appeared to be the motto for the day.

Ginali wants to talk to you when we get back.

Tell him to have kipatchya ready and I'll think about it.

Done. I could practically feel her smiling.

We had this. We could do this. I just needed to get out of my own doomsday forecasts. I focused on where Kyle was steering our vehicle along Quarry Road and out toward Ford Road to check out the nature preserves around there. The Mana around us appeared to be calm, or at least as calm as wild ambient Mana habitually behaved.

It wove in and out, over trees and brush, skimming the road for the gods knew what reason, and lingered whenever it approached any type of structure or sign as if trying to assess how best to approach it.

Out here, there were few signs of civilization, even though it was only a few minutes to get there by car. Vehicles didn't line the streets here, but soon, those few that were scattered along the roads would begin to decay as the mutating vegetation claimed back the world. Would we be able to maintain roads? I knew the settlement could, but what about the rest of them?

Soon, any out-of-settlement homes would be overrun with nature, and modes of transportation would give way to rust and other evidence of the passage of time. All of it sped up because of the mutant apocalypse.

Suddenly, a flash of strobing Mana practically blinded me from up a ways.

"Shit. Kyle, pull over!" I gasped out, each breath causing me pain. The brightness left that image at the end of my vision like when you stepped out from darkness into the sun. I forced the panic out of my mind. This was what I had been studying, why I'd even taken on Dequasha's training.

In my brother's favor, he pulled over calmly, not letting my outburst affect him into panicked action. Because we'd been the head of the convoy, the others pulled over with us, exiting the vehicles as they did so.

The Mana burst hadn't exactly faded, but it wasn't as bright as that initial information influx. There were traps ahead, on the actual road from what I could tell. Intricate in their complexity if the waves of power that bound them had anything to do with it. Heavy lines, leading lightly to their users who hid off a ways.

I had a bad feeling about this, about what type of beast would be able to lay traps like these.

Panic, though? I hadn't really done that in a while. All of this, of everything, led to a need to react and act. To stay alive—and we didn't do that by screaming and hiding. No, we did that by evaluating, assessing, and trying our best to kick ass even if it meant losing people sometimes.

"There's a set of traps out there." I spoke as softly as I could, gesturing beyond to where the bend of the road appeared to disappear into the trees. "They're intricate and woven with powerful strands of Mana. The way they're laid out likely means that whatever did it is hiding near to us. We will need to be careful as we approach. Any form of stealth is appreciated. You might want to scout out ahead, Gemma."

She nodded, and a moment later vanished. The Mana down the road wasn't fluctuating, just a constant presence of power and tricks, danger and death. I shuddered as a breeze passed through the trees, reminding me that we were in the dead of winter despite what the good-old Aussie sun was trying to tell me.

Time dragged on as we waited. I tried to tease more information from the damn Mana sphere, but it was being as obtuse as a six-year-old asked about who ate the candy.

"Kira!"

There was panic in her voice as Gemma gasped out my name, her face ashen. She was gasping for air like she'd never run faster in her life as she skidded to a stop before me. "Trapdoor spider mutation of some sort. There are so many traps there."

She bent over, her hands on her knees, shaking as she dragged in ragged breaths. I absentmindedly rubbed her back for her. I know it helped me when I had panic attacks.

Being a mutation meant it was combined with something else. Until we fought it or them, we wouldn't know what it was mutated with, because if it was obvious, then Gemma would have told us. There wasn't an option of just leaving it either. We had to clear the nest.

Because that's why we patrolled.

Damn it.

Spiders. Why did it have to be fucking spiders?

Chapter Eleven:

Trapdoors

15 Weeks, 3 Days Post-System Onset

9 a.m.

Trapickyzer

Level 43

The thing about being faced with a mutated spider was that I hated spiders when they were like three to five centimeters big, like a couple of inches. Sure, I was good with that, and extremely adept at keeping my distance. They needed their space to kill all the bugs trying to eat my plant life, and I respected their process enough not to interfere.

At least that's the way it used to be.

But mutated trapdoor spiders meant they were huge, Mana-enlarged creatures. And that was *so* not right.

"Watch out, there's another one of them! Left!" Evelyn called out from her perch high upon a small hill overlooking the Ford Road carpark area. The landscape had changed, and though the swampy water was still there, the stench rising from it now was close to unbearable. The water itself was almost unreachable from the way the webs interwove from the trees, through their branches, and hung like a safety net between each of the trunks and over the pond.

Looking to the left, over one of the mounds of woven path, was another of these massive trapdoor mutations. At least I think they'd been trapdoor spiders. They were so huge now, spanning about three meters instead of centimeters. Massive mixes of brown and black instead of just one, and they had those little boxing gloves up near their mandibles. Or that's what it always looked like to me.

But there was something else about them that I couldn't put my finger on. They had to be mutations crossed with some other type of creature.

There were highlighted areas of intense Mana concentration all around us on the ground that I assumed meant traps. It lulled you into a false sense of security because the webs around those areas didn't appear to be webs. They just looked like every other stretch of ground—dirt, leaves, even some asphalt.

But my implants allowed me to see past that. Hundreds of thousands of Credits well spent.

Note to self: hammers were not a good close combat weapon when you had to dive in amongst the fray of a very nimble, eight-legged creature intent on pushing you into its extremely sticky trap.

Webbing was just everywhere around us. It almost appeared to have a life of its own, which was terrifying in and of itself. Strand of webbing got caught around my Warhammer grip and for a few seconds there, I panicked because it felt like the actual web was trying to reel me in, that it was able to react to my movements.

Pretty sure I might have peed myself a little, it startled me so badly.

A second Trapickyzer approached and stood about five feet tall, a bit on the taller side than the first one we were currently fighting with Molly and Sange. At least, I thought it was about that tall. Frankly, it might not have been, considering it was actually maneuvering through the webs. I shot out Planted in Place, but that wasn't going to stop it casting more webs in our direction.

My root didn't hold like I wanted it to, and true to my logical brain, the creature could indeed still fire off webs in our direction. Planted in Place barely held it for a few seconds.

The spider moved forward, its massive legs just that much scarier because of the overall size. Its mandibles moved, and its head seemed to swell a little. No fucking way. Not even the System would have done that, would it? Why on earth would you cross a spider with a tick?

But I guess the System had nothing to do with Earth, did it?

Backing away, keeping my mental map of the trapdoors all around me so I would stay safe, I made sure to stick with the way Molly moved. We needed to stick together. No pun intended.

All the while, I kept my eyes on the monster approaching me. If my suspicions were correct, the size was even worse considering the other creature it was mutated with.

Just as I was about to call out, the second Trapickyzer shot something at me. It caught me while I was threading my way delicately between traps and webs, leaving me no place to hide but take it. At least I got a hand up in time to cover my face.

At first, I thought it was just a web with an oddly slick dripping liquid on it, as it stuck to my body, soaking through my jeans when it hit my legs. But as my body began to numb, I realized it wasn't. Shit. My left leg gave out, losing the power to hold me up. I shot out Planted in Place, hoping against hope that the creature was close enough to the ground this time for my spell to actually be effective.

It screeched in a high-pitched warble as roots shot up, grabbing hold of most of its legs and I sighed with relief even as I felt my other leg go numb. Out of the corner of my eyes, I could see a flashing notification. No shit I was poisoned.

This wasn't the most favorable predicament for me to be in.

"What the hell?" Evelyn was next to me, and I found I couldn't speak. Bad, bad, bad. Voice box too? I needed to warn them about the paralysis tick portion of the mutation. Because if you got close enough to inspect that damned face, it wasn't just a spider.

"Kyle!" she called out, not even attempting to calm her panic.

He pulled his attention away from healing the group, and his face paled when he saw me lying motionless on the ground. Now, don't get me wrong, I was in a bit of pain, but System healing was kicking in, as well as my own Blood Transfer, so it's not like I was dying. Still, my root wasn't going to hold the second creature for much longer, and unless I could get out of the way . . .

"Fuck." He rushed over and placed his hands on my chest. "Can you guide me?"

Well, we were making contact, so why the hell not.

I closed my eyes, feeling for that contact. Luckily, the paralysis hadn't quite made it to my chest yet and I focused on finding the poison in my system with Mana Purification and guiding Kyle through it. Not a moment too soon because almost immediately after we'd done that, I could feel my chest begin to tingle, and I knew, without a shadow of doubt, that my root was about to wear off.

A flash of warmth spread through my body as the toxins left it, dispelled by Kyle. At the same moment, the damned spider broke free of my root.

Hurriedly, I cast another Planted in Place on it, but not before it managed to shoot out and hit Evelyn in the foot. For crying out loud!

She yelped and it was only because Kyle and I were there that we got it done fast enough to back away before the damned thing shot another projectile web out at us. Definitely keeping the bugger tied down at a distance. Its range seemed short at best with that paralyzing agent.

Small mercies and all.

My brother had always been a good multitasker, and his boost to the system healing over time were easily maintained while he helped me. My body still felt tingly and sluggish, but I was just glad to be able to move again.

Implantation in place on the main one, and Blood Transfer on both of them, I got to work piling on debuffs to weaken these damned spiders. Considering the System wasn't shy about regeneration for all living things, it was a constant uphill battle to maintain damage output. Earthen Barrier raised just enough that the second Trapickyzer couldn't aim its web over the top of it, proved to be one of my better calls.

Spider legs are damned scary when they're a couple of inches big. Make that a meter or two long, and it was enough to make me gag. Those huntsman mutations we'd encountered a while ago had nothing on this. In fact, if I could have a Huntion come over here and start whacking on me, I'd be much happier.

Luckily, Molly's shielding capabilities were superhuman and so far, the paralysis shots hadn't hit any of the people within her protection. But those legs with their furry little bristles, hurt like hell when they cut into our skin. Those tiny feet had sharp claws that raked against metal, dug into flesh, and ripped us apart.

It was more difficult for Drake, Gemma, and Tasha to flit in and out, and for segments of the fight they had to resort to throwing weapons. Good thing those skills were just a part of their Classes. Especially Tasha with her ability to throw spells with her swords as she danced around the perimeter of the fight. Being effective in and out of direct melee was the dream.

When the first Trapickyzer hit about half of its life, it righted itself up on its hind two legs, and let out a bellow. One of the legs buckled precariously, having been the focus of most of our attacks so far. It's what trapdoor spiders looked like when threatened—only these mutations didn't really need to make themselves larger.

The sound of the bellow resembled that of a shoebill stalk. If you've never heard that, imagine a velociraptor sound as you know it from a particular movie franchise, dial it up about half an octave, and make it a lot louder.

It sent fucking icicles down my spine.

I knew what it was doing because the way the Mana waves spread out from it, in a rippling of information, of power, and of calling to all its goddamned friends.

"Shit. It's calling the others." I'm not even sure how I managed to choke out the words, how I managed to get the warning off. It felt like parts of my throat were frozen in fear. There was far too much webbing around us to make a run for it, so we needed to kill this thing as quickly as possible. Not that we'd been slacking, just cautious.

Gemma flashed in and appeared right next to the already injured back right leg and hacked away at the joint with a quick flurry of movement and dashing back out again before the creature could respond.

Drake mimicked her movements and did the same to the back left, and so they continued to hack at it methodically. The coarse hairs on those legs scratched them up something fierce when it hit actual skin, but their armor and cybernetic protections held off the bulk of the damage.

Evelyn and Dannin focus-fired the same joints, honing in on as much damage to the soft bits as quickly as possible. It made the most sense. Their arrows hit true to the mark most of the time, anyway, breaking down the joints in the back two legs on each side. When its back legs crumpled under the onslaught, the creature let out another of its dinosaur roars and staggered, its balance momentarily off as it adjusted to only having six working limbs for now.

Ray and Eritia continued to focus fire, helping Molly with the front legs and the separation where the body met the legs, while Sange and Kyle provided the healing back up and Hirish and Piola dashed into the fray with abandon.

The blast gun Hirish favored needed recharge time, and it wasn't the best at pinpoint precision. This time he'd chosen what appeared to be a sword with a laser-edged blade that dug in deep every time he struck. Piola dual wielded axes today, hacking and slashing wherever she could find an opening, whenever she could squeeze it in.

Meanwhile, I continued to keep Water Siphon, Implantation, and Mana and Blood Transfer active on the creature, while tapping into the one I still kept rooted and weakened. Not to mention keeping it partially at bay with Earthen Barrier.

The Trapickyzer we were all fighting keened as its second pair of legs collapsed, followed closely by the front pair giving it no way to really support its huge weight. It crashed to the ground with only its torso and mandibles active moments later.

The trick to avoiding web coated in paralyzing toxins hitting us was basically for Molly to use her shield wall, or else just to dodge it. The latter was monumentally more difficult.

I found myself in a loop of watching for Mana color changes that might give me more warning, so it was easier to avoid the paralysis and casting all of my debuffs and defensive abilities to keep us safe as well. The paralysis toxin gave normal Mana a sickly green tint, offering me a split second more warning, which wasn't always enough.

Flashes of color exploded around us as our ranged casters, Ray and Eritia, let loose with their ice and fire spells. Slowing the creatures, exploding them, and taking chunks out of their health. Arrows flew true to target, thunking into the segmented body's joints with sickening heaviness.

Hirish got too close to one of the flailing mandibles, getting caught by that boxing glove like portion of the appendage. The contact carved out a portion of his arm's skin. But the Hakarta merely grunted, and before I could blink, Kyle's healing removed what would have been a grievous wound six months ago.

The roar from the dying Trapickzyer's throat rang out again, though feebler this time as it entered its death throes. Still, though, the one behind my Earthen Barrier broke free just in time for me to slam another one up, but I knew more were on their way.

By now the ground was vibrating, and I shuddered to think just how many more of these creatures were coming. I reached out, sensing the movement of all of them through the Mana disruption in the immediate vicinity.

Two more were incoming, and if I timed it just right . . .

There, right there, I caught all two of them in quick succession with Planted in Place before they could even round the bend and potentially run into us. The Mana felt slick in my hands, at home in my mind, and for the first time I realized that this Mana Sense had the potential to save us all.

Track prey. Use skills.

Yeah, yeah, I answered the voices that were overlayed like a hundred people whispering at once in my mind. Maybe I was finally starting to understand the messages.

One monster down—or at least, neutralized—and one more to kill before the others arrived. We turned our attention to it, and I pushed aside worries about Mana messages. Kill now, listen later.

We were late returning to the settlement, and I don't think I'd ever felt so exhausted. It was the first day I'd ever used my Mana Sense in such a continuous and fluid manner. Every portion of me ached, from my mind right down to the soles of my feet, and all I wanted to do was crash into bed and sleep for days on end.

Even as we poured into the library, to food set up on the tables because Red always knew when we'd need it the most, I realized that the people in the room were worried. The aura of their power hummed around them, filled with concern and agitation.

Uh-oh.

Dolores cleared her throat. "We're glad you guys made it. It's been one of those mornings, days . . . whatever."

She flipped through things in front of her, probably her view of the admin panel and squared her shoulders before speaking again. "We've had daily updates as a general rule from Carindale since the day you guys made contact. Occasionally there's been a day's lull, but nothing more than that. And they've always answered relatively fast when we've contacted them to check.

"With it being two days yesterday, I didn't think much, but this morning when they usually just do a quick check in there was nothing as well. Add to that the disruptions we had up around the Newnham and Creek Road area, as you know that's directly on the path to Carindale, and I thought something might be up." I could hear the worry in her voice. They might not be our settlement, but they were other Brisbanites, other humans.

Sienna continued as Dor sat down. "We tried to contact them at ten-thirty this morning. And again, an hour later, and then another hour. So far, we've had no responses at all. Nothing."

"Going on day three of no contact?" Kyle frowned, his arms crossed as if he was trying to stop himself fiddling with his hands. "I mean, that's more than what we require to report missing people, right? Let alone missing settlements."

A murmur of uneasy laughter permeated the room, and I could sense why. It didn't take an empath to understand it. We'd left it several weeks now since we'd first visited. Intent on making our own home secure, we'd not yet undertaken the rescue mission we were fairly positive had to happen.

Mike stepped forward. "I vote we keep trying to contact them today, and then, if we have no response by patrol time tomorrow, we send out two patrols? So around thirty people to go and check? Numbers will give our people some form of security and hopefully end up giving us answers as well."

"Could their communication device have stopped working?" I asked, really hoping someone acted like I'd said the cleverest thing.

Chris shook her head, her blond hair bobbing with the action. "No. There's really no way for it to do that. It's a solid communication device, big and bulky. The odds of it being dropped and accidentally breaking are so minimal. Plus, last time I spoke to Lance, their head of tech, he'd mentioned that they'd managed to replicate two of them. So they have three now. One for the tech station, one for their council room, and one for Joshua's—the settlement owner's—office."

Well, that put a damper on my trying to smooth things over.

"Okay, I second Mike's proposal, then." I felt crust in my clothing, like all of me needed a wash. Damn it, I was going to get that freaking dermal underlayer like my kids managed to get with a perk. Sure, it was super expensive to do it now that it had to be paid in Credits, but I needed to prevent damage to myself every way possible.

"Which patrols?" Hirish sounded gruff. "I suggest whoever we send have at least two members from Pirra, Zarrie, and IRSHA."

"Good idea." Mike frowned as he went over his notes. "Sending out six experienced Dungeon Worlders with maybe fifteen of our adventurers should be enough to go check on Carindale and reactivate whatever happened to the communications systems, right?"

"Yeah." Chris grimaced. "I still don't think it's the comms, though. Mark my words, there's something wrong with the people. Something has happened and they're not able to get to us."

Rin, who seemed to shadow Chris and Sarah wherever they went, piped up. Her brown hair was pulled back in a bun today, and slowly but surely, she was gaining the confidence to make eye contact when she spoke. Not for long, though.

"I'm quite certain that the walkies have been removed from Carindale's direct vicinity." She paused, glancing at Chris. "I just asked the System via the Shop."

Chris grinned at her protégé. "Nice job."

Rin shrugged. "Seemed the logical option. Either they lost them, or the items were taken from them by force?"

"Not fond of that last option. Thanks for letting us know." Mike continued perusing his list. "I'll go over this party listing with Kyle—Dale, will you help?"

"Sure thing." Dale paused and turned to the whole group. "Just wanted to note—there are more monsters around the residential areas beyond our borders and leading to Carindale now. Just a word to the wise that it might actually take a full day or so to get to the other settlement this time. Things have been hectic in the mutation world for a while now, and I'm not sure how these creatures will react to a large group of fighters walking in through them."

"Have Carindale not been pruning?" I asked, a little shocked, remembering the group of their very own security force that had encountered us on our way last time.

Dale shrugged. "I assume they might be, but it's not having an impact on how many mutation variations are making their way down toward us."

I nodded. He had a really damned good point. And no matter what, I couldn't get this feeling of impending tragedy out of my head. It was best to get this sorted sooner rather than later.

"Fine. Now you just need to decide on who to send out tomorrow. Make it a strong group but make sure we don't leave ourselves under defended." It sounded logical in my head even if it made my insides clamp up. I wasn't about to let our settlement become a sitting duck.

"Does that mean you're free for that chat you promised me?" Ginali was suddenly at my side, looking up at me with a grin. Damn it.

"Yeah. But I'm bringing Dor because sometimes I think you like to pull the wool over my eyes." I grinned at him but meant every single word of it.

He sighed theatrically. "Would I do that to you?"

"Yes." I replied, "yes, you would."

Chapter Twelve:
Crafty Cartel

15 Weeks, 3 Days Post-System Onset

5 p.m.

Ginali brought his own person with him. I hadn't had many dealings with Ciago yet, but from what I'd seen of them, they were pretty decent. Perhaps a bit less sociable and a lot more business oriented. Add to that the alchemist Malina, with her armadilloesque appearance, was there too, and I felt comfortable enough.

The seats outside in the middle of the courtyard were cozy and soft. Probably meant to lull you into a false sense of security so you'd buy more. Around us, the bustling of the Cartel's operations was almost soothing.

The way welding gave an almost white noise like buzz, the ring of the occasional hammer like a metronome of industry, and the underlying chatter amongst the crafters that felt more at home than crickets chirping. Dolores sat next to me, an unimpressed scowl on her face, and I elbowed her gently in the side.

"Stop it. They'll think we don't want to have things discussed with us."

She let out a harrumph of breath and side-eyed me. "It's been a long day for all of us. I'm older, and despite the System, I'm tired, Kira. Don't take it personally, but let's just get this over with."

A pang of guilt shot through me. Yeah, I was exhausted. We'd all been up since four this morning. But this was necessary and Ginali wouldn't call a meeting unless he thought it directly relating to current circumstances or the growth of the settlement as a whole. Still, Dor was older, I wasn't even sure how much, and I hadn't asked if she'd like to come, I'd just sort of expected her to.

"Sorry. Next time, I'll ask."

"Good. That's the best we can do." Then she smiled at me, right up to her tired eyes, making them kind of sparkle with mirth. "Sometimes you're too serious, kid."

She wasn't wrong.

Ginali cleared his throat. "The agenda I have for this discussion revolves around our expansion as a Cartel including our needs, and the benefits we can provide to the settlement." He sounded all businesslike, and Ciago and Malina, the apothecary, looked upon him with approval. I think he even preened a little.

There was so much to unwrap there, and I was going nowhere near it.

I motioned for him to carry on, a little tired myself now after Dor reminded me just how exhausted we all should feel.

"As you know, when the expansion took place, the Cartel purchased multiple formerly commercial locations from the human world." He paused, making sure I was following, and then continued. "We did this as we're considered a part of the settlement and frankly, while this is a fantastic middle of the hub location to sell our goods, we are running out of space for all of the workshops as we grow, not only in what we produce, but the number of people we require to produce those items."

"Okay." I wasn't trying to be mean, but like Dor so helpfully pointed out, I was tired. I just wanted him to get to the point. "What is the news you have for me?"

Something passed through his expression. It wasn't a bad thing, more of a realization that he was excited, and we were exhausted.

"I apologize for bringing you out here when you've been up clearing monsters since the alarm sounded. There is so much happening for the Crafting Cartel right now that I just wanted to share. Sit a bit and we'll have some food and drink so you can at least replenish some energy." He sounded contrite, and I'd not seen the Pharyleri like that before.

It was marginally refreshing.

Not ten minutes later, we had steaming bowls of what looked like a beef stew sitting in front of us, with glasses of . . . chilled kipatchya? My eyes widened and I knew I must look shocked. "You can have cold kipatchya?"

Oh wow, why had I not thought of that before? I mean, I could chill coffee, right? I could take it everywhere with me!

Ginali's eyes sparkled. "There are a lot of things you can do with it. Stick with me and I'll introduce you to a whole new galaxy of the best cuisines."

Taking a sip, I could tell he wasn't bullshitting. The flavors were that much crisper with it cold. I glanced at him suspiciously. "You had an Ice Mage adjust the temperature, right?"

His grin widened. "You're getting good at that sort of thing."

I smiled, picked up the bread roll that came with the stew and began to eat. Speaking around my first delicious mouthful, I motioned to him. "Go on. Speak!"

For a moment it looked like a thousand thoughts were flowing through his head, but the Mana aura around him remained calm and unperturbed, so maybe he was just trying to figure out how best to phrase things.

"Some opportunities have opened up for the Cartel, and by extension for the Garden City Settlement." He paused, like he was double checking our reaction, and apparently encouraged, continued. "These include, but are not limited to, contracts offered to us asking us to supply certain large conglomerates with exclusive access after a certain new element, item, or piece of gear that has been discovered or crafted."

"Wait." Dor waved her spoon to and fro while she swallowed her food. "Doesn't that limit our potential income, and give those people an unfair advantage over others depending on what it is you're allowing them access to?"

Ginali nodded. "That it does. Which is why it's not my favorite of the options. Providing intergalactic goods is one thing. But the Coefficient Crafting Cartel is known for its neutral standings in matters of politics and war, and to accept such contracts would go against our code of conduct. But I did want you to know such offers exist."

This was actually interesting. It also shed light on why IRSHA had paid so handsomely for exclusive access within some parameters on this new continent. Seriously, galactic ramifications and red tape were just scary.

"Okay, so if that's not the offer or information that has you all excited, then tell us what is, please."

To be honest, the stew was delightful. Even if I wasn't sure what it was made of, I didn't care. The spices they'd used, the veggies they'd chucked into it, especially something that if it wasn't potato, was damned close to it. Yeah, this was good food, but I was going to get that sleepy after the full feeling hit me in the next twenty-odd minutes. He only had so much time with me before my eyes tried to close involuntarily.

He glanced at both of his companions like he wasn't certain how to say this. But then his contagious excitement shone through, and he beamed.

"There have been some crafting items traded to us that have allowed us to form several new enhancements on weapons and armor. Enchantments that help with restrictions otherwise placed on those types of items. Because of this, the Galactic Council has given us permission to work toward establishing an actual permanent trade portal."

Ginali stopped expectantly, like I knew what the hell he was talking about or something. All I heard when he said that was that there would then be a faster way for people to get to our settlement and thus more potential invaders. Nothing about that made me happy, nothing about it shouted that

129

we'd be safe, and a part of me even felt a little angry.

"Was that it?" I asked, realizing belatedly just how irritated I sounded. Then I sighed, put down my spoon and leaned back. "I'm not sure how I should feel about this. You're going to need to explain portals and how they work and why I should feel happy that we might be getting a permanent one. Also—just where do you plan to put such a thing, would it have guards, how easy is it to travel by portal? Those sorts of things."

"I told you, the humans wouldn't know," Ciago said with what I think was a chuckle, even though her face remained less than expressive. "Sorry. Ginali gets excited about the possibilities and doesn't stop to think that there might be other ways to interpret things."

"As the acquiring agent for the Cartel, all the delicious and completely new mutation variants this country is producing is a veritable smorgasbord of potential. You have to understand that when the System classified you as a Class-7 inhospitable ZFQ rating, there was all too good a reason for it to do this. The rate at which your mutations are occurring, and the items they're producing, well. It's fast, and it's deadly . . . and has the potential to be highly profitable for all of us."

"Tell us something we don't know, love," Dor drawled out, finally finished with her own stew.

I wondered if I'd be able to order some of this to keep in a cold box at our new house. This stuff was heavenly.

Ciago flashed us a brief grimace and continued. "The portal would need to be set up with the perimeters of the settlement. It would likely be a Class-2 portal and require round-the-clock monitoring. This is something the Cartel would take upon itself, though we would ask for permission and assistance should we need it. Not all portals are trading portals. Simple travel portals have fewer permissions and less . . . shall we say, permanence."

I nodded, sort of with her so far.

"I actually have an excellent idea of where to put such a portal, but you have to understand one other thing. Just because we have the potential to get one doesn't mean we *will* in fact get one. There are certain things that must first be fulfilled for us to establish the 'correct' surroundings."

"It's not an immediate sort of next week thing, but more an if we do A, B, and C, then in this much time we'll have a permanent portal?" I asked, seeing where she was going with it.

"Yes. Precisely." Ciago appeared to be pleased with my quick adjustment. "It should take maybe three to six months, perhaps even a little longer depending."

"Okay, so that's great and all, but what is it you need from us?" Dolores interrupted, a smile on her face that reminded me of Cheshire cats.

Ginali spoke up again at this point, and I'll admit there was some hesitation in his response as he formed it. "We need to strike a deal where the patrols deliver all of the rarer crafting materials only to us. I realize that sometimes the Shop pays a little better, but right now we will match the Shop. For a period of six months or until the portal gateway is implemented."

That was a pretty decent offer when all was said and done. He really wanted what we collected from the mutations.

"So if it takes longer than six months this is valid *until* we get the portal. But if it's shorter than six months you'll still honor the six-month time period?" I was so tired, he could have been trying to sell me a pink turtle for all my brain was taking at face value.

"Yes. That is correct."

My Diviner skill picked up no elements of subterfuge, nothing that might lead me to think he was trying to pull one over on us. Truth be told, Ginali didn't appear to be like that, but I'd also only known the Pharyleri for three months, so I wasn't betting anything on trust.

"Well, some of the items are rarer than others, as in they drop less frequently. What about those?" I asked, pushing the point.

He frowned for a moment, as if he was calculating something in his mind. I knew the Cartel was making good money off us through trades and purchasing items they required. This portal thing had to be truly lucrative. "Everything. Also—caveat that any newly discovered items from new creations such as that Trapickyzer you came across today. We would like first access to those crafting materials to see if they are something we can work with."

I glanced at Dor, who just nodded at me, her eyelids making it appear like she was in a sleepy haze, even though I knew she was paying attention to every word.

"Done, then," I answered, and the Contract appeared almost out of nowhere. Thing was, even if we'd discussed things, I always read a contract in full. And when it was a System Contract, that went doubly so. "Give me another iced kipatchya, thanks. I'm going to have to go through this before I sign it."

"Of course!" Ginali didn't even attempt to hide his smile as he motioned over one of the crafters and placed the order.

Damn little money-driven Pharyleri. He'd end up being the death of me, and probably craft an enchantment out of my pancreas after my funeral.

❖

Dor headed out before I finished signing the Contract. I went to find her and let her know I really did appreciate everything she did.

I flopped down on a chair next to her in what used to be the amazing

8 Street Eatery pre-apocalypse. Now? Now it was dim and wasn't conducive to living quarters. No one had done anything with it yet, although Paul and Red were talking about bringing back some of the Asian cuisines that had been housed there. I really hoped they did.

"You look exhausted. Shouldn't you be at home relaxing?" She didn't look up from the book in front of her as she spoke.

"I am, and I should, but it's effort to walk that far. Besides, I wanted to make sure you know how much I am grateful for everything you do." I paused for a moment, watching her.

Dor chuckled. "I know you are. I'm just grumpy in my old age."

How I could relate to that. "I'm also waiting on Chris, Sarah, and Rin to be done with a chunk of the new communication watches. Once they're done, I'll feel a hell of a lot better about the patrols going to Carindale tomorrow."

"Worried?" She finally looked up at me.

I paused for a moment to really think about it. We'd had mutations over near the Creek Road boundary of our patrols—at least more than usual anyway. Those came from the Carindale direction, even though we regularly cleared out several roads over. So yes, I was kind of worried. "Yep."

Dor flashed me a tired smile. "Well, think of it this way. We wanted to go and help them originally, and now we have our own shit together we can probably better help them anyway. Plus, I'll go create a little quest for you guys to investigate Carindale's lack of communication. There's no time like the present, right, mate?"

"Right." And she was, but there was still something about it truly bugging me. "Maybe it's the silence. We're going on a few days now. Just hope the same doesn't happen to our patrol."

Because that was the crux of it. Even though trying to keep track of all the people we had in my head was hella difficult, I still got this overall sense of belonging from them. Sending them out to potential doom instead of just possible doom. Well, that was more difficult than I liked to admit.

"It's one of those calls you just sometimes have to make. Doesn't make it easy, only necessary." Dor leaned back and nodded at me.

Damn it. Did she always have to be so bloody right?

"Necessary doesn't make people any less dead on my watch though." Which was the crux of my problem with the whole situation.

"But Kira, it's something you're going to have to get used to. Unless you pull your kids out of here and go live like a hermit. Somewhere where there won't be a heap of other people looking out for them, mind you, you're going to be in the center of shit whether you like it or not."

What were her abilities again? Because mind reader was apparently one of them.

It had been over three months, and nothing was changing. This wasn't some nightmare we'd wake up from.

The world we knew had ended, and I couldn't help the parts of me that wanted it to be easier, that wished I hadn't put myself out there when we all first met, that I couldn't help just wishfully thinking sometimes.

I pushed myself up, just suddenly exhausted in more ways than just the physical. "I know you're right, Dor. It doesn't mean I can't have wishful thoughts, and I don't have to like the reality to know it's the reality."

"We're all there with you, you know."

I did, and I also knew that everyone was suffering this mental fatigue of just surviving, too. "Yeah. If you can't beat them, right?"

Dor nodded, gulping down another swig of whatever she was drinking. "Then we surprise the hell out of them."

I laughed and headed up to the tech department, my work here done. Perhaps it was all just about supporting each other in any way we could.

Chapter Thirteen:
Dungeons and Levels

Week 16 Post-System Onset

8 a.m.

Wisp wouldn't let go of my hand as she stood next to me, gripping it tightly, like she thought I was about to leave her. I squeezed her hand back, trying to reassure her while the council and I handed out organized rations and weapons and everything we could think of for the patrol that was about to head out.

Tasha, Ray, Dale, Lousesh, and Zyrilian were all going along with the others. Declan was headed out too, and he'd become a strong tank able to keep monsters' focus despite not having to take hits.

They were taking people I knew were strong and able to hold their own. Even Mon'swkinon was going to go with them. We were sending three of our best aliens, I guess? Not to mention one of our best healers, our major Ice Mage, and our Spellsword. Even Rin was going to make sure they could fix any tech problems that arose. That gave me hope that communications would remain open.

Sending all those people gave me confidence that they'd be okay since I was staying back at the settlement. Not that I felt I was make or break. I definitely wasn't the only leader among us, and even then not the best.

It had taken me a couple of months to realize it, but I didn't always have to be out there on the new and unknown front lines. Because when all was said and done, my priority was the survival of my kids. Staying here for now, learning more from Dequasha about how to best utilize my abilities for the benefit of the entire settlement including my kids? Well, that was the current best usage of my time.

And I'd argue that until I was blue in the face.

Still, it felt weird not getting ready to go with the group myself, and it also filled me with a strange fear that they might not make it back. Perhaps it would be better to send someone else in Dale's place. He had his son here, after all. Orphaning Darren completely wasn't something I wanted to be responsible for.

But in this post-apocalyptic era, we all had to readjust. Like I did every single day when I went out on patrol. Second guessing myself this time wasn't going to help any of us, least of all Carindale.

I took a breath and approached the group, putting my false confidence on display.

"You come back now, you hear?" I could see a flash of fear through the human's eyes as I said it and realized immediately that I maybe shouldn't have.

Dale stepped closer to me, his gaze avoiding mine. He lowered his voice so only I could hear. "If I don't return, take care of Darren for me?"

"Of course." I breathed the words out, hating myself for not risking my own kids orphaning, and at the same time grateful that I had to work on mastering my Mana Sense and that it was logical for me to stay behind. I pushed down the guilt. I'd deal with that later.

Then I noticed that Morton was going too. His salt-and-pepper three-blade cut reminded me of gunpowder, and his eyes crinkled at the corners every time he spoke, like he was just this side of laughing on a consistent basis. I did like our Gunslinger, though I'd realized lately that he wasn't the only one we had.

There were several others of them scattered throughout our ranks. Maybe we'd bring some of them with us on patrol for training, help them get experience too. I raked through the group, trying to see if anyone else I knew well was going.

Dannin stood at the edge, talking to Evelyn, and while I knew there was nothing between them that wasn't just Ranger-type camaraderie, a pang of jealousy shot through me anyway. She appeared to be irritated with him, and I walked over to quietly join them.

". . . they need a better archer than the one they've got, Evelyn." I'd never really heard him assert himself like that. Just seen how well he worked with a bow, his proficiency up there with Evelyn's.

"I know," she muttered in response. "But we've been working so well together, I don't want to lose that for our patrol."

She had a point, but at the same time, the whole reason for our increased-in-size patrols was to train those who weren't yet as good as those of us more seasoned.

"Evelyn?" I let them know I was there, though I was fairly certain they were already aware of me.

She glanced at me, like telling me to butt out. Good thing I was stubborn too.

"He has a point. They're going out there, in an environment that's changed in the last what one or two months? The mutations are overrunning everything. And we want this group back with as good a chance as we can give them." I turned to Dannin, letting my words sink in. "You be your awesome self. Come back to us."

He nodded, and for a second I thought maybe there were tears in his eyes, but he blinked them away before I could get a proper look. Yep. Everyone was scared. We'd been holed up in our little haven for too long. Even our patrols were, for the most part, reinforced and comfortable.

Safe.

"We gotta move out," Dannin said, as Lousesh walked over, beckoning to him.

The massive Hakarta was one of the members of the Pirra clan I liked the most. He was about as friendly as they got, and always logical. Always willing to consider the other side of the bad—the worse.

"I'll bring them all back safely, if at all possible, Kira." He smiled down at me, the weathered skin of his face crinkling in all the wrong spots. Like I'd mentioned before, Hakartas' smiles are pretty terrifying. Something to do with tusks and alien skin colors.

Then he held his hand up, showing off the communicator the tech department had finally been able to produce a few dozen of. "We will be in constant contact."

I nodded, choking down a sudden lump in my throat. It bothered me that I wasn't sure if I felt so uneasy because I wasn't going, or if it was due to something just feeling off about the whole set of circumstances. No matter what, I couldn't help feeling like they had to be extra cautious on the way to Carindale. "Got it. Be careful out there."

Lousesh grinned at me again. "Never and always," he said before turning and leading his group of adventures out the gate.

Damn it. I needed all these people to return.

Why did I feel like it was almost a suicide mission?

❖

16 Weeks Post-System Onset

11 a.m.

I stood back panting, using my Warhammer as a leaning post as Gemma drove her knife through the underbelly of the Tetchrihorn we were concentrating on.

Damn it. Sharp implements seemed so much more viable as a weapon. Turning, I refreshed Planted in Place to make sure the other creature stayed rooted. Two of these things at once would probably kill us.

The Tetchrihorn looked sort of like a rhinoceros if you squinted really hard. There was a vague resemblance to alligator-patterned skin, but in bigger sections. Almost prehistoric in appearance, to be honest. The horn on its head gleamed in the sunlight that shone through a gap in the trees, and I couldn't believe the relief I felt at not fighting a mutation of some beloved childhood furry species.

I had no idea how Gemma's blade managed to cut through the plated skin like that, but I was glad for whatever reinforcement spell she'd used. When it finally fell to the ground with a thud that made the earth beneath us shake slightly, I inspected it.

Tetchrihorn Corpse

Level 47

Interesting. A flickering notification in the bottom right corner of my eyesight alerted me to the fact that my Planted in Place spell was wearing off the other target. And that Tetchrihorn was pissed—at us.

We probably killed its mate.

It broke free a split second before I could get my cast off and managed to leap two massive strides before my root snapped it back to the ground. But the force it had been running with ended up breaking the Skill before it could properly take hold and all it ended up doing was slowing the creature down some.

At least I gave Molly enough time to plant her shield in the ground and activate the massive sphere to protect all of us within it. The Tetchrihorn rebounded off it, fell to its butt, and shook its head before lumbering back into a standing position, only for my root spell to finally hit again and take hold.

It keened in anger, perhaps also in mourning, and the bronzed horn on its head began to glow. Great, an ability we hadn't seen before.

"Stand back," I called, tracing the power it used. Definitely offensive, explosively at that. "That horn is a ticking time bomb."

Everyone backed up, activating their long-range skills. Even Drake and Gemma. The creature stomped one of its front legs three times, frustration clear in its panicked eyes. Maybe if we'd left all these creatures alone, they'd have thrived and created their own ecosystem, much like if humans hadn't have developed the land so much the circle of life would have continued far less interrupted than with us.

But that was a philosophical debate for another time.

Right now, this thing might be frustrated and wanting to break free, but it also wanted to impale and explode us with its horn. So really, we needed to concentrate on keeping ourselves alive.

Molly planted herself front and center, her sturdy stance ready to brace her shield and block anything that tried to get past her. Sange stood about five feet back from her, their own healer's shield held tightly across their body, while the other hand wove protections with their wand. The rest of us hid behind them.

Well, except for Hirish and Piola.

Hirish stood on the opposite side of Sange, firing at will, an expression of grim determination making the wrinkles on his face sneer into a frightening mask. His favored pulse rifle had been replaced with a more maneuverable pulse pistol, and the brief bursts of blue power thudded into the thick hides of the Tetchrihorns in an even cadence.

Piola, on the other hand, dashed in so fast I could barely track her form and carved intricate patterns into the skin of our opponent, as if it spelled out something more powerful in culmination.

Kyle wove and released reverse healing spells, undoing natural regeneration in ways that I knew made his skin crawl. I needed to speak to him about how he was coping with his Class's capabilities because it hadn't been long ago he was struggling with them.

So many of my regular patrol members were headed to Carindale, and I felt a little lost without their back up. There were missed beats, openings in the salvo, or places where people like Piola or Gemma would take advantage of, to attack up close. Heals that came a little late, gaps in positioning that had people shuffle around wrong.

Wrong, wrong, wrong—because we'd gotten so used to working together. In and out of rotation. Removing too many of them, replacing too many of them—it left us vulnerable in a way I think we needed to rectify sooner rather than later.

Chris and Sarah were out with us today, testing several new devices they'd created. Their Level 32 selves had me worried for their safety, but their armor was solid, and they weren't weak. Another Archer type had joined Evelyn, and she was running through shots with them, helping them tweak their Skill order and get the most out of each cast of Mana.

I kind of missed Declan because I enjoyed watching his tanking style. If I'd been a tank, that's the type I'd have liked to be.

From the flow around the newbie Archer, whose name I believe was Marie, she was a fast learner. Her hair hung to her waist in a long, blond braid, clear blue eyes focused on her target, using a type of cybernetic visor I'd not seen before. From what I could tell, it allowed her pinpoint accuracy when firing, because I never once saw one of her arrows miss.

I could practically feel Evelyn salivating and anticipated a Shop visit from her as soon as we got back.

The Tetchrihorn's horn continued to glow, brighter and brighter, until it was almost blinding.

Three things happened at once.

Molly's shield slammed into the ground, creating a ripple effect that tripped up the Tetchrihorn's balance; Hirish shot a pulse rifle blast directly into the shining horn, causing sparks to fly in such a way it felt like fireworks had gone off far too close to us. And lastly, one of Marie's arrows hit it directly in the right eye, causing a massive keening sound to erupt from the creature.

As the sound traveled, the Mana fueling the beast began to act erratically, like it was trying to fit into spaces that were too small for it. Pulsating with uncertainty, power lingered around the creature as it began to stampede and flail around shaking its head where the horn now appeared to sputter like a flare.

Oh shit.

Like a flare.

Like a warning flare.

No. No. No. What was with all these bloody creatures calling in back up lately?

I could feel the sound of more incoming Tetchrihorns long before we saw them. Without a word both Marie and Evelyn split to different sides and laid traps on the ground. We'd need all the help we could get in order to break their charge.

Reaching out with my senses, I tracked the direction and number of incoming reinforcements. "Four incoming. Maybe more from farther away—I can't tell yet."

Damn it. Where were those mind-control Classes like they used to have in some of those MMORPGs? Why couldn't I restrict Mana flow as well as read it? Damned preset Skill trees.

Traps set, I turned to see everyone dog piling on top of the one in front of us, almost frenzy like in an effort to diminish the amount of these creatures we'd face at once. Only the Rangers, ranged Classes, and I stood back from everything.

Tracking the flow of incoming Mana, I got ready to shoot out two of my roots in quick succession. If that failed, I might block them off with Earthen Barrier to stop their initial roll. If I could catch the ones the traps didn't, we might even get out of this with little damage. The Tetchrihorns were huge and trampled like stampeding rhinos.

Evelyn's ice trap caught the first one, snaring it in place like she'd flash frozen it. But I could see the ice begin to spider from within and knew it wouldn't hold for long. A split second later, one of Marie's traps triggered.

I couldn't quite tell what it was, but my Mana Sense showed me this black, Mana-woven ropey appendage that shot out of the trap and began to encase the same creature, doing damage as it did so.

There were some definite differences in Marie's Class.

The Tetchrihorns, now aware of the traps, sidestepped the next two, but I shot out Planted in Place and managed to snag its legs, which left two of them still running toward us. With about ten feet left between it and Molly's defense line, I managed another root, barely holding onto one of the back feet. Smashing Earthen Barrier into place with it, my spell bashed the creature's nose and had it shaking its head so that the tentative root hold didn't matter long enough for me to refresh it. My Mana dropped precipitously, and I suppressed a groan. Mana regeneration still wasn't fast enough despite my upgrades.

In the meantime, Evelyn shot another ice trap at the feet of the almost-broken first ice trap, and Marie . . . well she didn't need to do anything other than riddle the creature Molly tanked with arrows.

Gemma and Drake worked like a well-oiled machine now, their blades whirling as they danced in and out. Fully aware that we had to kill it before it could activate the come rescue me flare, it was easier for us to focus down the one target without having to worry about the crowd-controlled ones.

Evelyn's controlled creature broke out of its hold first but stepped straight into the path of her next trap, and this time, perhaps because it was already freezing cold, the ice block that snapped around it didn't immediately begin to spider web fracture again.

Small mercies.

I wondered if she had timers flashing in her face like I did all around the corner of my vision. Like the Mana waves undulating through all the different blues of the spectrum all around me. Like the massive attack I could see Molly's current target—we'll call him Tetchrihorn Number One—building up toward, even as I refreshed my own roots.

Tetchrihorns Four and Five were being ice trapped, and Tetchrihorns Three and Four were rooted by *moi* with Earthen Barrier smushed into their faces so their vision was blocked. It felt like we were drowning in enemies.

"Can you interrupt it? Stun it?" I called out to Molly, knowing we had maybe a few seconds leeway.

Molly did exactly that, hefting her massive shield and slamming the creature in the chest bone. She stopped the casting Tetchrihorn Number One had been about to finish so suddenly that I could almost see little birds and stars flying around its head.

Not to mention the massive *whoosh* of Mana she expelled by doing so. Now I could see why she didn't build it into regular rotations. The built-up power around the Tetchrihorn dissipated, and I tapped all five of the creatures with Mana Stone to help bolster Molly's Mana regeneration.

I needed to figure out how to specifically target the recipients of my

Mana regeneration spells for better results. A cloud of power was already starting to gather up around her target again. She was going to need to build that slam into her rotation for this fight and for that, she needed Mana regen.

"Duration?" she grunted out under the weight of one of Tetchrihorn One's attacks.

"About a thirty-second buildup, I think?" I said, not entirely sure since I wasn't an expert at my skill yet. But our tank nodded, and I could tell she would make it work.

Directing my attention back to the two I held in place, I checked the root timers to see if I needed to refresh them and noticed Evelyn had put down another trap.

From the way Marie's trap's Mana signature was beginning to flicker, it looked like it would break soon. "Can you refresh that, Marie?"

She shook her head in the corner of my vision. "No. But I can kite it."

Another shot landed at the feet of her creature, with an appearance like tar. Probably a snare or slowing trap. Nice. Where had we picked her up? And why couldn't she trap it again? The questions built up and got jotted down on that "ask questions later" tab in my head.

The Mana faded completely around the trap and as the creature stepped forward, straight into the tarry substance on the ground in front of it. Marie shot off three successive arrows, raining down with her impressive accuracy, and took off running at high speed. The creature didn't even give Molly or the rest of us a second glance but dove straight into stampede mode after her. Except due to stepping through the tar, it ran in slow motion.

If I'd found this video on the internet prior to everything, I think the slow-motion effect of it all would have had me in stitches.

Molly's use of Shield Slam against her target had taken a toll on her Mana despite my best efforts, but we weren't in dire straits yet.

Evelyn's ice trap triggered for the third time, and I could see by the way it held that it was going to start having diminishing returns. I was definitely getting better at reading ability-related Mana signatures.

Planted in Place had the added irritation of allowing the creatures to move what body parts of theirs weren't tied down, which meant I needed to interrupt them intermittently with something else, considering my Stone's Throw and Rock Slide both did too much damage and were more likely to interrupt and break the root.

Gemma worked well enough with me when I asked for an interrupt that I could rely on her to track the creature's casting. Still, that meant I had to depend on someone else, which was always difficult for me.

Suffice it to say, I didn't like this type of monster at all.

This was an "interrupt, Mana conservation, keep the enemy moving" fight. If they were moving, they couldn't stop to cast that horn rainbow thing. At least from what we'd observed, anyway.

"Evelyn, can you fire two ice traps at my targets please?" I needed a quick break.

I tapped my good old Mana Cloak to give me a chunk of Mana. I loved that it gave me greater interpretation skills when it came to divining the Mana around us, and with a two-hour recharge, it was as close to Mana cheating as I was going to get. Not to mention that it periodically upgraded.

Its current stats surprised me a bit. I hadn't been expecting it to give me 250 Mana, but here we were. I think I'd just been blinking away the updates. Still didn't make much of a dent, but it helped.

The ice traps were fired before I got done replenishing my Mana, and Evelyn moved forward, dropping a tar trap in front of her creature. "The other one is almost dead, I'll kite mine and try to keep those two frozen for a bit. But it's best if Molly tags one of the one's we're kiting, because right now they're pissed at us."

I grinned at her and nodded. Evelyn probably wasn't even aware of how much she spoke like she was playing a game. I guess being a game developer was ingrained in her. At least most of us understood it though, having previously played some sorts of games ourselves.

She sounded tired and I couldn't blame her. Sometimes I wish I'd chosen a purely dedicated crowd-control Class. If only I'd known then what I know now. Still, her and Marie's kiting allowed me to focus on Mana Stone and Blood Transfer, which I couldn't place on the ones in the ice for fear of damage breaking the trap—or myself getting too much of that good old aggro. I could, however, leach life from the ones being kited.

It wasn't like my heals would ever replace a healer, but every little bit helped.

Implantation and Water Siphon helped keep the main creature weakened, and I did what I could to aid the two kiters.

Multitasking was becoming my bane.

Apart from the Mana-gathering explosion the Tetchrihorns had, and the fireworks flare of "come and help me," they weren't complicated monsters. They basically did short and sweet stampedes toward whomever had pissed them off the most.

Timed right, our melee fighters could jump out of the way, dodging the attacks and letting the Tetchrihorns run past, not hitting anyone including Molly as they tried to impale the tank. Their turning radius was shit, and we could easily still attack Tetchrihorn Number One while it maneuvered. Adding Earthen Barrier to guide where the current main target could or could not move gave us a bit of extra time.

Number One fell, and I thought we might have the fight under control as Molly pulled Evelyn's kiting target over to her with the Taunt from hell. Evelyn grabbed Tetchrihorn Four from the ice blocks as soon as her coast was clear.

Once Tetchrihorn Number Two was in place, I took a chance.

Hefting my Warhammer, I ran into the fray. I could even feel the ribs crunch under my swings as I drew back and wielded it with all my might. Though I didn't break the skin or cause wounds, it was still a satisfying way to work out my frustrations at the whole Carindale situation and the general overall sense of foreboding I felt because of it.

Maybe the group got too far into a groove, perhaps we just got complacent as we methodically worked our way through each of the creatures. Whatever it was, I couldn't quite understand what happened next.

We were on the Tetchrihorn Number Three, which Marie had originally been kiting and Tetchrihorns Four and Five were being snare-kited by our Archers, when Marie screamed.

Her scream cut off abruptly as she went down under the thundering feet of the beast she'd been kiting, blood flying into the sky and splashing the ground.

Then there was only deafening silence in my ears.

Chapter Fourteen:

Trampled

It only took Evelyn a split second to react, and I was still scrambling to see what had happened. With my root in place, Evelyn smashed an ice trap into Tetchrihorn Five and turned to re-snare the one she was kiting. Marie's chest still rose and fell, and I couldn't believe the sensations of relief running through me. If she was breathing, Kyle could fix her enough that the System would heal her.

Fuck. Didn't need those five years of life that shock just cost me.

Tracing around the amount of Mana being used in our area was difficult now. So many strands interwoven with others, where we assisted and bolstered one another. Trying to focus was starting to strain my head and I could feel the ache beginning right behind my eyes. But I had to get better at this. We had to get through this. Surely, I should have seen that break in control coming before it happened.

I should have been able to warn her.

Damn it.

Kyle was with her now, bending over her form just as the ice trap cracked, releasing the creature which stumbled first into a well-aimed tar trap and then another ice trap. I glanced over at Evelyn, who was still kiting her own. Damn, she was good at multitasking.

"DoTs. Broke the first one. I knew they would. Wore off now," Evelyn gasped out, and I realized that System assisted or not, she was going to run out of energy soon, let alone Mana.

Warier now, we attacked the current target with abandon. I leached what I could off it for all of us, implanted it to help with healing and small amounts of damage, and Water Siphoned it to weaken it. They were my easiest and most Mana-efficient spells to use when we were in prolonged battles. Most bang for my buck.

Once it was dead, falling where it stood with a shake of the ground next to the previous few like a domino that would never get back up, Molly taunted the one-off Evelyn with her Roar.

Of course, the thing you have to understand about taunts in the real post-apocalyptic world is that they don't work like they do in videogames. It's like a hormone inducer or something. Wasn't about to work on another sapient creature, but at least Molly could rile up the Tetchrihorn so that it looked at her long enough for it to get good and angry with her.

I cast root back on the frozen one and Evelyn shot two more traps at its feet. Ice and snare. This time she focused on assisting the DPS considering we were down Kyle. But I knew Sange was up for the healing task. They were one of the best healers I'd ever seen in this new world.

Watching my twin from the corner of my eye, I could see Marie moving now. Still lying on her back but stirring slightly. I should have looked away, but the way her obviously skewed bones shifted back into and beneath her skin to snap back into place was fascinating. The way the wounds on her body sealed themselves up as Kyle continued to heal her where bones had broken through was equal parts fascinating and sickening.

Whimpers of pain escaped her, and I didn't think she was completely conscious. Small mercies.

I'd hate to think what being trampled by a rhino creature felt like. From the way the Mana bled around her, I think she 'd been at death's door. Such a sobering thought. I'd barely known her a day and her potential death shook me more than I liked.

In the background while I'd been watching her wounds heal, the rest of the team had continued the fight.

I tore my attention away from her, directing it back to the fight where I was needed. Mana Stone replenished, I dove into the fray again, my attacks coordinating with Piola and Gemma. You couldn't have too many melee underfoot. These creatures didn't have hit boxes; you actually had to come into contact with them to do damage.

The accuracy our ranged casters showed was something to be grateful for. Arcane missiles and fiery death hammered into the creature without causing us any echoed damage. Hirish and his pulse pistol hammered shots into that tough hide without any danger of ever coming into contact with ours.

We kept at the rotations, the damage output, until both Tetchrihorn Four and Five were dead, sinking ourselves into pure damage, debuffs, and buffing rotations to block out the screams I was fairly sure would keep us all awake tonight.

❖

Marie was still sore when she got back to the settlement and Kyle seemed extremely concerned by it.

"You shouldn't be feeling residual pain, the System usually kicks in and takes over after I do the worst of it." He hovered at her side, brows furrowed.

Marie shrugged. "Some of it might be in my head. Those damned hooves were hard."

"Yeah, not something I'd recommend you do again any time soon." Kyle's tone was dry, but I could still hear the worry in it.

"Guess that's why no one puts getting trampled by a rhino on their bucket list," she said in a completely deadpan manner as we wheeled her into the center's medical bay. Marie still seemed to feel weak, and maybe that was an in her head type of thing. Which I got. It's just not natural to heal that fast from so much damage. Sometimes I think the System's need to keep everyone alive for whatever reason was going to ruin our mental capacity to deal with trauma and tragedy.

Evelyn grinned in response. "Told you you were cutting it close with the tar traps."

"Yeah. Rub it in. Told you so is exactly what I need right now." Marie closed her eyes a moment, and I could see the regret flit across her face before she opened them again. "You should be going to the Shop and getting upgrades, or next time I'm going to kill you in the damage output again. There's no next time to my getting trampled."

"Ha!" Evelyn turned on her heel and grabbed me by the arm. "Come with me. I need to see about implants."

I flashed Marie a grin, but her eyes were already closed again. It took the body a lot of energy to heal, and she'd just done a heap of it very rapidly. If it wasn't all the System's fault anyway, I'd almost say thank you for stitching her back together.

We were back an hour earlier than usual, having downed the Tetchrihorn nest anyway. We'd just opted to get Marie back to safety.

Wisp was still in school, and Jackson still out on his own patrol. It was odd not having my daughter greet me with her oversized companions, or a flip right up to my face.

"Store?" I asked Evelyn as I grabbed her elbow and steered her toward the Shop orb.

"Yeah. I never realized we could get enhancements like Marie has. Not that I've really looked before. Although, I mean, look at your eyes; they're freaking amazing to look at now. All the information you get from them. I'm not sure why I didn't use logic. *And* I've seen Gemma. I should have thought of it. The idea that another Archer is that much ahead of me because I didn't consider getting otherworldly help? It just irks me."

Still with one hand on my arm, she placed her free hand on the orb, making sure we both got yanked into her Shop. It wasn't really different from mine, and Shi'enah was still there. But I'd noticed on occasion that they had different shops leading off their hallway. So strange how everything was almost tailor made.

How did that even work on an intergalactic level?

I waited while Evelyn sold some stuff and spoke to the Shopkeeper, glancing around trying to discern an actual difference to the place I experienced. Once Evelyn was done, I waved at Shi'enah and followed my friend into a Shop.

It wasn't as bright as the one I'd gotten my implants in. There was a section over at the wall that was cordoned off. Perhaps a small room's size. If there were surgeries involved, I got the feeling they took place in there instead.

The rest of the Shop had several white shelves with what appeared to be high-tech virtual-reality-looking headsets on them. But if they'd been high tech for Earth . . . how high tech did that make them here and now?

Anyway, they were more like sunglasses; it seemed they tapped into your visual cortex in a less invasive way than my implants worked.

But Evelyn just *tsk*ed under her breath like she couldn't find what she was looking for. "I want what Marie has. At least that level of sophistication. She has this clip that goes over her ear and taps into her mind. Like it sort of plugs in when she needs it at the top where the temple meets the ear. And then allows her to project a focusing target over her left eye. That's the minimum of what I want."

"And I have exactly that here."

We both started and looked over to see a man standing behind one of the shelves that I now realized was a counter, dressed all in white. He blended in so perfectly that I hadn't noticed him. Upon closer inspection I realized his eyes were slitted like a cat's and his skin wasn't actually skin, but close shaved fur instead.

Evelyn brightened. "You have it?"

"Yes, we do." He reminded me of a kitten, right before it reached out and knocked a cup full of water off your counter and onto your beautifully porous tile. Yeah, he looked kind of harmless, but there were evil machinations underneath that smile.

"How much?" She tapped her foot with impatience, narrowing her eyes, and I could see the waves of determination coming off her.

The man in front of her grimaced for a moment, like he was reading her aura too. I chanced to Analyze him.

Degrash Inih

Felinious

Shopkeeper

Level 52

Interesting. I hadn't seen anything above level fifty yet. Not even the Advanced Classes. Those all started back at one. Well, unless you counted the Magon.

His sigh pulled me away from my musings. "It depends on what you're going to wear it for and what types of interface you will be using." He motioned Evelyn over and they began to browse what I assumed were specifications in a catalogue.

I decided to browse the shelves. This place was fascinating, like a mix between an old video game shop and a high-tech gadget place. I think Jackson needed to come here with Evelyn. I'd have to ask her about that later.

Wait, maybe my son had his own version of the Shop too. Ack. These trains of thought just made my head ache.

Glancing at the time in the corner of my screen, I noticed a message from Dolores about incoming communications from the patrol sent to Carindale. My body tried to freeze in place as it attempted to push my heart through my throat. Not literally, of course, just that sudden oh-shit feeling.

I managed to move despite that, motioning to Evelyn until she gave me her attention.

"Gotta dash. Dolores needs me." I tried to shoot her an apologetic look, but my friend just waved me away and turned back to Degrash to continue discussing this visual targeting system she wanted.

I ran all the way to the library. Yep, all like thirty meters. Didn't even wind me. Which is saying something. Hiking I'd always been able to do, but running? I was definitely not a runner. Dor looked up as I came into the room and motioned for me to sit.

Beanbag chairs for the win. I wondered if we could order these through the Shop because I would love to have them in my new house. "What?" I asked with none of the preamble.

"Last message said they'd been attacked as soon as they crossed the Creek Road line. Even though we took care of that area yesterday. I should have another communication coming in shortly, but it's looking like it'll take them days to get to the actual settlement."

I closed my eyes for a moment, trying to picture the area they'd been in when they got attacked. Creek Road marked the unofficial edge of our territory. If you followed it up to Logan Road, where we'd encountered the original Rigoll mind-control beast, we'd pretty much taken on patrols of everything around there.

Beyond the Creek and Newnham Road juncture where Creek continued on, it took us all the way to Carindale. Close to our borders there was residential housing, and I think one of those Bunnings hardware stores.

"What sort of creatures attacked them, do we know? How does the area down there look?"

Dor glanced over at me. "They said most of the buildings around the area were flattened, like completely in crumbled ruins, and that they were making their way up the road with extreme caution so they don't get jumped unexpectedly."

The communications set up chose that moment to crackle.

"Dolores?" I could tell that was Dale's voice coming through.

"We're here. Report." I could hear the relief even if it was subtle. Dor cared no matter how much she pretended to be gruff.

"We're working our way up Creek Road now." There was some static in the background and I could hear some yelling. "Just got attacked by a nest of Caneglobulous. Sorry. Talk soon."

I frowned. "They're on the main road, right?"

Dolores nodded. "From what I can tell."

"I mean, I guess those creatures came and attacked us last time when we went to locate Carindale initially, but for the most part, they'll stay where they are, yeah? We have to hunt their nests, right?" Thoughts were spiraling in my head, and I didn't like the way they were churning.

"Yes. That's why we've got the patrols organized the way we do. To keep the herds thinned and be on the lookout for disturbances. You know I know this, Kira."

"Then why are these particular mobs different? They're inspecting as the same species; then shouldn't its habits be the same?" There was only one answer, and I didn't want to be the one to say it out loud. But it scared the shit out of me.

She watched me thoughtfully, and I could see the same train of thought clicking into place rapidly. "You don't really think it could be, do you?"

Shrugging, I began to leaf through the database we'd been compiling on alien resources. It wasn't huge yet. Some information on the Dash'Kiri, more about IRSHA, some stuff about Mana, basically all the books any of us had thought to buy and share. But none of us had looked up the *Mormaturian Blobnecked Rigoll* since we'd fought it before we'd even properly established the settlement.

I shuddered at the memory of the kookaburra projectile jutting out of Barry's chest. Just one of the lovely scars this world left on us all.

"I have to go to the Shop. I have a really bad feeling about this." I stood up and headed out.

"Good luck!"

I knew Dor meant every single letter.

Chapter Fifteen:
Revelation

I barely spared Shi'enah a second glance as I ran into the Shop. A brief wave and there I was in Chjaveen's store pulling up all the information I could find on that damned beast we'd fought. Our first elite experience.

It seriously felt like a lifetime ago.

This was odd, though, and nothing like the experience I'd had when researching IRSHA. First up, depending on how I phrased the search, it yielded different results. And secondly, the prices weren't going to kill me.

Mormaturian Blobnecked Rigoll

Levels of Mind Control and Resistance Boosting
Cost: 6,265 Credits

Mormaturian Blobnecked Rigoll

Having a Rigoll in Your Immediate Vicinity and What to Do About It
Cost: 4,198 Credits

Mormaturian Blobnecked Rigoll

Mind-Control Hallucinogenic Effects
Cost: 3,723 Credits

The information in those books would download directly into my brain from what I could tell. We needed to know as much about the creature we were about to encounter as I could gather. I could feel it in my bones.

I tried a couple of other searches, but all I got after the initial information wave was a few books. They appeared to be bedtime books, or fairy-tale compendiums for the most part. But wasn't there always some truth in myths and legends?

At those low costs, I was willing to take the chance that they were crap. Even one tiny hint in them could help.

Mormaturian Blobnecked Rigoll

Myth or Legend?
Cost: 456 Credits

Mormaturian Blobnecked Rigoll

Bedtime Tales for the Fearless
Cost: 333 Credits

Mormaturian Blobnecked Rigoll

The Fascinating Beast of Old
Cost: 258 Credits

Yeah, those last few results were definitely more fiction than fact. Sure, great scare-your-kids bedtime stories, but that wasn't going to save our patrol or Carindale if what was creeping in the back of my mind was true. Still . . . any little tidbit might help.

Damn, I hoped I was wrong.

I was quite relieved that the cost was so much lower than I'd anticipated since I guess this was coming out of my own savings. Either way, I'd have the information and could go about figuring out if I was right.

I grabbed the books walked up to pay Chjaveen, so I could also get the downloaded information.

Before accepting payment, he eyed me with a knowing stare that made me far too uncomfortable. It was like he knew I was brimming with questions.

I sighed before speaking, gathering my thoughts. "Is there a reason this is so much cheaper than when I researched IRSHA and the Dash'Kiri?"

He kept staring at me, those reptilian eyes unblinking. Just when I thought he wasn't going to answer, he did. "The Rigoll is a monsssster, not a ssssentient, politically affiliated being. It can't really pay the Sssyssssstem to withhold information. However, otherssss technically could."

"Oh." Well, that was a lot more complex than I'd anticipated, and made a hell of a lot more sense. Just like I could pay to keep my family's information safe, I guessed others could do the same. Whole organizations, really. Fascinating.

Chjaveen was still watching me. "You realisssse once you know all thissss, you can't unknow it, right?" he asked, as if he were trying to bore his eyes into my soul.

"Yes." I gulped.

"Did you specifically ask the Sssyssstem if there was a mind-controlling alien hunting you?"

"Wait. What? I can do that?"

"Hirishhh did not mention thisss?"

I shook my head, feeling all too stupid right then. Moving to the side, I inputted my question into the system. All righty, then, time to ask.

Is there a mind-controlling alien specifically hunting the humans in Carindale?

481 Credits for the answer to this question.

Fine. I paid it, only to simply have my suspicions confirmed, but not specifically enough. It took a bit of the wind out of my sails that it had given me the information so easily, so willingly, and relatively cheaply. Still, I needed more.

So, I thought for a bit and asked another question.

What type of mind control creature is hunting the humans in Carindale?

572 Credits for the answer to this question.

A large mind-control creature exceeding level 50.

Damn it. Okay, so I needed to watch my phrasing. Thinking about it for several seconds I finally decided to just ask it straight up if I was right.

Is a Mormaturian Blobnecked Rigoll hunting the humans of Carindale?

2842 Credits for the answer to this question.

Ouch. That one hurt. But I paid it.

Yes.

Well, that answer hit me right in the gut. It was weird just being able to ask for information like this. Maybe that meant no one was trying to keep it from us. I'd take that as a good sign.

"I still need these anyway," I said to the Shopkeep. Now that my theory had proven correct, my need to know more about the damned creature increased tenfold.

"Come back alive," Chjaveen said as I gathered the books into my arms and watched my Credits drain out of my balance. I'd even taken the crappy ones, just in case there was something in the myths and legends of the beast that could give us clues for now. We never knew, right?

I almost ran into Chris on my way out of the Shop, dropping two of the cheaper books and glad that the damned things didn't break.

"Sorry!" I said reflexively.

"No. I was waiting for you. Should have maybe stood back a bit. I know how it can sometimes just pop people out like it spat gum." She smiled, but I could tell there was something behind her expression, something worried and dark, like she was fighting back anger or rage.

"Want to talk?" I asked, knowing that time was of the essence, but Chris and her partner were such an integral part of our tech team that I needed to make sure she was firing on all cylinders.

Relief washed over her in a wave of light ambient Mana and she hedged a smile, even as she twisted a longer strand of her blond hair about her finger. "Yeah. I really do. So many theories and so little time."

"Raybucks okay?" I asked, clutching my book hoard like a lifeline.

She glanced at them and pursed her lips like she'd wanted to ask if I needed help carrying them and then realized I might be a tad possessive. "Yeah. I could really do with a drink. Maybe kipatchya?"

Not having expected anyone else to really have tried it and loved it, I laughed. The expulsion of that pent-up energy really helped. Maybe laughter truly was medicine, or else I was so tightly wound right now . . . anything helped.

I motioned to Red whose coffee far outshone Ray's, to bring us the usual, secretly glad that it was the cook and not the Ice Mage behind the counter. Until I remembered that Ray was out with the Carindale patrol and the guilt at my pleasure began to seep in. Shit in a bucket.

Finally seated, I rested my arm atop my prized purchases and looked Chris in the face. She had bags under her eyes and her hair seemed oily and less fuzzy breezy than usual. I'm not a hair person, so my ability to classify hair wasn't the best. But it seemed to me like she had less joy all around her.

"Spill. What is it? Because this seems to be worrying you," I asked, catching a glimpse of Red and Leena, Ray's sister, flirting majorly behind the counter as they cooked up meals and made coffee and other drinks.

Hmmm. That was a kind of awesome pairing.

Chris fidgeted, sighed, and finally met my eyes. "The watch's range is maybe, ten kilometers right now, and to be honest, we should have tested them more. If it comes into contact with enemy fire . . . wait, I'm not saying it right."

She gathered herself and I waited as Leena brought over our order, her face full of smiles. It was nice some of us could forget we were stuck in this hell hole. "Thanks, Leena", I muttered, giving her hand a squeeze.

Her smile lit up the area and she let out a happy giggle. "Thanks, Kira."

I knew she was aware that I'd seen and was happy for her. Good. Sometimes knowing others were happy for you just put the icing the cake.

Directing my attention back to Chris, I waited while she formulated exactly what it was she wanted to say. All the while trying to ignore the pit of dread forming in my stomach.

"When they come under enemy fire, when it's directed against them, there's a subtle Mana shift, which I'm sure you're aware of." She took a breath. "Since the bands have been calibrated to fit each person individually for this trip . . . that energy can likely disrupt them if they're hit and don't dodge or deflect it."

"Ahh." It wasn't as bad as I'd first thought. That was, until she said:

"But . . ." She wouldn't meet my eyes, and the pit in my stomach began to turn into a black hole.

Chris took a breath before continuing. "While most of the people wearing the bands have the ability to dodge, deflect, do anything not to be hit by incoming attacks, I wasn't too worried. However, it appears, after communication with them and further testing, that when damaged, they emit a frequency that interferes with the other communicators. So that means in order to communicate with us, they're going to have to move out of range of the other devices if theirs gets damaged."

"Which can leave them vulnerable to surprise attack." I rubbed my temples slowly. It wasn't a complete disaster. We'd just hoped that everyone could have their own individual way to warn us or communicate with us. We still had that, just not as reliably as we'd anticipated.

"They still have a couple of walkie-talkies with them, so not all is lost. Dale can also reach us through the admin console for the settlement. Don't stress so much about it. Plus, Rin should be able to help with the tech, right?" I smiled at her, knowing just how much pressure we'd all put on the tech department to get us gadgets in this new world. Gadgets that we could afford instead of paying exorbitant prices through the Shop.

Chris shook her head at me slowly. "Sadly, I don't think she can fix them on the go. There's too many intricate parts that she just won't have the tools for on the road."

"Okay. That's still fine. They can still reach us in other ways." As long as we didn't panic and approached this logically, we should be fine.

We didn't have the money as a settlement to provide our people with Shop-bought things that could do the same, because those items were hella expensive. Something about dealing with the excessive Mana of a Dungeon World and Australia in particular. Yay for being special.

Instead, Chris and her group of techies had been cobbling things together that I sometimes felt were even better and more personally calibrated to work for humans.

"Seriously. The communicators aren't going to make or break anything. They were for peace of mind and easier contact. We still have some easy communication options with them. Besides, Tarin went with them, and Talia is still here, so we always have that way to communicate open to us. It's okay." Even as I said the words and saw some of the tension leave her shoulders, I didn't quite believe it myself. But Chris didn't need to know that.

She didn't need to know that our patrol wasn't just facing creatures like the ones we'd been clearing out, like the nests and new mutations and alien insertions we'd been killing.

Nope. Knowing now what I'd paid to find out, our people stood to be attacked by whatever species the Rigoll was controlling. And that—that was truly terrifying.

❖

I threw the books down in front of Dor as soon as I'd finished my lunch at Raybucks. Chris was on her way back to the tech station with a slew of ideas and determination, and I think we were actually looking pretty good in that respect. I hadn't had the heart to tell her that there were bigger and badder things out there, because she didn't need to know that until I had an actual plan.

Dolores grinned at my hoard and Sienna wandered over, sitting on the desk and crossing her legs. She arched an eyebrow at me. "You're not serious? Not another one of these?"

I sighed. "Look. I now know for certain that my hunch was correct. There is a Rigoll out there hunting the humans in Carindale. Knowing more about the creature is only going to help us. The Caneglobulous are acting out of character for what we know of them now. We can surmise that the Rigoll changes their innate patterns of attack. If we can figure out more of how this creature operates and what its potential weaknesses are, we stand a better chance of not only helping our patrol, but also saving Carindale from complete takeover."

Sienna glanced out of the glass doors to where Rolo stood staring at the ground. He was probably waiting for Wisp. They had one of those kid friendship connections where they were best friends in many ways and fought like siblings in others.

"We'll do everything to keep them safe, you know." Dolores said it gently before I could even form the thoughts I wanted to vocalize.

She was right. We would.

Sienna nodded. "I know, and yet. Stupid damn System."

I knew exactly what she meant. But cursing the System wasn't going to get us anywhere. Information on our target, however, that had potential. I pulled the first book into my lap. Then I stopped for a moment. "This is going to upload to my brain and probably put me out of it for several seconds to a few minutes. But with all this—" I gestured around me and shrugged. "Well, I really don't know do I?"

"We'll keep an eye on you, love," Dor said, her tone kind.

"Okay. Here goes nothing." I placed my hand on the first book.

Mormaturian Blobnecked Rigoll

Levels of Mind Control and Resistance Boosting

Information rushed through my brain like a high-speed train through European countryside and my temples immediately began to thrum. So much knowledge to sort through, so many things to process. And none of it reassuring in the least.

This gave me so much information about the Rigoll's powers. What we'd witnessed initially barely seemed to scratch the surface. The main thing standing out to me in this book was the fact that Rigolls were actually huge and had a massive range of telepathic abilities.

While it seemed they couldn't infringe on sapience, it was theorized that eventually, if the creature was allowed enough freedom to grow, to move, and to conquer minds, then it would be able to.

Starting with the young and impressionable, and also the elderly whose minds were starting to weaken.

Oh, hello, red fucking flag.

That's why we hadn't seen any kids or elderly in Carindale when we visited. Of course, I'd assumed something a little more human-monster-centric, and couldn't help the relief that it was actually alien-centric instead.

The Mormaturian Blobnecked Rigoll wasn't just one creature; it was a hive mind operating through numerous subordinates with a queen of sorts overseeing everything. The one we'd killed. Yeah, it had only been a subordinate. And that was not good.

Fuck.

I should have looked into this earlier, but in my defense, the original attack occurred before we even had a settlement or Shop. And once we got them both, I hadn't given it a second thought. Sort of like every single monster we encountered out there. I hadn't researched Huntions or magpie mutations either.

Settle.

Dwelling on the past changed nothing.

I opened my eyes to see Dolores watching me with quiet concern. She smiled tightly when I met her gaze, like she'd just been checking I was okay. Sienna stood on the other side of the room quietly talking to Mike. They stood closer than I remembered seeing them before several days ago. It gave me a warm fuzzy feeling.

People were starting to let others in, to let them be a part of our new lives now that we'd lost so much. Maybe it was time I stopped putting off how I felt about Evelyn. Or . . . maybe it was time for me to concentrate on the impending disaster first, and if we were still alive, I could worry about feelings then. Mine, at least.

I could still get all excited for my friends.

"One down." I breathed out, hoping that the budding headache held out long enough for me to absorb and sort all this information. I didn't feel like we had the time to wait.

"Too many to go." Dor leaned forward, her hands on her knees. "You sure I can't help?"

I shook my head. "No. I have like . . . extra storage capacity since getting my implant. I don't really trust this stuff just inserted into a normal brain anymore. The headaches I got from learning all that stuff I did a few months ago . . . not really worth it. Just got to let my brain settle a little bit. So much information."

"Hm." Dor stood up and went to the office area she used as a small apartment and emerged again holding a bottle of water. "Hydration can't hurt."

"Where are the other patrols?" I asked, noticing the time as I gulped down the water. "Shouldn't we be having the meeting?"

"Postponed it for a few hours. Figured it was better to have it once you had all the information you were after."

"Good point." I drained the rest of the bottle and there was no more time to ignore it. Onto the next book it was.

This one was much thicker than the study on how its mind control worked, and it was difficult to prepare myself for the influx of information I knew was about to pour into my head. Taking a deep breath, I opened the front page of . . .

Mormaturian Blobnecked Rigoll

Having a Rigoll in Your Immediate Vicinity and What to Do About It

And I let the information flood into me.

Everything in this was darker, with science I didn't understand. There was so much knowledge in this universe that I didn't comprehend because our Earth, as I was coming to realize, was somewhat primitive. But there was the gist of it, the overarching understanding that the Rigoll was doing exactly what this book said it was.

And there was the complete and utter realization that we may already be too late to stop it. With its powers of mind control, the creature, as it leveled up, was able to move from simple control like it had had with the native and smaller wildlife, right up to more complex creatures.

Those included new mutations of fauna and extended out to those newer monsters that the Dungeon World spawned.

It was powering up—*had* powered up considerably already—if it was affecting humans of any type. Mind magic was strong, but it couldn't work well with sentient and sapient creatures that possessed their own form of natural defenses. The young and the simple, those were easier to control.

It stood to reason that the thing must have made somewhere near Cardinale its home. Somewhere likely between the Creek Road shopping center and Carindale. That at least gave us somewhere to begin the search.

Wait. Maybe that was something else I could ask the Shop. I'd have to head back there and see. If I could figure out a way to get us enough mental resistance—like our entire group—then maybe we would stand a chance of resisting whatever it threw at us.

My hammer and my ring helped me. But I got the distinct feeling from all my new knowledge that forty percent wasn't even nearly enough. Not for this creature. And I was well aware that other humans might not even have the protection I did.

Slowly, I opened my eyes to find Dor scrolling through settlement information. As soon as I moved, she came over and felt my head as if she was searching for a fever.

"You're sweating. Have another water." And there was a bottle miraculously in her hand.

Bless her.

"Okay, just one more. And then we should be good for a bit. Not going to look into the legends until tonight." The water wasn't cold this time but lukewarm, and I didn't care. It slid right down with such ease and felt so damned good.

I glanced at my health and winced. Definitely taken some damage from all this downloading. I debated how much longer I could wait, gave it a few ticks, and wondered if magic healing would help in this case. Something to test for another time. Hopefully this book wasn't about to kill me.

Mormaturian Blobnecked Rigoll

Mind Control Hallucinogenic Effects

"In for a penny, right?" I muttered, ignoring Dolores's snort of laughter, and placed my hand on the title page.

This whoosh of information was different. It bled into my brain like an insidious snake, winding its path through all of my information to settle like lead at the bottom of my stomach. I retched without warning, bringing up some of that water mixed with a bit of my lunch.

Fantastic.

The smell hit me, even as Dolores cast a Cleanse spell, wiping it all away moments later. She targeted me right after, but I still wiped at my mouth. Didn't do much for the smells that had escaped, but at least that was dispersing.

The Rigoll would be somewhere it could hide both in plain sight and blend in with its surroundings. Given that it was a giant blob, there couldn't be too many places we'd find it. Still, I'd check in the Shop to see if I could actually pinpoint it before we headed out. Hopefully, it wouldn't cost too much. But knowledge was power, right?

The part that made my stomach churn and want to regurgitate? That had nothing to do with where it might be found, but what might happen if we couldn't get enough mental protection to help us battle it.

Its control worked like a hallucinogenic drug on sapient minds. Tests had been done—and I didn't want to know how these people came about this knowledge, to what extent they'd had to go to uncover all of this—but they knew it and it was horrific.

Minds affected by the Rigoll hormone, let's call it that for sake of expediency, were sent into a spiral of whatever made it easiest for the creature to infiltrate its victim's mind. Self-recrimination? Guilt about something?

It used whatever mind weakness it found to gain a foothold and tormented its captives with that weakness. That's how it kept control, sending them into repetitious spirals of their trauma, weakness, or pain.

Before it could do that, the Rigoll needed to be strong, to gain and maintain strength.

If one of the beings it controlled managed to break its mental hold, it would create a momentary opening for others to do the same. That's what we had to focus on.

We needed to get our hands on mental resistance gear. Anything to boost our resistances. And some rings or bracelets or even potions we could feed to, or attach to, those kids and other victims who'd been mind-fucked.

A plan, a hope was coming together.

If we could coordinate everything at once—boosting captive resistances as well as our own attacks, then maybe, just maybe we'd cause it enough pain that it had to let go en masse.

Maybe then we'd have a chance.

Finally, after what seemed like an age and a horrific headache to boot while I waited for my health to tick up, I opened my eyes and focused on Dor.

"I think I know what we have to do."

She grinned at me, relief in her gaze. "Good. Took you long enough.

Now let's tell the others."

Chapter Sixteen:
Plan of Action

16 Weeks, 3 Days Post-System Onset

7 a.m.

Preparation day. That's what I was calling it, anyway. We'd been up until late into the night discussing all the possible strategies or what we might be potentially overlooking. But finally, we'd agreed we needed to have a plan of action.

From what I'd been able to purchase from the System, the creature appeared to be located around the area I'd calculated it would be. Though as far as Chjaveen had imparted, getting exact information when a creature was capable of concealing itself could be difficult.

The general location was all we needed.

Wisp stood next to me, sulking quite loudly. Not complaining verbally or anything, but she was a hundred percent not happy with the current situation, and it fed through to the animals too. Dog sat with his butt to me, ignoring the fact that my foot was underneath it. He was successfully and completely ignoring the rest of me, too.

Great. Now I'd gotten on the bad side of Dog for doing things that were necessary.

I crouched down so I could look my kid directly in the eye. "Whisper. I need you to listen to me. I need you to understand that we have to take action as quickly as possible to prevent really bad things from happening."

She sighed, in that theatrical eight-year-old way, and met my gaze. "Fine. But I don't like it. You should take Mumma Wombutt with you and I'll feel like you're safer."

I paused at the thought for a moment. It wasn't the worst idea floated on the table in the last fifteen hours. She could definitely come in handy when fighting creatures, and her armor plating had extended now from the ridge on her back all the way down to her hind feet.

"I'm not sure how logistics will work, but if I can, I'll take her, okay?"

Wisp looked at me, like she was trying to see if maybe I was lying and then she nodded once. "If you don't take her, you're taking my protective bracer."

I opened my mouth to argue, but my headstrong kid just shushed me. We'd have to talk about that later, but she obviously felt strongly enough to do something she knew I didn't like.

"Mum. I want you to be as safe as you can. We will be okay here. Jana and Avery take us through safety drill and stuff. You know, like those drills we used to hear of in US schools, active shooter or something? Like that.

"We know how to pick up and hide and disguise our smells even so creatures might not sniff us out." She bit her lip, staring at me. "If you don't take Mumma, let me give you something that might help."

I sighed. "You realize I wouldn't be going if I could avoid it, right?"

"Yeah, I know, and I think if I begged you to stay and you did . . . I might feel bad about it." She smiled wanly and hugged Dog against her. "I just don't want to be left alone, Mum."

Her tiny voice was almost too low to hear, and I pulled her into a super tight hug. If I didn't have this stupid Mana Sense ability, I wouldn't be such a crucial part of the plan and I could stay here and hole up and pretend everything hadn't stopped.

"It's okay. I'm coming back to you," I said, holding her at arm's length.

"I know," she said, giving me another huge hug, but for some reason she didn't sound like she believed her own words.

Damn it.

"I'm going in to help Jana and Avery with the little kids. They're so annoying in the mornings." One more quick hug and my brave kid was gone.

We weren't leaving yet, not without ample protection. Like I'd said, it was prep day. We were still receiving communications from our initial team. There were no fatalities, and they were slowly making their way closer to Carindale.

Now that we'd been able to inform them of just what we were about to face, they were taking it slower, being more careful, and attempting to thin out some of the swarms of creatures for when we got there with reinforcements.

"Kira."

Ginali's sudden presence at my side scared the hell out of me. I hadn't been expecting him to pop up. He looked worn out and I wondered if he'd been up all night since we'd talked about our plan to free Carindale and stop the spread of the Rigoll influence.

If we didn't get this sorted, the damned thing was going to encroach on our space. And the last thing we needed was Caneglobulous, Emugators, and Koalzillas coordinated by a Rigoll in their attacks on our settlement. While they were willing to fight anything—including each other—first, that gave us an advantage, but the moment they gathered together . . . we were screwed.

"What's up?"

The gnomelike Pharyleri frowned, as if he was trying to figure out how best to give me what was probably going to be bad news if his hesitance was anything to go on. "There are several items and potions we can create that will lend some mental resistance. But we're talking potions that can't give you more than a few hours of protection and not more than ten percent. The rings and accessories will have maybe two to four percent per item. Likely with a lot of the baser versions just giving one percent per ring depending on the materials we can source.

"They're relatively cheap to make, but we have to depend on the skill level of the crafter to determine the amount per ring, and we have too short a production window for our top crafter to produce them all. People will likely have a mixture of one- and two-percent protection rings. With a few fours mixed in here and there."

"That sounds better than you realize, considering what we're working with right now." But I knew he was about to drop another bomb.

"Rings are our best bet. People can wear what, eight to ten of them? With ones and twos more prevalent, I'd say it's more like that we'll get ten to twelve percent extra per person." He pushed some of his hair behind his ears. "It might be an idea for people to search the Shop for a cape of magic protection. It has elemental affinities on it and will cost a pretty penny. Maybe twenty thousand credits or so. But if you can afford it, that's likely your best bet. It could have anything from ten to fifteen points of mental resistance on it, depending on cost."

I mulled that over. Twenty thousand wasn't completely prohibitive or anything, though it was a lot of money. With rings and one of those capes, I should be able to get mine to maybe sixty-four percent. Still not perfect, but a lot better than I had now. "Thanks, Ginali. We won't count on the potions. Just use them in a pinch, then?"

He nodded. "With more time, I could have done a lot more. I could have sent you out with lists of ingredients needed, and work on crafting mental resistance in new ways, but we do not have time right now. I can only do what we are."

His tone was so apologetic I just wanted to give him a hug, but since I didn't feel we knew each other well enough for that, I smiled instead. "Hey, if we can get everyone boosted up to even fifty percent, we might even stand a chance."

"You know what, that might be true. Little bits stacked up add up. I'll still see if there's anything I've overlooked. Ciago has been delving into some research about it herself. If anyone can find something I've missed, it's her." With that, he took a few steps, waved, and disappeared back through the settlement to the Crafting Cartel's domain.

What sort of shitstorm would we be in now if we'd never gotten that damned Crafting Cartel add-on to our initial quest?

Also damn it. I'd totally forgotten to get the dermal underarmor in the wake of that terrifying spider attack. I was going to the Shop and getting it now. I still had a chunk of Credits, may as well spend them on something that'd help keep me alive.

While the rest of us gathered up supplies and gear to increase mental resistance modifiers, I was going to the damned Shop to get my reinforced skin. If it was good enough for my kids, it was good enough for me.

Dermal Underarmor

This thin layer of super-strong, under-skin protection can be enhanced and upgraded through Artisan-based Skills, providing a less bulky and always-present layer of added protection equal to 800 physical defense, 250 Mana defense. Can be damaged. Regenerates damage from ambient Mana within the vicinity over a period of 32 minutes.

Dermal Underarmor - Upgraded (Level 2)

This thin layer of super-strong, under-skin protection has been enhanced and upgraded through Artisan-based Skills up to Level 2. It provides a more refined and always-present layer of added protection equal to 950 physical defense, 300 Mana defense, and 50% stunning effect resistance.

Due to dermal sheathing disrupting external, unsafe Mana Flow and System-Assisted Skills along with a boost in confidence due to increased safety level, this upgrade increases Mental Resistance by 5%.

Can be damaged. Regenerates damage from ambient Mana over a period of 29 standard minutes.

That was going to have to do me. It took longer and almost two hundred thousand Credits to get the upgraded version. Now that I realized it could be upgraded that simply, I'd save to get the kids' reinforced too. My coffers were almost empty now, jangling down in the lower six figures. I needed to sell things and approached Shi'enah on the way out of the Shop.

Tetchrihorns were apparently a well-selling item, netting me a total of forty thousand Credits each for the two I had, not to mention some of the Trapickyzer parts I hadn't sold yet. A bit more and I could afford the upgrades for the kids. Mum guilt was a terrible thing. Even though I was about to go out there and fight for more than just my life, I felt guilty that my Dermal Underarmor was now a higher grade than that of my children.

But I was as prepared as I was ever going to be to get out there and fight the Rigoll in its chosen habitat. And for now, that had to be enough.

It was one in the afternoon when I finally emerged from the Shop complete with my new upgrades and temporarily dwindled cash supply. Jackson stood outside, like he'd been waiting for me. Although he was talking to Darren, Dale's son, so the latter was probably in my head.

"Mum!" he shouted, his tone eager, and he looped one arm around me briefly for a side hug.

A thought occurred to me. "How much do you have saved up?" I mean when he went out on patrol, I didn't expect him to pay a tithe to me or anything with the loot he got. He had to have some savings.

He stepped away and eyed me suspiciously. "Enough. Why?"

"Don't be coy. Tell me. There's an upgrade I need you to get for yourself, and my cash is running low."

Jackson stood there for a moment, and I couldn't tell if he was inspecting or analyzing me or whatever, but he smiled. "You finally got the underlayer. About time, Mum."

"That's just it. It's expensive to upgrade. Since I'm going on this mission, I did. But I want you two to get the upgrade too." I said it softly. Mum guilt divvied out its own particular brand of shame. I felt so bad about putting my upgrade before theirs; it was really eating at me.

Jackson grinned at me. "There's some tech stuff I wanted to tinker with, so if I get that I'm a bit short for the armor. Should be able to afford it in a patrol or two."

"Oh, I don't expect you to pay for the whole thing yourself. Just to help out until I can make it back with more shit to sell and pay you back." Then I took a deep breath because raising kids can be the scariest shit out there. Even more so than giant emu-based mutants who had Gumby necks. "You're going out on patrols even while I'm gone, and I just want to make sure you're as safe as we can make you."

"Oh. In that case, I'll wait to get the tech toys and go get my armor upgrade right now!" His eyes shone, and he'd probably thought I was going to ask him not to go while I was away.

"And keep an eye out for your sister," I said, transferring him half the Credits for the upgrade.

"Always, Mum. You never even have to ask."

I watched as he disappeared back into the Shop. Jackson was a typical big brother. They'd rough-housed and fought, argued and had popcorn movie nights together before everything went up the creek without the paddle. Now, he was far more protective than I'd ever imagined, and right when I needed him to be.

Turning around, I walked outside the center to see how the rest of the preparations were going. With Jackson upgrading his Dermal Underlayer, at least I could breathe easy about one thing.

16 Weeks, 3 Days Post-System Onset
7 p.m.

I glanced around my kitchen in the house we called home now. We didn't have that modern open-concept look, but a kitchen that was separated from the living room, with a small area that had room enough for a table.

The island in the center was long enough for four chairs, though, and that's where I sat the majority of the time, elbows on the tiled countertops. I had no doubt the System would let me remodel it for a fee of Credits, but there was something about this late-eighties kitchen that just made it feel more like a home. It didn't feel like ours, yet. It was what we had; that would come.

Jackson and Kyle roasted some sort of meat over the fire pit they'd created just outside the entrance. Australians didn't have or need fireplaces. Well, at any rate, we didn't need them here in Brisbane. Our weather never got cold enough for that. The smoke was far better outside than in.

Wisp sat at the breakfast bar, her chin on her hands, brown eyes bright as they studied my every move. Evelyn was packing essentials upstairs.

My daughter continued to watch me as I tossed the salad with "vegetables" that vaguely resembled those we'd eaten four months ago. I even added a light sprinkling of an oil- and herb-based dressing. She continued to watch me when the boys brought the food inside, and only glanced away as her dinner was placed down next to her.

Finally done, I grabbed my plate and sat beside her, watching her push her food around the plate, even as she now avoided my gaze.

"You're still worried, huh?" I asked, giving her a quiet nudge.

All she did was give me a nod and continue to push her food around, making tiny piles in each corner.

Kyle, Jackson, and Evelyn were discussing routes and possible rescue scenarios, which meant that five of us were gathered around the island meant for four. It wasn't really the best place for Wisp to be when she had so much going on in that young mind of hers.

I jumped up, grabbed her plate, and motioned for her to come with me before picking up my own and heading into what would have been the lounge room, den . . . something or other. We settled onto the couch, meals balanced on our knees, and I waited for her to speak.

It took a few minutes.

"Growing up is scary now."

Oh yeah, honey, even more than it used to be. She didn't need her mum's sarcasm, though. "It is. The world has changed. We're fighting monsters and mutations who think we're in the way, or else think we're food."

She nodded, and actually ate a bite. "But you keep having to go out there and help. Couldn't you have been a teacher like Jana? She has to teach us all to read, write, math, and stuff. That's important too!"

"Yeah, it really is. Keeping kids safe and occupied is what she's excellent at. But you know how I've always worked with the earth and soil, the plants and their environment?"

Wisp nodded, her eyes on mine, like she was sure I was about to trick her.

"When the System took over, I got a skill in line with what I used to do. It allows me to see the Mana, the power that is causing all these changes. To read it and what it can do.

"I can warn our fighters about things trying to attack them, and I'm learning more and more each day about it." When I said it out loud, it actually sounded like a valid reason to leave my current eight-year-old in the base camp.

Almost.

"So you can really help them out there. Make it easier so that they can . . ." And she gulped. "Come back safely."

"It's what I try to do. Uncle Kyle is really good at healing, too. We all work together. And if I can tell where danger might come from, it's that much easier for us to win." I leaned in and gave her a hug. "Do you get it?"

"Yeah." She sighed, but it was one of those genuine ones this time. Then she grabbed a piece of meat, popped it in her mouth, before nonchalantly handing a piece to Dog who'd followed us in here. "I get it, Mum. I just don't like it. But I think I understand a bit now."

"I'll come back. You're not getting rid of me that easily." I grinned tightly, trying to put a lighter tone into the conversation.

"Oh, you bet you're coming back." She turned to me. "You really don't have an option."

Wisp shook her head and cracked her neck from side to side. "Growing up in the apocalypse kinda sucks, Mum. It really sucks."

From the mouth of an eight-year-old. Nothing but truth.

Chapter Seventeen:
Moving Out

16 Weeks, 5 Days Post-System Onset
6 a.m.

Being up at the butt crack of dawn let me see the sunrise over the Mount Gravatt skyline, down toward the M1. There was a simplistic beauty about it as we all crossed over and to the main portion of our settlement. Just that feel of nature, that touch of what had always been made me feel so much better about not giving up on what we'd always had, that drop of beauty in this proverbial bucket of shit.

I couldn't help the nerves. They crept up on me like a spider stalking a fly. Already in its web, I had no choice but to wait for it to get me.

"We got this." Evelyn nudged my elbow, but I could tell she was feeling it too. This whole blanket of trepidation that hung over all of us, suffocating us all.

There were a lot of us too.

Lousesh was already out with the first group, Hirish was coming with us, along with four other Hakarta. Paoli was quietly instructing the Zarrie she was leaving behind and prepping the four she was bringing with her.

Dequasha stood there silently, her petal-like limbs raised to the sky as the sun lit the atmosphere. I hadn't realized she was coming with us, but a part of me was grateful. We'd barely had time to go over my training since the patrol to Carindale left. Considering I still needed to learn so much, I was hoping she could help me while we were underway to lend them back up. Nothing like hands-on learning.

Several IRSHA members I didn't know personally were readying themselves as well. In total it looked like we had five Hakarta, five Zarrie, and about eight IRSHA members. Not to mention a nice chunk of humans.

Evelyn and I, Drake and Kyle, Gemma and Marie. The second Archer was well enough to come, even though I felt like her confidence had taken a bit of a hit. The System really needed to do something more than just taking care of the physical. Thank you, System, for letting us live through shit we should never have had to experience.

We definitely had a love-hate relationship.

Molly and Sange were coming too. I had a distinct feeling we'd end up needing our best tank and healer duo.

But we weren't leaving our settlement undefended. There were still a few dozen aliens here to help our humans protect our settlement. Mike and his enforcers, Eritia and her mages, and several healers Kyle had been instructing.

And Jackson. He was staying, of course. I wouldn't have let him come out with us.

It took every bit of willpower I had not to make him stay in the settlement and promise not to venture out at all while I was gone. Having that new armor upgrade definitely helped me bite my tongue. Still, I felt uneasy. He should be skateboarding, or science experimenting, just being a teen. Instead, he was eager to go out hunting monsters and building machines and gadgets that could better protect us, or better take down the beasts.

Then again, I guess he was living every kid's dream—being a superhero. Except this was the real world and superheroes could die here.

Hirish came to stand on my other side, and I glanced around trying to find Evelyn. She was grabbing several things another of the Pirra Clan had brought out for our little troop. Dasesh, I think his name was?

Replicating arrows that were reinforced from what I could see, and some other handy things for ranged weapon and skill users. I didn't even want to contemplate where we'd be if our alien allies hadn't practically fallen into our laps.

"This will be dangerous. Taking such a large force means everything will hear us coming." The Hakarta's tone made me look at his face. He was frowning, those bushy eyebrows like some massive hairy caterpillars.

"Yes, but it might not know we're coming for it." I glanced around to see Ginali in the midst of us all, handing out a bunch of silver rings for people to put on. They'd managed a lot of them with one or two percent resistance. There were only a handful of those with plus four.

"If we can get everyone up to around fifty percent resistance, we might even stand a chance when we go into battle." My voice shook, and I was grateful that Hirish chose to ignore it, or at least not comment on it.

"It might be enough, but more would be ideal." He glanced at me and nodded gruffly. "Good choice to upgrade your armor. I have a feeling we'll need your abilities out there more than we ever have before."

"No pressure or anything," I muttered.

He turned to me, and not for the first time, I wondered if the Hakarta just didn't quite get when humans were flippant or sarcastic. "Oh, there'll be a lot of pressure. But you will rise above it, because you are better than the pressure."

"Thanks." I breathed out, feeling a little awkward and surveyed our progress.

"Are you bringing the wombat?" he asked after several seconds of silence. Maybe he felt the weird too.

I shook my head. "I don't think it's a good idea to put her in the way of something that might control her mind. She's got decent resistances from what I can tell, but she is a mutation, and that might mean something else to a creature like the one we're going up against. I'm not going to risk turning her against us and us having to kill her."

The lump in my throat threatened to choke me, and I realized just how attached I'd grown to our Mumma Wombutt. So much that I wasn't willing to risk her in a battle with a mind-controlling blob that might take her away from us.

Hirish was watching me, a look on his face that I couldn't decipher. "What?"

He shrugged. "Nothing. It's a sound decision. Don't take things with us that might be used as a weapon against us."

"Sure." I'd let him think that was my reasoning if it made him happy.

"Dequasha will work with you to provide a protective Mana shield?" He looked at me as if I knew what he was talking about.

She hadn't spoken to me about it yet, but that wasn't surprising. "Whatever we need to do to make sure most of us make it back alive."

There was a tap on my shoulder, and I spun around to face Jackson, with Wisp clinging to him, balanced on his hip.

"She wanted to hug you for luck." His voice sounded huskier than usual, and I thought I might spy a tear in his eyes.

Damn it. Kids. I found myself unable to breathe for a second, my stomach and chest clenching tight.

I reached in and took Wisp from him, giving her the most encompassing hug I could. She was this tiny bright light and needed to stay that way. "You stay safe for me, right? Gather bugs, listen to Jana and Avery, play with your friends and take care of our pet companions, okay?"

She nodded, all of her bravado gone and, in its place, an eight-year-old girl who didn't understand the world yet. Not really. Definitely not this one. "Stay safe, Mum," she muttered into my hair.

It took all my strength to tear myself away from her.

Fuck this blob. I wasn't about to let it come between me and my kids.

❖

The most difficult thing about getting out of the Center was just the leaving everything behind. Once we got out to Newnham Road, things started to feel real. Though I really thought we needed to discuss where we met and left from next time. Going to the old service station, servo, that IRSHA now owned on the outskirts of our new borders was a much better option than gathering back at the main settlement if we needed to head out this way again.

If we needed to, that was.

I could almost feel our own people watching us out of their house windows as we walked by. An eerie sensation at best, like they couldn't bring themselves to come out and see us off just in case that made everything more real.

As we passed the threshold of our expanded settlement, I looked back through the gates to see the current guards looking down at us, a hint of fear emanating from them. Couldn't blame them really. Mike's guards needed to help us keep the settlement safe, but we couldn't even really say from what.

Kyle and Hirish rode in the first vehicle, leaving Evelyn, Gemma, Drake, and I in our own with Dequasha sitting in the open cargo area. As far as I could tell, she was meditating, and it made me realize how lucky we were to have these vehicles. The tech team had established a whole division to work on these, making them actually affordable to produce.

The Shop had everything you could think of, if you were willing to pay the price. Australians were pretty good with some hard yakka, so putting these babies together didn't faze most of the tech team.

"It's too damned quiet." Gemma spoke softly, as if she didn't want to interfere with the natural state of things.

I nodded. "This area, though, I get it. We've swept through most of these streets every few days, finding nests and clearing out any monster we came across, grabbing the few people who managed to survive. It's not completely safe or anything, but I feel like we've given the area approaching our settlement a bit of breathing room."

"Maybe." She still sounded gruff, but then it was rare for her not to.

Drake didn't say anything, just watched the horizon with a forlorn gaze. I could tell he missed Gary and was still hoping against hope that the system was right, and his friend really was alive. I wondered how often he checked. Gary had paid to have his information concealed apparently, but at least Drake had been able to find out if he was alive.

With the vehicles able to move at around thirty kilometers per hour and keep formation on the roads, we made it to the Creek-Newnham Road intersection in just under ten minutes.

My brain processed the destruction in front of it slowly, sort of like we were in a stop-motion video. From the once-massive Bunnings Hardware Store to the right, and over the and across to the beauty place, the buildings were crushed. A ton of damage that didn't hold with the housing areas we'd just come from.

Ambient Mana flowed with no real direction, just existing. Only a low level of it with nothing to suggest that there was anything around but us and the wreckage.

Nothing moved, there were none of our vehicles amongst the abandoned ones scattered along the road, and there was enough room for us to maneuver up Creek Road and toward Carindale.

"Watch out for survivors, or hidden monsters," Hirish called out, stating the bloody obvious even though it may have made me feel that little bit safer.

Our convoy of twelve vehicles wove its way through the debris before finally making it to the incline up toward Carindale. My stomach tied itself in knots as we headed deeper in, and I eyed my walkie-talkie, hoping the range held out and that Dor could get word to us if needed.

Every movement, every leaf that fell from a tree out of the corner of my eye. It all made me jumpy.

Dequasha chose that moment to approach me, her petal like appendages still something that filled me with wonder. "Can you feel the darkness in the Mana up ahead?" she asked me softly, wedging herself between where Evelyn drove and I sat.

Focusing into the distance, I could see it more than I could feel it. A darker cloud of power nestled up a ways ahead of us.

"If we aren't careful, that will sense us, just as we sense it. We need to hide from that," she continued as if it were the easiest thing in the world.

"All righty, then. What do I do?" Because hell, lady, we hadn't worked on this yet.

"Gather ambient Mana around you and coax it into shielding you. Make it appear as if you are ambient yourself."

I frowned, trying to grasp at the Mana to cloak me, and then I realized she didn't mean that. She just meant for me to ask the Mana already around us to project our presence as ambient.

Well, that was easier bloody said than done, wasn't it? Sometimes I might hear the Mana whispering, but the Mana definitely didn't listen to me in return. It had this slippery quality, like I'd almost grasp it, but it ran through my fingers before I could get a good grip. Like trying to pick up an octopus by the legs with a pair of chopsticks.

I tried again, and this time was even worse. My fingers burned, like I'd let a rope slip through them too fast and gotten rope burn. The third time I attempted to coax the ambient Mana around us into helping us hide, I finally felt it respond.

The mana slithered its blue light around us, weaving to and fro, up and down, all around us until we blended. That was the best way I could describe how it felt. It wasn't foolproof if someone was really looking for us, but it should help a bit and pass a perfunctory check.

"Done." I felt a little proud of myself.

Dequasha nodded, not one word about how long that took me. "Now do it for all the others."

Great, I knew there had to be a catch. Still, after the first couple of vehicles were taken care of, it took much less time. Practice made perfect— and made us all a lot safer.

A few more kilometers and we'd make it to the other settlement, driving through residential areas long since abandoned. There were no real parks or gatherings of trees for a while yet, not until we got closer. And while the center was likely under the control of the Mormaturian Blobnecked Rigoll, the mind-controlling little shit wasn't located directly near to the center at all.

No, it was out of sight, hiding away and biding its time while it controlled from the shadows. We had the approximate location thanks to the System, and it wouldn't take Dequasha and I very long to locate it precisely once we got a little closer to its location.

We finally arrived at the Golden Arches on the corner of Creek and Pine Mountain where I could hear the sounds of fighting up ahead. Surely that wasn't our initial group? Maybe it had been so quiet before now because all of the creatures were gathering at our other group. They didn't have the protections that myself and Dequasha could provide.

They hadn't been able to hide.

My walkie-talkie crackled, letting through cut out words from sentences, barely discernible through the static.

". . . attacked . . . ambush. Holding up . . ."

"Help . . . not long . . ."

"Shit," I muttered as we approached, and the sounds grew louder.

Hirish motioned for us to prepare ourselves and I could only hope we hadn't taken too long. Two days and they'd only made it this far? Had they managed to sleep at all? No one had let us know there were casualties, so I had to hope that everyone was accounted for.

The questions bombarded my mind despite the fact that I needed it clear to think. Because all of this flashed up a huge warning for me, letting me know that wherever they were stuck fighting, was somewhere the Mormaturian Blobnecked Rigoll was trying to keep them away from. And if so, then that had to mean the nest was close, the base, or whatever it was that this mind controlling blob called home.

Which meant the System had indeed been correct, as well as where we'd calculated she might be. This whole buying information from the System might actually have its perks.

We closed in on the fighting, the sounds closer, the ripping of flesh, the hacking of blades, and the distinct yelling of orders coming from Lousesh. They were caught close to where we'd been ambushed on our initial visit to Carindale.

First of all, we'd need to help get this under control. I couldn't believe the number of different creatures standing in front of us. Sure, the Caneglobulous were in abundance, but there were also massive MMNs—my good old mutant magpie nightmares—divebombing our people, and occasionally getting a nip in on the toads.

Couldn't fight nature completely, it appeared.

When I say massive, these were much larger than the ones we'd originally fought with the first Rigoll. They were the size of Dog, but with huge wings. Almost like small Magons. Which was *truly* the last thing we needed. There weren't many of them. Only about five, but it was all Dale and the Zarrie healer could do to keep the damage at bay.

"Get the flying ones first," I called out, and Hirish nodded, raising his pulse rifle. The Hakarta rarely missed, and today was no exception.

I could spy Ray amongst the group, his left arm dangling at his side. It looked like it had been dislocated or broken, perhaps both, but he was still fighting, a look of grim determination over his face. Even as I watched, the arm popped itself back into the socket, causing the Ice Mage to grimace with pain.

Morton fired shots at the birds above, his ranged attacks far more effective against them than the mutated cane toads. He held his pistols loosely in either hand, like he'd been firing them all his life. But the birds above him dove down consistently, divebombing him, and it was all he could do to keep them at bay.

His right forearm was a bloody mess of skin and material mixing together without time to heal because the attacks never stopped.

Dannin's shots were aimed at the ground, and I couldn't tell why until I noticed that something kept poking its head up through the ground, kind of like a Whack-A-Mole at an arcade.

Centiwormilia

Level 43

Oh joy, that did not look good. My bet was a centipede crossed with one of the massive earthworms we sometimes found in the more tropical regions. I wasn't about to ask how this had happened; I knew better by now.

At least it wasn't a few kilometers long and able to swallow moving miners. Yet. I bet it was just a matter of time.

With our fresh patrol reinforcements dashing into the original patrol's ranks now, the relief was practically palpable. For a moment I realized they'd really doubted we'd make it in time.

I counted at least five Caneglobulous, four MMNs now that one was down, and several of those Centiworm things attacking as if they were in practiced formation. All I could think of was how well Dale's group had performed. Declan fought tooth and nail to keep the attention of the Caneglobulous that weren't freeze trapped or rooted, but he was only one tank.

How they'd survived this long, I couldn't say.

Evelyn, Dannin, and Marie dove in to keep the Centiwormilia's slowed. Kiting them appeared to be the best possible solution since it kept them away from the main group of fighters while still whittling them down. And ranged weapons were the best way to deal with the things due to their popping-in-and-out nature.

Snare traps, ice traps, and rains of arrows in between. The Centiwormilias never stood a chance. Well, at least once our ranged forces managed to pick each other up, anyway.

Gemma and Drake jumped in with Tasha and began chopping down the Caneglobulous methodically. They darted in and out with practiced ease, just as if we were clearing one of the nests back home. There were others of course who followed their lead, but we had almost fifty people out here now, and I didn't know everyone's names.

Mana Stone allowed me to divvy out Mana regen to those I chose. At least that made the healers and I able to regenerate Mana. Still, I decided right then and there that I didn't like fights with this many participants.

Molly and Sange stationed themselves front and center, pulling some of the heat off the exhausted member of Dale's group who'd been serving as the bait—tank—until now. Molly slammed her shield into the ground, extending it and suddenly blood and other fluids boiled up through the ground.

She'd managed to sever one of those Centiwormilias, but she didn't even spare the spreading mess beneath her a glance. Instead, she focused on Roaring at anything within range, and pulled their ire for as long as she could. Sange, behind her, always healing, never missed a beat.

That's when I noticed Zyrilian. Kyle was attempting to heal him, and the Zarrie's left arm was gone. Nothing Kyle did seemed to help, and I could see the strain on Zyrilian's face as he endured the attempted healing spell. Apparently, it had been too long since he'd lost it for Kyle to help him grow it back.

Shit.

I couldn't see Mon'swkinon, but he had to be around somewhere—at least I hoped he was. It wasn't like I could miss him if he'd been there in the fray.

To the left of us, Ray gathered together all of the mages and began to hyper focus down the birds. Fireballs, Ice Lances, Arcane Missiles. You name it, they flew through the air with focused precision, striking the MMNs through wings, heads, and sometimes even eyes. I was surprised to see Rin using ranged magic, although I shouldn't have been, considering Jackson had offensive Skills as well. Rin's appeared electrical in nature, and I really wanted to ask her about them. Just needed some time.

Our arrival helped rejuvenate the energy levels of the previous patrol.

It all seemed like it might be under control, but there was a part of me certain than there were more creatures incoming. Which only meant that we had to find the damned Mormaturian Blobnecked Rigoll and kill the damned thing before they wore us all down completely.

This specific area appeared to be where it wanted to protect most. Even if I hadn't checked for the approximate location with the System, attacking us here was a mistake and a dead giveaway.

I needed to speak to Dequasha and figure out exactly how we were going to approach this.

Chapter Eighteen
Mind Control Beasty

There was a park between Boundary and Creek Roads. It didn't actually butt up to Creek, but it was only a subdivision away. All things considered, being in the middle of the suburbs and everything, it was a damned large park. Several street parks converged to form this one large chunk of greenery, frequented by kids and adults alike. We could get to it through Bendena Terrace, and then we'd have to go by foot.

"Are you sure that's where this thing is?" Hirish asked, his focus mainly on firing at the new MMNs who were incoming to attack our expanded patrols position.

The constant barrage of creatures was never ending. It was like the Rigoll knew we were closing in and was doing everything it could to stall us.

"Yes. Not only did the System give us this general area, but the attack patterns would suggest that we're in the right spot too." I paused and reached out with Mana Sense. Power flowed, subtly, from the direction of the park, blues swirling until they became dark and almost sluggish. Which either indicated a deep well of ambient, malevolent Mana, or else a gathering of many power-consuming creatures.

All of those things together led me to believe that the System estimation had been entirely correct. And now it was easy enough to narrow it down to exactly where the Rigoll was located, nestled in away from civilization. Away but still close enough that it could easily control creatures from the ground level up and bend them to its will.

Mind-control creatures were definitely on my shitlist.

I turned to look directly at both Dequasha and Hirish. "Everything points to it being there. While I'm fairly sure it can tell we are here, there has to be a way to keep it guessing as to our exact location as we approach. Can we disguise our footprint enough?"

Dequasha sighed, her eyes growing distant for several moments. Long enough that I had to fight down the urge to fidget.

"We can conceal perhaps ten people, or two vehicles if we each take one. Your coverage will be more effective, so if you go in the first vehicle, then perhaps it might be possible."

"Ten won't be enough," Hirish said, shooting at yet another MMN.

I didn't like the sound of the pulse rifle, and the bright spark of Mana that poured out of it with every shot momentarily blinded me. Not that I could argue with the weapon's effectiveness. As a long-distance one, it was stellar. And expensive. We had the Hakarta to thank that we could come with any at all.

"Ten won't be enough, but if we have everyone on standby for when we engage, perhaps they can speed down Bendena and then through the park. After all, they're four-wheel drives, right?" It was the only idea I had. Surely it wouldn't take more than ten, perhaps fifteen minutes at most to navigate their way to us.

"Leave those attempting to regrow limbs behind," Hirish barked out as he fired off yet another shot. "Take only those who can move fast and efficiently."

He made sense, as usual, and I tried to urge the rest of our main group to hurry up. "If it gains too much more power, it's going to be able to control more than just the young and elderly. Obviously, it's not powerful enough yet, or our first patrol would already have succumbed." The reality of those words sank down my toes, bottoming out my stomach completely.

"We're already handing out the rings Ginali had made. The more we can resist, the better." Evelyn shot me a quick grin as she drew her bowstring back again effortlessly.

"Going to need all the help we can get, right?" Kyle was suddenly there, right next to me. Maybe he'd just wanted to join in the chatter; perhaps it was easier now there was a whole gang of us out here, or, and more realistically, he could probably sense me stressing about everything from a kilometer away.

"How is everything?" I asked quietly.

He sighed. "Couldn't save Zyrilian's arm. There are several other missing fingers, a couple of missing leg portions, like calves and down. Things that the Shop will of course have cybernetic options for, but . . . things I was too late to heal."

"Actually," Hirish said just before firing off another shot. "If they're willing to pay the price, the Shop can just replace their limbs. It will be expensive. But it does have everything."

Kyle blinked at the Hakarta, and I watched as if I could see the cogs spinning in his brain. Maybe he wouldn't beat himself up now that he knew limbs could be replaced. At least that gave us more bandwidth to focus on fighting the big Rigoll we were about to hunt down.

We were bigger and badder than we had been, but to cause the disturbances it had, I also knew that this version of the Rigoll we were about to fight was just as big and possibly much badder than we were.

"I need Ray, Evelyn, maybe Marie, Dequasha, myself—and grab Molly and Sange, please. Kyle, come with. And Hirish?" I glanced around, still not seeing my granite IRSHA friend. It was starting to make me worry. "Does anyone know where Mon'swkinon is?"

Ray shook his head. "He headed off with a small patrol to see if he could find the nest the Caneglobulous were spawning from. It hasn't been long. I'm sure they're fine."

I nodded, even if them being separated from the main group made me feel uneasy. "Okay. Piola, we'll need you too. Let's leave the rest of our troop with the initial one, and signal for them to leave when we give the word."

I was confident those we left behind would know when to head to us because once we'd begun our attack, I had a feeling that the Mormaturian Blobnecked Rigoll would pull everything back to her. All of her power and concentration and monsters and everything would return to defend her.

Well, either she'd call them back to help defend her position, or else she'd release the creatures she'd been controlling and they'd hopefully turn on each other. Either way, it should make it easier for our backup to make it through to the rest of the fight.

A few minutes later we were off, down Bendena Street, Dequasha and I throwing our subtle ambient Mana fudging around us for all we were worth. In a way, it felt like cheating, being all stealthy Mana-blanket wrapped. But in reality, it was just using every advantage we could.

I really hoped having Dequasha and her flesh melting powers, Hirish and his pulse rifles, and Piola and her sneak skills on our side would turn the tables for this battle sooner than later.

Otherwise, I wasn't sure anything we did was going to hurt this thing. As long as we could launch enough of a surprise attack so that it let us hold out for the rest of our group to arrive, we should be good.

Technically. We had a lot riding on maybes here.

The White Hills Reserve at the end of Bendena Terrace had a couple of gate entrances into the wooded area. We chose the path off to the right a little so we could drive farther into the park. I didn't realize how many trees dotted this property, so traveling by foot might end up being quieter and faster.

About half a kilometer in, that's exactly what we did. Exiting the vehicles, we moved as quietly as we could, using ambient Mana to cushion our passage.

It was difficult to utilize the element for that, because we weren't actually consuming it, but instead sort of hid our presence behind it. With each step we took toward the middle of the park, I could feel the mind control presence growing. It exuded this pressure, much like the smaller one had so many months ago.

The air all around us grew heavier, a weight that threatened willpower to give into it and just let it crush you because that might be easier. I hadn't understood Mana as well when we'd fought the first one, but now, I could see just how much that wave of potential influence fluctuated through dark and sludge-like blues.

Coercion wasn't a pretty shade.

The Mormaturian Blobnecked Rigoll was so close I could taste it. And it stank.

The stench reached us several seconds after the mind-scanning pressure did. It smelled like decaying, bloated fat on apocalypse victims left in the sun too long. It wore down its victim's will to resist by constantly applying pressure to the mind. I'd hate to think what might have happened if we hadn't armed ourselves with protection.

The Mana pulsed, an angry underlying current whipping it about as it failed to find purchase in the group of us approaching. I could tell its efforts were in vain, and its attempts to subvert the thoughts even skimming along the top of our minds failed.

There was nothing for it to gain a foothold in, no way for it to enter and turn our own fears against us. Nothing it could do to take us over.

For now.

I focused my intention back on the path in front of us. Kids used to play cricket and even rugby in this park, but now it was the home of a massive blobfish-esque beast. Probably leaching off moisture through the ground from where the water reserve was a kilometer or so away. It was the perfect hiding spot out here amongst the trees and fields.

From what I could see of the park, it appeared to be hunkered down in amongst a group of closely planted trees, thus potentially restricting incoming attacks. Its ability to sense incoming creatures was a huge boon for it, and for the most part it would be able to take them over and coerce them into submission.

Hirish stepped on a stick, and the crack it made was so loud I almost shat myself. Taking a deep breath, I steadied my hand and kept moving. The complete and utter feeling of despair that I felt trying to weigh in on us alerted me to how close we must be.

And perhaps how frustrated the creature was getting that it couldn't seem to penetrate our minds. Now it was resorting to invoking pity in us— toward itself, if the pure desolation trying to crush my mind was anything to go by. Thank the Shop I was able to differentiate it enough not to fall for it.

Mental Resistance 101. Get it high enough that people can't fuck with you.

Maybe *that* was a book idea for the Shop.

Coming in here without beefing it up would have been foolhardy at best, and more than likely deadly for all of us.

That was when the pressure changed. Subtly, but it wasn't worth us coaxing the ambient Mana to hide us anymore, because the creature definitely knew we were there.

The suggestions trying to press into my head told me subtly that I was headed the wrong way and to go back where I'd come from. There was such a gentle push to it that I got angry.

There was no fucking way we were going back.

We moved as quietly as possible, heading for the place where all the dark Mana gathered, where the toxicity of power leaked from it. Just because it knew we were here now didn't mean we should run around like a herd of elephants.

It took me several moments to realize we'd arrived, because the entire circumference around the Mormaturian Blobnecked Rigoll was encircled. Encircled by the missing children and elderly of the Carindale settlement.

They stood there, like statues, their eyes glazed over with a film of grey. Staring at us. Through us. They wavered, slowly swaying as if there was a gentle breeze constantly blowing at them. But the air was still; not even a bird chirped above us.

I looked to the side of me only to see Kyle, Evelyn, and Maria shaking their heads, growing more agitated each second. Acting like they were trying to stop something buzzing around their heads.

I thanked my hammer for its extra protection. I'd only taken a few rings since I already had my plus five mental resistance one, and then the Dermal Armor upgrade too. Enough, for now, to bring me to fifty-two percent. What did the pressure feel like for those under what I had?

Between one breath and the next, the controlled people began to move toward us.

"It knows we're here," Dequasha whispered.

I bit back the *no shit* comment. My sarcasm wasn't going to help the situation any.

Saying that they moved wasn't quite accurate. Their limbs jerked with each step that they took, stilted in their movements. Like actual automatons. With their glazed-over eyes and puppetted motions, I felt like there should be strings attached to them from above.

Whatever this mind control did, it accessed their motor cortex and went on a wild joy ride regardless of whether the bodies were capable of it, of whether the minds were fighting the control. The children mimicked broken dolls in those horror movies, where the head is turned at an off angle that had to be painful, and the arms and legs jolted with every bit of momentum.

But it was the elderly that made my blood boil over. Some of them had enough mind left that it was obvious they were fighting for control, yet none of them could maintain it. Legs and arms jutted out as each step was pulled painfully from each of them. They staggered, almost like mindless zombies directed with unspoken commands.

"Keep them safe. As safe as we can," I whispered, wanting to end this creature we still had yet to see.

"Well," Kyle commented, dryly. "Maybe we should try the good old arrow to the knee and see if that stops the movement enough. Then again, they're not moving fast. We can out-jog them."

I gave it some thought as Evelyn spoke up. "Let's outrun them and use the arrows as a last resort."

"Done." Hirish didn't need a second invitation and instead began jogging toward the center. We all knew it was the right direction because all of the humans coming toward us were walking away from us. Sort of like they were trying to divert our attention from the center.

As soon as we got to it, I was going to Water Siphon the living daylights out of it, because I remembered just how much the little one we'd killed hated that shit. Mercy was for creatures who didn't fuck with the young and the old.

Today I wasn't feeling any of it.

I'd forgotten how horrible these things looked. Like I tried to use ugly sparingly, but this thing . . . it was probably in the dictionary under that word.

Where the first one we'd ever encountered had been about the size of three elephants combined and could have probably devoured a modest-sized house, this one . . . well, this one towered above that.

But where the other one was visible once we found its hiding spot, this one appeared to be capable of blending with the surroundings, morphing its appearance into a semblance to reflect its immediate area. The Mana diving around it made me think it had a similar capability to how Dequasha and I asked ambient Mana to aid us in concealing our presence.

This Rigoll still resembled a blobfish. Its dead, flabby face with a parasite hanging out of the corner of its mouth was almost exactly like the baby one we'd encountered previously. But this thing was at least twice as large, hunkered down amidst several trees, probably almost as long as a cricket pitch.

It squelched as it moved ever so slightly, the acidic liquid that spilled around it eating into the earth beneath it. It made me shudder with revulsion, and I barely avoided triggering my gag reflex.

Everything about it was disgusting, but also scary, even though some of that was obviously from residual mind control efforts. I vowed to spend the next six months finding everything I could to boost my mental resistance even more.

"Fight any fear you feel, any inclination to run from this and never look back. That's how it works, that's how it gets into your head. Don't let it best us." And even as I said the words, there was a part of me that just wanted to let it take control, make it so much easier than having to deal with the day-by-day shit of the new world.

It would all be so much easier if we just let Mr. Blobby here take over. There'd be no more worries ever. This creature was even more dangerous than we'd realized, because right now I knew there were probably thousands of people who'd take it up on its offer.

Analyze engaged:

Mormaturian Blobnecked Rigoll Queen—Elite, Level 52.

Well, shit.

This thing was going to be tough, and I wasn't even sure if the ten of us would be able to hold it at bay until the rest of our force got here, but it didn't need to know that.

I slammed Water Siphon into the creature so fast I almost gave myself whiplash. The effect wasn't as instantaneous as it had been when we'd fought the smaller version, but it did hit, and began to slowly suck the moisture out of the creature, making it more fragile. Keeping that spell on it was the only trump card I had.

That and knowing . . .

You have resisted Mind Blast

I staggered slightly with the force of this one. Apparently, the bigger the Rigoll, the more damage the Mind Blast actually did. Luckily, I resisted the influence and just took about ten percent physical damage. Yay for healing types. My brother patched me up.

Thank whatever gods were currently not on my shit list.

Glancing around, I noticed that Marie seemed to be having a hell of a time shaking loose on the Mind Blast. It didn't get her by the looks of it, but the constant pressure was wearing on her.

The others seemed fine for the most part. Evelyn fired her arrows while Molly used her shield slams, always ready to back off so she could protect those behind her. And if this version of the blob had the same acid-spraying breath, we were going to need that shield.

Sange hung back with the ranged, more cautious this time. We all remembered the bodies who'd melted right in front of our eyes, and how Sange had needed to regrow a limb. They wouldn't want to go through that sort of pain again.

Ray's ice bolts always worked well, but this time he had a new ability, Freeze Frame, and it shot out and began to spiderweb freeze all of the moisture around and protruding from the creature.

The Mormaturian Blobnecked Rigoll was a damp creature, and that spiderwebbed freezing caused it to call out in pain. The keening sound recalled all the humans, and they turned back, beginning a slow and marionette like wobbling return to their controller.

"Watch for the puppets!" Hirish called, and a part of me could appreciate that distancing ourselves from their humanity for the duration of the fight might even help us survive.

I tapped into the creature with Mana Stone, dissipating Mana regen all over the rest of my team. Implantation came next, as well as Blood Transfer to assist with any damage we took. Water Siphon continued to weaken our opponent so we could methodically beat it down.

Waiting for the Rush move the smaller version of the creature had exhibited was difficult. Was this one too large to rush us? And even as I had that thought, I saw it bunch up with a sudden influx of Mana streaming into it.

"Incoming!" was all I had time to yell out, but it was enough to put everyone on guard. It raised itself ever so slightly from the ground and moved so fast I think it hovered over the earth.

The gelatinous nature of its body meant the momentum made it slosh around as speed took over. Its abrupt stop and narrow miss of crushing any of our people made the fat roll to the front and then slam to the back again, brushing past several of its own victims as well as one of our attackers before it returned to its original position.

It happened so quickly, I barely had time to gag.

Paoli barely dodged the fat roll, as she leapt to the side and took about twenty percent damage from the side swipe before the creature settled back in its original place. At least it hadn't managed to suck life force from her and heal itself.

"Nice dive," I called out, not liking the close call that had been. Surely the acid attack would come soon. Out of the corner of my eyes I could see the helpless puppets it had created still approaching us.

Damn it. I didn't want to have to fight them, and I didn't want to have to hurt them. Aiming as well as I could, I erected an Earthen Wall about five feet tall, spanning down about ten meters. The Rigoll didn't appear to have enough finesse to make the humans climb or jump something, so this way they'd have to go round the entire structure to get to us.

That bought us time and me peace of mind in that we wouldn't have to hurt helpless people.

With no sign of attack Mana gathering, I rushed in and smashed the Rigoll with my hammer only to realize belatedly that a heavy hammer wasn't going to do any solid damage in a buoyant, fatty body like that.

I yanked my Warhammer out and if the feeling was anything to go by, tore something in my shoulder as the monster's body refused to give my Warhammer back. Couldn't leave it inside—I needed that Mental Resistance. Clamping down on the pain, I knew that the System and my brother's next heal would take care of the damage.

Water Siphon reactivated. There had to be something I could do with the soil underneath it. I had enough of those damn abilities. But I'd need to stack it correctly.

"Incoming!" I called out again, as the Mana preempting the rush attack activated around the Rigoll again. The more I saw it use Mana, the more in tune with its castings I became.

This time the attack seemed faster, and not as many of us managed to dart out of the way in time. Evelyn and Marie stood, letting arrows rain down on the creature as it barreled toward them, barely diving to the side in time.

Gemma wasn't so lucky. The hulking Rigoll managed to wedge one of her ankles between it and the earth beneath it, eliciting a scream from the Rogue. Her face paled for a moment before Sange's next heal hit her and she was able to pull herself away from the creature, slicing effectively with one of her daggers as she moved away.

The arrow that whizzed past my face took me by surprise and I searched for where it came from only to find Marie facing me down with that grey film over her eyes.

Shit.

Before I could react, the next arrow embedded itself in my shoulder, just under the collarbone. A scream tore from my throat, and I stumbled. Kyle rushed to my side, grabbing at the arrow to break it and tug it out.

But Marie raised her hand again, almost quicker than I could follow, and it felt like everything was going in slow motion. I could practically hear the bowstring pull back, hear the *twang* as it released, and felt Kyle's hands around my waist as he pulled me to the ground barely in time to avoid another hit.

"Snap out of it!" he yelled gruffly, even as I watched Evelyn and Gemma tackle Marie to the ground. The Archer shook her head as if she was trying to dislodge something from it while the others snatched her bow out of her hands.

Close call, that one. Marie was still fighting the others while Kyle healed me, but by the time the arrow was removed and healed, she was herself again.

In the meantime, the Rigoll had returned to her original spot, where she could search for her next weakest link. Even as brief as the possession had been, a sense of nervousness passed through the rest of us. If it could get to Marie, it could get to anyone of us.

"Bring her down," Hirish snapped out, and I had to wonder if Marie had startled him too.

I tapped into the Top Soil to coach the vegetation the blob was sitting on to do my bidding and then activated Treesong. I requested that the flora around us do what I ask. None of these gum trees and other plants were the same as they'd been four months ago. They were hungrier now, out for blood, and the massive blob sucking up all of their moisture was the perfect target to sic them on.

They fell about its base with abandon, eliciting another keening cry from the creature. I could practically feel the frustration welling up inside it as it listed to the side, roots and branches, grass and flower stalks pushing up from below and into it.

Treesong had a specific use, and it wasn't against anything too mobile, so the Queen Rigoll right here was the perfect target, even if it drained a substantial chunk of Mana. After about twelve seconds I stopped, having done a nice portion of damage to it, and hopefully let it know that this wasn't going to be an easy fight.

I could practically feel Marie's anger from where I stood as she released torrent after torrent of arrows into it. Delayed explosion arrows, acid punch arrows . . . you name it, she punched the arrow type into it.

Evelyn followed her example. Molly's Roar wasn't as effective in this type of fight as it was in others, but she still did a heap of damage with her shield when she used it offensively.

Gemma and Drake worked in concert to inflict all the damage they could, not caring that this particular target lessened their slicing damage.

Ray's freezing web still took the cake, periodically causing the creature to cry out in pain, like music to the vindictive soul.

And suddenly I felt them.

The others were coming. They were only a few minutes away. Maybe we had bought enough time. In the same moment I sensed a rumble, a massive and sudden amassing of Mana and I just knew that this queen didn't need to say the words; she didn't need to announce the offense spit shower like the little guy had.

"Shields!" I called out. Even as I finished my shout, the queen opened her mouth to expel bone-melting acid over my family and friends.

Chapter Nineteen:

New and Old

Molly dug her shield into the ground as most of us managed to pile behind her. I pulled an Earthen Barrier up to the side of the shield, barely covering myself and Evelyn in time. Even as I did, I could feel the splashing around us, see a deep black shine to the Mana used to project the acid.

My barrier barely held up, and if we hadn't moved to duck into Molly's shield while it was doing its job, we still would have been hit. Getting my skin melted off my bones wasn't exactly my idea of fun.

And then the screams reached my ears.

The puppets had come in close enough that some of the droplets hit them too. Just a few here and there, but even one drop was enough to dig into the skin and begin melting the person from the inside out. Both Sange and Kyle splashed heals all over the place, cleanses, trying to combat the sheer damage.

Right then, I remembered Dequasha's Skill that had melted the skin off that Zarrie's bones all those weeks ago. It was somewhat similar to the Rigoll's current attack. I'd talk about that with her later.

And then the rest of our troops were suddenly there with us. Another twenty or so. I couldn't quite count as we stood there, our attention still on the fight in front of us.

The acid splashes might have hurt those who were being puppetted, but it had also broken several of them free from the Rigoll Queen's control, and she didn't currently have the facilities to bring them back into her fold.

To the side I could see Tasha gathering those who'd woken up from the control into a group and leading them away, and I was glad I didn't have to worry about them. Another casting of Water Siphon, and the queen actually began to look like I'd drained some of the life-force out of her. Her health was finally sub fifty percent. We were whittling her down.

Finally.

I replenished from my Mana Cloak, refreshing Mana Stone to make sure the regeneration hit everyone in the raid now that we'd grown so much bigger. The lack of Dale's and Zyrilian's presence wasn't lost on me, and I hoped they were taking care of the others back at the road.

But I didn't have time to split my attention, as I needed all of it to focus on the different colors of blue surrounding the Rigoll Queen for incoming attacks. She was bigger, and more powerful, and the last thing we needed was a surprise attack before she exploded at the end.

Another Rush, this time toward Hirish, who dove out of the way with perfect timing like he'd been doing it most of his life. The queen returned to her spot just as fast as she'd left it, but as her health whittled down, I could practically feel the waves of concern washing out from her.

Just below forty percent now, the dark lines of Mana flashed around her again, and I knew their pattern now.

"Incoming acid!" I called out, pushing up my Earthen Barrier to offer whatever extra protection I could manage for the puppetted people who still swayed in their trances. Then the rest of us dove behind Molly's shield. I wasn't sure if we'd fit, but now wasn't the time to lament the lack of personal space.

I could feel the sizzles as the acid rained down on the ground around us, felt the reaction as the dome repelled the attack, and luckily couldn't smell any burning flesh anywhere near me.

But I did hear a strange rumbling sound in the distance, something that sounded familiar, yet I couldn't spare the time to figure out why.

Five seconds of acid-spit rain sure seemed like an eternity, and the dome only lasted eight. Just enough. I shuddered to think how it would go down if Molly ever mistimed it. It sure wasn't Jules's shield, that's for sure, but it was what we had.

Once we were clear, we jumped back out and began the attack anew. Water Siphon every time I could cast it with effect. I even cast Planted in Place on the chance it might offset the creature's Rush ability.

The rumbling grew closer, more like a growl now and I spared a glance to see if I could recognize whatever it was. There was no Mana flash, or signature for me to go on.

The Archers, or Rangers, or hell, the ranged arrow people lined up back about fifty meters or so. They didn't even need to risk being close enough to get hit by that acid. All three of them released a barrage of arrows which exploded once they'd wedged themselves into the creature's blob-like skin.

Ray led Rin and a few mages I hadn't seen before, his ice powers lending amazing preparation to the earth mages next to him. Their abilities drove rock through and into the frozen sections, obliterating parts of the creature's cells and stopping immediate regeneration for a time.

Every little bit helped.

The rumbling grew louder, and that's when I realized what it was. Or, I should say, I realized what it was only when the dark blue jeep catapulted from the trees, going at a solid speed with a direct trajectory toward the Rigoll.

Dale threw himself from the vehicle about ten meters before it careened straight into the creature, hitting it head on. His impact onto the ground let out a snap, but he didn't seem perturbed when he stood up. He'd be able to heal himself.

However, the Rigoll took a load of damage, plummeting her health down a good ten percent. Nice to know if we ever really had the vehicles to spare.

"Nice shot," Kyle commented. Dale only grunted in reply and retreated to stand with Sange.

That's when I noticed Dequasha.

She stood behind Molly's protective ring of shield planting—not the dome, that was a different Skill. But Molly was able to plant her shield into the ground and extend it around her somewhat. It meant that Skills and abilities couldn't breach her protection.

Dequasha's eyes were closed, and she made an intricate weaving with her petal fingers. It seemed delicate and beautiful, but underlying it all there was a dark Mana aura. It bled into the air around her, only slowly dissipating.

"Incoming Rush!" I called out, sensing the skill approaching but never once taking my eyes off the way Dequasha wove her power in that foreboding manner.

Timing Planted in Place's release helped a little, the Rush falling short of its intended target and leaving Gemma to dive back in and utilize her own slashing skills to pierce the unrelenting globby hide of the creature. Drake dove in after her followed by Piola, inching the queen's health down even more. Even Declan had switched to damage mode, considering he didn't have the same shielding abilities as Molly.

A rumble of power alerted me to Dequasha, still standing in place, completely vulnerable now because Molly had moved slightly while the Mitoi-Aral was casting. I glanced at the queen, knowing she was close to another acid spit onset, and headed towards Dequasha to catch her in the same Earthen Barrier as myself if needed. Maybe if I doubled and put up two quickly after one another, we'd survive through it.

About two meters away from her, raw Mana pushed me back, and I barely escaped the shot of dark, deadly magic Dequasha unleashed at the queen.

I'd never seen anything like it before, not even atop the parapets when we fought together.

The power streamed out ahead of her, taking the queen directly between her eyes, with trails of blackened and purple-tinged Mana in its wake. Once it made contact the queen's skin, it began to bubble, like when someone gets into a whirlpool with the jets going full speed. Except this was skin.

It bubbled from the underneath like all the remaining moisture in its body was being boiled on a stove. The creature's mouth, still with globules hanging from it, opened in a silent scream until it wasn't silent anymore and the sound threatened to burst my eardrums.

When the boiling of its innards underneath the confines of the flesh had reached a splitting point, the bubbles began to pop. At the same time, those people it had in its thrall started to break free. Their disorientation made it difficult for Tasha to corral them, so all I could do was throw up an Earthen Barrier to stop them from stumbling into the path of the oncoming damage.

"Take cover," Dequasha managed to squeak out, and Hirish immediately repeated the phrase in his loudest and most commanding tone.

People dove for cover even as the Mind Blasts rolled out in quick succession without any real target, as if it just hoped people would be in a place it reached. Several people took damage, but not enough that our healers couldn't compensate. If a bunch of us had been hit, it could have healed the Rigoll.

But Molly activated her shield again, and we hid inside it, behind her. I continued to push out as many Earthen Barriers as I could, attempting to mitigate any potential damage to those who hadn't moved fast enough.

The bubbles underneath the queen's skin grew, massive putrescent blind pimples just waiting to shower us with acid and goop. It was the most disgusting and vile-smelling thing I'd ever witnessed. And as someone who worked with vegetation, often rotting, that was saying something.

Dequasha was almost limp, like a wilted flower, and it was all Hirish could do to lay her down where she wouldn't get trampled. There was a concerned expression on his face that I hadn't seen before, and it made me wonder about a lot of things I didn't have time for.

The Rigoll Queen continued to squeal in that high-pitched, piercing way, rolling from side to side like she was trying to get the boiling pustules out of her yet yelping evermore when they vacated her by exploding outward. She didn't even appear to have the mental capacity to shoot out Mind Blasts in the hopes of catching someone to leach off anymore.

Out of the range of immediate danger, Ray and his mages didn't let up; neither did our group of highly experienced Archer Ranger people. Evelyn and Marie utilized their Shop-bought focusing devices for deadly aim, sinking arrow after arrow into those black, fathomless eyes, while Dannin continued to fire out his own explosive shots into the body.

It was then I realized he was kneeling, and belatedly realized why. His left calf was missing, and he hadn't said a damned word. Fucking acid monsters were the worst.

The queen's health continued to tick down, and we didn't let up on damage, even as acid and pus rained down all around us. The mess was deadly as complete sections of her flesh exploded outward.

Her health ticked down, all the way to around five percent before the deluge of disgusting finally ran out. Our barrage of damage didn't, but I remembered the last fight, and this time we were prepared.

No one else was losing a limb on my watch. Even if they could purchase a new one in the Shop.

"Back up! Ranged attacks only—she's about to explode." And I actually took my own advice for once. I was rather partial to my own limbs and didn't relish having to give the Shop any more Credits than necessary.

The thing was, the queen was at least double the size of previous Rigoll we'd fought. Her blast radius was likely huge, and I didn't know how well we'd be able to outrun it, but we had to try.

The Rangers had a head start, even Dannin, partially crawling through the underbrush. Evelyn and Marie continued to walk backward, never taking their eyes off their target, while Ray and his mages did the exact same thing.

Tasha, now back in the fray, used her spell abilities from her Spellsword Class, and the Hakarta who were with us all pulse rifled the fuck out of the queen.

The melee? Well, those who needed to be closer just bolted back to catch up to where the ranged groupings were. I just hoped we went far enough.

All of the ranged we had did what they could, myself included. Water Siphon always made it more brittle, while Planted in Place meant that its Rush, if activated, wouldn't be as accurate. I glanced at my Mana and cringed. Only 250 left. My coat was tapped out, and my regeneration was having a hard time keeping up with my output.

It should be enough, though, if I timed it right. With one percent left to go, I shot up four Earthen Barrier walls around it, as thick and tough as I could make them. If nothing else, maybe the brunt of the damage would stay within those walls.

When the explosion happened, Molly triggered her barrier again, still backpedaling slowly with as many of us as could fit behind her moving in sync.

The blast splintered the earthen walls apart, sending dirt and debris scattering all over the area. Evelyn was hit by a shard, as was Ray. Hirish was still out there, firing with his fellow Pirra Clan members and a couple of the other Hakarta. But those wounds were healable, and dirt was a thousand times less dangerous than that acid.

And finally, the damned mind-control beast died, releasing all of those who were still under its control at the same time. Not to mention the fetid smell that puffed out of what remained of the Rigoll like a bag of broken rotten eggs.

I gagged, but at least I couldn't smell any burning flesh.

It took several seconds for the shock of the battle ending to wear off all of us. And then the sobbing began to echo through the trees. From grandmothers, grandfathers, other elderly, right down to the pitiful sobbing of a five-year-old who'd been forced to move against her will for the last couple of months.

I sat down, panting, watching as the Mana that the Rigoll had taken up dissipated into the surroundings so it could be used by something else. The way these Dungeon Worlds worked fascinated me; the fact that Mana existed was simply enthralling, but I couldn't shake the danger this creature had posed to all of us.

And we'd almost not realized it in time.

How much larger would the queen have had to grow before she was capable of taking us all over?

A flashing flickered at the corner of my vision, and I reluctantly signaled for it to open.

What is Mana?

Update: You're beginning to understand the cycle of Mana and the purpose it pursues. Keep going.

Level of Quest: Unnecessary

Reward: Knowledge

Warnings: Curiosity killed lots of cats. Will you be satisfied?

Great. That was no help at all. As usual.

Dequasha literally flopped down next to me, what I thought was a smile tugging at her delicate mouth. "I thought it would work, but I wasn't entirely sure. That particular Skill can be . . . volatile." She breathed out, looking around at everyone who was gathered together getting ready to head back to the road.

"Is that a Class thing?" I asked, wondering if there was a way I could get my hands on it easily. Because that sure as hell would come in handy.

She nodded. "That it is."

Damn. We sat in a comfortable silence, and I scanned around us, only just realizing how spent I actually was.

Kyle was going around to all the injured, seeing if he could help them regrow limbs, or if there was anything that required my help with toxic elements, but so far it seemed there was nothing. Dannin began screaming the moment Kyle touched him, so I assumed he was going through what Sange had gone through all those months ago and was regrowing his leg.

Hey, at least he'd save some Credits, right?

I didn't think everyone would be so lucky. A couple of the elderly were still in shock, and parts of their bodies were long gone. We'd only had one death, a rogue I didn't know, but Gemma was taking it hard.

I think she thought every single rogue out there was her responsibility to protect. Not that I could blame her, I felt like that about every person I'd dragged to Garbo with me.

"Thanks for using that skill, even though it was dangerous." I said it quietly, realizing I hadn't really given Dequasha a thank you.

"Species superpower." Her visage darkened slightly. "That creature is the result of experiments performed millennia ago by people who should have known better."

"I'm glad you're on our side," I said, meaning it. Without her ability, this could have dragged on and taken a lot more casualties. "You saved lives with that."

"I'm just glad it worked." She shrugged, an oddly fluid and pretty gesture. "What is next?"

"Carindale." I nodded emphatically, making the decision then and there that we had to head in and give them back their people, and make sure everything was fixed now.

Hirish harrumphed next to me. "This sounds like an excellent plan. We will see to gathering the patrols and transports and head out as soon as possible."

"Better to stick together than send people home before we know that all the threats have been neutralized." I thought over what I'd said and groaned. "I mean the mind-control, sic-all-the-animals-on-us-together type of danger."

Hirish nodded. "I know what you meant."

I was glad one of us did.

Putting my head in my hands, I gave myself a moment. Massive Queen Rigoll dead, looted, and hopefully going to refill some of the Credits that we'd spent financing the mental resistance gear we got. I'd hate to think what could have happened if we'd given into her thinly veiled suggestions.

A Mana signature approached, Marie's if I was right. Which I was. Of course.

"Kira?" There was hesitance in her voice, none of that usual confidence.

"It's okay, Marie. I know you didn't mean it." I knew why she was there. Didn't have to be a mind reader for that.

She offered me a wan smile. "It felt so . . . wrong. I couldn't control anything. All there was was this compulsion to move exactly as directed, to do what I had to. I didn't want to."

"I know." I pushed myself up and brushed off the grass and leaves. "All bets are off. Everything has changed. We survived and that's what counts."

Marie nodded. "Yeah. Thanks."

I watched her go, clamping down on the trembling I could feel coming on. There wasn't time to dwell on near misses, close deaths, or anything else. The fact was that I was still here, and I was still alive, and my kids hadn't lost their mum.

Keep on staying alive; that was all we could do. That way we'd be there for the next shitstorm thrown at us.

Chapter Twenty:
Carindale

16 Weeks, 5 Days Post-System Onset

7 p.m.

The sun snuck behind the horizon as we finally crested the Carindale carparks. How the fuck was it still the same day?

Our little convoy took a lot longer to get to the settlement, what with all of the injured, those in need of Shop visits so they could replace limbs, and little kids we had with us.

Every time I looked at one of them, I felt my heart hurt. It could have been us. They could have been Wisp.

Fuck the apocalypse.

Carindale knew we were coming. Our communications were back in place. Joshua, the settlement admin we'd met all those weeks ago, was eagerly awaiting us, his hands clasped in front of him, his mop of red hair blowing in the light breeze.

Jake Manly, if I remembered correctly, his head of security, stood next to him, tightlipped as he held his gun loosely in one hand. There was no sweat on his dark brow in this meeting, but his bright brown eyes were even more piercing than the first time I'd met him.

When they spied us and our cargo, dozens of other people began streaming out to help us get the injured and elderly back into the settlement. I was so tired; I think I could have dropped right there and slept on the cement.

Joshua suddenly stood beside me, and my reflexes were on such a hair trigger that I scanned him, making sure this wasn't a trap. His Mana was quiet, not readying to do anything. Which was good, because this wasn't something that could be healed, and I had nothing left in me despite my Mana well slowly refilling. This was far too much concentration on tracing Mana lines. I hadn't realized how much it took out of me before today.

"Thank you," he said simply, and I could feel the emotions bubbling just underneath the surface. "You saved my little sister, Jake's daughter, and grandmother . . . we owe you guys so much."

It all made sense now, the way they'd been so hesitant and blocked off from us when we visited the first time. Their overreaction to us having alien species with us. After all, an alien species had just taken so much from them.

"Why did the communications stop? We got worried," I asked, following him into their settlement. It took effort just to put one foot in front of the other.

Joshua hesitated for a moment. "Several of the elderly returned and confiscated our communicators. They were controlled, we could see that, and yet . . . what could we do? On one hand, we were angry; on the other, we hoped you'd care enough to check in on us when we didn't check in with you."

I choked out a laugh. "Well, we definitely did that. Our first patrol got beset by creatures in a constant stream of attacking and never made it here, so we had to come after them."

Joshua smiled. "For whatever the reason, we're grateful to you. We're taking care of the rest of the beasts now."

I nodded and followed him. Once inside the center, my knees threatened to buckle, yet I didn't really feel safe enough to just pull up a bench and sleep. Don't get me wrong, I wasn't injured—the System saw to that—but my brain felt numb.

My senses weren't up to their usual tasks. Tracking any Mana strands was giving me a headache. I'd definitely overused it and overextended myself.

But I was certain that with a full night's sleep I'd be able to bounce back.

The System wouldn't want any of us to die of exhaustion.

There was still something off about the center, but I couldn't put my finger on it. The quiet was gone, and people chattered excitedly with some of those who'd returned. Parents sobbed over their recovered kids. Others mourned those who didn't seem to be reappearing.

I knew from the number of bones scattered around the queen that there'd definitely been casualties. There was no avoiding it. Damn it, I was tired. I needed to contact Dor and check in on the kids. Though I was pretty certain my familial interface would alert me to anything too bad.

"How you holding up?" Kyle put his hand on my arm, and I stared up at him blearily. His black hair looked like someone had rubbed oil through it, and it stood out at odd angles, making me giggle. There were dark circles under his eyes, and his skin seemed paler than usual.

"I thought I was bad, but you look worse." Smirking was one of my hidden talents when overtired.

"Ha. Ha." He sat down next to me on the wooden bench, looking out at the sea of people with a perturbed expression before running his hands through his filthy hair. "Yeah. I could do with a shower. I could do with a week's sleep, too."

"That healing spell is hard, isn't it?" I asked, trying to be gentle considering how I knew he still struggled with his Class's damage abilities.

He shook his head. "It's not just that. It's that the pain they go through feeds back to me. Not in pain itself, but more the energy toll it takes on the patient to regrow the limb. I can sort of sense it, and whoa, I don't ever want to have to do that shit to myself. Remind me not to get limbs blown off, thanks."

Then he leaned back and stared at the ceiling. "Also—there's a definite limit on the time window after the injury occurs. I'm thinking it's around forty to forty-five minutes long. Sadly . . . sometimes I just can't fix it. Dannin seemed a little disappointed that I could regrow his leg. I think he wanted a cybernetic replacement."

"Well." I patted him on the shoulder. "You could always offer to chop it off for him again?"

Kyle chuckled softly, and we both sat wordlessly for several moments.

He finally spoke again, maybe more to himself than to me. "I still hate failing. I don't like losing people."

"None of us like losing people. But now?" And I realized that what I was about to say was truer than I'd been willing to admit previously. "Now . . . death, premature death, is all just a part of life. We shouldn't expect it all the time, but we have to learn to deal with it without it breaking us down."

Numbing. Yep. I think I was becoming numb to the death and mutilation all around me.

And wasn't that a thought to take to bed.

❖

16 Weeks, 6 Days Post-System Onset
8 a.m.

Carindale approached its days rather differently to ours. Several of our members had availed themselves of the Shop yesterday, and Dale and Zyrilian were sporting cybernetic adjustments to their missing limbs. Guess they felt that was an upgrade to their everyday limbs—or maybe it was cheaper.

Their new appendages looked like their skin, even felt mostly skin like, but there was extra strength in there now, and Dale even grabbed what appeared to be a medical upgrade to his, allowing for the ability to store vials of rejuvenation in his forearm. Like not a lot, just a few small vials. Still, though.

If I hadn't known they'd gotten skin grafts to cover their cybernetics, I wouldn't have been able to discern it. Alien technology was kinda creepy.

And I was more grateful than I liked to admit seeing Mon'swkinon in amidst the rest of our survivors. He didn't look like he'd been badly injured or had to replace anything, so he had to be fine, because the System wouldn't have it any other way.

The rest of the shopping center's inhabitants just milled around; they didn't really have a meeting, or anything as far as I could tell. Nor even really a council. Though, until last night, they had been under the threat of a mind-control beast, so . . . I shouldn't be judge-y.

Feeling mostly refreshed after some sleep, I called in to Dor and Sienna to check in on the kids again. No matter how sure I was that they were safe, no matter that I'd been able to check on them with the house info in my interface . . . I was still worried. Too much happened yesterday for me not to be, and I desperately wanted to get back home, but it seemed to me that there was a fair bit of stuff we had to check on here first.

I wasn't about to leave this settlement in a vulnerable state again. Today Dequasha and I would scour for signs of any other Rigolls and clear the buggers out if any of them remained. From what Mana fluctuations I'd managed to get a read on, I didn't think we were in any danger of another queen being present, but we couldn't be too cautious. Who knew how long it took for them to grow in strength?

While waiting for my Mana teacher, I wandered over to the tech area we'd visited briefly last time we were here. It was a hive of activity this morning. Para stood amidst a gathering of people, his head down. I could tell he'd cut his long black hair since the last time we'd been here. Now it was maybe at a three blade, and he didn't need to keep pushing it back up into a headband that was largely ineffectual.

There was a smile lingering on his lips, like he enjoyed what he was doing, and the people around him seemed happier, so much more relaxed than before.

"It's like night and day from yesterday." The voice at my shoulder wasn't unexpected. Mana tracing could pick up anyone anywhere. No one got close to me anymore without me noticing it unless I was engrossed in something.

"Hey, Joshua," I said without looking at the man.

He chuckled. "Yesterday we weren't sure how much longer we'd all be alive. Today . . . there's a new feeling throughout the settlement. A bit of hope, still some fear, but mostly determination to make the most out of this second . . . I guess third chance?"

Now I glanced at him. His hair fell to brush his shoulders, and the red curls were a shade that most women would have killed for. I wondered if that meant he had the stereotypical fiery temper. Probably not—that was prejudging—and despite our brief interactions, I was sure he was a lot more mellow than that.

More. Something more.

Yeah, Mana Sense. I got that. Thanks so much for the obvious hint. Note to self to figure out why I got these glimpses of Mana sentiment sometimes.

"What's bugging you then?" I tried to ask it gently, but it came out gruffer than intended. I guess I was more exhausted than I realized.

"That obvious?" he asked, his eyes following Para's every move. Maybe there was more there; he seemed a little bit preoccupied.

"Yeah. To me, anyway. What's the problem?" Maybe now I could get to the bottom of why the hell things still seemed to be off.

He sighed and motioned for me to follow him. We approached the rest of the food court, or what had been the food court in times gone by, and sat in a little booth next to what I think was their version of our Raybucks. Joshua motioned with his hand and received a nod from the girl behind the counter before steepling his fingers and looking at me.

"We know the location of two more Rigoll. These aren't as powerful, and we have people keeping them at bay. One is almost dead, but the other one. . . . Well, we only found it early this morning while patrolling our grounds. We could use a bit of help with it." I could see that he didn't want to ask for help. They were proud, but at the same time recognized that help was here, and it was better to take advantage of it.

"That's a long fight if you're keeping one at bay?" I couldn't wrap my head around that.

He frowned. "That might not be the best term. We found the first one last night and staked it out. Started attacking it with a small force several hours ago. Our fighters are likely a little less adventurous. We don't really know what they do except for the acid that burns us up from the inside out, melts our skin, and generally creates nightmare fodder for everyone involved."

"Ah, yes." I did know exactly what he meant.

"So. We've been depriving it of water sources, because we noticed that it sucks moisture in. And generally, just having ranged attacks whittle it down while hiding behind barriers. We don't really have the resources to do it for the one we found about an hour ago." He looked down at his hands as the girl brought over two coffees and left them with us. "So, if you can, we'd really appreciate some help just getting rid of these things and ending this whole ordeal."

Suppressing the sigh I felt wanting to escape, I offered him a smile. "We'll help. Just let me check in on my people and we'll go over patrols and organization with you. We should check with the Shop and specifically ask how many there are in and near this location."

Joshua blinked at me like I'd grown another head. "What now?"

There were no friendlier aliens around them here, so maybe they hadn't gotten chatty with their Shopkeeps. "Almost any information you can think of is available for purchase from the Shop. Given that you're willing to pay the price, that is. That's how we knew the approximate location of the queen. So it's probably a good idea to just go get the locations and then we can help you."

"That does sound like the best plan." He still seemed a little shellshocked. While we were used to the internet and all of its information, I guess we'd forgotten what it was like to just be able to google something.

Although in this case, it was expensive. I smiled. "It'll definitely help us make quicker work of whatever is left here. The least we can do is use our own experience to help you guys have the best chance of being free and clear."

Joshua laughed, and some of the tension in his shoulders eased up. "Thank you."

"We can help you set up to make sure your settlement thrives too. Just information and general things that have worked for us. Clear out everything so you can establish and maintain patrols. Because trust me, you'll need to. Apparently, our country was flagged as unsurvivable for a reason. Our mutations are super big, super complex, and grow with super speed." I grinned and watched his face fall a bit.

Then his eyes sparkled, life and good old Australian humor coming back into it. "Because living with deadly normal animals wasn't enough?"

"Precisely." It was good that he got it. We needed to keep that sense of humor alive. Better to laugh than cry, right?

17 Weeks Post-System Onset

We spent the next couple of days helping the Carindale troops figure out patrol areas, how to clean out nests and make better use of the Shop, and hook some of their lower Levels up with instruction from some of our higher Levels.

They weren't doing too badly. Sitting in the mid-high thirties was decent progress, considering all the impediments they'd had thrown at them. Way I heard it, the entirety of Australia was ahead of the curve by quite a bit even for Earth. More monsters, more mutations, higher levels of experience—all of that benefited us.

Also, higher death rate. Not exactly a pro column item though.

It was novel to see the way Joshua and Jake interacted with Hirish. After all, he was a nasty alien creature, right? Still, not all aliens were bad aliens, at least in my experience so far. I watched them interact as they discussed the various patrol areas we were helping divide their groups into. Hirish had that I-will-spell-it-out-to-you look on his face that rarely went down well with Piola.

"No. I would categorize your maps differently." Hirish crossed his arms with a frown, eyeing Jake critically.

"This area over here is still filled with civilians. We need to take care of them." The head of Carindale Security's frown outdid Hirish's and I found that an achievement of its own.

Hirish pointed to three different areas, sharing them with Jake. "If you wish to keep them safe, then you must extend your borders as we did ours. Expansion is necessary. The mutations are not slowing on this planet. Growth will continue at a rapid pace till the end of the Integration period, at which point mutations will slow in most locations. That might not be the case with this landmass. You must be ready, or you will be wiped out."

Ah. My Hakarta friend didn't seem to understand how to let people in on that sort of thing gently.

I stepped in.

"What he means to say is send out patrols in patterns that keep up with the nests we showed you. Extend patrols to keep the people in those subdivisions safe. And as soon as you can afford to, extend your actual gates and walls so that the general security patrols will then take care of those people still living in their houses." It wasn't rocket science. As much as I hated the System and the Dungeon World it created, it did have all the answers right there if you only searched for them.

Well, maybe not everything. But when it came to protecting a settlement, it really was all there.

Jake made to protest, and I held up a hand, watching Joshua and Dale discussing something off to the side.

"Look. This is the easiest way to do it. If you want to take more difficult approaches, that's up to you. But we will be reachable, and hopefully we'll have the networks up and running soon enough. Although regaining the Internet is still something I'm not sure we'll ever figure out. We probably won't need to—I'm sure once we have the Credits, we can leapfrog to the Galactic equivalent.

"But we aren't that far away, and we can communicate if needed. Ask us for advice, for help, for our chili recipe. Any of the above." I rolled my shoulders, feeling a little stiff after a half day of fighting. I knew it was mental—still didn't make it any less annoying.

I'd spoken to Wisp that morning, but I really just wanted to get home and hug her. Let her know I was truly okay and that I loved her. Meanwhile, I'd give Jackson a fist bump and ruffle his hair so much that he growled at me. All in a mum's day's work.

Jake relaxed a little. "Yeah. Okay. Sorry. It's just been a hell of a few months and I don't adjust well to change."

"This sort of change . . ." I swept my arm around to gesture vaguely at the world in general. "This is big stuff. None of us were prepared for this. So don't feel bad if you're not dealing with it in an 'ideal' manner. There is no actual textbook for this, only other recounting of their experiences. Trust me, I looked. Maybe we should write a technical manual."

That got a laugh out of him and a little bit more tension release. "Thanks. For the patience. We'll do our best to return the favor should you need it."

"I know," I said, nodded once and left the planning offices.

This wasn't my circus, and they definitely weren't my monkeys, but I felt like maybe I'd given them a bit of a shove onto the little trapeze we'd all be swinging on for the foreseeable future.

"Hey." Evelyn nudged my arm as I walked out, and I realized she'd been waiting for me.

"Hey yourself." I nudged her back and felt all of my own worries lift, just a tad.

"Think we'll make it out of here tomorrow morning?" She glanced around at the massive center, which was technically smaller than Garbo.

I looked too. This wasn't home, but I really hoped it could become that for this settlement. We still had to reach out to more potential survivors. But for now . . .

"Yeah. We'll all be heading home tomorrow."

And for the first time since this all began, I actually felt like we had a place in this world.

Chapter Twenty-One:
Downpour

17 Weeks, 1 Day Post-System Onset

11 a.m.

Brisbane is often so dry, you forget that water can actually pour from the sky. The poet in me found it beautiful.

The realist in me driving in a top-down Jeep on the way back to Garbo . . . despised it.

About twenty minutes after we set out from Carindale, the clouds opened up and let the rain pour down. Even in winter our city was dry as a bone, and the soil and earth got so parched that it cracked and had little room for the water to soak in. Instead, it ran off into storm drains that were easily overwhelmed, leading to flooded streets in most areas. Luckily, we were still a while away from that. This wasn't quite a torrential downpour.

Yet.

The thing was, Upper Mt. Gravatt had high elevation. If it went under water, the rest of the city was already fucked. So even as we drove with water sluicing down my back, dripping from my face, I knew that our settlement wasn't going to be in much trouble, and neither was Cardinale, but there were areas that we patrolled—and others beyond that—where the water levels would definitely rise.

Twenty minutes away from us was Wellington Point, the beauty of the bay that led out to Moreton and Stradbroke Islands. I didn't even want to think what horrors might mutate from out in the deeper ocean. Mutations that might come up our rivers and waterways with torrential flooding, bringing nightmares I couldn't even begin to fathom.

Even without an apocalypse mutating all the creatures around us, we'd often ended up with bull sharks and whatnot in waterways, including even some in golf course lakes. Try getting your ball out of *that* water trap.

Actually, I vaguely remember once seeing a video with an idiot doing just that . . . lost to the ether now, I guess. Was quite the hoot.

Luckily, we'd been helping Carindale's patrols the last couple of days. We'd cleared up in the direction we'd drive home, getting them on a regular schedule they could easily maintain without us.

Still. Water in winter made me shiver more than not. At least autumn would start in a few more weeks.

I couldn't wait to see our settlement's walls and maybe soak in a tub for the first time in what felt like forever. Probably wouldn't get to do it on my own. I mean, that's not something mums get. Regardless of going to the loo or taking a shower, there were always interruptions and questions that just couldn't wait.

Right now, I felt lucky that I still had that.

The worst thing about taking the main roads to get back home was that it left us out in the open. Perfect for a particular Magon to swoop overhead looking for prey. The vehicles stopped abruptly, and I'm really not sure why we thought it wouldn't notice us if we didn't move, but anything was worth a shot.

It wasn't directly over us, maybe a few kilometers to south, but we could see it, and we weren't risking it seeing us and deciding we were easy pickings. The tip of its wingspan sent shadows cascading over us, but no relief from the rain. I hoped that the dismal clouds with minimal lighting helped obscure our potentially tasty figures.

For once it wasn't howling into the sky but drifting silently along the stormy currents like it was prowling for something in particular.

It felt like forever before it was far enough away for us to feel safe starting the vehicles up again. The apocalypse would be so much more fun if we didn't constantly have to worry about getting picked off by an overgrown magpie. Maybe we needed to make a settlement quest for that.

Finally, our little convoy hit the turn off for Logan Road. The trip was uneventful mostly, just a few errant little Level 20 blobs and Magpie Nightmares. Nothing insanely difficult.

Just the rain reminding us that nature was still present.

Solar wasn't going to be a source of power for at least a few days or so, it seemed. The dark, roiling clouds above us looked to have no end. Ambient Mana should be sufficient to power most of our little town's needs. Or so I hoped.

I'm sure Dor had graphs and numbers for all that.

And then we were finally home.

Wisp barreled into my arms so fast I barely had enough time to exit the vehicle properly. Water streamed down on both of us, and I returned her bear hug fiercely for about half a minute before I got us inside the building.

"Mum! You'll never guess. Jana took us out on a school trip. Just beyond the borders yesterday. It was so cool. I got to pick some plants and items to sell in the Shop." She clung to my hand like it was a lifeline, and Dog trotted next to her like a worried Nanny. Wombie wasn't anywhere in sight, but I wasn't concerned. I'm sure I'd have been told if something happened to him.

"You had a school trip?" I commented, running through my brain to try and recall any vague information I might have had about it. Nothing came up, but that didn't mean Jana hadn't told me. Sometimes I walked into a room and forgot why I was there, after all.

"It was so much fun. Sort of scary too. But Dog came with me. So I wasn't too frightened." She grinned up at me.

I pulled the bracer off and handed it to her. "Well, if you're going to be a world explorer, you're going to need this a lot more than I will. No more giving it to me, okay?" I fought down the irrational fear I felt. She'd already gone beyond the walls; the danger was in the past. I couldn't change it, so I needed to accept it and move on—perhaps leaving a couple of years of my life expectancy behind with the almost heart attack.

Not to mention getting her that dermal underarmor upgrade to level two had just become a top priority.

"Fine. But I will still lend it to you if I think you might be in danger." Wisp pouted slightly as she reequipped her bracer, and I pulled her into a side hug. Though I knew Jackson was out on a patrol, I was a little nonplussed that he didn't seem to be around for a hug too. That was okay; I'd ambush him when he got back.

Mum stealth tactics, activate!

Though I didn't envy him being out in this weather, I suddenly realized that patrols had to happen regardless of weather. With our usual lack of rain, I just hadn't thought about it before.

The mutations and new monsters weren't going to just go "Hey, the weather is shit. Let's stop multiplying and wait it out." There were always going to be more monsters for us to deal with. I didn't see that ever stopping, and suddenly the whole situation felt even more exhausting.

"Everything okay, Mum?" Wisp tugged at me, and I realized I was thinking way too heavily.

"Fine, Buttercup. I'm absolutely fine. Just a little tired."

Her grip on my hand tightened. "Did you get to do what you set out to?"

"Yeah. And we saved lots of little kids, and heaps of older people too." I smiled at the thought. "Thank you for being here for hugs when I got back."

This time she grinned at me. "Well, of course. That's like my job. That and taking care of Dog and Wombie. He spent the day with Mumma. She seemed to be lonely without you here to check in on her. Plus, they're dry in their little house . . . though . . ." She paused, looking skeptically at me.

"What?" I wasn't sure I wanted to hear this.

"Well . . . I think they've dug tunnels down from one of the garage sides. I mean, it's what they do, right?"

I groaned. The last thing we needed was a wombutt-induced loss of structural integrity in the roads surrounding our branched-out settlement. But I guess that was something we could deal with when the rain stopped.

"I'm sure it'll be okay," I bluffed to my kid.

Her hugging of my arm told me she didn't believe a word I said, but really, that was okay.

I was home and could get dry and warm in just a little bit. And for now, just now, I could fool myself into thinking that everything felt right with the world.

❖

Rain has this dizzying effect for me. As if it's lulling me to sleep whether I'm moving, standing still, or lying down. This rain was no different, even if everything else was. On the bright side, it seemed that the repairs we'd done to our house when I purchased it were holding up under several hours of watery onslaught.

Jackson sat chatting with Kyle in soft tones in the den. Evelyn was upstairs taking a shower, while Wombie and Dog played with Wisp in the living area. All of it under clouded skies, as if nothing had ever happened.

Me? I was getting ready for a meeting we were having this evening.

Getting ready to go out and get drenched again, all in the name of settlement management. In total, we'd lost about five of our adventurers, but their names didn't register anything inside me, only a vague recollection of who they were.

If, however, someone closer to me were mangled . . . I'd probably have a hard time dealing with it. Maybe? Probably? I wasn't even sure anymore.

"Ready?"

I glanced behind me to see Evelyn standing in her Archer's gear. She'd upgraded her gear and seriously seemed like a female Robin Hood. Green leather, skintight, leaving little to the imagination and making me blush like I was back in high school.

Shit.

"That's new," I commented, floundering slightly.

She grinned. "Glad you like it."

Damn it. "Yeah. Glad I do too."

I stuck my tongue out, suddenly feeling all too juvenile and then laughed. It felt so freeing to laugh.

Evelyn finished pinning her brown hair back into a tight bun with what looked like those chopstick types of hair pins. Except they glinted strangely, more like steel.

I narrowed my eyes. "Are those throwing weapons?"

She nodded. "Yeah. Fling anything pointy hard enough and it's likely to penetrate a surface."

"Good to know."

Evelyn glanced sideways at me, a light smirk on her face. "You know I'll never fling it at you, right?"

"Whew," I said, wiping my brow theatrically. "Here I was worried for a moment."

There was a brief second of companionable silence before she broke it again. "We should probably jet out."

I sighed, not wanting to go out in the chilling rain. Evelyn silently handed me a coat, like she'd read my mind. I looked at it and laughed. Drizabone. Wow. These were heavy-duty, oiled canvas coats that the water just slid off while the interior kept you toasty warm. When I was a kid, I'd worked for a boutique retailer that stocked the brand. Always wanted one, never got around to it.

"Thanks," I whispered, somewhat touched.

"Got one for Kyle, too, and the kids. Don't feel too special," Evelyn quipped, but she winked at me while she did so, and yelled at Kyle to hurry up.

While he pulled his jacket on, Jackson came and gave me a quick hug. "I'll keep Wisp company. Darren was going to come over in a bit, is that okay?"

"Sure. No loud parties while I'm gone."

For some reason that sent my son into gales of laughter I hadn't anticipated, and it took a solid minute for him to calm down again. "None, Mum. I promise."

Yeah, I didn't actually think he was the sort of kid to throw wild parties, especially not now, but still. I didn't think it was *that* funny. Walking into where Wisp lay on the ground with her pet friends and a book, reading out loud to them, I ruffled her hair and leaned over to give her a hug which she returned somewhat absentmindedly.

"We'll be back later. Don't get in too much trouble.," I said quietly, not wanting to interrupt.

Without taking her eyes off the book, she responded quite dryly, "It's wet outside, Mum. I'm not going mud puddle jumping" before she promptly returned to reading to a mutant wombat who would barely fit through the door soon, and her pony-sized dog.

The scooters drove silently, powered as they were by Mana batteries, and I could see some people in front of us and behind us as we turned onto Tryon Street to make our way through the retirement village toward Garbo. Silent transport and the rain falling down on and around us held this eerie sort of foreboding. I didn't like the premonition it gave me and had a sudden feeling that this storm was actually building toward something that had nothing to do with the weather.

I tried to look inward and see if my Mana Sense was going to talk to me, but no luck there. Silence from all corners. Great, just when I needed it to actually pipe up and even give me a hint of what we were walking into.

It didn't seem to work that way.

The clouds were low and dark enough that it leant the world an early twilight, tinged with grey overtones to dampen the mood even further. Inside the center, the lights didn't feel as bright as usual, and everything just gave me this odd sensation of the worst was yet to come.

I could do doom and gloom perfectly well on my own, thank you very much, Mother Nature.

Tonight wasn't just for the council, but for all of us. Well, within reason. We were dividing up into groups. Representatives for the adventurers, crafters, admin, hospitality and food workers, other essential personal like those deeply involved in health care or the teaching of our kids.

Considering we were closing in on four thousand settlement members, we were really starting to get a huge chunk of children.

Once everyone had gathered in the food court, and Leena was passing out a heap of snacks and beverages that her staff at Raybucks produced, it was Jana who stood up first. Her dark hair was pulled back, as usual, in her tight ponytail, and her bronzed skin stood out against a simply lemon-colored cotton peasant blouse. It struck me as such a sunny thing to be wearing today of all days.

Jana cleared her throat before speaking and I could practically feel her nerves from where I sat. "We've reached a bit of a blockage."

Avery sat just to the side of Jana and nodded encouragement. There were other women and a few men around them both who I only vaguely recognized. But it sort of seemed like they were all funneling courage to her.

"We have several hundred kids now. Luckily, quite a few of us were teachers in our previous lives, so we've been making do as we can." She took a breath, glancing back at her support system again as if she really needed the strength and barreled on in.

"We need more space to educate them and have to make a definitive allocation of space for the kids that are about two to four or five. The kids we're not yet teaching to read and write regularly and learn about our old and this new world. Thing is . . . we're having to play this all by ear. It's lucky that the kids don't get their Classes until they're teenagers, but at the same time, it means we have to prepare these kids for everything. Their Perks are all already chosen, and so . . ." Jana stopped, gathering her breath and thoughts.

"Out in the southeast portion of the lot, where the main roads converge, and we have that little corner that's sort of part of Garbo out near the Travelodge. Where the old tax building used to be. It's pretty huge." She didn't wait for an answer to her question. "We would like to ask that the settlement consider helping us remodel and adjust that so that we might use it for an interim school building. Right now, it's just empty offices and we think that, with everything else going on, the kids need a place to call their school, a place that can have some measure of normalcy for them to be children."

There was a murmuring around, but for the most part I thought it was definitely an affirmative consensus.

"I don't see why not," I offered, wanting to get through the rest of the night.

Jana smiled at me, obviously relieved.

"We can talk about how to go about it after the meeting if you like," Sienna offered quietly, patting a seat beside her. "Now, Avery? You had something too?"

"Just about the Sunrise Kids Development place. We're going to repurpose it as exactly that. Though we'll be limited to how many kids it can hold unless it expands. We may want to look into using the half-demolished Travelodge building as another option for the schools. No matter what, we're going to have kids to take care of. We need to have the infrastructure in place."

"Makes sense." Chris stood up, obviously scrolling through some sort of information in her personal interface. "I have some tools I can use to help you figure out curriculum and sort of upload it for everyone who is a teacher. It'll take a bit, but I can get one of our tech teams working on it starting tomorrow."

Avery's face lit up and it was such a juxtaposition from when she'd almost lost her son that it made me smile. We might be at the end of the earth so to speak, but we could all think of the kids, right?

"Great. That's settled." Sienna went through her own list of things, ticking off a couple and making notes, and then stood up, her face grave.

"The Carindale patrol is back, and moving forward, our communication and cooperation with them to keep the area between us open will be extended." She glanced down as Dor spoke to her. "I know today's rain hasn't put us in the best of moods, but we have to go out in it. Nests aren't going to stop spawning just because we want to take a day off for rain."

A low murmur of irritation rumbled through the room, but nothing too bad. Sienna held her hand up. "We will be looking at the new people who've registered the last five days. If you are an adventurer Class, you will need to see Hirish, Kira, and Kyle after this meeting."

That was news to me, but I tried not to let my irritation show on my face. After all, I did manage time for a bath before this. It wasn't all bad.

She directed anyone with teaching or similar qualifications to go to Avery and Jana. Techies to Chris, healers to Dale, foodies to Red, crafters to Ginali. It never ceased to amaze me that we were building this community. From the ground up, adapting technologies to different power sources, and proving just how resilient and stubborn humans could be.

"What are you smiling about?" Hirish asked, his voice as gruff as usual.

I shrugged. "I dunno. Just thinking that sometimes it's kind of nice to be a cockroach."

Chapter Twenty-Two:

Intermittent

17 Weeks, 3 Days Post-System Onset
7 a.m.

Kipatchya tasted even better in the mornings after walking through the rain to get to it. Granted, I didn't have many other days to compare it to, but I was going to make this decision right now, considering I thought myself informed enough.

What I was more interested in, however, was my twin chatting to a lovely healer who I think had come with us from Carindale. I hadn't really paid too much attention at the time, too bothered by thoughts of rain and getting home to my kids, but now that I was sipping my drug of choice . . .

She stood maybe five-four . . . maybe a little less, with brightly colored rainbow hair that I wished I could get to take on mine without stripping it to death. Her skin was a beautiful medium brown with hints of a heritage I didn't want to guess lest I come across as rude, and her eyes were startlingly green.

She was gorgeous.

And apparently completely smitten with my brother.

That was definitely something I'd keep an eye on. He'd never made time with his career. Several partially serious relationships and that was it. I somehow doubted that an apocalypse was helping him free up time, not without some helpful prodding from a loving and not at all busybody sister.

All in a day's work, right?

They turned to make their way over to me and I busied myself with trying to look like I hadn't been spying on them. Pretty sure my brother knew I was full of shit.

"Hi!" I said, far too brightly for this time of morning, but I was in a good mood because we hadn't had a meeting this morning because of last night's. Win-win.

"Stop it." Kyle rolled his eyes and gestured to the woman next to him. "Kira, meet Melody."

"Nice to meet you." I held out my hand briefly which she squeezed and retracted. She seemed a mite nervous. "You came from Carindale, right?"

"Yeah. I . . . have several Skills in common with Kyle and wanted to learn more about them. We had to hold back a bit with all the . . ." She smiled somewhat shyly, gesturing vaguely around before glancing across to my twin.

Oh, how I could have butt loads of fun with this if I didn't have to eat and get to my patrol. I put on my adulting pants and decided not to tease the ever-living crap out of my brother. Yet. "Kyle's a good teacher, and a fantastic healer. It was a good choice."

She grinned, and it lit up her face even more. "I thought so too."

I shot a message to Kyle. So grateful for the familial messaging Perk we'd chosen when this all started.

Can she regrow?

Yeah.

Short and sweet. To the point, and now it made even more sense. Healers that could regrow limbs appeared to be rare. "Well, don't keep him too long; we have a patrol to go on shortly. Unless he's bringing you, in which case, don't be late."

I grabbed my drink and headed to the library to talk with Dor, without looking back. They didn't need my needling, even if it was a hell of a lot of fun. It took every ounce of willpower to walk away without several smart-arse comments. Kyle owed me one.

As I walked, I could still hear the ever-present tinker of light rain on the center roof. Even with all the other noise in the center it gave this underlying current of discordant music, sending chills down my spine like a portent of disaster.

Way to go, overactive imagination. I'd never liked the electrical storms we got. Where there was lightning and thunder without actual rain. But sometimes the downpours could ignite even worse possibilities in my brain.

Dor was waiting for me outside the library entrance. "Managed to raid the stores of the Driza-bones we had. All of it. There wasn't too much. We can replicate some of it through the crafters, but that's going to take time. And yes, the Store does have them, but I'm not inclined to spend the money we need for defenses on extra rain protection. People can do that themselves. I've grabbed raincoats too. First come, first served. You're lucky Evelyn nabbed you everything yesterday."

"Yep." I looked at the stack next to her. "Humans really aren't all that fond of rain. Are we?"

She chuckled. "It's not like it makes us grow. I wouldn't want to go out in it, let alone stay out in it and kill a heap of mutated creatures. So I guess I owe you and the others a thank you."

"Psh." I said, waving the compliment away. "There's never a time you need to thank us. Just keep on keeping on with all the admin stuff and we'll call it even."

She chuckled at that.

"How're the schoolhouses coming?" I asked, hoping it was all running smoothly.

Dor shrugged. "We're sending out people to activate the remodeling today. It's not too huge a cost, so we can afford it and frankly, for the experience and attention they're giving the kids . . . I think it's a necessity. We'll just have to end up shuttling the kids down to their new school."

Shuttling the kids to school. Giving them a half-normal existence up until the point they turned into teenagers with choices. "Sounds like a plan. Gotta have them literate enough to know what they're looking at when their Class choices come up, after all."

Dor's gaze bored into me, and I waited for her to speak because I knew it was coming. It's like she expected me to know what she was about to say and was marginally irritated when I didn't just prattle off what was in her head.

"I think most of the kids will show a . . . proclivity toward a certain Class. Like some certain almost-nine-year-old girl with a plethora of pets following her everywhere." The older woman raised an eyebrow at me.

Ah. She did have a good point. I'd not really thought about it before. Wisp had always saved every lizard, every frog, every bird who'd ever been injured throughout her entire childhood. Her affinity with animals wasn't a shock to me at all. If her Class ended up being something in tune with those same creatures, I wouldn't be surprised at all.

"You make a good point," I said quietly, suddenly contemplating how that might all work.

"Of course I do," Dor grumbled, but I could tell she wasn't in a bad mood.

I nudged her. "C'mon. Let's get all this shit sorted for the morning patrols. The quicker it gets done, the faster I get home and can take a nice, warm, bath."

❖

Koalzillas are terrifying to see on a normal day, but drenched by downpour, it's worse. The way their fur clings to their bodies gives them a hungry and rage-filled appearance. The damp layer hugging their bones and the rain washing away the blood and viscera previously clumping that fur together left rivulets of pink and bloody streams until they ran clear.

It left absolutely none of the cute in evidence around the jaws. With the hair of the creature matted around its mouth, there was little left to the imagination about how very powerful its jaws actually were. Teeth peeked out of overgrown, matted lips for some of the creatures, barely held in by their mouths considering the sheer growth they'd experienced during mutation.

Canines the size of my forearm did more to strike fear in me than the rising quagmire we fought them in. But I'd become an expert at pushing down fear and grasping onto logic and strategy after weeks—months!—of killing things.

At least, I hoped I had.

Changing my grip at the last second, I twirled around to gain momentum and slammed the head of my Warhammer into the ankle joint of the massive creature in front of me. It wedged in place and as the creature screamed, I flew up several feet as it yanked its now injured foot up.

Only when it touched back down did the impact allow me to pull out the damned hammer and roll away, not a moment too soon. The way the System worked, getting stomped on wasn't going to kill me outright, but it would sure as hell hurt.

Evelyn and Marie fired in unison, their targeting visors allowing them to adjust for the rainfall making it through the tree canopy. Ray's Ice Blasts took on more power as moisture gathered with his projectiles. The lingering clouds of ice particles left behind were almost pretty, even if they did fade fast.

I'm sure there was a metaphor about the apocalypse in that thought there.

Zyrilian had come with us today, testing out his new cybernetic attachment. I wasn't entirely certain the rain of the day was the best atmosphere to test it in . . . but he seemed to be handling it well, stopping occasionally to discuss something with Gemma.

All the while, I continued to root the second and third monsters that we couldn't get to yet. Their reach was huge, so Molly had to pull the main one we were fighting farther away to outrun their reach. Sange and Kyle banded together, their healing focus intent on those in close combat as that's where the Koalzillas wreaked the most havoc.

The rain continued to tumble down, lending a bleak and cold air to the whole situation even though winter would be coming to a close soon. I had to admit to disliking the ominous feeling I felt permeating through the Mana around us.

Like it knew something we didn't.

Which, of course, it sort of did. I mean, it was Mana's fault that we were a Dungeon World to begin with. In a way. Sort of. It wasn't so much a consciousness of its own, but instead a presence I could sometimes interpret. The messages I got were more interpretations.

Just a few more of these damned creatures and we could maybe head back home for the day. All I wanted was somewhere dry and welcoming. Not this quagmire of a eucalyptus forest with its mutating gum trees and underbrush where I kept thinking my feet would be sucked from legs if I wasn't careful. The underlying mud had clay qualities to it, reddish in nature the closer we got to the bay. It was cold; it was wet and squishy and just a little slimy and got in even through my pants, especially when I had to jump and dodge and roll.

Not a thing of fun.

Luckily, the squelch and sucking that annoyed me appeared to have the same effect on our opponents. I watched as Molly backed up, having difficulty maneuvering the shield when the slimy clay wanted to keep a hold of it. The Koalzilla whose ankle I'd recently punctured made to move after her, but the foot I hadn't injured refused to come free at first, until, with a sudden loud sucking pop, it did—and sent the massive creature plummeting face first into the ground as it overbalanced.

Molly, Gemma, Zyrilian, and two other rogues we had with us barely managed to get out of the way in time, but it was worth it watching them dive to the sides as the Koalzilla face planted.

Way to go, nature, helping us battle monsters.

If I hadn't had the cold mixture of sweat and rain leaking down every part of my body underneath my Driza-bone, I would have thanked it.

Fighting in a patrol, I often had a group of similar people with me. It became so mundane, so repetitive that everyone blurred into the background. We fell into a rhythm even while training lower Levels, teaching more people how to use and hone their Skills.

We dove in and out, used all our Skills to whittle down the health of our opponent even as it struggled up, crushed it eventually, and then finally moved onto the next. In the meantime, the healers with us would make sure we were patched up, and occasionally had to save lives if something went wrong like it had that day with Marie and the Tetchrihorns.

It worked for us. Even if I kept falling into a groove that might get too comfortable if we weren't careful. With these weather conditions, we had to be more alert, and not become complacent.

I couldn't imagine ever being so reckless as to venture out and take some of these on solo. Being in a large group provided a level of protection, the possibility of healing, less danger of death.

It'd take someone with a death wish to fight solo out here.

Blinking rain out of my eyes as the last Koalzilla fell to the ground, I realized I was panting. My shoulders hurt and I cringed, thinking I might need to pump some more Strength into myself if I was going to be wielding the damned hammer this much.

All I could hear around us was the patter of persistent rain on varying species of gum leaves above us and around us. Rain sank into the underbrush to further soften up the clay, pulling us and the monsters down.

It would be so easy to manipulate the ground into swallowing up opponents. I tried to figure out what combination of Skills I'd have to use to pull that off. Another Level and Cocoon would be mine. Then . . . then we could talk.

Perhaps.

I imagined the Koalzillas' faces, mud closing in on them, struggling. Mixing with the cuteness of the creatures I knew before. Gasping . . .

"Kira?"

The water running down my face was trying to blind me, and I felt like I'd come down with a chill if I wasn't careful. Though the System would likely cure me of that. I faced Evelyn, pushing the damp hair that had come out of my ponytail back out of my eyes. "Mm?"

And I realized that was all the energy I had in me. Stomping through muddy fields was a lot more difficult than when the ground was dry.

"We're heading back. It's almost three in the afternoon."

I looked at her like she had two heads. There was no way we'd been out here for over six hours, was there?

Shit.

Death and disaster had become such a part of our lives, I think we were all autopiloting through it. "Thanks. Don't know how I missed that."

She shot me a sympathetic look and ran ahead to catch one of the newer archers we'd brought with us today. I followed, not entirely sure how I'd come to feel so numb about everything. But right then, I decided that I needed to do something to maintain a handle on my own humanity. Something just for me, even if it might not be the most productive use of my time.

Muddy mosh-pit monster fights were now a part of my daily routine.

I shuddered.

Didn't have that on my life's bingo card now, did I?

Chapter Twenty-Three:
Alive

18 Weeks, 1 Day Post-System Onset

9 a.m.

Pinching the bridge of my nose, I considered, again, seeing if the Shop had a time machine. Jackson's scowl didn't change, however, and I was fairly certain if there was a time travel option, then someone would have already reversed every Dungeon World there ever was from coming into being.

"Mum. It doesn't matter if you like it. I have a Class that can fight as well as tinker. It doesn't make sense to keep me out of the thick of it." He crossed his arms and tapped his foot and wow, did he look like Mason when he was trying to get a point across.

The thing was, unlike his father when he was just being stubborn, my son was correct in this bit of obstinacy. I knew I was being a dick, a stick in the mud, helicopter parenting as much as I could in an apocalypse. But the other thing was, I couldn't help it. To me, he was still the baby boy I'd brought home from the hospital hoping I wouldn't fuck up his life.

Kudos to the aliens for doing that for me.

"Fine." I ground out the word, wishing I could take it back immediately. "You can come with us on our next patrol, but!" I held up my hand to forestall anything he'd been about to say.

"You will listen to Hirish and Kyle. You will not be treated specially, because out there we can't afford that, and you will take orders, even if it means taking cover. Do you understand that?" My tone was harsh, but this was my kid, and I couldn't have him thinking he had special privileges just because he was Kyle's nephew and my son.

"Of course I get it. What do you think I've been doing out there with

Lousesh's groups?" He seemed angry, and maybe he had the right to be.

Lousesh went out far, but not as far as us. They generally didn't encounter new creatures before we did, and their clearance routes were technically less dangerous. Still dangerous, mind you, but maybe not as much. Would having him with me help or hinder? I had no idea, but I guess he was coming with us next time.

"Don't be a smartass. I have to consider all of our safety and reactions to having you there." I said it quietly, and I hoped that he understood what I meant. Maybe he did, because for a moment his expression softened.

"I'll do what I'm told. I promise I'm an asset, Mum."

Ah, he was still such a kid. Needing such approval, and it was a shitty move of me to make him think I didn't value him. "I know you are. I'm just worried."

I pulled him into a hug, even though his first reaction was to pull against it. But then he relaxed, and so did I.

"You're infuriating!" Piola's voice carried across to us from Garbo's entrance and with it went the fleeting calm I'd felt.

"Your ways are archaic." While Hirish wasn't yelling, his voice had this quality that covered distances.

Both the Zarrie and Pirra Clan leaders were soaked through, glaring at each other even as they walked toward the library. I got the distinct feeling that rain wasn't one of their favorite things either. Way to have something in common with the aliens.

"What seems to be the issue?" Stepping forward, gently pushing my son half behind me. You just never knew. They might be allied with us because of some contract, oath, or whatever, but they were still aliens.

Hirish's temper boiled beneath the surface, and Piola struggled for a moment before throwing her hands up in the air. The fur on her muzzle was matted and let her canines peek out in a way that reminded me of the Koalzillas we'd fought a few days ago. Like her teeth didn't fit properly.

"We have developed several traps that could easily be deployed to help maintain the nestings." Piola crossed her arms, a slight snarl raising one corner of her mouth as she spoke. "He insists that this is an archaic way to go about it."

"That is not the entire story." Hirish didn't even appear to be ruffled by her complaint. I eyed him critically. He did often think that his way was the best way, and was often correct, but that didn't mean Piola didn't have an excellent point too.

"Then what is?" I asked quietly. Jackson squeezed my hand and ran off somewhere behind me, probably bored to death.

Hirish let out what sounded like a long-suffering sigh. "The point is that in all of this water, some elements of the traps will not function correctly and thus are a complete and utter waste of time for us to put in place."

Piola rolled her eyes, which was quite a comical thing to witness, though I didn't think she'd appreciate me laughing. "Not now. Once the rains clear." I could practically hear her adding, *you dimwit*, or something to the end of that in her own mind.

Hirish pondered that statement for a moment before replying. "Why didn't you say that in the first place?"

She squared her shoulders and took a deep breath before speaking through clenched teeth. "I did. As usual, you just weren't listening."

"Once the rains clear, we should attempt a few locations and track the progress, then. I'll leave that in your hands." He nodded at her and moved passed us into the library without an apology or anything.

I thought the Zarrie leader was about to pop a gasket. "Count to ten," I cautioned.

Piola glanced at me, confusion taking over her anger. "What was that?"

"Count to ten so you don't lose your temper." I shrugged. "It's a human emotion-controlling technique I guess."

"Interesting," she said and seemed to be mulling it over. "Count to ten. Maybe five. I'm too impatient for ten. Slowly but surely the Levels of the respawns are increasing. Usually, an area remains constant, but I'm not so sure this continent is going to stick to what is usual."

"Well, we're definitely unique," I said, a hint of pride in my voice.

Paoli watched me for several seconds. "You are resilient. Wily. And going against the assumed order of the System's calculations. That makes you rare, but not unique."

"I'll take it."

She smiled at me. The fur around her muzzle had begun to dry and fluff out again, so it wasn't a bloodcurdling sort of expression anymore. "Don't worry. We will make this alliance work."

"Even if we have to kick ass and take names to do so?" I asked.

She paused a second and grinned in response. "Yes. Even then."

We headed into the library in companionable silence.

Lousesh, Hirish, and Mon'swkinon stood together, gathered around behind Dor discussing something I decided I wanted to find out about. Trotting to stand with them, Lousesh turned to me. "We have received a . . . radio call for help."

"What?" Did he mean from more human survivors, not from Carindale?

Dor sighed. "On the way back, they received a two-way frequency interruption asking for help."

"Wait, who from?" I couldn't help being excited. After all, finding more humans out there meant more of us were sticking it to the takeover.

Dor looked up at me and shrugged. "Listen for yourself."

At first all I could hear was the crackling of the walkie, but then came the voice, breaking through the static like a clear picture.

. . . Gary to Garbo, do you copy?

Copy. That was Dor.

. . . relief, man! Stuck with a group . . . small settlement . . . need help.

Location?

Sheldon College. . . .Thornlands . . . surrounded.

Stay alert. Will respond.

And then the message went quiet.

I blinked at Dor and waited, knowing she'd fill me in without my having to ask the ten thousand questions already running through my head. Like how had he gotten a radio, and why had it taken so long to contact us?

"We haven't been out quite that far with clearing, so whatever they've encountered, whatever has them hemmed in . . . the Levels are likely to be some of the highest we've seen." Her voice held a quiet urgency. "If we want a chance of saving them, we have to go as soon as we can make the right preparations."

"Even in this rain?" Mon'swkinon's question was full of disdain. I'd noticed the Dash'Kiri held a mild hatred for this water-ridden landscape we found ourselves in. Their heavy bodies didn't do well with the sodden, clay-like mud the earth had become.

To prone to sinking.

"Especially in this rain." Dor leveled a look at him that brooked no nonsense. "If it's not something you can help with, there is plenty more for you to do around here."

And just like that, she'd made it less awkward for him to not head out.

"Plenty else to do around here? What did I miss?" Kyle stood, chomping into something that vaguely resembled a sausage roll. Damn, I hadn't had one of those in ages, and my stomach was rumbling.

Wordlessly, he held out one for me. Sometimes having a twin was awesome.

"Next time bring enough for all of us, Kyle." Gemma sat herself down on the floor, stretching out like she did when she was winding down.

"No." He stopped chewing. "Now what did I miss?"

"Gary radioed in," Dolores said, cutting straight to the point. "It appears he was picked up by other survivors and they've gotten themselves hemmed in."

"Gary really is alive?" Suddenly Drake was there, and I don't think I'd ever seen so many emotions play over the man's face before.

"It would appear so," Dor said gently, a kind smile creeping over her lips.

"Is he . . . okay?" It was strange to watch as the tension left his shoulders and he sat down on the floor next to Gemma like he couldn't maintain his own weight.

"We hope so. As long as we begin mounting a patrol as soon as possible," Hirish commented. "We will map out a rescue mission. Piola and I will head the patrol with Kira and Kyle. If that is acceptable?"

"I'm coming," Drake said.

No one argued with him.

Mounting a rescue mission was a lot more difficult than my eager brain realized. Not that I thought it would be easy, but we had to map out the nests we knew about along the way and make sure they were clear before we reached the college where Gary said they were. Running a train of monsters on ourselves and the people we intended to save was probably a bad idea.

In order to make it back with any survivors we found, we'd have to get as close to them as we could with vehicles and hope that our transports stayed intact while we battled through whatever creatures surrounded them.

Gary radioed in several times over the rest of the day while we got supplies ready. In that time the downpour receded, letting up enough that there were multiple hours of only grey clouds in the sky with nothing falling from them.

I really hated dreary days.

Each hour that passed brought more nervousness with it, and Drake paced the halls of Garbo restlessly. I tried to shoot him sympathetic glances whenever I saw him, but he wouldn't meet my eyes. His best friend had been gone for weeks by this stage. We'd all thought he was dead despite what the Shop told us. In a way, it was like he'd come back from the afterlife.

I left the packing to everyone else and concentrated on gleaning what I could from Dequasha. Honing my skills was my best contribution, and we'd be leaving bright and early the next day.

"You should be concentrating on developing your Mana Sense," Dequasha admonished me as I looked wistfully toward the Raybucks. She was right.

"I know." I closed my eyes again, resetting what I'd been tracking throughout the center. It was one of her favorite tests to give me. She'd point out a person, and I'd have to tell her what they were or were not doing with Mana in that given instant.

Reflexes. That's what I needed to develop. An instant understanding of the incoming spells, attacks, and other ways that Mana moved. It was getting there, but I was far from being an expert with it, and I needed to be.

Concentrating, I picked up on strands of Mana, following them to their owners, discerning their purposes.

"Kira!" Mike's voice broke through my concentration. I could practically feel Dequasha's annoyance radiating from her.

I turned standing over near the coffee shop, beckoning me toward him. There was this sense of urgency about him. Like there were things he needed to say five minutes ago but didn't want to yell across the center.

"Sorry. I'll be back."

I didn't wait for Dequasha to shoot me another one of her disapproving looks. I already knew them far too well.

Mike's serious face hid just underneath the excitement, so I approached hesitantly. "Spill it."

He frowned at me, but then shrugged good-naturedly. "We've been tracking the nests over the last five weeks since we increased our patrol numbers and frequencies. The path to meet Gary and the others isn't quite as bad as we first thought."

"Define quite."

Mike chuckled. "There are several routes we can take. Right now, we're leaning toward splitting the force to take care of the nests and then meeting up closer to the rendezvous point."

"Splitting up doesn't sound like the wisest choice," I muttered, a weird unease gnawing at my gut. This just didn't feel right. Like splitting up was the exact thing those creatures wanted us to do, encouraged even. Of course, that made no sense. Not like the monsters were working together. "Why do we need to clear out two paths there, anyway?"

The head of security paused for a moment, like no one had asked that question yet and he wasn't sure why I was. "You know . . . that didn't come up in the discussion. It just felt like it might be the most logical way to approach this. Give us a couple of options on the way back."

"Us? Hirish, Piola?" I glanced at him, and he truly seemed genuinely flummoxed. It wasn't like Mike to go into something willy-nilly. He thought things through, checked and triple checked stuff. Unless he was maybe thinking with his heart a little more than his actual head?

"Sienna?" I asked, as gently as I could.

The flush that spread over his face was enough of an answer. Sienna's Class was about as politician like as anyone in the settlement had. It came with a large dose of Charisma—and she could make dirt sandwiches sound appetizing if she wasn't careful. While she'd been better about accidentally pushing her opinion on people, sometimes she could slip up.

Rummaging in my inventory, I pulled out two of the two percent mental resistance rings from the Rigoll fight and handed them to him. "She means well, but you always need to double check that you're thinking for yourself. Even when she doesn't mean to exert it, her Charisma can do a number on your head."

"Shit." A flash of irritation passed over his expression before he choked it back down. Mike was a good sort. Thorough, dedicated, and sometimes downright scary when it came to the seriousness with which he performed his security job. I could see the gears working and knew that he was probably questioning a lot right then.

"Hey. She doesn't use it deliberately. I've only ever seen her activate it consciously when trying to calm people down if they're scared. Which is a fantastic way to use it because we don't want things happening as reactive actions that could damage a whole lot of things."

I took a breath, trying to use my own, I don't know, reasoning to soothe him. "Her Class makes her Charisma high, which automatically affects everything she says and how it comes across to people. She would never manipulate you, but she can't help how the stats impact her everyday communications."

"Yeah." He ran a hand through his short hair and sighed. "I know you're right, but at the same time it makes me question everything she says and how I feel . . ."

Mike caught himself and blushed slightly.

"Mate? From what I've seen, all of that is reciprocated tenfold. No need to worry there. What you *should* do, though? Get some mental resistance going. Once you've got that, you'll be aware of when her Charisma is attempting to put weight behind her words, and it'll be a lot easier for you to acknowledge what is real, and what's maybe a bit of a reach."

He frowned for a moment and glanced toward the Shop. "Guess I've got a stop to make before I get back to the drawing board."

"Right on. But it's not that hard. Just have the patrols going out this afternoon switch it up a bit and clear where we need cleared."

He took a deep breath and smiled somewhat bashfully. "Yeah. That makes a lot more sense than splitting forces. Thanks."

I watched him head toward the Shop and turned back to Dequasha, but she had disappeared. Fine by me; I could really do with a cup of the good stuff right about now. And a scone. I definitely wanted a scone. Cracking my neck from side to side, I turned back around and walked the short distance to Raybucks.

"Mum!" Jackson stood in front of my regular table at the coffee shop with his hands on his hips, getting close to my height now, with a totally teenage expression on his face. You know the one? The one where they know everything, and even maybe kind of have a point that the parents don't want to admit to? Yeah . . . that one.

I knew what was coming, but that didn't help soften the blow of my growing-up-way-too-fast kid confronting me. So I did what any stubborn adult would do and cut it off at the head. "I'm not arguing about this. You're not coming. You can go out on regular patrol while we're gone. We still need to be clearing nests."

If thunder could have rolled in those dark brown eyes of his, he would have shot electricity out at me. "Stop treating me like a kid."

"But you are *my* kid."

"Kids in an apocalypse are something totally different. Stop acting like I'm asking for a midnight curfew back before all of this happened!" He paused and I stood there, quite shellshocked, unsure of how to respond.

Because above all, he wasn't completely wrong.

"None of this"—he gestured around with sharp movements at the world and beyond—"none of this is normal. None of this is 'how you raised me.' This is all new, and you have to adapt too."

I swallowed the suddenly huge lump in my throat, fighting back a well of emotions I really just didn't want to deal with. I did what any good adult would do and pushed them down into denial.

"I know." It came out quieter than intended, not in my usual mum-knows-better-than-you tone, and maybe a little more bewildered than I would usually admit to being in front of my kid.

But he was right about a lot of what he said. Four and a half months into the apocalypse and life was definitely different. We couldn't do things the way they'd been done before. There wasn't any way to define the new normal yet because we were constantly in flux and changing.

"I know, and you are right, but you're also a bit wrong." I held up my hand and pulled up a chair, motioning for him to do the same. It allowed me a few more precious seconds to gather my thoughts together and not to just react to his outburst. He deserved better than that.

"You're still thirteen. You're a child still, even if you don't like it, even if you're having to grow up faster than we'd like." I took a deep breath knowing he wouldn't like what I was about to say but hoping that he'd understand. "You are *my* child. It is still my job to keep you safe. Every person here? Technically? Also, my job, but they are not my kid, and I don't have the bond to them I have to you. Will I pull rank and make you stay when others might let their kids go out into hefty danger? Sure as hell, I will. Because even in an apocalypse, I want you to be as safe as possible."

The smoldering indignation in his eyes began to recede and left a deflated expression in its place. Even a glimpse of the fear he thought he was hiding so well. Ah, shit. Still, there was a fine line of mollycoddling and treating your kid like the grownup they were pretending to be.

"Listen, mate. I don't want to cut your wings, but right now, as this weirdly mutating planet gets going and all, it's super unpredictable. And losing you? It's just not a part of my survival plan, okay?"

"Yeah. I get it. I just want to do more." He wouldn't look at me, and from the slump to his shoulders, I could tell he was frustrated. Not at me necessarily, but at the world . . . or I guess in this case, the galaxy.

And that right there was the crux of the matter for him. We'd raised him to believe that he could change the world, and here he was at thirteen in a drastically different world than we'd predicted, not entirely sure of himself or anything about his future.

Me too, mate. Me too.

"You already do a lot, and I know you'll do so much more. Just don't be in such a hurry to grow up that you die in the process. Please?" Because that was my greatest fear. I think it was every parent's greatest fear.

I didn't plan on burying my children.

"Survive and fight back?" he asked, and there was hope in his eyes again.

I nodded. "Survive, grow, and fight back."

He sighed, and shook his head, a sheepish smile spreading across his face. "You have no idea how intimidating it is to try and stand up to you, Mum."

I wasn't sure how that made me feel, but I was proud of him for speaking his mind. "Just reason out your decisions and be careful. Too eager to go out before you're ready can mean an early death none of us want."

That sobered him up and he nodded. "Yeah. I get it, I just don't like feeling useless."

"Clearing nests and keeping them cleared isn't useless. It's necessary. Sometimes tedious, sometimes messy, often muddy lately. But it's never useless." I hoped he couldn't hear the sliver of doubt I felt about the whole thing. "Frankly, being an adult? It's about doing all the boring necessary shit."

Jackson laughed and pushed himself up with both hands, like he was gathering strength. "I'll try to remember that. Thanks, Mum."

He dashed away before I could say anything, and I realized I hadn't even gotten my bloody kipatchya yet.

Chapter Twenty-Four:
Detour

18 Weeks, 2 Days Post-System Onset
7 a.m.

Bright and early, that's when we headed out. Not as literally bright as usual, with the overcast sky still threatening to open up and spill rain all over us. Jackson stood to the side, Wisp clasping his hand, but this time neither of them seemed as emotionally charged as when I'd headed to Carindale.

A moment of guilt hit me. That I should be here with them more than I was, that I was missing chunks of their lives. But this was just like work.

I'd always worked, and been there in the evenings, for sports, for activities, to talk, to console. It was important that I show them that single-minded preservation was nothing without protecting our pack, our fold, the other humans around us.

Caring for other humans is one of the best signs of humanity. It's the difference between civilization and chaos. It's amazing how many of us only care about those in our immediate circle.

Dor and Sienna were seeing to defense upgrades again, now that we'd had a bit of time go by and the settlement treasury had some Credits in it. They'd be done by the time we returned, or at least I was optimistic that they would be.

I watched everyone gather around our patrol, out here near the Officeworx. We'd have to use this exit which was fine. The constant grey skies were bugging me though. Give us some sun damn it.

Lousesh and Zyrilian were to remain behind, along with Mon'swkinon and a chunk of IRSHA. I didn't recognize all the Hakarta and the Zarrie that we were taking with us. But Hirish and Piola were each speaking to a group of seven others from their clans in tones that didn't quite reach my ears. Dequasha was nowhere in sight, and a thrill ran through me.

Without her there, it was up to me to manipulate Mana energies in the ways I needed to. That was kind of exciting, to be honest.

Offensive and defensive were fairly easy to recognize, but getting inside those abilities to the nitty-gritty of why they were being cast, and specifically what was being cast? My information was about fifty-fifty. Fifty percent not a guess, that is. Practice would make perfect; it had to.

"You're on edge." Kyle, my ever-sarcastic sibling, moved up next to me.

"No shit," I snapped out at him. Not that he really deserved it, but he was more forgiving than most others. Also. He deserved it.

He chuckled, and I couldn't resist a moment longer.

"You and Melody getting along?"

I swear he blushed right up to the tips of his ears. Oh, this was going to be fun. Once we'd mounted this rescue. Once we'd returned safely. Once there wasn't something threatening to kill us all just around the corner every single day.

Who was I kidding? That wouldn't happen, so I should just tease him now.

"Shut it. I don't tease you and Evelyn," he quipped very belatedly.

"Yes, you do, and you know it," I said, nonplussed. "How you feeling about this trip?"

He mulled my words over for a lot longer than I expected he would. Kyle was usually the jolly one, the one who saw the best in things, whereas I was often more practical. Looking out over the sea of people we were taking sent stabs of nervousness up my back. It wasn't fear, just caution. Maybe it wasn't the right thing to do, bringing so many people.

Hirish and Piola brought five scouts each with them. Our main rangers:

Evelyn, Marie, and Dannin with his reinforced calf. Gemma, Drake, Tasha, Molly, Sange, Ray, Eritia, Morton . . . so many damned people. And others I knew vaguely in passing. But one thing made me feel better about recent decisions. I was fairly certain the youngest member of our group was maybe seventeen. Jackson might be Level 37 as were Darren and some of the other kids. But we were still parents regardless of the end of the world, and we weren't about to let our kids perish with it.

"I'm worried about the trek. We haven't ventured out this far yet . . . we haven't seen the Levels these things might be. Gary seemed sure we'd be fine with more numbers, but . . ." Kyle finally responded to my question, even as his eyes raked over everyone. "Dale is staying to help coordinate the remaining patrols and help Mike with the settlement."

"We can't keep taking both of you out with us."

"I know. Someone else needs to pick up your Skill." There was a cloud over his expression like he wanted to say something he knew I wouldn't approve of.

"Say it before it chokes you."

He barked a laugh and then looked at me, seriousness taking him over. "Everyone might die. It's no different to prior to the apocalypse in that, I guess. Just more chances of it now. But I don't think any of our group, and definitely not me, would do well if you die. I don't like you always having to go out with the groups just because of this weird hocus-focus fortunetelling thing you can do."

"But it helps save so many lives." Didn't he understand that's why I did this? I could help so many people with this Skill I had, with this Class. Save so many of us.

"Yeah. It does save lives." Kyle gave me another long look, like a thousand things were running through his mind right then. "Until it doesn't."

❖

"Remember, we're going up Newnham Road, onto Mt. Gravatt Capalaba Road, and through to Highway 21 right until we get to Sheldon College. Stay vigilant. Keep an eye out—be ready to disembark at any time and engage!" Hirish's voice rang out clear through the morning air, cutting through the gloom with authority. "Convoy, keep it tight! Move out!"

Our jeep was second in line and contained myself for my Mana Sense ability, Evelyn utilizing her Sharp-Shooting Skills, and Molly and Sange, lest they have to jump out and engage. I didn't really expect anything for the first, say, two-thirds of the journey.

The nests were cleared and should take a couple of days to replenish, and we were as well prepared as less than twenty-four hours could make us.

There were no incidents as we headed onto Mt. Gravatt Capalaba Road, and it was almost easy to forget we were part of a convoy and not just out for a nice morning drive. The trees that lined the sides of the roads cast beautiful patterns of leaves over us.

Except I swear they weren't the gum trees we were used to. This constant evolution of our natural resources flummoxed me. I wanted our flora to stay the same.

Tingalpa Reservoir was pretty to look at. Trees and the like, paths . . . beautiful water. Everywhere you looked, nature was at its best. Although some of the ripples out toward the middle of the water were far larger than I'd ever seen there before. Mana tinged the edges with a deep, dripping blackness. At least I didn't think the rains had flooded us enough leave ocean visitors in our waterways. Leaving the aquatic areas to themselves just seemed like the clever solution.

We worked our way past the Brisbane Koala Bushlands. That was the farthest point we regularly cleared really. Except the time we ran into the Trapickzyers.

And then we passed into the unknown. The area we hadn't reached with regular clearing, and a few kilometers from where we needed to get to so we could help Gary and the new people he'd ended up with.

Saving even a dozen people would be worth it.

The dark clouds hung heavy with unspent rain, but I wasn't sure if it was ever going to spill, or if they were perhaps just waiting for the exact right moment. We'd had nothing but occasional drizzles over the last day, and some of the quagmires were beginning to dry up.

A sudden flash of bright Mana ahead of us had me standing in my seat. Hirish motioned for the convoy to stop, and it echoed down the line. Still trying to get my bearings as my eyes got used to the normal ambience of Mana around us again, I could feel the gathering of power still a ways off.

"Trap up ahead," I snapped out, trying to keep my voice down as my temples began to attack my head with pain I didn't want. Really needed to figure out how to compensate for the occasional flash of Mana like that.

Hirish nodded. "Scouts. Head out."

Ah, that's why he'd brought so many of his own people, and why Piola had brought hers. Three of each, making two groups of six stood at the ready, their weapons in plain sight. They blended into the greyness of the morning, even though I knew they were still standing there.

"Which directions, Kira?" The Hakarta Pirra Clan leader was all business. After all, the lives of his men in this weird Aussie wilderness 2.0 depended on it.

Closing my eyes, I pulled the overlap map in my interface up, so I could try to pinpoint the exact directions of the Mana fluctuations.

I suddenly knew, with a sickening lurch to my stomach, that the Greenacres Caravan Park was the source, and in that suddenly overgrown area was a pit of sludge like Mana being gobbled up and used. Being used always made Mana happy, but this felt sickly to me. Mana never seemed to have an actual preference. Being used was its purpose.

"Ahead at the . . . where the caravan park used to be, and up farther at the baseball club too." I choked the words out, the taste of the tainted Mana stuck in my throat. Vile. Noxious.

The tail end of our convoy pulled up along the freeway where we'd halted by a roundabout. It wasn't like we had to be careful of oncoming traffic. Keeping the vehicles together was our best bet of keeping them whole. It was way too far to walk home from here.

We waited there for word from the scouts about just what awaited us. I fiddled with a strand of hair that had fallen out of my ponytail while we watched and waited. It didn't take long for the scouts to return and one of the Hakarta reported to Hirish, his chest rapidly rising and falling with the exertion of running back to us.

Hirish eyed me warily. "It seems there might be some type of tree mutations up ahead."

"Great." I didn't mean it, in fact the whole thing made me angry. Couldn't we just let the trees be trees?

"Proceeding with caution," Hirish said, half to himself before turning his attention back to the road in front of him, making the vehicle practically crawl.

We crept along the road, my trepidation trying to sit in my throat. No matter what, I had to be prepared to see what was coming up. Except I wasn't; none of us were.

We stopped the cars, slowly disembarking our gazes all focused on the site down the road. The extent of the mutations. Not the wildlife, the flora.

The plants and trees.

There were massive vines slithering across the road, branches that moved more than the slight breeze allowed for. All things that would have fascinated me if we hadn't been in the middle of an apocalypse.

Nature had been subverted, and it bothered me more than with animals, more than with people. Plants had always been a constant in my life, and now, they were dangerous. They moved with a slithering grace that reminded me of a cobra. Deadly and ready to strike.

Maybe this was revenge for all the paper products we humans used.

Even as we spread out along the highway making our way toward the caravan park, it felt like a trap. But I couldn't sense or see anything around us that spoke to that. My attempts to coax the Mana into concealing our movements was clumsy at best. Without Dequasha here to back me up, my confidence in being able to do so flailed. This entire scenario felt like I was coming up on a Little Shop of Horrors of my very own.

Not to mention the Mana just felt like it didn't want to do as I asked, which could entirely be the case.

Ahead of us, Hirish halted, holding up one hand in a gesture to slow us down. *Don't worry mate, I wasn't planning on rushing in head on.* Evelyn crept next to me, her face pale enough that her freckles stood out more than usual. I gave her a quick shoulder hug, never once taking my eyes off the grotesque plants in front of us.

There were two that caught my attention. The first appeared to be a mutation of a bottlebrush tree. I remember growing up and climbing in the branches of one in our front yard back in the eighties. Beautiful trees with cylindrical flowers that bloomed in bright red with tiny straight petals jutting out from the center completing the spiral. When I was a kid, I'd sworn they looked like fairy lights scattered amongst the branches.

Nether Bottle

Animated

Level 48 (Elite)

Not now, though. The bottlebrush flower had grown to such a proportion it was easily the size of my head instead of my fist. What used to be delicate points like those fairy lights now appeared sharp and dangerous. Yet the scent of citrus wafted over to us, like nothing had changed at all.

The damn tree appeared to joyously womp and flail about with its blossoms, cutting into one of the fences nearby. It wrenched itself back out of the wooden posts with a splintering crunch of destruction.

Gone were the beautiful palms and fronds, the light and airy feeling that was once a part of this little park. In its place were monstrous mutated flora.

Which brought me to the second former tree I couldn't take my eyes off. The spider flower, silky oak, whatever the fuck you wanted to call it. Usually, the tree was just beautiful with slender leaves and delicate flowers, depending on species, of varying sizes. The soft flower clusters resembled spider legs and thus it was named.

Except now the blossoms were the size of a large cat and dragged on the ground, crawling on all of its petals as if they were spider's legs. It used its flowers now as a form of propulsion to drag itself forward through the rain-softened ground.

Spider Oak

Animated

Level 46 (Elite)

The things of nightmares right before my eyes.

Maybe the rain had done this; perhaps in all of its flooding the Tingalpa Reservoir infected all the plant life on its shores. Maybe there was a spore spread by water. Maybe it was just another random series of mutations. I had no clue.

What I did know was the Mana surrounding it dripped black like tar-infested magic, and each of the former trees were so intent on each other, they didn't actually notice us coming.

Strike one for recent sentience, I guess?

Just as the realization hit me, Hirish fired a pulse into the tangled mess of the two trees, blasting away tree limbs, spider-legged blossoms, effectively halting the battle that had been about to flare.

Trees weren't animals. And whatever had happened to mutate these two didn't have a baser instinct to tap into. But they definitely wouldn't be happy with the dude who'd just fired a laser ball directly into their midst.

The higher point of their branches whipped around as a keening squeal echoed toward us. I couldn't tell if they had mouths, but the sound definitely emanated from the mutated trees. If they'd had eyes, they would have been staring us down. The thing was, they weren't the only things that turned and looked at us.

From all around the caravan park heavy movement could be heard, and it wasn't until more of them pulled into view up that I realized a lot more vegetation had come to life than I'd originally thought.

And Hirish had just really pissed them off. Especially the two he'd separated who were already pulling their roots along with them and heading our way.

"Not the smartest move," Kyle hissed out between his teeth.

Hirish shrugged, even though I could tell he'd rattled himself a little. "No matter how we look at it, they're in the way, and it's time to move."

True to his word, he motioned toward the scouts. I hadn't seen them since they'd reappeared earlier. They blinked out of my vision, and I was fairly certain Hirish was having them circle around the back of the approaching creatures to check on whether we had more than just the two approaching us incoming.

At least, I hope that's what he was doing. We didn't need to anger more of these . . . things.

The trees moved with remarkable speed, closing the distance faster than I'd anticipated. One Bottle and one Spider. Fantastic.

The Zarrie with us flung throwing knives; our archers began to open fire, as did our mages. And the scouts reappeared, wielding their pulse rifles. Watching what used to be a brilliant examples of our country's local flora advance on us as if their roots were running on a rail saddened me in ways I hadn't thought it would.

My sadness only lasted until the first head-sized Nether Bottle flung one of its blooms, which exploded just meters away from me in an eruption of sharpened needles, directly into the side of Tasha's face.

The Spellsword screamed so loudly I thought my eardrums would burst. Kyle was next to her so fast I barely had time to blink as he reached out with a covered hand and pulled what remained of the former flower from her cheek. It came off with a loud squishing sound as the blossom relinquished its hold on spikes that were now stuck firmly in her cheek.

She staggered back, blood pouring from the wound as I wrenched my eyes away to focus on the impending monsters.

Mana flooded out from the creatures, all around them, like waves lapping at a shore—angry, frothing at the bit in their desperation to be used. I could practically see it flowing up through the roots into the limbs and leaves, the branches bulging with their own type of power.

But there was only one thing that really meant that was of any consequence. "Incoming attacks! Shields up!"

It felt like the most useless thing to yell out right then. Of course, they were going to attack, they weren't about to stop and wait for us to make the first move. I'd never in my life imagined that I'd see creatures in front of me capable of unfurling branches with lightning-quick speed and accuracy. The only thing that saved Gemma as the Bottlebrush snapped a whiplike branch at her was her own speedy reflexes.

That particular Nether Bottle bloom exploded without hitting anyone directly.

And then Molly was there, digging her shield into the bitumen like it was raw cookie dough in the nick of time. Slamming the shield far and wide, stretching its capabilities, and her own. It was the kick in the ass we all needed.

These definitely weren't your friendly Ents.

I reached out, implanting into both of the trees that had approached us. I threw up Mana Stone straight away to blanket over all of our healers and casters. We were going to need all the Mana we could maintain, and all the healing I could contribute.

Planted in Place broke the first two times I tried to cast it on the second tree. We were going to have to dual tank this, and I wasn't sure how that would work. Tank it, whatever—we needed someone else who could take hits and anger the Spider tree.

Piola jumped into the fray with Drake, Gemma, and Tasha right alongside them. Hirish ordered his troops into formation while barking out an order to two people I didn't recognize.

The first man who stepped forward looked pale and somewhat familiar. I vaguely recognized him from when he'd returned several times with Jackson's groups, so he had experience.

Tanner Smith

Knight

Level 38

He didn't move the way Molly did, but a frown of determination edged onto his face, and he took a deep breath before hefting his shield and approaching his target. I didn't have time to watch him taunt or activate his Skills, but if Hirish called him out, he had to be solid.

The second person who stepped out made me smile. Declan. He'd come with us several times and learned from Molly. He was a great freaking tank. Very different, and relied mainly on avoidance, but super effective when it came down to it. It gave me hope to know Molly wasn't alone.

Even if I should have known it anyway. There was no way we would have taken this many people with us without considering all setups.

Pulse rifles fired, mages shot spells, and most of our melee combatants used whatever ranged abilities they had while we figured out exactly what we were facing.

Rangers and Archers opened fire from behind us, fire arrows flying through the sky over me, over the protective shielding and straight into the branches of our enemies, skillfully avoiding those of us fighting close to the target.

Except once in the trees' canopy, the fire sputtered and died in the wet branches.

Because of course it fucking did.

Chapter Twenty-Five:
Soggy

Gemma and Drake, along with the Zarrie flanking them, had a difficult time getting in for melee combat because of the tentacle-like roots defending every aspect of the tree. They slapped and darted out, retracting themselves.

I cast Water Siphon because damn this stupid rain and all its annoyances. There was a lot to suck out of the trees, but the sooner I started, the more likely we were to kill them faster. Next, I needed to analyze Top Soil and see if instead of providing the earth around me with more nutrient-rich soil, I could perhaps deprive the area around the trees.

Their rippling roots kept reaching down into the ground, like they were tapping into a source of power. And that's what the earth was. It would feed them what they needed to heal and regenerate, so it was up to me to stop that, if only I could figure out how to adapt my Skills.

One of those roots snapped out and grabbed a hold of Tasha's leg, tugging her to the ground as it furled back in on itself. She screamed, and that's when I noticed the side of her face wasn't healing. Which meant there was something toxic in whatever those bottlebrush flowers had on them.

Thing was, right then, I couldn't take the time to guide Kyle, but even as Tasha flailed against the tree, I could see the wound decay progressing right in front of my eyes. She wouldn't have long. If we could even get her out of the grasp of the roots.

Drake sped over, his short sword and dagger raised as he slashed almost ineffectually at the roots holding her.

Acid. Fire wasn't going to work because of the damp, but acid should cut through. I called it out, pushing down my panic at the growing holes in her face to find the logic I needed to operate through this fight.

"Acid attacks on the wood." And even as I spoke the words, I cast Vine

Defense on Trisha, trying to lend her more armor rating and allow the degradation to maybe eat away at her slower. Arrows rained overhead again, whistling through the air to land in the branches, sinking into the bark of the trees.

A lengthy hiss emanated from the Nether Bottle, like a snake ready to pounce. But it withdrew several of its limbs including the one holding Tasha without taking her with it. Evelyn and the others must have applied an acid topical to their arrows. Or however that worked. I knew there were potions that could do that. There were potions and tinctures that could do everything.

For a price, there was nothing the System couldn't enable.

Kyle scooped Tasha up in his arms, signaling as he ran to the other healers with us. I refreshed my Blood Dispersion, knowing we needed as much help as we could get.

He knelt next to me and waited for me to crouch down. Taking a deep breath, I placed my hand on her arm, trying not to look at the way her skin was slowly peeling back from her jaw in all the wrong ways, and closed my eyes.

I found Kyle and guided him through to the source of the infection, making sure he had a good grasp on it before I left him to do what needed to be done. I only hoped we'd managed to stop it before it did irreparable damage.

Blinking away the doubt, I pushed myself back up to standing and threw out another Water Siphon, making the damned tree keen once again. This wasn't a fight that my hammer would help. I was far better suited to keeping the rounds of debuffs active, doing damage where I could, cutting off external healing sources, and making sure the whole raid had some sort of leveled up Mana regeneration.

Mana Purification

Level 2

The notification popped up in my vision, just brief enough for me to see before I flicked the damn thing away in irritation. Great. I wasn't sure what that meant, but I'd take all the upgrades I could get that might help my friends faces not get eaten away by rot.

Chunks of the Nether Bottle were flying off now, its limbs separated much easier now that they were brittle, thanks to my Water Siphon sucking a copious amount of water out of them. It worked, but it became super Mana intensive for me to maintain all the debuffs. There was one opponent after this we had to contend with, and I'd be spent . . . I just had to hope none of the others would come up our way before we could recuperate.

"Shit," I heard Kyle next to me, and the word sank to the bottom of my stomach like a stone. I knew, even just instinctively, why he was cursing, and that it couldn't be good. But we had fifty-odd people out here, with even more people depending on us to get there.

I couldn't let one emotional roadblock get in my way.

A sudden surge of bright blue outline around the massive deeper chunks of Mana surrounding the Nether Bottle gave me the only warning we are getting. "Shielding!" I screamed out, hoping my voice would carry.

Molly groaned under the heft of the onslaught on her shield, but the golden dome appeared momentarily thereafter, followed only a split second later by a knightly contribution from Tanner just beyond her. His was more shimmery and less solid, but combined with the damage repellant that Declan threw into the mix, it still saved the hell out of us.

A split second after the shieldings were slammed into place, a flying barrage of bottlebrush blossoms flew toward us, their poisonous little spikes reaching out for anything they could dig into. Molly's shield held them at bay, but Tanner's wasn't quite so lucky.

Several dozen of them rebounded off the protection, but about half a dozen or so didn't. They shot through instead. A couple of them hit the ground with a dull thud, but the remainder were more troublesome.

One of the Zarrie I didn't recognize went down in a scream of agony, a blossom jutting out of her bicep. Morton, our Gunslinger, went down with a yell of terror as one of them hit his left calf and sent him crashing to the ground. And the last one who went down took a blossom straight to the face. I'm not talking the cheek, I'm talking smack bang right between the eyes.

The scream cut off as they hit the ground, and I knew we'd lost another. Damned apocalypse killing my people, mutating my plants. I shoved out another wave of Water Siphon, my will to conserve Mana barely still present, and tapped my Cloak.

275 Mana Replenished.
Mana Cloak Empty
Ambient Mana Recharging

Gee thanks for the fucking obvious, but I guess it had leveled up again, so at least that was something. The last casting of Water Siphon worked like a charm and dried up the trunk of the tree so much that the next time it tried to unfurl a root, the damned thing snapped off.

"It's weakened. Dive in while you still can," Hirish called forth the attack, and every single melee we'd had who'd been holding back because of the tentacles ran in to hack away at the offending tree's appendages.

Kyle stood next to me, his face grim, sucking what life he could from the Nether Bottle and redistributing it to the rest of us. I watched him out of the corner of my eye knowing that he'd need to talk later. We probably both would. But I got the sneaking suspicion later was going to be far longer than either of us liked.

And that's when I noticed the blossoms of the other tree, detached from their branches, but creeping along the floor like centipede spiders and making their way slowly, stealthily around the ranks toward like they were intent on encircling us so they could attack.

What you have to understand about Brisbane is that it's an evergreen climate. The seasons don't change enough for the trees to ever lose their foliage. Hell, we once drove all the way down to Stanthorpe just to witness the changing of the leaves. Not that we hadn't seen it in the USA before we moved, but seeing that it could happen in Australia, just not where we lived, held this kind of magic.

Not so much right now.

These blossoms used to have gorgeous, delicate protrusions that rounded out the flower, making it and its kind uniquely beautiful. Now those same protrusions acted as legs, and the blossoms moved quietly and fast, with way more than eight legs.

"Hold your breath!" came a cry from a voice I recognized but couldn't quite place.

It held an oddly melodic sound to it, like they were singing the words rather than speaking them, yet there was this haunting familiarity about the sound. Still, I didn't need to go asking questions like why, so I just held my breath and shut up.

A misty cloud formed around our feet, spreading out like a rolling storm. Each of the blossoms that it touched withered instantly. I wasn't sure about anyone else, but after twenty or so seconds, I wanted to breathe so badly. It was inordinately difficult to function when not breathing.

What seemed like suffocation levels of time later, when in reality it had been a total of maybe forty-five seconds, the same voice spoke out again.

"Breathe. It's all clear." This time, though, the voice sounded tired, almost worn out, like creating that noxious mist had somehow drained all of their strength—or perhaps in this case, Mana. The voice's familiarity tugged at my tired and preoccupied brain.

I turned slightly, after casting another Water Siphon on our friendly neighborhood Spider Oak, to catch a glimpse of our savior. Except while the voice had tickled my memories, I'd still not been expecting to turn and stare into the ridiculously bright hazel eyes of my ex-husband, Mason.

There wasn't time to process it, not with the other creature still raring to fight us, even if the Nether Bottle was barely this side of still alive.

"Focus," I muttered to myself. Giving into my confusion, the *what the hell* going through my mind, was not an option.

The Spider Oak wasn't the same formidable opponent the Nether Bottle had been. Not only were its blossoms more easily dispatched, but it just didn't have the same level of ferocity in its attacks. It made me wonder if these mutated flora had a hierarchy when they decided to become sentient. Or did the two fewer Levels really make all that difference?

Top Soil manipulation seriously helped. When the opponent couldn't activate its regeneration by plunging its roots back into the earth, I got a feeling of triumph. It was the little things.

Then the Spider Oak hit about thirty percent health and I glanced back at where Tasha lay for the first time since realizing nothing Kyle nor I did seemed to have healed her. My stomach churned, and I almost threw up all the bile my stomach held.

Choking it down, I cast rapidly. Once both Water Siphon, Implantation, and my other debuffs were applied again, I fell to my knees next to her.

Her chest rose and fell to a staccato beat, and a whimper escaped her lips with every breath. At least what was left of them. Half of the upper right one was already gone, and the degradation had spread all up around her right eye and was intruding onto her nose now.

Even being super careful not to touch her wound lest whatever it was getting onto me, I tried to sit with her, to make her know that she wasn't alone. With her right eye gone, I crouched to her left side, and she focused the remaining eye blearily on me.

Words didn't come out; maybe it had already worked its way back inside to where her voice box was. But her left hand gripped mine tightly, like a lifeline offered to her. What did I say? What do you say when someone is dying and none of the magic, none of the gifts, none of the potions are working to help her come back to life?

Was the poison actively resisting our effects? Was the damage debuff that high that even reduced, the damage was overriding her own System regeneration? If we threw enough healing at her, would it help or would it just prolong the agony?

There had to be something we'd missed, had to be something that could have prevented whatever aspect of those bombs had decayed her face to this extent and begun to ravage her body.

It was difficult to read an expression in someone's eyes when there's only one to focus on, when there's not enough of their face left to read how they're feeling or responding to what you're saying or doing.

But I was fairly sure she was relieved not to have her last few minutes alone.

I shut out the world, making sure that Water Siphon and Mana Stone were maintained on the last target. Molly's shield never fell, and I knew she had to be getting low on Mana, but it would probably last just long enough.

"I'm here, Tasha." I whispered, noticing the tear that rolled down my cheek somewhat belatedly. Not that I'd cried when Jules died. Not that I'd actually cried since the whole damn thing began.

She blinked, or I guess winked, since the other eyelid was already gone, very slowly and opened her eye again at the same speed. Like she'd acknowledged me and knew everything was over for her. The groaning of the great tree behind me lent a melancholy air to the wake I held.

Tasha's last breath sputtered, heaving like she was fighting to cling to life and then thought what the hell, why not.

It took several seconds for me to realize she was truly gone as the grip in her hand loosened and the rot began to eat away at what was left of her good eye. I scrambled away, putting a few feet's distance in between myself and her corpse as I realized that the rot wasn't about to stop just because she was dead.

There was no healing something that moved that quickly.

If she'd been hit in any other appendage, like the Zarrie and Morton, Kyle could have amputated the limb and helped regrow it. But the head? Decapitation wasn't exactly something someone came back from.

I was still sitting on my knees, half upright, just not quite to my feet yet as the massive Spider Oak behind me fell to the ground. The rumble as it impacted the earth tingled through to my spine. Kyle placed his hand on my shoulder, and I squeezed it with my own.

Damn it. You'd think I'd be desensitized by now.

Tasha was gone. Not one of my best friends in this new place, but definitely one of my friends. And definitely someone I'd miss. Just like everyone else we'd lost.

"There was nothing we could do with what we had," Kyle spoke so softly I could almost imagine it was the wind. "Thanks for sitting with her for the last few minutes."

"Yeah. Couldn't let her die alone, right?" My voice didn't even sound like my own.

The thing was, she wasn't the only death of the fight. Two deaths, two amputations who were painfully growing limbs back. If we kept on this way, we were never going to make down the road to where we needed to rescue others. So much for reinforcements, right?

Kyle tugged at me, willing me to stand. It was odd how sibling bonds worked like that. At least ours did. Almost like he loaned me strength.

"Hey. You know you need to go talk to him, right?"

I blinked and it flooded back. It seemed like an hour ago, but that had definitely been Mason, and he was still here. Slowly, I turned around to scan the area for him. He stood over with Hirish, his arms crossed and his chestnut hair blowing in the faint breeze. I could feel the smile spreading across my face already.

The lute strung loosely across his back reminded me of our college days, and if there was one thing about my ex-husband that I still loved, it was that he'd been one of my friends for longer than I could remember.

❖

Mason's hugs have always been able to make me feel better. Just like Kyle's, they have this medicinal purpose for my soul. He was just always the friend parent, the no-consequences parent, and frankly, a big brother to the children and a third kid for me. Which wasn't so bad before we had the kids . . . but yeah.

"Explain," I said, feeling remarkably like I was teetering on the edge of a bit of a breakdown. My brain had moved so far past tired it wasn't even funny.

He shrugged. "We're a part of a scouting team the Pacific Fair settlement set up. We were actually coming up here to see . . . anyway. We ran into some trouble down Coomera way and had to cut across to Beenleigh Redland Road. Much more roundabout than intended . . . guess that was a blessing in disguise."

Then he took a step back and held me at arm's length. He'd only ever been a couple of inches taller than me, and now I was almost the same height. "How did you grow so . . . wait, genome treatment?"

I nodded, activating my Mana visions to check out the flow of Mana around him. As always it lit up my eyes for a moment.

His next step back was completely involuntary. "Whoa, Kira. What the fuck is that?"

"Just one of the many perks of the apocalypse." Go me with the sarcasm-tinged bitterness.

"The kids?" He asked the words hesitantly, like he was almost scared to. If he'd been traveling for a couple of days, he wouldn't have had access to a Shop to check in on them.

"Safe and sound at home."

The relief practically rolled off him. "I thought they'd be fine, but their identities were protected as minors. I couldn't tell anything except that you were alive."

"If they'd been dead, the System would have just told you. It doesn't really care about your feelings." Kyle gave Mason a gruff hug and moved to stand next to me.

Mason blanched. "Well, I guess that's good to know, right?"

"So, why are you here?" Yeah, mate, I noticed you skirting the actual question earlier. I plastered my know-it-all grin on my face.

"Let's just focus on the crap you guys seem to have going on here. Your Pirra Clan Leader? Mentioned that you're on your way to retrieve some people who got caught up behind a wall of monsters?"

"We are and would love some help." Kyle rolled his shoulders. "If you're offering, that is."

"Of course. The more of us survive, the better, right, mate? Aussies are made of stronger stuff." Despite the smile on his face, there was this tightness to Mason's words that said he was pissed off.

"You're more than welcome to help out. I'm not about to turn down help." I held up a hand as he made to speak. "But no more avoiding the question."

He sighed a little awkwardly. "Yeah. Well . . . we could use with some help down the coast, but it's not dire. Not like this. You were alive—I figured you'd be somewhere near work . . . so I offered to head out with our scouting party."

He gestured to about a dozen people including him. The others were talking to Hirish and Piola.

They didn't appear to be uncomfortable with aliens like the people at Carindale had been initially. But from the looks on a few of the faces, they weren't completely used to being around them, either. From simply avoiding eye contact to rapidly blinking every time they spoke, the people Mason brought with him were doing their best not to stare at the alien species.

I frowned. They all appeared to be rogue and bard types. Classes that were stealth based or existed to move quickly.

Mason Kent

Bard

Level 39

Darna Jason

Speedwalker

Level 37

Ezra Djones

Rogue

Level 38

Hmm. "You're all stealth Classes? No dedicated healers or like tank-type Classes or anything ranged?"

Mason smiled. "You missed a couple of them, but we do have two hybrid archer Classes. No, we came up here with survival in mind. We have abilities that obfuscate, turn a blind eye, that sort of stuff. We also have a few of us who can hasten the movement of our party members. Makes for excellent fleeing enemy tactics."

"Obfuscate." I couldn't help it, I let out a laugh. "You still use that every chance, eh?"

"Of course I do."

I'd give him one thing. I didn't think the apocalypse had changed Mason much at all.

I wasn't sure if that was a good thing or not.

After that, we moved the convoy carefully past the caravan park, piling our new friends into the first few vehicles with us. It wasn't like we were going at breakneck speeds. No one was about to give us a ticket.

The trees moved uneasily, but I couldn't see any of them pulling up roots to run after us. Maybe the lack of rain was making that less possible. This could have been something that only happened if there was a torrential downpour. Definitely food for thought.

I could be full of shit, and they could have just been waiting for us to let our guard down completely.

We stopped next to the baseball field, and I frowned. I could have sworn there'd been wild Mana signatures emanating from here earlier, but now it was calm. "Did you come from here?" I asked Mason suddenly.

"Yeah, this is where we were when we heard the commotion. Why?"

"Nothing. Just explains a lot." There was no small relief running through me that they'd already taken out some of the creatures I'd felt. "How many were there?"

Mason paused for a moment while he thought about it. "About twelve. They were about Level 35 but wispy and not strong at all. Barely even normal monsters from what we could tell. Usually, we'd have run away from that, but yeah."

He shrugged like it was just an odd thing and not worth thinking about.

Climbing back into the convoy, we set off continuing on, navigating slowly enough that we could stop and abandon the vehicles at any moment we needed to. It was a short ride, maybe a kilometer at most before we realized just why Gary had radioed for help.

Turning off the vehicles, we disembarked and headed down to where the college was. But we stopped on the entranceway. The cricket field, everything that wasn't a building—they were all teeming with monsters. There were ones I hadn't seen before, and a few just like the trees we'd fought.

Most of them were fighting each other, except the trees. The trees were, as usual, behaving oddly. Just like the ones who continued to sway back and forth while we killed the two who fought us. Silent. Watching something I couldn't see from where we stood.

A large rodent, or so I thought it could be from the back of it, fought with a blob about twenty times the ones we'd fought near MacGregor when we first cleared the streets behind Garden City. Squelching noises emanated from it every time it jumped forward trying to entrap the rodent within its gelatinous folds. The sound made my stomach churn.

I could spy a group of Caneglobulous fighting with an Emugator off in one of the farther areas. The Emugator's slinky neck and harsh beak had a lot less impact on the spongy body of the toad and made a pop loud enough for us to hear where we stood when it pulled itself free. They eyed each other warily, clashing again as if they'd learned nothing.

The trees we'd seen waved ominously, scratching feebly at the glass windowpanes of one of the college buildings as if they were trying to get inside.

"We need to know what those bottlebrush blossoms excrete. We can't fight those again if our only solution is amputating the effected limbs and regrowing them," I muttered, more to myself than anything else, but Hirish grunted a nod at me.

"We're trying to figure that out now."

I nodded, focusing in closer on the view in front of us.

There was a glow suffusing two of the buildings in the middle level floors, a glow that felt like us. That felt like all the humans I'd met once Dequasha began teaching me how to read the Mana flows. The calmer I felt, the easier it was to trace their magic, their Skills. I could practically reach out and pinpoint where Gary was.

"They're in those buildings." I knew it. Without a shadow of a doubt.

Mason scoffed. "You can't possibly know that without getting closer to the action."

Kyle grinned. "Yes, she can."

"How can she possibly . . ." But he stopped and watched me, like he finally understood that the world really had changed us all.

I smiled, and maybe there was a sadness somewhere inside me that wished we could all just go back to the way things were. Most of me, especially the part of me that counted was finally starting to understand the new world and how I could make a difference, how we could all say fuck you to everything about the System's calculations. How everything we'd done, and all the people we'd lost, along with everything we'd managed to build was only going to make us more formidable.

I reached out and gave Mason's arm a squeeze. "I can tell. With absolute clarity. It just takes a little bit of magic."

Chapter Twenty-Six:
Rescue

The best strategy is sometimes the simplest.

We chose to circle around and take out those creatures on the outskirts first, slowly working our way inward. Caneglobulous were easier these days, now we'd been faced with bigger and worse mutations. Their oozing toxins easy enough to avoid when you'd danced with them dozens of times before.

With the sheer number of them, however, I found it more difficult to jump into the fray and, instead, watched from farther back than usual, standing with the ranged casters while idly drumming my fingers on my Warhammer. It was a better way to get an overview of the entire battlefield and to watch for potential incoming monsters that I might be able to at least head off with Planted in Place.

As my Class progressed, I noticed that it appeared less about combat and more about controlling aspects of fights. Healing and Mana taps, down to roots and weakening or draining spells. Understanding the emerging world around me so that I could better use to help us all survive.

"Incoming to the left!" I called out, feeling the flow of the Mana as I did so. Following that stream of power allowed me to interpret the potential powers we'd be facing. "Two Rangers tag and kite."

The incoming four creatures were aiming for the fray of people and Caneglobulous, in all their blobby, toad-like glory, who were duking it out for all they were worth. Their dedicated path showed that they didn't differentiate between us, but that everything in their path was considered expendable. These new creatures were similar to the Tetchrihorns we'd seen before with one, massive difference.

They were about twice the size of the ones we'd fought before. Their skin was still patterned like an alligator and most of them resembled a rhinoceros, but these ones had even more of a dinosaur vibe than the smaller versions we'd encountered weeks ago. While a relief to see a creature that wasn't a mutation of a beloved Australian animal, these things were terrifying in their own right. Their horns bristled with a sickly green glow as well, and they had hooves, not split toes.

Malihorn

Level 49

Evelyn and Marie broke away from the group, each of them having chosen their own Malihorn target to kite. They proceeded to kite, but they'd both learned from Marie's earlier faux pas and kept their distance and traps on a better rotation.

Which left the rest of us to fight the remaining two hellbent on the path toward the Caneglobulous. While Declan and Tanner took on one of them, Molly let out a cry as she planted her shield in place, beckoning one of the two not being kited.

And that's when we found out that the blasted things could stomp out magic. Granted, they had to stop in order to do so, which meant that while being kited and constantly in motion, our Archers were mostly safe from that particular attack. But the rest of us weren't.

The Malihorn that Molly angered stopped about ten feet away from us, reared high, and came down with both front feet at once, smashing into the ground like the earth had done something to offend it. The resulting rumble was strong enough that several of us lost our footing. Gemma and Drake barely managed to keep theirs, even having to put out a hand to steady themselves, and they were the most flexible in our group.

Molly almost buckled and only managed to keep her stance thanks to her shield. But I could see the grimace of determination on her face. She didn't give in to shows of strength like that. In fact, I always got the feeling that she prided herself on taking those species down a notch.

I tried to cast Planted in Place, realizing only belatedly that the stomp didn't just cause the ground to rumble, but also slowed my spell casting ability. "Interrupt the stomp if possible. I'll warn."

The thing about a large fighting force out in the real world is that it has absolutely nothing in common with fighting in a computer game. Out here in the *real* apocalyptic world, Ray could accidentally hit me in the back with an icicle if he lost his focus for a moment.

We couldn't all just gather on one spot and recklessly aim our Skills at the creatures we were fighting. It was better for us to divide ourselves into groups so that the damage was better distributed, the area less busy, and the target less obscured by forty-odd other fighters.

I glanced over to where the Archer and Ranger were kiting the other creatures and was quite pleased to see that we had several similar Classes assisting them. Kiting as a group, working in concert to keep the creatures snared, and whittling down on their health with barrages of arrows as they did so.

Mana Stone in place, meted out to our healers, tanks, and myself, I tapped out what I could. There were only so many people I could hit with the Skill. This was what I should have been saving points to boost the entire time I was leveling. But hindsight was always perfect, right?

It made me wonder if, for the right price, the Shop would allow me to redistribute the points I'd spent. Something to file away for later.

Keeping my eye on the Mana usage flashes from the Malihorns, I raised my left hand high for the ranged Classes to see an interrupt was needed. Thing was, it was damn difficult to keep my eyes on both of the ones we were fighting.

And then the Caneglobulous joined the fray. Luckily for us, Declan peeled off, leaving Tanner to tank the other Malihorn and ran to gather what Caneglobulous he could. The once-a-cane-toad mutants felt the wrath of my Water Siphon. Having amphibious heritage was a definite downside for them.

I scanned the area for other incoming, but right now all we had was what was in front of us. Luckily. It let me relax slightly, concentrating on both Malihorns to stop that damned stomp from happening. Occasionally I glanced over where the Archers and Rangers were kiting and whittling their targets down, just to make sure they were still handling it.

With the fights broken up like that, the odds of being hit with friendly fire diminished.

It was so much easier when we were out on patrols. While I would have preferred just to concentrate on my usual group, I couldn't afford to do that in this situation. Not and keep a solid overview of the battlefield for potential incoming monsters, or even for incoming attacks that could take us by surprise.

So I stepped back farther, coming to stand just beyond Ray and the ranged casters he directed. He shot me a glance like he wasn't sure why I was so far back. I gestured briefly around us. "I'll call out stun when it's necessary," was all I said to him.

He cracked half a smile before returning to bark out casting and stun rotations.

Taking a deep breath, I settled into the overview. Gemma and Drake dashed in and out from the one Malihorn that Molly was tanking with Piola and Ezra, who'd come with Mason, doing the same. They worked in unison, having filled the hole left by Tasha already. While I knew they felt her absence, they were also being pragmatic. We didn't have time to mourn while out in the field.

That could come later. But the more we did this, the more I knew the more time went by, the less we'd weep for the fallen.

Desensitizing at its finest.

Marie and Evelyn and the other archers that I didn't know the names of, continued their focused kiting and I realized that Mason was helping slow the beasts too. I could see him out of the corner of my vision strumming that lute, which just felt so out of place in the middle of a battle. Sitting there playing a damned song. At the same time, I couldn't explain quite how that simply *was* Mason. I guess that made him a pure support Class. Entertainment Class? I had no idea what to call it.

His face scrunched up in the way it always did when he concentrated, a hint of childish glee in every musical accomplishment. The man was endearing, and I had missed him a bunch. Now we just needed to survive through this so he could come back with us and hug his kids.

Tanner and his healer had the dwindling number of Caneglobulous under control.

Ray, Eritia, and Morgan switched their targets from the Caneglobulous just before it died, focusing down Molly's Malihorn. As soon as the last toad hit the ground, Tanner stepped forward and called out.

"Marie's target in five!"

In response she reslowed the target and pulled a color of arrow I hadn't seen before, waiting a couple of seconds before loosing it. "Redirected, you have eight."

The redirect had the creature heading over to Tanner before he could throw a taunt or anything else at it. And those eight seconds were more than Tanner needed to make the Malihorn remember him. He flashed a bright golden light at the creature, catching it directly in the eyes and making it stumble. The thing was down to thirty percent anyway. Maybe we should have just kept kiting the damned creature.

Except in all the swapping kerfuffle that was going far too smoothly for my liking, I'd completely forgotten to time the stomp, and the next one got away from me.

The ground shook again, sending several of us down to one knee, slowing our casting abilities in the process. Damn it, I needed to get better at severely multitasking. It wasn't like the Malihorn did it out of the blue. You could see him prepping for it even if you couldn't read Mana waves. I wasn't the only one who could give warning, but I really should be better about being on top of their skills.

Tanner was struggling under the weight of the attack to push back up to two feet while the Malihorn bore down on his shield. I could see him straining under the pressure of it all. One of the melee fighters I didn't know the name of dove into the fight, barreling directly into the side of the Malihorn.

While he barely made it blink, he did hit it with enough force that it budged slightly, enough so that Tanner could right himself and dig his heels back in. The Malihorn let out a deep squeal and trampled to the side, hitting the brave melee fighter directly in the torso. The guy went down as the trampling continued, and only Gemma's quick reactions managed to retrieve him before it stepped on his head.

Kyle dashed in to pull the fallen rogue out of further harm's way and help heal him up. There was a small whiff of fear coming off all the remaining fighters in the thick of it, but it dwindled as they threw themselves back into the fight. And then it was like no one had even been trampled. We were nothing if not stubborn.

Truth be told, I didn't like fighting with a group this size. There was far too much to keep an eye on, and way too much that could go wrong.

Once all three Malihorns were defeated and all of the corpses looted, I glanced through my inventory. Another reason to hate large group sizes. I just wasn't getting as much loot as usual, and thus my income was down. Still, this was a rescue mission, not our usual patrols.

Still. Whatever.

"You okay?" Evelyn spoke from next to me as everyone got their bearings before we moved onto the next group of creatures impeding our way into our target building. I think she tried to sneak up and see whether or not she could surprise me. Not going to happen as long as Mana existed.

"Yep," I answered before giving her a sideways glance. "You do realize I know your Mana signature, right? I can tell whenever you're around me."

"Oh, do I have a stalker?" she asked, half laughing. "Do I need to watch out?"

I smiled. "Depends on your definition of both."

She laughed softly, a grin on her face, and continued whatever she was doing with her interface while I finished taking stock of my gear and stats. Standing next to Evelyn always felt right, comfortable. And yet laughing when we'd lost a friend not even two hours ago? That . . . that felt all too surreal.

I sighed.

"Now that doesn't sound fine."

"Yeah. It is, and it's not. There are still monsters we have to kill. I think we're almost to Gary's building, and I can tell where creatures are, but that doesn't mean something out there can't mask itself from me." Mana was fluctuating nearby, and I knew that was the least of our problems. Once we retrieved the guys, we had to make sure we didn't anger the trees or else they'd smash through the windows to get at us while we retreated.

Apparently, trees could leave now. Literally. In all ways.

"That sounds like a plan. You're just really organized." Evelyn gave my shoulder a squeeze. "It's okay, Kira. You can't save everyone."

The chill that passed through me felt like premonition of a haunting and I shuddered, hoping those words wouldn't become prophetic. Remembering that I'd just entirely failed to save Tasha. "Maybe not. But I can damn well try."

"Just don't lose yourself to save others." She shrugged and stepped away to talk to Dannin, Marie, and a couple of other bow wielders. I watched her go, pondering her last words. She had a good point. Again.

Kyle. I needed to go talk to Kyle about better ways to utilize my Mana Purification, but it struck me as less important in the face of everything right now. We'd have to figure it out eventually, but right now, from the way the Mana fluctuated all around us—I was fairly certain our brief reprieve was about to be over.

Scanning the Mana oscillations around the front entrance to the building, I couldn't immediately see anything. The trees were on the other side of the building, so if we could avoid those, we should be done sooner rather than later, but the way to the was visually empty, yet the Mana said something totally different.

Something was definitely there.

And that's when I realized that whatever was lying in wait was invisible.

I raised my hand slightly, trying to catch Gemma's eye, but she was in a huddle with several other rogues.

Piola suddenly stood by my side. By suddenly, I mean she moved so fast I wouldn't have noticed without reading her Mana. Her seven-foot frame and the sleek Anubis-like appearance always gave me a surge of the impossible every time I stood next to her. We rarely talked alone, so I had to push down on the intimidation I could feel ringing through my soul.

"Yes?" she asked, and I think she smiled. Those canine teeth always held a glint of danger, but not necessarily directed at me.

"Can you see the invisible? I know Gemma has a skill that allows her to see stealthed monsters, creatures, people even."

"Of course." She glanced at where my gaze was directed and then gasped ever so softly. "I see."

"Then tell me what you see because I very obviously cannot." Way to go with the patience there, Kira.

And I kept telling my kids they needed to be patient. Attempting to emulate the role model I wanted them both to have, I waited while Piola gathered her thoughts.

"They're large rodents, sort of. But they look like I should be stuffing them for the young to learn how to hunt. They sort of look like they could be related to that kangaroo type of creature, but they have sharp teeth when they open their mouths. I would have thought they'd be larger, though."

No way. There's no way they could be what I thought they might be. Those were native to Perth for crying out loud, related to wallabies and kangaroos, but not them. Perth was four thousand kilometers away. Though . . . there were enough animal sanctuaries around here that I wouldn't put them past it to have the creature here.

"Exactly how large are they?" I asked, hoping against hope that I wasn't about to have to fight yet another beloved native animal.

Piola paused and held out her hand coming up to the bottom of my ribcage. "Yay high. There are about nine of them."

I sighed. Again.

Today was a sighing fucking day.

"Well, we need to get a plan of action sorted out. Do they look like they have any other type of animal mixed in with them?" Shit. Shit. Shit.

The Zarrie shook her head. "I believe Wallaradiance is what they are called."

"Th-thanks," I stammered, now unsure about my original idea. I'd been certain we were about to fight a mutated bloody quokka. That's how she described it, but if it was analyzing as a Wallaradiance?

Still, wouldn't that mean it was at least related to a wallaby, just like the quokka? And wallabies were so cute. Nothing like those hulking red kangaroos.

❖

It was ridiculous for me to be relieved that I was about ninety percent certain these creatures wouldn't resemble the cute little quokka at all. To avoid setting expectations low, I stuck to the name Piola had given me instead.

Wallaradiance still sounded far too pretty a creature for us to have to kill, but at least it wouldn't look up at us with a smiling face that we'd have to smash in. Small mercies still counted.

We prepared to fight, trying not to let on that we knew they were there. It was Evelyn who broke their stealth ranks for us, firing a shower of fire arrows toward the front of the building—the same place we needed to rescue Gary and his friends from. Let's hope the dampness won out and nothing caught fire.

When the stealth dropped, I realized that Piola's jaded view of what entailed scary and mine . . . were universes apart. What she thought was cute and should have been stuffed training toys, I would be having nightmares about for coming months.

While based on wallabies, or perhaps having some of the DNA of wallabies—these were no longer cute and cuddly. Where their small mouths had been, it looked like someone had artificially elongated the jaw, making it open far wider to reveal rows and rows of sharp little teeth. Sort of like a shark.

"That's definitely not a quokka," I muttered to Piola, who shrugged.

"You said it, not me. It is rodent-like in appearance." And then she followed the other rogues into battle, attacking with such swift movements that I couldn't see her blade.

Still, almost chest-high brush wallabies with shark teeth and a bladed tail made me step back again with the ranged folk. All of the ranged spread out, while the melee Classes bided their time, alternating between rushing in during a firing lull and utilizing what ranged abilities they had. Hirish had a solid grasp of organizing a battlefield, and I was truly grateful for it. His group of the Pirra Clan used their rifles like the experts they were. Firing on the creatures with deadly accuracy without taking down our own people.

It struck me as odd that a mere nine Wallaradiances were keeping Gary and the others at bay. Surely they could have come out by now? It was obvious we were here. We weren't being quiet about it. Maybe the creatures were higher level than I'd realized.

Wallaradience

Level 46

Nope. That wasn't it. I was definitely missing something.

With nine of the little buggers attacking us, I'd never been so glad to have three dedicated tanks. In fact, we really should have had more. These creatures, with the way they leveraged their tails to jump, weren't good candidates for snare. Slowing Skills didn't appear to have any effect on them.

And rooting them had less-than-stellar effect. Not even Mason's Bard slow worked effectively. Our bow wielders utilized their ice traps. Or to be more specific, Evelyn, Marie, and Dannin had those traps which took care of three of the creatures allowing Molly, Declan, and Tanner to take on two of the critters each, thus making their jobs easier.

Area effect spells that taunted had to be so well aimed to make sure they weren't affecting each other. Each of the tanks spread out, and that allowed us to divide our forces up and avoid shooting each other with friendly fire.

Wallaradience was the strangest name I'd heard yet. It pretty much made no sense. Usually, I thought the System was pretty unimaginative with its naming procedures for mutated native animals. After all, those animals were often hybrids of two types, or else there was a mutated element of the name inserted with that of the original.

But what the hell did Wallaradience have to do with wallaby apart from the *walla*? Radiance implied that there was some brightness or light. As I watched them fight, though, I saw none of it. Their long feet were more claw-like than soft like I'd usually expect, and I cringed as one turned quickly on Piola, slicing her calf from ankle to knee, causing her to hiss and back away.

Heals and System-based regeneration were a lucky thing. We'd have been up shit's creek well before this if the System didn't seem to want to keep us alive.

Mana pooled around the creatures, extending their energy, and helping them do physical damage, but there was nothing magical about them. No spell outputs, nothing. Which led me to believe that these guys were a decoy.

Not like mind-controlled decoy, but perhaps more of a pack control thing. After all, kangaroos moved in packs with an alpha male.

Scanning the area while making sure that Mana Stone was active, I searched close by for the apex predator of this pack. These guys had to have a boss. Somewhere around here.

Yet there was nothing anywhere around them, except for . . .

I focused on the building, trying to see if I could go into an X-ray mode or something. It was like the sensations just stopped. I should have been able to see what the Mana flow was like beyond some glass windows. Except right now, I couldn't even detect the ambient flow beyond the current fight. Meanwhile, the poor little Wallaradiances' health was truly dropping.

Then two things happened.

I finally managed to attune my sight to the hidden Mana flow and got blasted with a burning blue so bright that I staggered to one knee.

Secondly, the first Wallaradience died, and as it did, it exuded an explosion of bright, white light, momentarily blinding the rest of the raid group and rendering us all momentarily helpless.

Chapter Twenty-Seven:
Of Circumstance

Molly screamed out what I knew was the command for her shield to expand not only its size but to extend its dome of protection.

It took several second for my eyes to get used to normal sight again, which was much faster than anyone else, and I shot out several roots to keep the Wallaradiance in their spots so as to protect the others, even knowing they weren't as effective on these creatures.

My mind barely registered that Sange and Ray, who shouldn't have been up the front so close anyway, were lying on the ground bleeding from tail-inflicted damage.

Thankfully, Sange was a healer and managed to get to both themselves and Ray.

What bugged me was the slowly opening door from the building we needed to enter.

"Pull back," I called out. Tanner, Declan, and Molly did exactly as that with a finesse and unison movement that would have been nice to watch under other circumstances. They really were a good team.

The walkie-talkie in my pocket went all static, and I knew I'd need to answer it shortly, but right now we needed to live through whatever was about to come through those front doors. Because that thing's Mana signature had hurt my eyes worse than the Wallaradience death explosion.

Whatever it was moved slowly. Perhaps it'd been locked in or something.

"Eyes!" Molly yelled out about two seconds before the next Wallaradiance went down, giving us just enough time to react and shield our eyes from the incoming blinding death attack.

This time we weren't caught off guard, and our groups continued to work at downing the rest of them.

I sent a message to Molly through party chat.

Big monster incoming shortly.

Got it.

Ah, always one of few words, that was Molly. Not really. She definitely talked more than Sange when she had something to say, anyway. I watched as she worked with the other tanks to hand off the creatures she'd been tanking while she prepped for a bigger bad.

As the Wallaradiences fell, the Mana behind the door built up to such a threshold that there was this keening sort of hiccup of sound and the double entrance doors smashed open, sending glass flying far out into the front lines to reveal a massive kangaroo.

It stood about twelve feet tall when it righted itself fully, and I really had to wonder how it got into the building in the first place. Perhaps it grew after it entered. Its eyes weren't brown or black but shone down like red-eyed photographs come to life.

Poetic really, since this was a red kangaroo.

Big Red

Level 49 (Elite)

If you've ever seen the normal brown kangaroos and whatnot, or even the redder ones they keep in zoos, then you still haven't really seen a red kangaroo. The ones I'm talking about grow to be six feet tall, and their tails were lethal weapons even *before* the apocalypse.

I still have a memory of driving down to Sydney when I was about eight and being blindsided by a big red. He crashed into our tiny little Ford Laser while we were driving, pushing in the driver's side door so badly it couldn't be opened, and my dad had to climb out of the passenger seat.

This thing stood a hulking twelve feet tall, with a tail that dragged behind it. Except instead of just one tail, where it reached the ground, it split into several and splayed out in such a way that I didn't think this thing would ever lose its balance.

When it opened its mouth, there was no doubt it was now a carnivore. Intelligence shone in its eyes, and the remaining five Wallaradiances appeared to receive a surge of energy at its presence, as if they were buffed by it.

Shit.

I stepped back, instinctually knowing what it was about to do as it ever so briefly crouched into its jump and then sailed right over the front line, to land directly in front of me. Its bright red eyes focused on me, freezing me to the spot.

Until Molly was suddenly there, planting her shield down with a loud thud into the earth and aimed her Taunt at it. Thank the gods for Molly. I hadn't been watching her and had no idea how she'd gotten over to me so fast, but I was glad she had.

Except even with her there, roaring at it, the damned thing didn't take its eyes off me. It felt like time was passing in a vacuum, just it and me standing there while others bashed on an invisible barrier trying to get in to help me. There was something about the sheer intelligence in its eyes that shook me to the core.

It lifted one foot so fast, that I didn't see it coming as it darted out, smashing into me before I could react. The air whooshed out of my lungs as I went flying backwards, the strange trance finally broken. And maybe a few of my ribs too.

I gasped in pain, coughed up an immediate splash of blood, and then healing hit me as the System knit me back together in lightning-fast time with the help of my brother. Still recovering mentally, I scrambled back to my feet, watching as the creature finally turned its attention to Molly and her taunts.

It leaned back, its tails supporting all of its weight, hefted both its massive, clawed feet back, and kicked out at Molly's shield. The huge tower shield groaned, and our tank got pushed back several feet. I'd never seen anything make Molly and her shield retreat without her deliberately activating it to do so.

I could tell she was irritated by it, too. There wasn't much we'd encountered along the way that could push Molly back, at least not since we'd all hit the forties.

Still, Molly dug in and stood her ground, and our Archer types fired off flame, ice, and bomb arrows. At least that's what they looked like, so that's how I described them.

The target was large enough that we could fire on it as long as we spread out, as long as the ranged Classes aimed for the top of the creature while the melee dove into the bottom.

Morton fired shots, fitting in perfectly with Hirish and the other Hakarta. The mages threw out their entire arsenal. From Arcane Missiles right through to Ice Lances from Ray. The melee Classes rotated in and out due to their numbers and limited space. It meant they constantly had enough Mana and melee attacks would continue through rotations.

After the rest of the Wallaradiances were felled, anyway. For now, Declan and Tanner held them at bay and the melee rotations contributed damage.

But our attacks made such tiny dents in Big Red that his health hadn't dwindled significantly at all. He had to have weaknesses, but I was at a loss as to what they were. Mana fussed around him in a frenzy, like it wasn't sure what to fill up first.

Suddenly, he stepped one foot slightly forward and pivoted, sweeping his massive tails out around him. Molly jumped in time and most of our people were ranged for now, but the handful of melee close enough to get hit were sent flying like I had been several minutes ago.

Healers frantically filled hit points back up, and it took mere seconds for our melee to be up and combat ready again.

I guess Big Red had a spin as well, then.

Now all I was waiting for was for him to have a boxing attack, because of course we had to fill the kangaroo stereotype, right?

The last of the Wallaradiance fell in a blinding flash of light, freeing up the rest of our melee to jump into rotation on our Big Red fight. No sooner had they moved into place than did the damned monster decide to prove me right.

So many cartoons get kangaroo boxing incorrect. It's not like you expect. Essentially, most kangaroos balance with their tail and punch with both feet, lending it a powerful impact that often hits below the belt. There are no rules in kangaroo fights, at least not when they're against each other. And punching with their paws is less an actual thing, and more like a grappling for purchase on the opponent.

Eyes, mouth, ears—nothing is above being gouged out if the kangaroo can manage it. It's almost like their arms flail with purpose. But true kangaroo boxing is done with the feet, and those hits are powerful.

This time the launch into the kick was subtly different in that I could see the Mana pooling around the base of the tail, leading up and into the feet. "Incoming attack!" I yelled out, way too sure about my kangaroo knowledge to second guess myself.

Molly activated her shield just in time for the punch kick to impact. It made the whole dome of protection she activated reverberate, even through to the shield itself, letting ripples of power echo down the line.

Hirish and his Pirra Clan opened up fire again once the attack was passed, pulse rifle shots catching the creature in the chest and face.

Lowering itself back onto its feet with a thud, Big Red roared loudly. Well, a bleating cry sort of roar. Kangaroos make super weird noises. Either way, he was angry.

He raised his front paws, and a swell of Mana gathered around them. "Incoming magic attack!"

I barely got the words out in time, before the first pulse of . . . whatever type of power that was struck right into the middle of our archers, forcing them to scatter, heal, and regroup before they could begin their barrage again.

Hirish's group never let up with their firing, and Morton stuck with them to join the gun brigade. The flatter arc of bullets and laser beams meant they needed to spread out and gain a higher angle of attack normally, unlike our archers who could literally drop their arrows on our opponents if they needed to.

Ray motioned for his casters to fan out, thus giving Big Red less of a group target, making the kangaroo have to pick exactly where to aim those shots. It was beginning to get crowded around the creature, and Ray began to call out rotations for casters to minimize possible accidental damage to our allies.

From what I could tell, Big Red couldn't use that ability all the time. Perhaps a prerequisite meant it needed to charge, I didn't know. But his massive kick, that was something different. He could pull out that at any time, and with the amount of melee we had in the mix, that was going to get dangerous.

"Piola!" I called out, motioning her to me while I tried desperately to keep my eye on Mana fluctuations. "Watch for tail movement. When it spans out, make sure you all retreat."

She nodded and dove back in. I knew Gemma would be pissed with me for asking the alien to watch for it, but Piola had all of her Zarrie to think about too. She was a commander. Gemma still worked in concert with Drake, and they'd pulled more of our rogues into the fray too. I only hope she listened to Piola's directions on when to clear out.

Big Red was anything but predictable. Paw Orbs, Tail Swipe, Kangaroo Boxer . . . I had no idea what his abilities were called, but I was naming them for all I was worth. He threw those orbs out about every forty seconds or so; the tail swipe didn't appear to need to recharge or anything, and the Kangaroo Boxer was all willy-nilly too.

He took out multiple of our people several times, knocking them back twenty, even thirty meters sometimes.

It almost became a game of tag. Big Red spun, catapulting his tail through the few melee fighters who weren't able to get out in time. They shot through the air briefly, hitting the ground and rolling for the rest of the way. It broke limbs, gravel rashed up their entire bodies, and in some cases mangled faces, wearing away at the skin until it got down to the bone. Each time they'd get healed up and go back to getting ready to rotate back into the fight.

Mana Stone had never felt like a wiser choice in my life. I should have saved all the points for this one. Still. Hindsight.

More Paw Orbs shot out, catching the occasional ranged person completely by surprise because they were engrossed in their casting rotations. But spreading them all out had been a brilliant idea, and Big Red was less able to hit many of them in one target.

We fell into a groove of fighting, being hit, healing, and throwing ourselves back into the fight until time didn't even matter anymore.

Suddenly, the doors behind Big Red opened again, almost giving me a heart attack, and Gary stood there. Dried blood was caked on his shirt, but he was fine, and the relief on his face made all of this worthwhile. Sort of.

Even though Tasha was dead.

Behind him came about a dozen others, all in varying stages of undress, but more from clothes being ripped than anything kinky going on. They dodged and wove out to where Big Red couldn't reach them with his tail, and then jogged their way over to where I stood in the middle of it all.

"We have a few more, but they're unable to come and help until we can get them to a Shop." He was just as gruff as always. A college student, he was big and burly, and never the brightest, but since we'd fought him and Drake all those months ago when we first founded Garden City, they'd become reliable allies and almost—dare I say it?—friends.

"If you're able, get into the fray and dodge the abilities. Work with Piola and get out when she tells you so we can avoid damage we don't need to be taking." I patted him on the back and continued to concentrate on the Mana waves so I could call out warnings. Water Siphon wasn't as effective on this beast as it was on those who required moisture like trees, or blobs, but it did help weaken Big Red somewhat.

Implantation, Blood Dispersion, and Mana Stone were my best bets to contribute to the whole fight. But with a dozen more people joining us, I was fairly certain that Mana Stone and Blood Dispersion weren't going to contribute much to overall damage or healing. There had to be ways I could separate them out, or control exactly who I was targeting, but maybe that was a next level thing, or perhaps I just needed to play with it out of combat more.

Big Red's health was slowly dwindling. We needed it to dwindle faster. Before the trees got wind of what we were doing, and before we ran out of Mana.

When he hit about fifty percent, it was like a light went on in his head. He looked around himself and I could practically see the cogs whirring as

Mana gathered around him, but in a different way this time.

He wasn't about to hit us with Skills or Abilities; it was something else.

And then he pushed off with those damned powerful legs, and help from his massive split tail, and jumped. Now, you don't understand what I mean by that. This thing was a few feet taller than your average kangaroo even when *not* leveraging with its tail. He bounced over and came to rest about twenty-five meters away, just beyond a group of our mages.

Now in their defense, they pivoted quite fast, but not before Big Red gathered a Paw Orb in his little tyrannosaurus arms and flung it at them. It sent them flying backwards, a couple of them releasing their own Skills as they did so. They rolled over and over, gathering gravel rash and broken limbs as they did so.

But Big Red wasn't finished, because he gathered himself again, and jumped.

Shit. We were going to have to change tactics to compensate. And I didn't think we'd be sending in any melee now. They'd never make it to the target in time before he jumped away again.

I had to give it to the massive kangaroo mutation. He'd definitely retained some of his smarts.

"Back up!" Molly called out, retracting her shield and moving herself. She was closer, so she'd be able to see anything not directly Mana related. We all needed to reorient ourselves.

Hirish's voice boomed over the battlefield, which meant Big Red could hear him too, and I had a sneaking suspicion the huge kangaroo would get the gist of it.

"Melee, resort to whatever ranged options you have." Hirish positioned himself down with Molly. "Tanks will be using any and all taunts in rotation. Ranged Classes track Big Red as it moves. Be aware of your positions."

Yeah, that ought to do it. We all switched tactics. I kept Mana Stone, Blood Dispersion, and Implantation on the damned bouncy little bugger. Even though I wasn't sure how Implantation would work if it went off while Red was in the air.

The second jump only ended up knocking about three bow users off their feet and sent the rest scrambling just this side of being hit. But now that we knew what it could do, ranged Classes were doing their best to track the creature as it bounced to its next perch. Once it touched down, they released their Skills, bombarding Big Red with as much damage as we could.

Damn, he was so mobile; he only spent about thirty seconds on the ground each time, and his usage of Mana with each bounce was so light, I didn't think he'd ever run out.

Mages, Archers, Shooters—all of them could track the creature, but shooting while it was airborne? That was best left to those with guns and rifles. Melee fighters contributed with smaller damage Skills, a few of them having their own low Bow skills usually better for hunting.

And so, the damned massive kangaroo began a game of bounce. More agile than we'd given it credit for, it led us on a merry chase all around the front of the college building. Bounding from one group of us to the next, gathering energy, and doing it again. If it hadn't been so damned infuriating, it would have been comical.

Okay, so it was a little comical.

Big Red's health continued to go down. It just took longer than any of us would have liked. It crawled, and I felt like he wanted to just hop away, but there was some sort of compulsion not to. In a way, it made me a little sad.

At least until he landed in the middle of the group he jumped to and sent Mason skittering across the parking lot like he was a skimming stone on a lake. Now, I just wanted the fight to stop.

Not only was the fight drawing out, but Mana was becoming a problem. "Drink up!" I yelled out, knowing that it gave us that bit more time. I only had the Mana regeneration going out to healers, and a few select ranged Classes, but I was sorely tempted to take it from the healers. No matter how much healing we had. If we weren't doing damage the thing wasn't going to die.

At about ten percent health, Big Red was visibly tired. His bouncing jumps lost some of their zest and the size of them lost some bite. He'd land now, and kick out all around him, using the Tail Whip too, trying to dislodge any of us that he could.

Balls of blue Paw Orbs rained overhead like he was trying to take us all out at once in moves of sheer desperation. Ray and two other Ice Mages managed to head those off, searing off the heat with ice cold so that the orbs dropped uselessly onto the ground like big snowy balls.

That didn't deter Big Red from firing them out. And his Tail Swipe knocked more of our people on their butts than I'd like to admit. But we wore him down and kept at him like scarabs on a corpse determined to pick it clean.

Only then we had to shift all of our attacks again because he'd jumped again. As the fight wound down, he became more sluggish, having used up enormous amounts of energy to bounce between us all.

Finally, he fell, and everyone around him had to run out from underneath as he came slowly crashing to the ground. When he hit, the surface under us all rumbled with the impact and we too allowed ourselves to sit down with the effort that whole fight took.

I walked forward, touching him on his huge nose, his eyes now closed and no longer showing that sickening red light from them. Poor boy. Wasn't his fault the big bad apocalypse came along and turned him into a monster.

He'd probably been the leader of his pack originally. Not a hair over eight feet, well-muscled and built. Just like any good kangaroo boy.

Looting the corpse, I paused, going over a couple of things that caught my eye.

Big Red Brain

Weight 1.5kg
Use: Crafting, Enhancement

Big Red Laser Ball

Weight 0.5kg
Use: Skill, Crafting, Enhancement

There were a few other things like tail, upgraded biceps, weird stuff like that. But the first two stuck in my mind and I felt that weird sadness wash over me. Maybe if we'd got to him first like we had to Mumma Wombutt— maybe he didn't have to devolve into such a menacing foe. Maybe we could have become friends too.

❖

We sat around cleaning up for the most part. Evelyn walked over and just gave me a huge hug. Damn did I need that. Sometimes, just sometimes, that whole adrenaline thing was hiding a lot more exhaustion than I realized. Fighting for our lives was becoming common place, but I still wasn't used to it.

"You okay?" she asked, letting go and holding me at arm's length.
"As expected."

She raised an eyebrow at me as if calling me on my bullshit, and then just shrugged. "You're going to get yourself in trouble pulling this I'm fine shit all the time."

"Maybe." I knew she was right. That whole burnout thing loomed. But there was still a lot to do. "But first we've got to make sure our little settlement is actually safe and that my kids can handle me taking a few days off."

Evelyn just looked at me for a few seconds. So long that it almost became uncomfortable. "You know, you don't give them enough credit. I think you'd be pretty surprised how well they could do if you needed them to step up." And she walked away to where the other ranged Classes were having a discussion.

"She seemed a bit intense," Mason said, suddenly at my shoulder.

His Mana hue was a little more to the green spectrum than others, so it'd been easier to tell he was there. He was just looking out for me, like usual. "She's pretty focused on the things that matter to her."

"Ah," he said, looking around the clean up a little more. Then he nudged me slyly. "Things like you, eh?"

I paused for a moment contemplating that. He was right, at least I thought he might be. "Yeah—I hope so, anyway."

He chuckled softly before speaking. "What's the plan then?"

I was about to speak when my walkie flared to life again. Frowning, I pulled it out and held it up.

Yes?

Dor's voice came crackling over the speaker. Frankly, I was impressed she could reach us out here. *Our patrols are struggling. Overwhelming numbers.*

Wait. What? Are we being attacked? Cold ran down my spine as panic tried to set in. The kids would be fine; they had to be.

Her next words soothed me. *No. But we have to keep the nests in check. We're also fighting fleeing monsters.*

Shit. I took a breath and scanned around me. Fleeing monsters? I didn't even want to contemplate what they could be fleeing from. *Will be back as soon as possible.*

Got it.

The crackling stopped, and I glanced toward my brother, holding up my hand for him to come. He did, bringing Hirish and Piola with him. "We have to get back. The patrols are having trouble keeping up because . . . I think fleeing monsters are overrunning the nests we otherwise had under control."

"That is not surprising." Hirish and his matter-of-factness were going to make me want to punch him one of these days. "There are areas we have not cleared. The creatures there will have leveled higher and likely be looking for more sources of food. They are, thus, moving toward your settlement and sending other creatures fleeing them."

Great. That didn't sound like a barrel of laughs. "Okay, then. Where's Gary?"

Kyle gestured over his shoulder at the building with its front entrance demolished. "He went in to fetch the others. Once they get to the Shop, they'll be able to replace missing limbs at least."

I shook my head. I guess that had been the real problem. They hadn't been able to fight out of there and take the injured with them.

"We've been fighting all day. Although . . ." I glanced at Hirish. "As long as we don't fire and pulses directly into them, I get the feeling the trees aren't about to attack us."

Hirish shrugged. "Perhaps. Perhaps not. They do not appear to be as contentious as the two we met on the road."

"What's the plan then?" Kyle asked, crossing his arms. "We've been fighting most of the day. We need to rest, and escort these guys back to their settlement?"

Gary had wandered over and stood just behind the Hakarta. "If you could lend us maybe a dozen people—including a Hakarta or Zarrie or two—we survivors could easily make it back to the settlement." He paused, glancing back at where he'd left their ragtag little group of about twelve people. "Do you think it would be okay if we came back to Garbo with you in the end?"

"They want to come stay with us?" I asked, trying to mentally calculate the room we'd need. "How many people?"

He shrugged. "All in all, about another sixty on top of us. It's not a big settlement, and they don't have a Shop or an orb or anything. They've just been surviving."

"With the way cleared by you guys"—he gestured toward the road— "we should have another maybe thirty-six to forty-eight hours before the nests respawn. We can make it to the settlement before nightfall if we can take a few of the vehicles? Then leave in the morning and head to Garbo."

I mulled it over, glancing at Kyle who nodded. He was right. Including the survivors, we found that'd be about seventy-five people. I mean, it was a lot, but the center could definitely handle that amount of people. Not to mention I was aware of quite a few apartments that still needed residents.

Without a Shop, their inventories must be overflowing. "Okay. I think that'll work."

Kyle piped up, saving me. "We'll send twelve people, including what, two Hakarta and Zarrie each?" He glanced at the respective captains and both Hirish and Piola nodded their assent.

"Do you guys have *any* vehicles?" I asked softly.

Gary shook his head. "No. Bikes and stuff, though."

Kyle nodded. "We can spare . . . maybe ten? You could overload them a bit. Chuck people in the truck beds if needed. The back of a ute will hold a lot of you. Have some people ride on bicycles. It'd be quicker getting back to Garbo that way."

I cringed. That was going to make the odd eight vehicles we had left very full for our groups to get back home with. But it was worth it. "Sure. Maybe we can get them home before nightfall."

Kyle set off to take care of metering out just who would go where, while I sank to the ground, ready to sleep. Constantly using Mana Vision felt like it drained my brain. I had to be able to do something about the strain it put on my eyes. Yet another thing to research.

Mason had wandered off to his own little group of people. I couldn't wait to surprise the kids, to see that happiness spread over their faces. Even if I felt like he wasn't going to stick around, for now, it would do.

We were going home with a lot more humans than we'd headed out with. But damn, it felt good to still be alive.

Chapter Twenty-Eight:

Return

18 Weeks, 3 Days Post-System Onset
6 p.m.

I rode through the gate down near the Officeworx just as the sun was setting, fully determined to find my kids. We were expecting the newcomers to make it back here in by early morning tomorrow. Hirish was about to send another convoy of vehicles out to help pick them up. The ones we'd used, however, they needed to charge still.

Thank the hells that the damned clouds had buggered off. Today was the first day of sunshine in like . . . a week or something.

I needn't have worried about my kids.

Jackson walked toward me while Wisp rode on top of Wombie. The young wombat had grown since we left early that morning, I swear.

"Mom!" Wisp preened as I raked my eyes over her, watching at the way she was secured with a type of harness that appeared to have one of those easy release clasps. Damn. That was an excellent idea—and one I was going to steal.

"Well! Do you like it?" She was beside herself with excitement, so much that she hadn't even noticed her dad was standing behind me yet.

Jackson, on the other hand, hadn't moved for several seconds, like he'd been rooted to the spot. "Dad?"

The word came out in a whisper, like he didn't quite trust himself with what he was seeing.

"In the flesh, mate."

I could hear the emotion in Mason's voice, and my chest tightened. He'd really missed the kids like I'd known he would. Damn, was I glad he wasn't dead.

Jackson, my least emotional child, took three steps forward, broke into a short run, and flung his arms around his dad's neck. Mason, for what it's worth, stood there, just hugging his son, tears welling in the corner of his eyes.

Ah, reunions. I refused to cry. I would not.

Wisp wasn't acting like I expected her to. She raised an eyebrow and eyed her father critically. Then she leaned forward and spoke in a really low voice. "Mum. Are you sure it's him? There are alien species who can take on any form, you know."

Oh, my.

What sort of reading had she been doing in my absence? "It's okay, Buttercup. It's really your dad. I checked."

Which I had—mostly, anyway. I'd analyzed him and spoken at length with him. If this was an alien impersonation, it had even taken on his annoying habits. Like humming tunes when everyone else around him was talking or checking to see if his armpits stank by craning his neck down without bothering to be discreet.

Wisp's expression changed in an instant. From suspicious to eight-year-old kid just wanting to see her dad.

"Daddy?" she whispered.

He lifted his face long enough to look her square in the eyes, and that quick release tab on the harness had never been used so fast as she slid down the side of her giant wombat and ran to him. Dog followed at a respectful distance, standing guard with the wombat just in case.

I rested my hand on Wombie, scratching behind his ears like he liked. He huffed out wombat breath on me and leaned into it. Wombat breath had a soft sort of baby puppy smell. It didn't smell godawful, but with his huge mouth, Wombie had a *lot* of that breath. I'd remember not to stand as close next time.

Finally, after what seemed like forever, they broke their little huddle. Wisp clung to Mason's hand like it was a lifeline she never wanted to let go and Jackson, his cheeks a little flushed and his eyes a tad bit red, shoved his hands in his pockets as we all walked back to the center.

Wisp chattered away at him nineteen to the dozen, her face bright and excited, her grip deathlike. Jackson glanced over at me and smiled.

That was a reunion I hadn't thought would happen for a long time, if ever.

"Hey. I have to check in with Dor and Sienna. They called us back sooner than expected."

Jackson nodded, while I could tell Mason was sort of listening, he was also doing his best to give Wisp a lot of attention.

"While you were gone, we started witnessing really strange nest patterns. Not necessarily dangerous, but different enough that we're going to have to modify patrols." Jackson spoke well and confidently about the circumstances, and while I'd already known that much it still impressed me.

Damn, when did he grow up so much?

"Will you guys show your dad around?" I asked as we entered the center.

Mason's eyes grew wide at the suggestion. I knew he'd been with a large settlement on the Gold Coast, but I guess Pacific Fair was a more open-sky sort of shopping center than this one. Totally different layout.

"Of course, Mum! Can we show him the Shop too!" Wisp's eyes were so bright, I didn't have the heart to tell her that her dad had a hundred percent already witnessed a Shop. His might be entirely different than mine, even.

In fact, I would bet on it.

Luckily, her dad didn't tell her either.

"He might even show you his Shop." I winked at her, ignoring Mason's pleading look. "Just go have fun."

Nope, I wasn't going to help him at all. They hadn't seen their dad since three months before the Apocalypse hit. Closing in on a total of seven months now. They needed to spend time with him, to know that he truly was there. In the midst of all this death and change, that was the *least* Mason could do for them.

Once they were out of sight, I forced my bone-weary body to toward the library so I could find out just what sort of shit storm awaited us. While I knew Mason hadn't just come up to see his family, I'd talk to him about that once my settlement was safe again.

That was my plan, anyway.

Dor beckoned to me as soon as the doors closed behind me. She sat at her desk with Sienna, Mike, and Dale gathered around her. Kyle would join us soon, as would Hirish and Piola. I scanned the room, not finding anyone from IRSHA and frowned.

"IRSHA are off trying to help contain several of the nesting grounds that have . . . become overrun," Dor said without even lifting her head from whatever she was concentrating on.

"Dequasha needs to see you this evening. Your Mumma Wombutt did not like you leaving and has been camped out in the carpark again ever since you left. And we have a hell of a lot of displaced monsters that are at least the same level or some of them higher level than the nests they've been disrupting." Dor finally swiveled in her chair to look at me, and for once, she seemed tired.

"No more leaving for you. You go away and shit hits the fan."

"Damn. There goes that beach vacation I'd been planning for," I quipped, snatching one of the more comfortable chairs and rolling over to see what had their attention so captivated.

"Beach might be a colossal bad idea anyway," Dale shot back. "If the creatures around here have mutated, just imagine what the coast looks like right now."

I shuddered. "Just the nightmare fuel I needed. Thanks, Dale."

"Always willing to oblige." He grinned at me, and I glanced at his hands, unable to distinguish which was the cybernetic version he'd got from the Shop. Damn, that shit was good.

I looked at the map and groaned. "So are they just disrupting, or killing, or taking, or . . . what exactly is going on?"

"All of the above." Mike flipped over to the Daisy Hill portion of the map, where the Dungeon was and pointed. "Here . . . especially. There are creatures just flooding toward the conservation Dungeon like rats before a flood."

The image that conjured didn't do me any favors, but at least I could understand it.

"Are they ignoring each other and attacking only us?"

"No." Dale paused for a moment. "So far, they seem to simply be fighting. But with the increased monster population, we're needing to up our nest-clearing patrols. If we don't, especially with this influx, we're going to fall behind and be overrun again, because even when we clear the nests, another group of fleeing monsters just comes in and takes the space."

"Defenses?" I asked, directing the question to Dor as I pulled up the settlement interface to get a closer look, happy to note that level three defenses were now in place. We'd regained what ground we lost when we expanded. That was good to know . . .

She shrugged. "Level three is in place now. It's a lot of Credits to get the walls up another level, but we're working on it. And, by the looks of things and the influx of people you just brought back with you, we're going to need to expand again soon-ish."

"Can't blame me for bringing people to safety," I grumbled, but she was right. Sure, these odd seventy people weren't going to overflow us anytime soon. But we would eventually need to expand again.

From everything I could tell in the interface, our current expansion had room for around eight hundred more people to move into apartments or houses. Those extra taxes would help fund the growing need to expand more. Damn, this shit was complicated. I was just glad Dor and Sienna had a good handle on it.

Dor smiled. "I'm not blaming you for bringing them, just pointing out that we're going to have to expand again."

"Maybe wait to push defenses to the next level after we expand the settlement?"

"Maybe." Dor pursed her lips, obviously thinking it over.

"Strategies for the nests?" Frankly, I was toast. I couldn't get my brain to work even pushing it to do so. All I wanted to do was sleep.

Kyle flopped down next to me in another rolly chair, pulling up like he wanted us to chair race. Well, joke's on him; I didn't have the energy. "Keep sending clearing out teams and just be more on our guard?"

"Getting caught in the middle of these creatures fighting isn't a fun romp in the park, Kyle." Dale sounded like he'd been in the thick of it himself. "A group of middling-Levels got stuck in one of the nests yesterday and got out by sheer luck, but not before Melody had to regrow several limbs."

Kyle sucked in a breath. He understood how painful that could be. "Okay, so it's more serious than I thought."

That's all he needed to put his thinking cap back on. "Can we send out scouts to well . . . scout the area and identify interlopers before they arrive?

Or else, it might be best to just let the creatures take care of each other as much as possible and let us swoop in and finish off once they've whittled each other down. Take advantage of what some of them are doing for us, so to speak."

Dale pondered that as more people streamed into our cramped little meeting place. Lousesh was back now and looking decidedly pissed off. Piola and Zyrilian spoke in low tones as they entered, too. Evelyn, Ray, and Eritia also filed in. Still no IRSHA in sight. I tried not to feel worried about them. They were intergalactic hunters, after all.

Many of the IRSHA were from the Dash'Kiri clan and were hardy little bastards. Still. Mon'swkinon had been badly injured when we fought Carindale, so despite my thoughts they were nigh invincible, the truth was that they weren't indestructible.

Sienna stood up, glanced at Mike—who nodded almost imperceptibly—and cleared her throat. "We've sent out a minimal patrols of nest clearers this afternoon while we try to figure out a better strategy to clearing our surrounding areas."

"What is scaring them so much that they're stampeding into regularly cleared grounds?" Eritia asked a question I hadn't wanted to consider.

Zyrilian piped up, his dark eyes gleaming from out of the white spots that encircled them. "Predators. There's always a need for something bigger and stronger out there. Here it could be anything. From the Magon right through to a creature or five that has gotten out of control. Just because we have not yet seen it, does not mean it isn't there. The possibilities are endless."

He shrugged and his sleek black fur glistened momentarily with the movement.

"You're saying that despite clearing everything within a ten-kilometer or so radius, there's things beyond that who've leveled and grown enough that they can now threaten within this radius?" I could hear the confusion in Dale's voice. Or maybe it was just fear tinged with willing disbelief.

Could have been a bit of both.

"Yes. Do not forget we are still undergoing System integration. Monsters continue to spawn, outside of your current radius. These monsters will grow with strength and range farther, forcing other, weaker monsters out of their original habitat. Fleeing to the next, safest zone is common." Zyrilian turned to Piola. "Have you not been informing them how the System works?"

His commander sighed. "Yes, but we hadn't reached this level of saturation yet, and were on a mission."

Zyrilian rolled his eyes at Piola. "That's how it is. The System is still integrating your world into it. You should be increasing your defenses through the use of turrets and other automatic protection options. Make your base your stronghold. Build it up."

Hirish cleared his throat. "Credits will allow you to buy most anything. You just have to pay for it."

I glanced at the treasury balance and tried not to groan. This felt like a pay-to-play game, where you just had to keep sinking money into the damned thing until you overpowered your character or settlement enough that it could be fun to play.

"Wait, so we're always going to get influxes like this?" Evelyn piped up, and I could hear the irritation in her voice. Seriously, we all wanted to know if this was ever going to end, but I didn't think any of us were ready for the more likely than not answer of no, this was just our lives now.

Maybe the System had just got the timeline wrong. Australians wouldn't die in the initial onslaught, just over time under the weight of all this constantly, speedily mutating crap that didn't appear to need to rest.

Eventually, there'd be too many of these high Levels and we'd fall under the rampage of creatures the System kept creating.

Shit.

❖

18 Weeks, 4 Days Post-System Onset
10 a.m.

Mason's presence, and the children's overwhelming joy in seeing their father helped give me time to get done what I needed to.

Sitting in strategizing meetings for most of the next day was never my idea of fun. Leena even brought us all sustenance from Raybucks.

She brought me a chilled version of my beverage of choice along with something that resembled a cheese danish. At least it took the sting out of the fact that it was looking like we'd wear out before we died of old age.

The only thing that broke the monotony was the arrival of the rest of our little rescues. We broke the meeting up long enough to go and welcome them to the settlement. Frankly, I was glad of the reprieve.

Drake and Gary were almost attached at the hip, so glad were they to have found each other again. Their bromance brought a smile to my face. As far as I'd been able to tell, they'd been college roomies when all this hit.

"That's a lot of people, Kira." Dor spoke softly next to me.

"Yeah. That's also a nice chunk on its way to the next quest."

She chuckled. "Touché."

I pulled up the information as they filtered in, giving their names and Classes to our welcome wagon as they did so.

A Habitable Safe Zone

Part Four B: Just a few more!

Goals:

1 - Gather 5,000 total inhabitants. This may include visiting species. Current population 4,394/5,000

2 - Completed: Expand your Township to the first extension point

3—In Progress: Utilize the Town's Quest-giving system more efficiently. Now make it a habit!

4 - Survive 6 months as a Township

Reward: 25,000 Credits for your city Treasury

That's it. Nothing else. It is just a bonus quest.

"Getting close. Could probably give them some of those town quests?" Dor glanced at me as she'd obviously had the same idea to check the quest as I had.

"Couple of nest-clearing ones should do. Maybe some of the crafting material gathering too. Ginali loves getting those." I activated a few of them through the settlement control panel. "What do you think?"

She chuckled. "Yeah, that looks good. I'll insert a couple that have to do with helping take care of the kids, too."

The settlement interface had so many options in it now we were growing as a town. There had to be better ways to handle all of this than the small group of us scrambling to take care of certain aspects.

"Here's a thought. There has to be someone else in our settlement with a planning, city planning, or some sort of management Class. Go find them and apprentice them or something and help take a load off yourself and Sienna—hell, make them the quest person."

"That's a bloody brilliant idea." Dor gave me a quick hug and headed over to where Ray and Mike stood surveying the list of incoming Classes.

I chuckled softly.

Well, that was something else to thank Mason for. He'd freed up a touch of worry about the kids for me, so why shouldn't we administrators have someone that could do the same for us?

It wasn't as if we didn't have any help as far as admin went. For the most part we had security and defenses, settler intake, food storage, food production and procurement, crafting liaisons, healthcare . . . it was, for all intents and purposes, like a real little city government. Sort of.

Eight more weeks to find another six hundred-odd people. We were going to be pushing it, and really, for twenty-five thousand Credits, I wasn't even sure it was worth it. Mulling it over, I turned and followed Dor back into the library now the excitement of the newcomers had waned sufficiently.

Dor was frowning. "Carindale just contacted us. Joshua says they're seeing some signs of monsters outside of their usual patrols, but nothing like what we've got. They'll try to up patrols through to us, to help free up some of our resources to deal with everything here."

"Great." See, saving Carindale had been a good idea in the end. Even if it cost a lot of time and a literal arm and leg or three.

I watched as Dor and Sienna went through what I believed to be the listing of available Classes our residents had. Kyle and Hirish worked with Piola, Dale, and Mike to go over expanding the patrols so we could keep up with the increased monster presence. And I sat here like a good little settlement owner, flipping idly through the interface and creating small beginner quests that could help the settlement overall.

Blissful moments of peace.

Perhaps the first real ones I'd had since the whole apocalypse thing started. Watching the people I'd come to call my friends and colleagues. There was an oddly surreal vibe to the whole situation. Because right now, we were faced with what we'd been fighting against for so long.

Being completely overrun by the damned monsters. Hell, it was the whole reason the Hakarta and Zarrie had agreed to work together in the first place.

"Hey." Kyle nudged me and held out another drink. This one just water. "No use in dehydrating yourself."

"Wasn't planning on it." I grunted as I took the drink and gulped half of it down in about three seconds flat. "Okay, so I was thirsty."

"You're being awfully quiet."

He was right; I was. "There's not much I can contribute right now. Not unless I get out there and see if I can plot a path using Mana Sense to figure out how the damned creatures are traveling?"

Kyle laughed, and I wished that my abilities were that far along, that I could do something that useful with it.

"Are you sure that's *not* something you can do?" he asked, his mood sobering slightly.

About to shake my head, I realized that I didn't actually know that at all. "I'm really not sure. There's so much to it that I don't understand. Little offshoots that keep developing. It could be possible. I'd have to ask Dequasha." I glanced around trying to find her, but she still wasn't in the room. No one from IRSHA was.

Granted, her abilities didn't work exactly like mine, but they had enough similarities that she was able to help me gain better control over it. Maybe she did know.

"IRSHA are still out fighting the last of the fleeing monsters they could find." Kyle answered my unspoken question.

"But it'll be dark out soon." Worry shot through me, and for a moment I felt ashamed, because I wasn't worried for their sake, but for mine and not being able to figure out some of my abilities on my own without the flower lady.

"They'll be fine. They've been checking in with Dor. If you weren't sitting here daydreaming, you'd have realized that." He ruffled the hair on my head, like he hadn't done for ages, and it took the sting out of his words. Even if they had been partially correct. After all, relaxing and idly creating new settlement quests was exactly what I'd been doing for a while now.

What I wouldn't give for more time to myself than that.

The plight of motherhood, and now the responsibilities of a settlement owner. Brilliant.

Speaking of which, I wanted to sit down with my whole family.

It was late when I got back home, and I was tired, but I wanted to make time for my family. Including Mason.

To my surprise when I walked in, a bundle of child rushed into me, enveloping me in a massive bear hug. "Hey there!" I couldn't help the laugh that escaped me.

"Mum, you'll never believe it. Dad can like, charm animals." Wisp's eyes were big as saucers as she regaled me with her father's surprise talent. "You should see the way Wombie warmed up to him!"

Mason was grinning from ear to ear, like his big kid self. "She's exaggerating. I just played a song the wombat liked."

"Let her exaggerate," I whispered, leaning over the counter to snatch one of the chips out of the bag, suddenly realizing I was famished.

Jackson laughed. "No, don't say that. She'll make up crazy stories if you let her." But that smile was genuine.

My kids were happy.

I couldn't tell anyone what we talked about. We watched Wisp and Dog perform feats of agility. We listened to Mason weave tales of some of the beasts they'd run from on the way up the coast.

And we sat together, in a precious moment of cohesion that I knew couldn't last, and yet I'd fight to preserve.

❖

It was late by the time I climbed the stairs to bed, leaving Mason to sleep in the living room on the couch. I still had stuff to do, like making sure all my points were distributed since I'd leveled somewhere along the way.

With how long it was taking us all to level, it was difficult to remember to check a status screen that just wasn't changing. Even when it did, it ended up being in a heap of notifications that I just pushed to the side.

In fact, I'd almost missed hitting Level 42.

Cocoon

Effect: Wraps your opponent in an earth cocoon for up to 42 seconds. This prevents them from moving, casting, or any combination of this. They will not regenerate Mana or Life while contained in the cocoon.
Mana Cost: 90 Mana

Cocoon was an excellent choice. Better than Ecological Outreach which I was now not as certain about getting as I had been originally. It took so damned long to level with all the extra patrol members and higher Levels sucking up portions of the experience.

At least Cocoon was potentially lifesaving. So I chose it over Ecological Outreach. I wished I could save points for the next Class Level. But apparently you had to distribute them all in each tier and couldn't use the previous tier's points to buy stuff in the new tier you advanced to. This Class System was all so needlessly complicated.

Status Screen			
Name	Kira Kent	Class	Ecological Chain Specialist
Race	Human (Female)	Level	42 (1,894 XP to next Level)
Titles			
Diviner			
Health	530	Stamina	530
Mana	1200	Mana Regeneration	15.2ps*
Attributes			
Strength	35	Agility	30
Constitution	55	Perception	86
Intelligence	124	Willpower	79
Charisma	25	Luck	20
Class Skills			
Shield of Power		Leadership	5
Analyze	5	Mana Sense*	17
Diviner*	2	Mana Purification	2
Blunt Weapons	7	Mana Cloak	6
Combat Skills			
Mana Attunement	2	Water Siphon	2
Earth Barricade	2	Blood Transfer	1

Rock Slide	1	Mana Transfer	2	
Implantation	3	Treesong	2	
Top Soil	2	Mud Slide	1	
Planted in Place	1	Blood Dispersion	1	
Stone's Throw	1	Vine Defense	1	
Mana Stone	1	Cocoon	1	

Mana Sense was my thing. Sure, without it I could do a lot of stuff, but understanding and watching the Mana flow around me, how it worked in its ambient sense, always present, always moving, like a perpetual flow waterfall?

That's what I needed to pursue—just how to know it more intimately, how to understand it and its purpose, and just how my interpretation of it could benefit the people I needed to protect.

What is Mana?

Update: Your understanding of the cycle of Mana is growing. But do you realize just how integral it truly is? Keep going.

Level of Quest: Unnecessary

Reward: Knowledge

Warnings: Curiosity killed lots of cats. Will you be satisfied?

I choked back a lot of spicy words I wanted to throw at the System right then. The Mana Quest made no sense—hell, a lot of everything made no sense anymore. But that was just it, wasn't it? The end of the world wasn't supposed to make sense.

I threw myself onto my bed, dismissing the quest notification in the process.

Sadly, sleep took a lot longer than I wanted.

Chapter Twenty-Nine:
Planning

18 Weeks, 5 Days Post-System Onset

9 a.m.

While we waited on our patrols to set out for the day, I stood with Dequasha, discussing the probability of my being able to track creature's Mana usage from a long distance.

"Theoretically, it is possible to track potential paths of creatures through their Mana output and usage." Dequasha spoke softly, and I could just hear the massive but that was about to come.

"But it's an inefficient use of your time. The amount of time and precision that is required to trace and track using Mana in real time wouldn't be beneficial to what you're attempting to achieve." Her lilting voice was tinged with a patience I'm glad she had, because I sure as hell didn't.

I pinched the bridge of my nose, trying to figure out just how to phrase what I wanted to say. "So. I could trace them, but it wouldn't give us any real advantage because of how real time that tracing would be?"

"Exactly!" Her expression brightened, and I felt like I'd finally understood what she was saying.

While I could potentially trace, track, and predict how a pattern would emerge, the time it took was better used for preventing damage through immediate interpretation of Mana usage. At least, as far as her experience with Mana tracking and sensing went.

The early patrol left at six in the morning, and the second wave wasn't leaving for another hour. I'd volunteered for it and Jackson . . . well, considering his father was coming with us in the same patrol, there was no holding him back.

Which left me with my youngest child currently sulking as she leaned against Wombie, sinking in against his side.

"Wisp, love," I said as gently as possible, turning to give her my attention. "We'll be back before you know it."

She tossed me a glare. All right, then. This wasn't the right approach. Kiddo was definitely growing up. She'd be nine soon.

"Hey. I can't take you. Right now, there's nothing you can really do to help, and I would be far too worried about you. Okay? What you can do is stay here with the rest of your class that you're incidentally late for and do what Jana and Avery ask of you. Okay?" I reached down and gave her a tight hug, which it took several reluctant seconds for her to return.

"It's not fair. Jackson gets to spend time with you *and* Dad."

"Yes." I pondered. "But he could also lose a limb while we're out there. How would you fare if you couldn't flip around like you usually do?"

Her eyes were wide, and I kicked myself. I hadn't wanted to scare her. I'd wanted to out logic her. I was losing my touch.

"Could he really lose a limb?" Wisp asked, her voice small.

I nodded, doing my best to keep a grave expression on my face. "We all could. Some of us already have. But don't worry, the Shop can fix pretty much everything if you've got Credits." There, that should help.

She bobbed her head up and down for a couple of seconds as if taking that all in. "I'll stay here for now. But when I do get my Class and abilities, you have to take me with you too."

"Now that? That I can do. It's a deal." I held out my pinkie for her so she knew just how serious a promise it was.

Linking her tiny finger with my own, we shook on it. "Can't go back on that, Mum. You know it. I know it. The universe knows it now."

And then she enveloped me in the tightest hug I'd had from her in quite a while.

"Be careful," she whispered. "I need my mum."

Tears pricked at the corners of my eyes, but I blinked them back. "Of course! Just like I need my Wisp!" And I returned the hug before backing away lest she see me about to lose it myself.

Jackson stood with his dad and his uncle at the prepping area. Since we'd moved the defenses when we expanded, it gave us a lot more room to gather together before heading out, and this morning, we had several patrols going out at once.

Days off? Forget about that. Until we got this under control, there'd be none of that.

Maybe the apocalypse was trying to kill us by wearing us down until we all collapsed so that the mutations could overrun us. Solid plan with the way things were going, it wouldn't take much longer. It didn't seem to realize the mind needed healing too.

It was odd not seeing Tasha gathering with us. Even if she went off with one of the other groups, I saw her daily. All the time. Now she was just gone. Did it make me heartless that I hadn't had a good cry about it yet? Or was that part of me just hardened now?

"I miss her too," Evelyn said quietly, suddenly standing right next to me when I needed a shoulder to lean on. Pity it had to be figuratively since she was somewhat shorter than me. Still though.

"Impeccable timing," I said, flashing her a grin. "Thanks."

No one else seemed affected, except maybe Gemma. But then Gemma took every single death as a personal affront. One more notch she had to pay the System back for.

"You with me?" I asked Evelyn, keeping my voice low.

She scoffed. "Of course. Hirish and I have an understanding. Anything happens to you on his watch when I'm not there and I'll take it out on him."

I laughed, but her expression remained serious. Okay, then. "Good to know you've got my back."

"Naturally. And your kids. And anyone who's become part of our De Facto little family. Even your ex." She grinned at me.

I fingered the top of my Warhammer, sitting nicely there in its little loop around my waist. I'd realized by now that jumping into the fray wasn't my best option, best use of my powers, or my strength.

Being able to beat something to a bloody pulp if required was certainly a bonus, but no more points were going into Strength when I had so much more I could do with Intelligence and Willpower.

The decision felt like a turning point for me, a realization I should have had weeks ago. It wasn't the first time I wished the System was like a game and I could reset the attribute points I'd already spent without suffering consequences other than Credit cost. Still, we live, and we learn.

"You went quiet." Evelyn prodded my arm with a finger.

"I had thoughts."

"Ooo, secret stuff?"

I laughed. "No, just stupid, Class-defining things."

"Ah."

Hirish walked over to us, his eyes focused beyond him, obviously on a screen he'd pulled up from the system.

"Kira, Evelyn, Marie, Mason, Kyle, Jackson, Drake, Gemma, Molly, Sange, Ray . . . I'm wanting to keep you guys together for the time being. We have to work on developing a cohesive attack unit. We'll add two each of the Zarrie, Hakarta—me being one of them—and IRSHA. I need to go organize two other groups while Piola does the others. We'll be leaving at 10:00 a.m. and pushing down past the Sanctuary."

Checking my inventory, I made sure I had food for myself and others, just in case anyone forgot in their excitement to get going. Which my son likely had, and I didn't want to nag him while he was so excited to head out with his parents for the first time.

My only hope was that I didn't screw up because I was too concerned for him. At least this way his dad would be there to look out for him too, even if it felt completely surreal for us both to be here now.

❖

Past Daisy Hill, right through to Cornelia Forest Refuge, out near Shailer Park. Hell, we'd never come out this far. Loganholme had a small gathering of people that didn't qualify as a System settlement, if what I remembered was correct. It wasn't big enough for a Shop. The area around it was overrun with creatures, too.

The canopy was coming back fresh as what passed for winter here finally gave way to spring. Not that the leaves had ever fallen off. You have to understand that winter in Brissy isn't exactly cold by comparison to other places in the world, and spring temperatures last for about three weeks before they dive back into heat wave.

Well, maybe the latter was an exaggeration, but it was close.

My favorite part of Brisbane was the heat. It was rarely cold. And freezing weather and I were not friends. Although since the apocalypse, I had to admit I'd barely stood still enough for the cold to affect me.

The last patrol cleared past the Daisy Hill Dungeon and farther down than I expected, and the empty nest areas just left a cold chill in my stomach. Well, relatively empty. There were small monsters that popped up, things that would have been a problem months ago. Mutated ants, a giant rat or two. Level 1 to 5s. Nothing that was worth mentioning normally, except they all looked more nervous, if you could call giant mutated monsters nervous.

We were pushing out farther than usual, which meant potential new creatures and more danger. Our group was running toward the monsters that were chasing others out of the nests we'd been clearing.

Mason moved up to walk with me while we got out of the vehicles and moved onto the paths. There was no way to fight from the cars when we were amidst so much brush and trees. No good way at least, not without missing more shots than we hit.

"You're always up front," he stated after several steps.

My eyes focused on the Mana flows around us to give warning should we need it, I answered somewhat absentmindedly. "Yep. Early warning system."

"Is that why you have implants?"

"Partially. That or go blind." He should have asked me this back at the settlement. I didn't really have the time or patience to go over the intricacies of my Skills while on the lookout for new and dangerous creatures that were likely several Levels higher than we were used to. But then he had been catching up with and spoiling the kids. And I was grateful for that.

He didn't say anything for several steps. "Sort of like what you do for work then? Or . . . did, I guess?"

I smiled. He'd always found my penchant for plants and the earth bewildering, my ability to just go out and get dirty, but he'd always supported it. "Yeah. Except with Mana and not the earth now—or not *just* the earth."

"That's kind of cool," he said, and I could hear the slight awe in his voice.

For all most people knew, Mana was simply what powered our spells and abilities. They didn't realize just how much more Mana had to do with everything that had happened to us.

Frankly, this whole mess was Mana's fault. If it wasn't for the complete and utter saturation of it, we never would have evolved, though I use that term loosely, into a Dungeon World.

"Thanks." It was the only response I had for him. This took concentration, the following of Mana waves to where they might congregate with others, which would mean a gathering of creatures we had to watch out for. I'd become so accustomed to seeing the world through this strange lens of blue that anything else didn't seem to matter anymore.

I paused, placing a hand briefly on Hirish's forearm, and he motioned for the others to stop.

"Up ahead, maybe twenty or so meters, behind that fallen trunk. Several . . . I don't know what they are, but we haven't seen them before." I kept my words soft, trying not to alert anyone or the things beyond us. The last thing we needed was to lose the element of surprise especially given the power radiating off those creatures. "Six of them, I think. Higher Level than us."

Hirish motioned for everyone to fan out into formation, to get ready to take on whatever the creatures before us were, and the tingle of anticipation that raced up my spine took me by surprise. Perhaps I was getting a little too bloodthirsty.

The flow of blue lines around them were deep and dark, sparked occasionally with a bright counterpoint running through them. It didn't feel like some of the other tainted Mana I'd come across, like with Big Red, but it did have a sense of power about it, way in excess of what any of us could produce. Even taking the Hakarta and Zarrie into consideration.

Gemma vanished, activating her stealth mode as she scouted out our opponents. We weren't that far from them that I didn't think they could have told we were there. So that meant they were also waiting for us to make a move perhaps?

Maybe two minutes later, Gemma reappeared, her face so pale her freckles stood out more than usual. That couldn't be good.

"They're like . . . frilled neck lizards." She shook her head like that wasn't quite right. "No. Like massive ones, but sort of resembling that one dinosaur in Jurassic Park that spat at that guy."

I gulped reflexively. Bringing dinosaur comparisons into it only heightened my levels of anticipation.

"They're about three meters long, and their heads hit maybe one and a half meters high. There are six of them, three on sunning rocks where there's a break in the canopy, and the others appear to be standing guard." She finally got it all out, and relief crossed her face. "I hate lizards."

I got the distinct feeling that she just wanted to be able to slink back behind all of us and let us do the fighting. How the fuck were we going to manage six of those creatures at once? They were known for running away on their hind legs, which was decidedly cute and comical when they were all of thirty centimeters long.

What if they weren't predatory? "Is there a chance they don't want to attack? I mean, they're not known for being the most ferocious predators around."

Kyle raised an eyebrow at me. "Seriously? The System mutates them in size, but doesn't give them any drive to kill?"

I spoke somewhat defensively. "Mumma Wombutt doesn't want to eat us."

"True," he murmured. "But I'd think she's more the exception than the rule."

"We have two Rangers, and depending on their skills, we can probably freeze trap a couple with diminishing returns, or I can root or Cocoon them, while Marie and Evelyn kite a couple? Depending on the creatures' attacks, of course."

I could hope that the frill around their necks was just to scare off potential attackers like the original, right? They had two defenses in the wild. Their frill, and if that failed to scare off their potential attacker, they just hightailed it out of there.

I got the distinct feeling that wasn't going to happen with our new mutated friends.

"Oh." Gemma piped back up. "Level 52 . . . I analyzed one."

Shit. The Levels really were getting higher. Sheer firepower should be enough to take them down, and we did have the Hakarta and Zarrie who were technically in their 50s if the way I understood Advanced Classes was correct, but still. Six of them. Would the kiting plan even have a chance of working with those Levels? Wouldn't resistances be higher? That's how everything worked in a game.

Everything would be so much easier if this was just a game.

Chapter Thirty:
Lizard Fodder

Gemma's description did not prepare me for the reality when we finally rounded the bend. The creatures sat on large rocks in the middle of the forest, preening up at the sun shining down on them. Their frills were flat, and for a moment, I thought maybe they weren't hostile. Perhaps they hadn't seen us.

I scanned the one in front briefly, to get a general idea of the group.

Chlamydosaurus Kingly

Level 52

HP:

I frowned. The System had almost taken its Latin name exactly. Not quite, but still . . . maybe it wasn't above being lazy.

From one moment to the next, multiple things happened.

First up, Molly moved forward until she was within spitting distance and smashed her shield into the ground, activating one of her Taunt barriers. One of these days, I'd figure out all the shit she could do with that shield. Secondly, right on the tail of Molly's challenge, the closest frilly hissed and bared its fangs, letting all semblance of friendliness vanish.

And thirdly, perhaps a little prematurely, Marie loosed an arrow, encasing one of the topmost frillies in ice.

The one I'd scanned let out a wail that reverberated through to my spine, freezing me in place for just a second. It opened its mouth and extended the frills around its neck. At this size, the appearance was daunting, even to me, a human with weapons at my disposal.

If I'd been any less intelligent a creature, I probably would have turned tail and ran. As it was, I don't think any of us humans were too bright at that moment. Seconds later, the initial creature leapt at Molly's shield, clashing into it with a resounding thud of power as the rest of us hurried to catch up to our tank's lead.

By that time, Evelyn and Marie had two of them cased in ice, and one each that they were kiting. Marie was being extra careful ever since her run-in with the Tetchrihorn that trampled her, always erring on the side of caution.

I managed to shoot out Planted in Place in time to secure the fifth one just outside of its attack radius. Couldn't afford to let him break the root though considering he'd jump right inside of Molly's personal space if he broke free before I renewed the spell.

Fine lines everywhere here.

Lizards weren't the most dependent on water, and Water Siphon was great for whichever one we attacked, diminishing its natural defenses. Any damage inflicted on the creatures I rooted to the ground could break that root since the damage also reflected off the vines holding them in place.

Backing up past the casters, I kept an overview of everyone. It would be much easier if I was on higher ground. An idea occurred to me about perhaps using Mumma Wombutt to help me keep an eye on the battlefield and castings happening. That could work, much better than trying to remain mounted while she fought, even if that was a super badass idea.

I flung Implantation at our main target, while I kept an eye out for any other Mana disturbances. These creatures didn't appear to be harried, or worried. They definitely didn't seem to be fleeing anything.

I looked for Jackson, knowing I needed to keep the whole battlefield in view, I renewed my root and finally tracked him down. He stood next to Ray, aiming his offensive spells directly at Molly's target like any good fighter would. Bright light shot out of his hands, disrupting the dark Mana that surrounded our rather large enemy, giving me more ideas. I'd need to study his Skill tree in more detail than I had.

There weren't too many spells that could disrupt Mana flow. Not that his did for long, but something was always better than nothing when it came to control over Mana.

Evelyn and Marie continued to kite their targets, firing off ice traps at the feet of the other two lying in wait for when their current prisons broke. I made sure that all three of those who weren't imprisoned were tapped with Mana Stone. Three mobs made the Mana regeneration so much stronger, yet I still had to keep an eye on my own Mana levels.

These variations of the frilly lizard didn't turn tail and run away on their hind legs. Nope, they doubled down and brandished the frill around their necks like a rebounding trampoline. The first time liquid spurted out of it, I heard Molly curse. This wasn't something I could track with Mana. I think it was just a part of the way the mechanism that opened their frilly beards worked.

Acid droplets rained down around them in a small radius, so that anyone too close to them got burned by it. Nothing like those Nether Bottles that killed Tasha, though. A quick heal from Kyle or Sange and we were back in the game. The next time, Molly was ready for the attack, pushing up her shield, expanding it so that no one got hit.

Since the majority of the melee personnel fought around the side and behind of the creature, they weren't in danger of being hit by the acid shower, since that only opened out to the front.

These creatures weren't nearly as dangerous as I'd been expecting. Sure, they were a pain in the butt and the one I had locked down with a root never let his gaze waver from me as he tracked me with his eyes. I had no doubt that if my Planted in Place decided to break, he was coming straight for me, acid frilly and all.

But they didn't seem to be running in fear like I'd been led to believe.

Their attack range was short enough that Marie and Evelyn didn't have to worry about it while they kited, and Hirish and the other Hakarta could easily shoot down the one Molly tanked. The acid attack hurt, but Sange and Kyle had the actual damage under control.

It didn't add up. The first one went down, and Molly broke the ice trap of one of the others waiting in the wings and just let the two bow wielders continue kiting the ones they had.

I couldn't help the mental refrain that kept saying that this wasn't right.

These couldn't be the interlopers. We just hadn't been out this far to clear out this nest. They're just what we expected to see, for the kind of Levels in this region. I wish we had fought them previously; these guys weren't that difficult to kill.

I expanded my Mana Sense scan, pushing to try and find any sort of unsettling Mana aura. That's when I got a flash of why things felt wrong. It wasn't too far away, maybe half a click or so, and slowly creeping in on us.

A group of I had no idea what, but the power leaking through to me was maybe a hundred and fifty percent of what these guys exuded. Substantially stronger. They were closing in on us too. Subtly, slowly . . . maybe they'd been doing it the whole time.

Eyeing what we were fighting and where we were in the process of finishing them off, I didn't think we were going to make it before the next attackers made it to us.

"Conserve Mana—we have another wave incoming in about in a minute or two." I tried not to phrase it like a question; after all, this was my ability, not anyone else's. But I couldn't pinpoint exactly what time these creatures would arrive only generally. All I could do was warn our group that they were coming.

❖

The next bunch arrived when we were working our way through the second-last lizard. Upon seeing the new enemy, the frilly I had been holding down squealed and keened like it needed to get away, and I had to say that I felt that right through to my bones. The panic in its eyes gave me pause, but we didn't have any other choice because this migration of mutations and other creatures was happening all around us.

I'd hate to encounter what was forcing its hand.

At least it wasn't some fresh mutation from hell, but instead appeared to be some sort of alien creatures that had bubbled up out of the earth this time. Tar hung from its jowls, and each of the three newcomer creatures stood about twelve feet tall, not quite as high as our Koalzillas, yet far stockier and sturdier.

The tar dripped down from its chin, plopping to sizzle on the ground and remind me that just because it looked like tar and dripped like tar, didn't mean it *was* tar. Not to mention the smell, the sheer overwhelming scent of hot, fresh, bitumen.

Escridium Madeo

Level 54

All righty, then.

These guys . . . these ones were the danger we'd been expecting. One of them lumbered in, ignored every single weapon turned its way, and swiped directly at the frilly in my root. The swing of his tar hand took the lizard's health down by one-third. Something it took us like thirty seconds to do. Meanwhile, the Rangers had to double ice trap one of the three to get it to hold.

I scrambled to cast Cocoon on it but waited. It didn't even look at us yet, maybe the frilly could do some of the damage for us before it turned its attention our way.

The two creatures scrambled together, with the Escridium far outweighing the frilly. The fight ended faster than I'd have thought, though it wasn't too surprising given how quickly the tar monster did damage.

I finally cast Cocoon on one of the others, cringing at the sheer amount of Mana the bloody thing cost.

The earth beneath them rumbled, shooting up sheets of dirt that wrapped and enveloped the creature, just like a cocoon, allowing us to focus on finishing off the final frilly we'd had waiting in the wings. In the meantime, the Escridium who'd killed the last frilly was down about fifteen percent health. Molly dug her shield in, her stance changing to completely defensive as she activated one of her taunts.

"Behind me!" she called, even as we moved.

Always better to have said it unnecessarily than to have people caught unawares.

"I'll take over the ice-trapped one," I said. That way it'd free up more damage. I got the distinct feeling that we wanted the Escridium fights to be as short as possible. Glancing at the timer on the first Cocoon, I did some rough calculations in my head.

If I kept them sealed away, it was going to be super costly. I threw a Mana Transfer for myself, and Mana Stone onto the two creatures still in play as I cast Cocoon to take over the final Escridium just as the ice traps failed.

I had to keep them locked down. There was no way any of us could afford to be hit by the attack it used on the frilly. I didn't think we'd survive it. Higher Levels than we were used to, and not mutations of creatures we'd fought before. Were these some of the equalizing creatures the System brought in, like Zyrilian mentioned previously?

Even with the first attacks on the creature, I realized that my Mana probably wasn't going to hold out long enough, but I'd be damned if I wasn't going to try. This creature hit hard and fast, even to the point of driving Molly back with each blow on her shield.

Growing visibly frustrated, it lashed out with tar bullets—the only name I could give to them—as I rapidly dashed to avoid being hit. Ranged area-of-effect attacks and brutal close combat were the worst.

And that's when I realized that I wasn't the only thing with the power to drain Mana pools. Suddenly I had enough for two more refreshes and that was it. "About to be out of Mana."

I pushed the panicked laughing I felt bubbling inside down. There were mere seconds left on one of the Cocoons, so I made a split-second decision.

"Evelyn, Marie, kite the far one as soon as it breaks." Maybe, just maybe I could buy us enough time by keeping one of them under wraps.

The Escridium we fought was low on health, but I was about to be useless in keeping things at bay. One Cocoon cast down, and I noticed the beast Molly fought gathering Mana again, fearing for the worst.

But she lashed out at it, interrupting the Mana flow, and I sighed in relief. Still, these Escridium were hardy, and extremely accurate with their tar bullets. It shot Kyle through the shoulder, hit Gemma in the thigh.

It was a testament to both of them that they simply grunted in pain and waited for the healing to kick in. What did that say about us now?

Mana Stone caused my Mana to tick up way too slowly, and there was no way I'd get enough replenished before I needed to recast. All I could do to help was dive in with my hammer.

Evelyn and Marie had to kite in a way I'd never seen before, tagging in and out, barely able to remain out of range of the tar bullets. Occasionally I watched one of them take a hit, just to keep the creature focused on them.

They used the trees and brush covering all around us to lure the creature to them but used the obstacles as ways to avoid being shot. The tar bullets still ripped into the trunks, but often got wedged halfway through. Better than accidentally puncturing a heart. I wasn't sure even the system could recover from that.

Either Sange or Kyle replenished their health with a heal, and it just repeated from there.

I swung my Warhammer, using that good old force to dig in with it. Hefting it back out of the tar body was difficult, and it strained my muscles, fueling the anger I felt. There was a glimpse of the irrationality I'd had the first time I used the weapon, and I balked, baking up for it to wear off before diving in again.

Another cast of Cocoon and I knew there was no way this first one would go down before the second one broke free. "Second incoming, Molly."

She nodded, but that was the only sign that she'd heard me until she widened her stance to take them both.

None of us expected the second creature to catapult forward and slam into her shield in a coordinated attack with the first. Even the kited one slowed down and looked over, its expression unreadable. But as another flame arrow *thunk*ed into its eye, melting a portion of the socket, it reared up and began chasing the Ranger again.

Molly, on the other hand, got pushed back several feet, unheard of for her. All she did was grunt and pulled upon extending her protective field to help us all recover from the sudden barrage of tar bullets.

But not before one caught Gemma through the gut. She rolled out, crashing to her knees, coughing up blood. I dashed to her side automatically but had no idea what to do.

Kyle's heal hit her the same time I arrived, and between one second and the next, Gemma was fine. I needed to get my worrying sorted out, because wounds that would be fatal under normal circumstances, just weren't here if you had a half-competent healer.

And let's face it. We had two phenomenal healers.

Except I realized right then that there was nothing they could do when it appeared that the two creatures we were fighting fed off each other. The first that had almost been dead, was now back to ten percent health. Working together appeared to bolster their regeneration.

"Keep kiting. Don't let it get close," I yelled, and I could see Hirish had noticed what I had.

He spoke in that booming voice, modulated just right. "When I give the signal, shield scatter and gather behind Molly's shield."

I had no idea what the Hakarta was going to do, but if that's what he wanted, I was all for it.

"Push out now, Molly!"

And our tank wordlessly extended her shield, causing the creatures to bounce back off it. We didn't use that often because it was better to keep them within melee range.

"Scatter!"

And we did. We had to before the temporary stun wore off and the Escridium bounded back. All of us, except our kiters, hunkered down behind Molly's protective shielding as Hirish lobbed something overhead, and ducked down too.

A split second later, a massive explosion shook the area around us.

Chunks of earth flew up, trees fell over, and what I think was the remnants of an Escridium arm landed right next to me.

Moments later when the dust cleared, Hirish grunted. "I dislike chaos grenades. But sometimes they have purpose."

One of the creatures was dead, and the second one badly damaged. As long as we kept them separated, this might not be impossible. I definitely didn't dislike those grenades, unless . . .

Glancing at Hirish, I dared to ask, "Why do you hate them?"

He shrugged. "They are messy, only work with certain elements, and are known to often malfunction. Plus, they're expensive."

Focusing my attention on my combat ability I nodded. Time to kill these tar buggers so I could go home and scrub the smell of bitumen out of my skin.

Chapter Thirty-One:

Repeat

22 Weeks Post-System Onset

The Escridium Madeos weren't the only non-mutated monsters that emerged to give our native ones a run for their money. We spent the next few weeks barely able to keep our shit together.

The Shop ate every Credit we earned as we bought bigger, nastier weapons and defenses. The Hakarta leaned into high-tech improvements, including floating gun drones; the Zarrie seemed more interested in consumables that bumped up damage, and IRSHA . . . IRSHA went and did whatever each individual chose. We humans? We watched and learnt and upgraded too.

Me? I invested in a fucking pulse rifle.

Was it something my Class could specialize in? No, but with my ocular implants, I could buy a scope that synchronized with my own tech and allowed me to fire with precision. Standing in the back like I had to these days meant I could at least contribute some damage while maintaining my debuffs, buffs, and view of the battlefield—and all it cost me were some— okay loads of—Credits.

Each day bled into the next. Days off were a pipe dream. Falling into bed at night, waking up early and going out again. Repetitive, and hard on the body despite the System renewing us every moment of every day.

Perhaps it really was more of a mental thing, too. It'd take someone insane to be able to do this, day in and day out, without it wearing on them. I'm not sure I'd ever want to meet the kind of raging asshole who *could* do it.

I'm not sure I could stop myself becoming one if this was our lives now.

The one day we'd encountered the Escridium had been the farthest we'd been able to push out. Ever since then, the monsters were coming for us. To us. Butting right up to the domains of our mutated native fauna. The only small mercy that I could see was that at least it wasn't raining.

Under the guidance of the Hakarta, we tore down buildings, used Architects and Engineers and Techno Mages like my son to put up temporary redoubts, killing zones, and traps to slow down the monsters.

Channel our incoming aggressors a little by changing the terrain. It worked—sort of. Except for the big ones who just tore a hole through whatever we added.

However, now summer was approaching.

Five months into this and we'd gone from autumn verging on cold winter—cold for us anyway—to spring turning into our usual boiling-hot summer. Jackets were a thing no one wanted to wear, but we had to—all the more armor, all the more protection. Could we upgrade the items in the Shop? Sure, we could. But over the last few weeks we'd been spending every Credit we earned on items to increase our chances of survival. Or else, we'd traded every item we could for better potential damage.

Soon though, we'd need to make sure we were protected enough and not sweating ourselves to death. Bit of a Catch-22 right there.

As the summer months approached, so too did the possibility of mutated mosquitoes.

I was not looking forward to that. I'd better be able to buy something with a repellant built in.

Three and a half weeks of fighting, daily. I no longer worried about Jackson heading out there. He was either with me or he wasn't, but either way, he was as safe as he was going to get.

He'd almost hit Level 40. Everything after 40 felt like a complete and utter slog. Each damn tier increased the amount needed by a chunk, adding another huge burden on us.

Distributing the experience over the sheer amount of people we sent out in patrols, along with low-leveled Advanced Classes like we had from the Pirra Clan and the Zarrie, meant that everything trickling through to us was meager—even including the apparent bonus we were supposed to get from surviving on our inhospitable continent.

No surprise, with all the fighting, the litany of the dead grew. Someone in the shopping center had started a mural, a simple listing of those we'd lost. It started small and included the names of Barry and Julia.

I had a sneaking suspicion it was Leena's doing—our little resident Street Smartist. The names grew every time I walked pass it, and I had to each time I wanted a cup of kipatchya.

If there was one thing that could kill my addiction, it was that damn mural. There were too many people on there who I'd known.

The only plus to the whole thing was the people who'd still been out there holed up, fleeing toward our center, toward the hope of safety. Even with all the deaths, our population still grew. That was a dark-tinged silver lining right there.

And so it was that I stood there, sipping my favorite drink as I stared up at the names above me, seeing and not seeing them at the same time. Where was Leena going to paint the rest once we ran out of room on this section?

What were we even doing? Fighting tooth and nail, until our brains were numb, only to do it all over again? Should we just give in and let the System be right about our continent?

"You look tired."

Mason wasn't trying to start anything or be a dick, but right then all I wanted to do was snap "no shit, Sherlock" right at him. Instead, I took a breath and flashed him a wry grin—at least that's what I think it was. From his reaction, it could also have been closer to a grimace.

"Tired. Exhausted. Wondering if it'll ever end?" That wasn't combative, right? He didn't deserve my moods. He'd been nothing but helpful and supportive of our entire initiative at Garbo since arriving. Not to mention being a godsend with the kids so I didn't feel quite as guilty all the time for everything I had to do.

Not quite, anyway.

I mean, being a mum already comes with a large dose of guilt about every damn thing.

"I'd tell you to get some rest. But it doesn't appear like you can do that around here." He bit his bottom lip, like he was deep in thought about whatever was bugging him. I knew he'd tell me eventually, but I really wished that time could be now. I could use a distraction.

"Did you not think it would be like this?" I asked, my voice soft because to be honest, this wasn't how I'd envisioned an apocalypse either.

He shook his head. "No. I did not. I thought coming up here would show us how we could better manage the shitshow we have down the coast."

"And it's not helping?" I didn't have a heap of answers for him. It almost made me feel bad.

Mason chuckled dryly and looked around the center with its bustling people and the overhanging cloud of doom. It felt like it was just us two there right now. Jackson was with the tech group and Wisp was helping with the wombats.

"It's not *not* helping. You've all got your shit together; it's just that it doesn't seem to matter. All of this Mana mutation, alien monster crap? It's still coming no matter what you do. Hard and fast, and not leaving much room to breathe." He sighed before continuing. "Seems to be pretty much the same everywhere. At least here."

I nodded slowly. "Yeah. Carindale isn't any better off, either. I know IRSHA is having difficulties in the few other settlements in Brisbane that they took over. Right now, no one has numbers to spare for each other. It's all pretty much fend for yourselves and hope you survive."

And suddenly, I just didn't like this roll over and let this whole thing happen attitude. Because that's what it was, wasn't it? Right here, right now, with all these people who'd died staring down at me, I was giving up—I was resigning myself to how things were and would always be.

No. Just no!

Straightening my back, I rolled my shoulders and shot a message through the admin system to Hirish and Mon'swkinon. This could all be damned. There was no way I was letting this happen anymore. We had to be more proactive. Figure out bigger and better ways to address all of these invasions and attacks. We had to blow shit up with whatever means necessary.

"Fuck this," I said, skulling down the rest of my drink as I turned around. "We're in a rut. And we're not staying in one. You coming?"

Mason didn't say anything as he followed me past Raybucks, where I popped my empty cup down, and toward the center entrance.

There were kids all through the center, playing hide and seek, red rover, and a slew of other games. That was something I'd fight to protect, this haven for them, this way of living that they all should still get to experience.

Fighting like we were now wasn't getting us anywhere. All it did was delay the inevitable, letting it draw us inextricably closer to being devoured by the apocalypse just the way the System had foretold.

One inch at a time. One dead Aussie a day. Dead anyway. Only a bit slower than expected.

And damn it if I wasn't going down like that.

"What're you thinking?" Mason ventured the question almost like he didn't actually want the answer.

I grinned at him as we pushed out of the Center into the carpark. "I'm thinking that we haven't been approaching this correctly—and that maybe, just maybe we're going about this all wrong."

Hirish stood, his arms crossed, somehow always faster than me at getting to where I wanted to be. It was warm enough outside that I thought it would be better to gather here instead of inside. Not to mention it didn't get dark until much later these days.

Motioning him toward me, I dragged Hirish over to where our defensive gate initially stood. Now we just had the gate tower there, able to still keep a watch around the center and residential area. Mumma saw me and trotted over, offering her side for my leaning pleasure. Fluffy fur, warmth. Damn it if I didn't just love this wombat.

Mon'swkinon arrived several minutes later, and I could no longer remember which of his limbs had been so badly damaged in the Carindale attack that he'd needed to replace or enhance it. Sometimes the Shop's sheer scope scared me. Kyle and Mike arrived shortly thereafter.

"What's the deal?" The Hakarta seemed a little impatient. Maybe I'd interrupted his dinner or something. Perhaps he was just tired.

I raised an eyebrow and patted the ground next to me. Hirish scowled.

"Why are we just sending out patrols and fighting to clear nests and fight off any of the newer monsters that have pushed their way forward?"

"To keep the surrounding areas cleared." Hirish sounded utterly confused.

"Yes, but . . . we're not thinking ahead. We've just been plowing on, doing the same thing we do every day without truly strategizing, and that's not going to cut it anymore. We're just waiting to be killed." I watched Hirish, because I knew him and the Hakarta well enough to know that if it came to that, the Pirra Clan were out of here. Their obligation was mainly to the Crafting Cartel, and the moment it looked like their investments were no longer monetarily worth it, these allies we made, these aliens I sort of considered our friends. Well, they'd hightail it out of here on the next possible portal.

"How do you mean thinking ahead, then?" Hirish said. In his defense, no one expected the Australian native survival rate.

This sort of Mana saturation was apparently a rare occurrence and our continent had been given a mostly zero chance of survival. I got that, but that also meant the System counted us out before counting on us, and in a way, we could use that to our advantage.

"We've been fighting the problem from a perspective of survival. Only survival. We haven't been looking to expand. All along all we've wanted was to gather survivors and make a defensible town. But what if we look beyond that?"

"How do you mean?" Hirish crossed his arms and eyed me critically.

"We've been relieved that the creatures sometimes take a few of their numbers out for us when they clash, right? Like they kill off a few of each other's groups and we swoop in and down the rest, making it far easier on us." I didn't wait for an answer, because I knew that's how it was. "Like when we fought the first Escridium bunch."

"Yes, we've been lucky enough to have that happen several times now." Kyle frowned. "Come on, Kira, spit it out."

Making sure I had their attention, I tried to figure out exactly what to say before I said it. "What if we do that deliberately?"

"What do you mean?" Mon'swkinon cocked his head to one side. "If we let them fight each other on purpose?"

I probably should have talked this over with Ginali first to make sure what I wanted to do was even a possibility. But in for a penny . . .

"Instead of just using bombs to throw in and do as much damage as possible, or create a smoke cloud, or the plethora of different types that exist so we can finish them off—couldn't we use a type of bomb or explosive that draws the beasts to each other? That's got to be a scent thing, right?

"I mean, they're automatically attracted to each other if they're close enough. Why don't we just enhance that and make it happen? So instead of a stink bomb, couldn't we create a luring scent bomb?"

Perhaps I was too tired to get the words out in the way I needed to bring my point across. I tried it again. "Lure them into fighting each other instead of randomly being happy when they stumble into it themselves. Plan to use them against each other. We've been using more explosives these days anyway, but why not deliberately sic 'em on each other? Basically, choose our own battles."

I watched the Hakarta's expression closely, needing to know if he thought the idea stupid or brilliant, or if maybe he'd already thought of it but hadn't suggested it due to potential backfiring reasons.

"That could get very dangerous. Deliberately baiting monsters toward each other . . ." But I could see that spark in his eye. He liked the idea. No, he didn't just like it—it was giving him other ideas as well.

"You want them to basically have a creature battle to the death before we come along and destroy the leftovers?" Mon'swkinon leveled one of those stony grins in my direction.

Kyle practically vibrated on the spot. "Wait. That's kind of like a Monster Thunderdome! Like that's what you mean, right? Herd them all into one spot by luring them there with the scents of other monsters, right?"

He wasn't wrong, but I hadn't really thought of it that way until he mentioned it. "I guess, yeah."

"Best. Twin. Ever," Kyle said, grabbed my face, and kissed my cheek.

"We have to set up the perfect places for them to rumble in. Not that we can change the terrain like in a battle mode, but this could be so much fun."

Mason laughed. His eyes also lit up as he jumped on Kyle's bandwagon. "This could be epic, like those shows we watched when we were kids, right? Let the monsters duke it out."

Bewilderment spread over Hirish's face. "But the idea is that all of the creatures will clash with each other after they have been baited into the designated area, correct?"

Kyle cleared his throat. "Yes. Yes, that's correct." He even managed to look a little bit sheepish, if only for a few seconds before he and Mason began laughing again.

The grin that spread over my face felt a little unhinged, but that was okay. I did some of my best work when I was overtired and not quite with it. "Now all we have to do is talk to the tech team and maybe the crafters and see what ingredients we need to even do this sort of thing."

I'd had the idea; now we just needed to figure out how to execute it. This was the world of the System now, after all—there were probably twenty ways to do what I wanted done.

Garden City had far less foot traffic these days. Even with the excess people we were still bringing in and adding to the population, we had enough empty-shop converted apartments in the center that it didn't seem to post a problem.

Since the mass exodus when we bought housing, however, there was more room for the tech department to expand into, and damn did they make use of it. They'd combined several of the shops together where they'd initially set up, and we had about twenty-five or so people working under Chris and Sarah.

And so, it was I found myself with my friends talking about creating lures for monsters in order to create Monster Thunderdome.

"I mean, we've been making explosives for several of the different Classes that use them already." Chris still seemed somewhat confused by what I was asking, and I couldn't blame her.

Sarah, on the other hand, was practically bouncing off the walls. We'd established pretty early on that taking either or both of our tech engineers with us into battle on too regular a basis put their production behind. Making new things would help them level their skills up. They were still in their mid-thirties, and I got the feeling Sarah was competitive.

"We want to engineer a trap explosive—or if not an explosive, something that produces wafts of the scents of other creatures so that the targets think their territory is being invaded. That way, the target will follow the scent toward where the other creatures will also have been lured. Then the mutations, creatures can duke it out. Is that correct?"

Her eyes looked at me, but somehow through me at the same time, and I got the distinct feeling that she was already devising something or other in her interface. "Got it spot on."

Sarah's bubbliness took a back seat to her business manner, but her deep red hair and grin gave her this sort of gleeful air that I couldn't help but get infected with. It was difficult to stand still while I waited for her to continue. Rin worked quietly next to the redhead, tinkering with something while her expression remained serious.

Rin then turned to Sarah and shook her head, looking at me apologetically. "We can't get this to happen overnight. It's not going to be immediate."

I felt a little deflated, but Sarah hurried to reassure me. "Rin can be a little negative. She just means it will take a few days at least. And you're going to have to obtain the scent glands of a variety of creatures so we can use them to create accurate bait.

"If you've got them in Inventory, bring them to me. The more different types, the better. That way, we can engineer and build these, and they technically should do exactly what you're asking. Especially if that scent is smeared all over an area another species is trying to mark as its own."

She frowned for a moment, as if she was calculating something in her head to double check it and then glanced at Rin, who nodded.

"Yes. That's it. All the scent glands. The sooner the better." She smiled up at Chris, who returned the eagerness.

"Truth be told, we've been a little bored. The Shop has almost everything anyone could want, and just recreating what it has so we can all save some cash gets a bit tedious." Chris reached up to twirl a strand of her short blond hair. She seemed to do this when thinking. "Give us about two days once we get the scent glands and we should have everything figured out. But if we want to keep this up, scent glands will need to be delivered regularly."

I was already diving into my inventory since I knew I'd kept several things to the side from the Shop to talk with Ginali about. When I hit Level 40, my inventory jumped to 169 slots, which was plenty and quite difficult to fill up. So much I sort of forgot about things sometimes. It was a lot to go through. Pulling out a Koalzilla scent gland, a Caneglobulous, and a Tetchrihorn, I handed them over. "That'll get a start, right?"

Sarah's eyes just glowed with excitement. "This is going to be so much fun!"

I returned the smile. Playing with scent glands might not be *my* idea of fun, but the potential result from doing was exciting. I wasn't about to get down on what made someone else's day.

Mana flared to life around Sarah as she examined what I'd handed her, frizzing around her edges with almost as much energy as she exuded naturally. Kyle and Mason handed over what they had with them to Rin and Chris, but for the most part, we usually sold everything we got. Scent glands had never been high up on the need or want list for anything else.

"It's enough to get a good head start, Kira."

I started a little and noticed that Chris was focused on me. Teach me to get lost in my thoughts. "Thanks. Glad I hadn't emptied out from the last two days. Tomorrow's patrols will be under instruction to retrieve all scent glands possible."

Chris opened her mouth, like she was about to tell me something, and then thought better of it.

I nudged her with my elbow, only lightly, but she pretended it hurt, even while fighting a grin. "What is it?"

"I've got a few ideas to tinker with the established explosives you can get from the Shop. If that's okay? Ice blocking variations, that sort of thing. And I'll see if there are any ways we haven't thought of to distribute the scent traps."

"Sounds like a good idea to me." I really did think so. Maybe, just maybe, with all of this we could get our shit together and finally start to make actual headway on all of these damned creatures. "Don't know about you all, but I'm getting bloody sick of being on defense all the time."

❖

Watching Ginali and Hirish go at a discussion toe to toe was far too amusing. It was all I could do to keep the smile from my face. The Pharyleri barely reached the Hakarta's chest, but his presence made the height difference secondary.

"You cannot execute the rest of this plan effectively if you do not utilize the settlement's crafters for set up." Ginali tapped his foot so fast, I thought it was going to break through the carpet and tile in the library.

Hirish crossed his arms, and I got the feeling it was more defensive than usual. "We don't have that sort of time."

"Make time." Ginali's glare reminded me of a cat when you forgot to feed it soft food. Demanding, and fully capable of crawling. "Do it the right way, and it should help more in the long run."

He did have a point, and I could see the begrudging realization dawning on Hirish too. Tension loosened in his shoulders, and he left out a pent-up breath. "Fine. What do you suggest?"

Ginali's eyes sparkled, and it made him seem two feet taller. Momentarily, anyway. "I'm so glad you asked. We have carpenters, stonemasons, earthmovers, you name it—your settlement has so many people who have non-combatant Skills. Those people can form terrain, change the rock landscapes, and basically build this Monster Thunderdome Kyle speaks of."

My brother gave a little arm pump off in the corner where he was ostensibly in discussions with Dale. I knew they'd been eavesdropping anyway.

"Basically, you're saying we prep the area to better contain the fights we're going to force?" Mike butted in, a thoughtful frown on his face. "Make it an actual battle zone?"

Ginali thought the words over, like he wasn't quite sure Mike got exactly what he meant. "More like, reinforce the area you're wanting to use for battle in a way that doesn't seem like it's reinforced."

"So it's less easily destroyed?" Mike pushed the question.

Ginali shrugged. "Yes, in a way. But also, so it's easier to have a definitive place to lure the combatant creatures into. We need to create obstacles for them to navigate, to slowly funnel each of the species through to each other. Doing this in an uncontrolled environment will yield less than ideal results."

"Timeline?" Hirish barked out, and I knew the Pharyleri crafter was going to get his way.

"Give us two to three days." Ginali nodded. "Yes, that sounds about right. It might take less, but it shouldn't take more. That way you also have more time to amass more of those scent gadgets."

So that was it. We were going to have an actual Thunderdome. Although not really. More of a nature-based arena for the creatures to fight in, but I wasn't about to burst my brother's bubble. I could practically see him salivating.

Plus, this way it allowed our crafters to contribute more. So many of our settlement residents seemed restless; this would be a good way to have everyone involved in protecting what we'd built.

Now we just had to prune nests while we waited. Violence might not have solved everything on the old Earth, but at least here in the Dungeon World version of Australia—violence was our new best friend.

Especially organized violence.

Chapter Thirty-Two:
Scented

22 Weeks, 3 days Post-System Onset
3 p.m.

It took closer to three days for the crafters to get the area ready. In the meantime, the tech team pumped out a heap of scent trap devices, while we sent out patrols to guard the non-combatant workers and to clear the other nests that wouldn't be in our initial test zone.

So it was that we sat in the library looking at detailed diagrams and pictures of the new and improved Koala Bushlands area we'd specifically curated for our little test trap.

No trees directly in the way, but instead they scattered back around the perimeter. Boulders and rockfall were strategically placed throughout to provide some cover and breaks to line of sight should we need them.

They'd managed to create natural-seeming, yet strategically well-formed paths that should funnel creatures into combat areas. None of it looked unnatural, unless you knew how it had been before they remolded it. They'd done a really good job.

I hefted a small grenade device in my hand as I surveyed the work they'd done. The thing was solid, and sincerely like the grenades I'd seen in television shows, except this was distinctly silver, and the pin was a button underneath a small, clear plastic cover that you had to flip open. No accidental setting it off, which was fine by me. Each top was a different color to signify a different type of creature's scent marker.

Hirish was looking over one of the other devices. He turned over what looked like a pressure plate to me. It was larger and flatter and meant to be dug into the ground. I had visions of exploding body parts flying all around in my head.

"These are meant to be planted so that you can run through a previously established path to lead one set of enemies to the next without getting the scent on you. Once the pressure is applied, there's a three second delay before the scent will waft up and out of the ground." Chris winked at me while she explained, and either I had the worst poker face ever, or else, she could just read me like an open book. Probably a little of both.

Kyle and Melody walked over. I'll give them timing. I was far too engrossed in checking out all of the scent weapons to actually consider heckling them much. That was okay; I could bide my time.

"What do you think?" my twin asked me.

I shrugged. "It was sort of my idea, in a way, so I think it's bloody brilliant." There, I was being modest and everything.

Kyle chuckled softly. "I know it was your idea. You haven't let me forget it for the last few days. Just keep in mind, we haven't tested it yet."

"I know, I know." I waved his concern away. The last thing I needed was negative energy interfering with this master plan. There was a lot that could go wrong. And it didn't mean we wouldn't have to fight, it just hopefully meant that we could get away with less constant patrolling.

Maybe I could help direct the flow of the scent path with the help of Mana, or hell, what if I could trigger traps remotely that way? We'd see when we tested this out.

Maybe this could save us all a little from the patrol burnout I knew we were all experiencing. Okay. I was experiencing it. It was all me. I hadn't really talked to anyone else about it.

Dolores hit the desk with a gavel. Now, I'm not sure where she got it from, but the sound definitely shut the room up a lot faster than it did when she cleared her throat. "Distribution starts tonight for implementation tomorrow. We have seven sectors marked out for the initial run. Koalzillas, Caneglobulous, Emugators, Tetchrihorns, and several others. The aim is to lure in monsters whose nests we haven't been clearing so they do it for us."

There was a part of me ridiculously excited about this, and another part of me that just hoped it worked. Theory was one thing; this . . . this was entirely another.

Hirish raised his hand, a grenade clenched loosely in it. "Group leaders will be given several of each ground mine, but only one of the grenades. Grenades must be detonated in the correct direction after all of the ground mines have been activated. For the first few rounds we will be observing to ensure this works as we're intending."

"Theoretically it should, right?" Dale spoke up, a grin on his face.

"Yes," Zyrilian responded, holding up his once-injured arm and clenching and unclenching his cybernetic fist. He hadn't opted to cover the device, so it looked like a part of him. "But we all know how theory works out sometimes—"

"Basically," Hirish interrupted, "be ready for anything and everything. We never know when it'll backfire so, for the first part of these tests, we'll be sending out the usual patrols just in case."

A chill made it down my spine as he said that. The "just in case" never sounded right to me. For all of my bravado, I just had to hope that this panned because we needed something to give.

"We'll have two runners with every group." I spoke up this time, willing myself to sound more confident than I suddenly felt. There was so much that could go wrong. But we had to do something so that the System mutations and monsters didn't keep trying to steamroll us. "Two runners, two rogues, and at least three ranged, just in case the weight of the runner doesn't set the traps off properly. We have to make sure the stench is released when it needs to be, or everything falls apart. It's a chain reaction sort of thing."

I took a breath and continued on. "If everything goes right with this test round, we'll set up another for remote detonation once we've tweaked the devices calibration with the manual trials."

I smiled, and Chris nodded at me. Sarah hadn't come with her wife, as she was still working on making more of the trigger plates and grenades. Rin, however, had accompanied Chris.

She cleared her throat now. "We are experimenting with adding an audible element to a few of the trigger plates and grenades. To help . . . entice the monsters into fighting with one another. This has taken a little more work than anticipated, but we should have several options ready for testing tomorrow."

A low murmur of approval circulated the room as Rin took a seat again. This was starting to get exciting. The more we could send out, the better idea we'd have of just how potentially effective the idea could be. If we could make it safer with precise remote triggering, all the better.

Mike bent over some sort of visual he was sharing with Sienna. She was usually our more levelheaded politician type. Excellent at keeping us all calmer, so I was surprised she hadn't spoken yet. Watching the two of them warmed my heart. They were both great people, and excellent at what they did. It was good that they found each other even in this hellhole of a future.

Sienna righted herself, a determined set to her jaw. "Okay. So that everyone knows just how serious this is."

Everyone stopped. Keep in mind that by everyone, I really only mean the council in this room. Sienna glanced at Mike, who nodded barely perceptibly.

"There is a possibility that this could cause the creatures to become enraged. Not that we know it for a fact, but with every type of new spell or technology, there's always the possibility it's not going to work as intended." Taking a breath, she looked around, making sure everyone was paying attention to what she said. "We need to have everything in place for round one of this tomorrow, and once we've ascertained that we're not pissing off the local wildlife mutations, we'll give the green light for the rest of the patrols to repeat it."

"Hear, hear to not dying!" Ray called out.

There was an undercurrent of uneasy laughter throughout the room. But at least the tension eased up a bit. Most of us filtered out, the Hakarta and Zarrie taking the trigger plates and grenades for the respective groups with them.

Don't get me wrong, I was proud of our human ingenuity that let us build these, and yet at the same time, if it was going to backfire, maybe it was better that it be one of our invader allies? Maybe that was callous of me. I'd never asked if they had family back home; I'd never even thought of it until now.

Just about to leave and follow Mason, Kyle, and Evelyn back to the house, Ginali cut me off.

"Kira, we need to talk." His eyes shone fiercely, and I knew this probably wasn't going to be good news and lollipops. Why couldn't I just ever get a rainbow?

"Hey. What's up?"

He glanced around, like he didn't want anyone to overhear, and noticed that Dor, Mike, and Sienna were deep in discussion, out of earshot if he kept his voice low.

"I'm not sure we can trust all of those people who came with your ex-husband."

Well, that wasn't the statement I'd been prepared for, or even expected. Not that it mattered, but Ginali didn't dramatize things, so that meant he was definitely sensing something. Thoughts whirled through my head, but I cleared them as best my overactive imagination let me and pushed on. "What makes you say that?"

"I heard a couple of them talking. I don't know any of them well, including Mason, so I thought I would talk to you."

"Well, I hate to burst your bubble, but the only one I know at all is Mason. But run it past me anyway." I tried to sound reassuring, but we'd all changed so much in this apocalypse that I had to confess that maybe none of us knew each other well anymore anyway.

"Ezra, the rogue they brought with them, was talking to Peter—he's their Archer. I don't think they thought anyone was listening, and you know I'm not a habitual eavesdropper."

It was all I could do not to guffaw out loud. Because as much as I loved Ginali, my Pharyleri little friend, he was amazingly gifted at eavesdropping, at knowing what people wanted before they even realized it was what they wanted themselves. That's what made him so damn good at what he did.

Still, I simply inclined my head and waited for him to finish. If he wanted to protest his innocence, I'd let him.

"They were speaking about needing to 'get back to the Gold Coast' as soon as possible." Ginali paused and looked up at me, his eyes questioning.

I shrugged. "I mean, that's where they came from, right? That's their home base, so it's not that unexpected. Did they mention what for? Is that what made you so curious?" Because I had utterly no clue why this should be a big deal. They probably had people they wanted to get back to. I could totally relate to that.

Ginali tsked in exasperation and threw his hands up in the air. "Not in so many words. But why would they be keeping it secret? They were whispering over near the street, away from all of the vendor's tables. Like they were trying to hide what they were talking about."

Well, that raised some red flags. Not that people didn't have secrets or that these guys wanted privacy, but that they'd gone to such an out of the way spot to discuss it. I looked at Ginali and pursed my lips. "And just how did they not see you?"

Ginali's eyes twinkled. "Sometimes being shorter in stature is a definite boon. After all, people who aren't accustomed to our presence don't really know how to look out for us, do they?"

This time I laughed. He wasn't wrong. It *had* taken me a while to always notice when he was around. Frankly, he was always so well dressed in robes that accentuated his features that I found it difficult not to see him now. But perhaps that was all about perception.

Just like his Mana signature was one of the more colorful ones I'd witnessed so far.

"What do you think we should do?" I asked. If they were up to something, and I wouldn't put it past them considering how we'd first met Drake and Gary after all, then I couldn't dismiss it, could I? None of us could.

"We should keep them separated. Not send them all out in one group. By doing so at least they'll have to meet up to discuss whatever it is they're needing to retrieve, and thus afford us the opportunity to perhaps overhear important information again?" I swear Ginali was a master spy on the side. He did have a solid plan and a semi decent idea. So why the hell not?

"Sure. I think that might be a good idea. I'll make sure Mason is with me, and perhaps take Peter or Ezra?" That sounded solid. Mason had always been super trusting. It was one of his best and worst traits. Not that I could talk much. I'd always tried to believe the best in people. Pity they oftentimes disappointed.

"Sounds like a fantastic plan." Ginali was happy, and a happy Ginali meant perhaps better prices for some of the stuff I'd been holding onto.

"Excellent. Now, do you have a few moments to look over some of my inventory?" I asked, pretty sure it was my eyes twinkling this time.

"Of course!" He grinned up at me. "I thought you'd never ask."

❖

22 Weeks, 4 Days Post-System Onset
8 a.m.

Gemma insisted that she be the one to set off the pressure plates in our trial run. Given her speed when she activated one of her Skills, I was glad she'd volunteered.

While I was still nervous about setting them off manually, this was all about calibration. Once this was done, we could remove yet another aspect of danger. Less potential death was a thing of joy.

We still had to keep the area clear of potential interlopers. There were so many other ways to just head straight through to our staging ground even without the paths we'd had designed. The Koala Bushlands was a huge area.

The whole morning was spent setting up the traps, digging them into place, mapping it out in the settlement defense system so we could potentially just deploy them once the tech department was done with the trap tweaks. We needed to get the distances between the traps perfect.

The better we timed the traps, the smoother the operation would go down. Trial and error.

We ended up putting down eleven Koalzilla-scented pressure plates over about a six-hundred-meter distance. We had to lure the creatures into our arena from outside of it. Rin assured me that the three closer to the

Thunderdome would also trigger the Koalzilla roar, and thus further anger the monster species that was drawn to it.

We hid them along the engineered path, slotting each trap into the designated holding space and hoping that all this work would be worth it. Trees and strategically placed underbrush hid the mesh that covered the spaces. Some of the holding areas were even hidden inside stones and rocks.

All in all, the non-combatants had more than pulled their weight with this setup. If it worked—if this did what we needed it to—well, we'd be setting these up all over the greater Brisbane area.

Once all of the plates had been placed, we worked our way backward to the vantage point we'd chosen where we could get a good view of the whole arena. Essentially, our little construction crew had built us an observation deck that frankly was camouflaged to appear like more of the surrounding eucalyptus and gum trees. Hirish and Gemma left us up there and moved out getting ready to trigger the first set of traps once Chris and Sarah gave them the go ahead for tracking the results.

I watched Gemma and the way her freckles stood out on her face even though the sunlight was scattering through the trees. It was one of those defining moments, right before something big happens. I could only hope it was going to be a *good* big.

She took in a deep breath, closed her eyes, and then exhaled. Mana gathered around her like a cozy blanket, as if it was used to the way she was, eager and willing to help her expend as much of it as she could.

When we used Mana the way it was organically meant to be distributed, it was a beautiful thing for me to watch.

And then, she raced off so fast, I couldn't keep track of her.

Only the Mana trace she left behind let me know that she'd already activated the first scent trap. We knew there was a better way to do this, but first we had to tweak it, make sure the whole concept worked the way we'd designed it to. Triggering, watching, and learning. Making the process smoother. Seeing if we could outsmart the mutations, outsmart the System that was trying to kill us with an overpopulation of monsters.

We sat up in our little perch as silently as we could. There was a faint rumbling in the distance as some of the creatures we'd begun to entice started moving. Koalzillas versus Tetchrihorns and Caneglobulous were round one.

Fight.

I had to choke down that giggle so I didn't spoil everything. My ocular implants zoomed in like binoculars; I could see flashes of the creatures beginning to run as they began to follow the scents. Just glimpses of them through the trees as they made their way into the gauntlet we'd created for them.

There were several Koalzillas emerging from their nest areas around us. We knew they moved fast, so their traps were triggered last. The toads and rhinos were going to take longer to get to us. I couldn't believe how much my stomach was tied in knots while we waited to see just how well the plan worked, if at all.

It was one thing for them to randomly encounter each other and try to devour the other creatures first, but deliberately enticing them into battles between species . . . well, that was something else entirely.

I knew it only took about three minutes for the whole chain to be set off, and for Hirish to toss his grenade into the middle of the whole thing, but it felt like an age to me. To all of us, I think.

We huddled involuntarily as the ground shook up into our stand. Staying close enough to the edge to observe but far enough away that we weren't going to be scented ourselves or for them to see us.

For a minute or two, despite feeling the approaching monsters, I didn't think the plan had worked. Nothing came into the arena via the preset paths . . . until they did.

Suddenly, two of the lanes I could see rampaged in toward the middle, carefully funneled into each other even before they'd arrive where the Koalzillas should gather once they got there. The Tetchrihorns and Caneglobulous clashed first, focusing on each other even as the pack leaders looked around for the source of the Koalzilla scent.

Suddenly, Hirish was up in the tree stand with us, watching just as closely as the rest of us. Gemma lingered down, close to where the action was.

Tetchrihorns with their alligator-like skin and piercing horns plunged into the sides of the Caneglobulous, activating their stuns as they did so. But the wobbly concoction that made up the latter just wasn't as affected by stuns as other creatures might be.

The Caneglobulous released their toxins before the Tetchrihorns managed to pull free, allowing the poison to leak down through the grooves in the horns, onto the heads of the creatures and into the skin. Wails of pain echoed up to us as we watched the fight progress, both species squaring off against each other, taking stock through all of their scent-driven frenzy.

Gemma threw one of her darts at that point, hitting one of the final traps they hadn't triggered yet, and a low keening sound like a Koalzilla in pain emanated from it. The two fighting species spun immediately toward it, their eyes wild as they sought the source of the sound.

Just in time for three Koalzillas to come rumbling into the center point of our little Thunderdome, their jowls soaked in the dried blood of other creatures like a portent of what was to come.

It felt surreal sitting up high and watching this happen. I imagined it might be like how the emperors felt when they watched the people fighting in the colosseum. A queasiness assailed me, because even though these things regularly tried to kill us, setting them against each other deliberately and then watching while we waited to take out the victors?

It felt like something alien to our own species.

Something far from human.

You okay? Evelyn mouthed at me, reaching over to squeeze my hand.

I nodded, directing my attention to the arena below us again as I watched the Koalzillas dive into the fray. Their big hands found easy purchase in griping Tetchrihorn horns. Though it didn't appear easy for them to fend off the creatures, they didn't lose much ground. Sparks couldn't call in back up if they couldn't be seen, and the biggest Koalzilla snapped the horn of the largest of the horse-like creatures with a snap so loud it reverberated through the treetops.

That Tetchrihorn screamed in so much pain I thought my blood would curdle. It left me with no doubt in my mind that the creatures we'd be clearing up in the aftermath would be the Koalzillas.

We watched as the Caneglobulous were splattered. We watched as the Tetchrihorns were smashed against rocks, dehorned and declawed. And we watched as the Koalzillas proved, beyond a shadow of doubt, that they were indeed the kings of Australia's new bushland.

And then we descended from our perch to finish off the forty-odd percent of life they each had, making them far easier prey than usual.

After which, we had to clear the arena and trial the second run of different species.

Death, blood, and corpses shouldn't have been so easy to clear away, but they were.

I just wasn't sure how I felt about that.

Chapter Thirty-Three:
Discombobulated

23 Weeks, 5 Days Post-System Onset
1 p.m.

The trial runs worked better than we'd ever imagined.

Once Gemma and Hirish were satisfied with the timing of the pressure plates, Chris and Rin set about working on remote detonation, even though remote deployment was going to take long.

This meant that it took a fraction of the time for us to clear the areas around us, and even less time for us to gather new scent glands needed for the next round of ammunition. We ended up with a beautiful, cohesive way to get the higher-Level incoming creatures to do away with the constantly leveling creatures we frequently cleared from their nests. Which left us with much less danger when facing off against the interlopers. As long as we timed it right and jumped in at the correct moment, they never had the time to regenerate.

We were starting to discuss how many more of these arenas we needed to establish. Because one of them was no longer enough. Ginali and Mike were in talks with all of our heads of crafts to get an estimate on cost of materials, sourcing of materials, and all the people we needed to pull these off. Credits were my one worry about this whole operation. It cost a lot if we wanted to keep developing these Thunderdomes.

With less time out on patrol, I sat at Raybucks having lunch with my littlest, and felt decidedly discombobulated.

I hadn't even headed out today. I'd gotten to spend the entire day with Wisp. And she was delighted.

Dog sat at my side, pushing his head under my hand any time I didn't have it on the table, demanding pets like an actual non-mutated animal. Wombie was outside with his mother, since he was too large to fit under the coffee table anymore.

"And we're going to go to the Crafting Cartel's new outlet that they built in the expanded settlement week! Miss Jana said we can all try out some different crafting things. Ginali is setting it all up for us." Wisp chattered on, picking at a cupcake Leena had given her.

Shit. Wisp would be nine soon.

"Mum. Are you listening to me?" She stopped me in my thoughts, staring at me accusingly.

"Of course I am. What craft do you think you'll try?" Because I did want to know. So far Jana and Avery had managed these kids amazingly. Now that the new school was in place, we were even getting kids progress reports.

Reading, writing, math. Things that would always come in handy. For older kids, there were mechanical options too that could help them navigate the entire System and this new world in the long run.

Surprisingly, some of the aliens had even been willing to chat with Jana and Avery about Galactic teaching standards. We didn't have the Credits for a lot of their suggestions, though the Galactic equivalent of tablets was on the table.

Still, I know I'd missed more than one meeting where things had gotten heated over the addition of early-on combat Classes. It was one thing to say we're doing modified stranger danger routines, another to have the kids calmly—or excitedly—discussing weapon choices for different monster types.

It really was a whole new world.

Wisp pursed her lips and reached down absentmindedly to scratch her dog. "I was thinking of looking at potions. You know they can do more than heal or give you Mana, right, Mum?"

I nodded. She wasn't the sort of kid you had to pretend had just taught you something new. "What sort of potions were you wanting to make?" I reached across and snagged some of the icing off her cupcake.

She glared at me but answered anyway. "I was thinking of something that might make Dog stronger, might help him be able to defend himself and maybe even me. That would be ideal, right?"

"You think Dog wants to fight?" I asked, looking down at the boy dubiously. Sure enough, he returned my expression quite solemnly.

"I think Dog wants to do whatever it takes to stay like he is. For us all to stay like this." Ah, there it was. That glimpse of her old soul.

"We all want to survive, love." I reached across and pulled her to me. She was growing, and it was more difficult to nestle her in my lap, but I managed it. Ha! I won.

What a weird day this was.

Mason and Jackson headed out with one of the patrols to set the final traps of the day. They were helping Rin and Chris figure out the best methods for remotely arming the traps. There were so many ways for it to go haywire. It was good to see my son and his father undertaking things together, but there was something Mason wasn't telling me, and the longer he didn't tell me, the more worried I was about it.

"Mum. Do you think things will be able to stay this new normal?" Wisp muttered into my neck as she continued to hug me.

"We're hoping so, Buttercup. That's the plan."

"Do you think Dad will stay here?" This question she asked in an even softer voice, like she wasn't even sure she wanted me to answer it for her.

Thing was, I didn't know if I had an answer for her, or if it would be one that she'd like. "He'll be here at least for a while, love."

She hugged me tighter, and I wished I'd had a better answer. Even with the end of the world happening, Mason was more of a wanderer, and being a bard, even ignoring all the stereotypes—he just wasn't a stay-in-one-place sort of guy. But I knew he felt an attachment to his kids. He did love them.

Not everyone was cut out to be a full-time parent.

"He's here now. That's an awesome thing, right?" I squeezed her shoulders and gave her a kiss on the cheek. She didn't say anything for a while, and Dog laid a massive paw on my knee, like he was checking to see if Wisp was okay. I'm not sure how we managed to luck into mutated animals that liked us, but I was glad she had Dog.

"Kira!" Avery jogged over to me, and I could see a group of school-age kids lined up neatly over by the food court.

"Hey!" I said, not moving my daughter even an inch. If she wanted hugs, that's what she got. "What's up?"

"We need to figure out how to get more people interested in helping out with the school and daycare. Too many kids, not enough adults." Her face was flushed, and I did a quick headcount of the kids lined up in twos that she'd left near the food. Sure enough. There were about thirty of them there. Ouch. Definitely not ideal, especially not in a Mana-fueled world with kid-unfriendly mutations.

"Have you talked to Ray?"

She shook her head. "I can never catch him. When I have time, he's off with patrols. When he's around, I assume I'm wrangling kids. And Jana hasn't had any luck either."

I mulled that over. Ray was up to his ears in shit. Red should have a fairly good grasp on all of the people we had, since they were technically one of our commodities. "Check with Red. He's been wandering around with Mike. They should have a clearer idea of the types of non-combatant Classes we have available to us. Want me to radio them over?"

Avery shook her head. "I can't leave the kids too long. If you could contact them, just send them over to where we will be shoveling food down their gullets?"

Hiding a laugh, I nodded. Before leaving however, Avery looked pointedly at Wisp who was still snuggled up against me, her head buried in my neck. She mouthed: *is she okay?*

I nodded in my best stealth mode. It was nice to know that others cared about my kids too. A sort of relief.

"Hey, Buttercup." I shook Wisp gently. "We have some outside work to do."

"Don't wanna." She snuggled closer, gripping me tighter in her tiny bear hug.

Why couldn't she do this when we were at home and there was more room to snuggle? Still, I wasn't looking this gift horse in the mouth. So, instead, I whispered to her, "We have to go take care of Mumma. I have a harness for us to try out."

That got her attention. All of her melancholy seemed to peel away, and my bright and bubbly little girl was there again. She pushed back from me, one eyebrow raised. "Why didn't you say so! Can I try the harness? Is it for riding? Is it better than the one I have for Wombie?"

The words tumbled out of her mouth like the inquisitive kid she'd always been. But I was glad I'd got a glimpse of what was going on in the back of her mind. I'd have to tread more carefully, give her more time, be there more. And maybe, with all of these changes we'd been able to make—well, maybe I really could.

❖

Mumma Wombutt really deserved a much more regal name than we'd given her. Realistically, her shoulders stood ten feet or so above the ground, and she was just a darling creature in magnified size. I pulled the harness I'd had Ginali make for me out of my inventory, with explicit instructions from him to let him know if it worked so he could patent it and have it as an option sold by the Cartel through the Shop. I really needed to ask him how that worked, because I believed we had a whole heap of shit we'd developed that would sell like hotcakes if we got it patented.

Were patents even a thing? In a System that allowed you to buy most answers, how did you stop others from using your work? How did that interact with Skills? Interstellar commerce was not something I expected to have to think about. I'd hated the international marketing subject I'd taken in college to satisfy my business elective.

Still, damn, could our town ever do with the income. Especially when it came to expanding to the next number of properties. What we needed was to find ways to use the System for our benefit instead of economic detriment.

Wisp eyed the contraption I held in my hands somewhat dubiously. Considering her imagination was always on fire, I wasn't sure how that made me feel.

"You sure that's going to work, Mum? It looks sort of . . . like a bundle of straps."

I looked at all the leather in my hands and just sighed. "It *is* a bundle of straps. Nothing is going to happen if she doesn't understand what it is that I want. I'll never get it on if I can't make her realize what I want to do with it."

Wisp watched me, considered me, and then stepped back about five steps, slowly and deliberately.

"Just going to keep my distance over here." Dog stood next to her, sort of positioning his body partially across the front of her like he was going to protect her if anything went wrong.

Me too, Dog. Me too.

I approached Mumma, trying to figure out how in the hell I was actually going to get this contraption on her anyway. She eyed me, but there wasn't any suspicion there, just that beautiful gold-tinged glow in her intelligent eyes. It really was amazing how she'd been affected by the mutation as opposed to so many other creatures. It made me wonder if all wombats reacted this way, or if she was an exception because of Wombie.

"So . . ."

It felt so weird talking to a wombat like she could understand me, but I'd already assumed she could anyway. In for a penny . . .

"This is a harness." I paused, and then motioned with my hands as if putting it over her head. "So I can sit up there—and not fall off, and not hurt you by gripping too hard."

Her gaze held mine, like she was trying to decipher what my words meant. She tilted her head to the left and then the right, before she bowed her massive head right down to the ground. I reached up, scritched her between the eyes like I'd done a thousand times before. She really did love that.

Then I looped the main portion behind her ears to her very thick neck, moving to either side to bring the relevant straps into place. When she righted herself, the straps dangled down, needing to be secured around her chest and under her forelegs.

It took me a little while, but eventually the harness was secured and in place, and the little ladder footholds that Ginali had built into the girth loomed in front of my face.

Wisp hadn't come any closer, but still stood watching the whole ordeal with Dog by her side.

"Here goes nothing," I muttered under my breath, and Mumma responded by sighing out a wuff of air. Maybe she really did understand me more than I realized.

Hauling myself up on top of her felt so surreal. Like in some ways I'd thought it would be like riding a very tall horse. Let me state now, for the record, sitting astride a massively mutated wombat is *nothing* like sitting on a horse.

For starters, her back is much broader, and I found myself super thankful that I was rather flexible because right now I was about twenty degrees shy of the splits. This would get uncomfortable fast, so I'd have to either sit cross-legged or figure out something else. Maybe side-saddle style?

Ginali had built in a quick-release strap that I wasn't sure would help me stay on top of here anymore than gravity would shoot me down to the ground. But there were grips for me to use, and those felt much safer. The view from up here was kind of wonderful, and Mumma shook herself slightly, like she was trying to get used to the new weight distribution or something, and then settled.

Now that I was up here, Wisp looked tiny down there, but I could tell she was grinning from ear to ear. I knew she'd be asking to clamber up here in no time . . .

One thing I hadn't thought of though: how was I supposed to make her move? Could I show her with Mana manipulation? Could I push her with my thighs? Like I'd already realized, she wasn't a horse, but we did have this sort of innate understanding of each other. Perhaps I could use that.

"Hey, Mumma." I said the words gently, and her ears flickered ever so slightly. "Do you think we could move forward a little?"

Her ears twitched again, and then she moved. I had to admit that the harness definitely helped. Before when I'd been trying this after using ten thousand different ways to get up here, I'd always been in danger of slipping off her smooth fur. This however, this felt kind of wonderful. Not that I was entirely sure what I would do with such power, but hey—I was riding a combat wombat, and I felt like all my birthdays had come at once.

We only did a little circle—I mean, she wasn't an amusement park ride—and to be honest, I'd really just done it to see if it *could* be done. The odds of me taking her into combat where she could get hurt, or where having me on her back might cause her to react differently than she otherwise would, didn't feel like it was the best idea if I wanted to keep her safe.

And I guess that's what I wanted. At least until I could figure out how we could be effective together without plunging us both into mortal danger.

Finally, I got her to stop, and half climbed, half slid down her side. I could feel the flush of excitement in my face and frankly, this was fun. Maybe when things calmed down and we established a new normal, I could take her on picnics to larger fields with Wombie, Dog, and my kids in tow. That would be something pretty wonderful.

"That looked like so much fun!" Wisp stood close to me now as I petted Mumma on her cheek again, motioning her down so I could remove the harness. I wasn't about to just leave it on her where it could get accidentally tangled or something.

Wisp's face fell a little as I took the harness off.

"Not right now. Later, when she's more used to it. This was just a test." I gave my kid a brief hug.

"But I've been riding Wombie, Mum." Wisp scowled slightly.

"Wombie is three feet from the ground. That's a world of difference."

She pouted for a second before brightening considerably as Wombie trotted over from where he'd been waiting on his Mum. "I don't have a little seat up top. Do you think I ca get one?"

I looked at the baby wombutt. He had really grown, and his back was almost up to my shoulders now, which made it more like a four-foot drop to the ground. I was pretty sure Ginali would make the change to her. Maybe he could even make it adjustable so it would grow with the little guy.

"We can ask Ginali," I said.

Wisp knew the Pharyleri well enough that she squealed because I'd pretty much just told her yes. "Thanks, Mum! I'm going to go find my friends in the food court and tell them—is that okay?"

"Hang on a second." Damn kids, always getting ahead of themselves. Still, it was nice to see her so enthused. "Just let us ask Ginali first."

"Fine." She mock pouted this time, but I could see the excitement practically bubbling out of her.

I continued to scritch the massive wombat behind the ears, just loving the peace I could feel, the sensation that we'd begun to figure out ways to work with this apocalypse instead of always racing to try and catch up to what it did.

The damned thing was like a runaway supply train with our only source of survival constantly dropping tidbits here and there, mostly down ravines where we couldn't get at it.

"Thanks for this morning, Mum," Wisp said, her expression full of love for the animals around her. "Sometimes it's just hard to be happy all the time."

Ouch. That hurt. Coming from my kid, it was like a sucker punch to the gut. "You know you don't have to be happy all the time, right?"

She hesitated and laughed softly. "I know, but sometimes it just feels easier for everyone including me if I just be happy."

"Ah, kiddo." That's the last thing I needed her to do, but didn't we all do it to some extent? "Just as long as you're honest with you and with me, okay? You know I'll always listen, and I'll always love you. No matter what."

"Yeah. I know, Mum." Then she grinned. "So, my birthday is in like two weeks, right?"

Sneaky little thing, knowing when to tug on my heartstrings. Still, I knew at least some of it was real. She was growing up, becoming a tween soon, and the world had changed, and all the big and horrific things we had now were overwhelming. I got it.

"Birthday? No. Didn't you know they're skipping that day this year?" It was a game we'd played so many times, such a nice little slice of normalcy.

Wisp giggled, and opened her mouth to say something else, except she never got to.

Sirens blared from down near the Officeworx. Not the alarms, but the incoming wounded. The break in the blanket of peace was shocking, like an ice bucket had just been emptied over my head. "Go inside and stay with Avery or Jana, okay?"

Wisp gave me a huge hug and then bolted for the entrance to the center while I moved toward the incoming wounded. Dog trotted after her whilst Wombie and Mumma Wombutt huddled together, looking towards the entrance, grouping together on instinct.

Off in the distance, I swore I could see smoke spires spiraling into the otherwise clear blue sky. Fire in the Australian bush was never a good thing. Not ever, not even now.

Not to mention it looked like it was right where we'd crafted the arena. *Please don't let it be destroyed.*

"Shit." I could feel Mumma waddling behind me, her footfalls much reduced to how she used to lumber around. Like she'd learned how to be stealthy now. It felt comforting to have her with me, not that she could help, but that I wasn't alone.

My heart jumped into my mouth as I reached the reception area and saw multiple patrols streaming in. Blood from gaping wounds the System was unable to close. It was strange how that had become the new normal and that anything *not* healing itself in a timely manner meant that something unnatural was interfering.

Piola and Dale directed the wounded through to one of our standard outside med tents. Off in the distance, I swear I heard a rumble, followed by another plume of smoke obscuring everything in sight, including most of the sky. "What the fuck is that?"

"That—" Evelyn spoke next to me, blood dripping from a gash in her forehead like it was just another day at the office. "That is the Magon."

Shit.

Chapter Thirty-Four:
Good Bait

I didn't have time to unpack the loaded statement Evelyn made before she wavered on her feet. The wound wasn't right, and Mana's attempt to heal it was sluggish at best. I needed Kyle, and I looked around trying to locate him, knowing he'd been out in that mess too. Shit. I didn't think my Mana Purification skill would work with Dale.

Then again, I was just going to have to try, wasn't I?

Mason and Jackson weren't back yet either. On the bright side, they weren't among the wounded sitting and being healed by multiple healers right now, so I had to cling to the hope that when they all got back, they'd be fine. They had to be.

Besides, I was fairly certain the familial portion of the System would tell me if one of my dependents was dead.

I motioned Dale over, trying to size up the other strands of sluggish Mana I could see around me. There were only about six people who'd been hit with the slowing toxin that needed explicit healing before the System could kick in. None of the wounds were ultimately life threatening from the looks of it, but they had to be hurting, and losing that much blood was never a good idea.

It'd probably time out or get fixed eventually. I had no doubt the System wouldn't let an ability exist that permanently disabled healing. With an oversized magpie dragon-wannabe in play, though, we couldn't afford to test it and wait it out.

"What's up?" Dale asked, breathless as he jogged over. He'd been barking out orders to the med teams and I'd only caught him in a lull.

"I haven't done this without Kyle, but Evelyn, Dannin, and those four other people over in that direction"—I pointed over the other side of the tent—"need a cleanse healing. And I don't know if this will work but I don't think we can afford to wait."

"Worth a shot?" He grimaced, and I remembered that Darren was out there with Jackson today, too.

Shit.

We were both on edge but had to take care of the people in front of us first.

I placed my hand along his good arm, following the flow of Mana through his body and tried to direct him in how to cleanse the Mana. Following the muck through where it leaked into Evelyn's body, threatening to taint the blood inside as well, to make everything move slower. Especially healing

"Wow." He breathed out. "That's pretty cool."

It took longer to use Mana Purification with Dale. Precious moments that I wanted to go and find my brother and child, my ex, even. But this is what we had to do to survive. Take care of those that we could and worry about the rest later.

After what felt like hours, but couldn't have been more than fifteen minutes, we'd managed to cleanse all the six people I'd noticed with the wrong Mana signature trying to leak into them.

Although, I guess that didn't explain it well. It was more that the Mana they had had been infected by a poison and was attempting to fight it off, and just needed a little more help than usual. That was all and everything.

Fatigue washed over me, and I watched as Evelyn righted herself, already recovered from the System's intervention once we'd cleared out the obstacle. Miracles everyday baby. Right here. Thanks to alien intervention.

You know, but for all the monsters and death and shit, the System would have been an amazing thing for any culture. It made me wonder if the

System only pulled this genocide-level shit on Dungeon Worlds.

Which in turn made me angry, until I heard Kyle's voice.

And then every other thought fled from my mind.

I turned to see him and Jackson first. The relief that flooded me at their apparent healthiness was nothing short of massive. And then my attention fell to the person they were supporting on either side. The person who could barely walk or support himself. Mason.

I pushed aside all the emotion I could feel welling up. It wasn't going to help any of us right now. Not the worry, not the anger, nothing.

Instead, I focused my implants on his wounds, noticing trace amounts of the poison. Luckily, it wasn't anything Kyle and I couldn't fix pretty quickly. Lucky this time.

Mason wasn't really a combat Class. He was more like mine, support in buckets. Hell, the group he was with had even been sent with the specific aim of avoiding as much combat as possible. Had we seriously just assumed everything was going to work out the way we wanted once we figured out the baiting game?

Fatigue was a bitch, and I was simply exhausted. Perhaps not physically, but mentally—that was something the System still couldn't fix. Come on, wasn't it supposed to be smart? It had spent almost six months with humans. You'd think it would have learned by now.

We got Mason settled, and I dove in with Kyle. It took mere seconds with my twin as opposed to the few minutes with Dale. In no time we were done.

"I'm going to be okay?" Mason breathed out the words from where he still lay on the table like he was all I was worrying about.

"Yep." I nodded. "We just fixed you."

Mason frowned, but he was tired too. "Thanks. I feel better already."

Being healed took energy, especially to close big wounds.

Granted, it came back pretty quickly—thanks, intrusive alien System.

Jackson gave me a sudden hug. So sudden I didn't see it coming. And he just sort of held on. "It was scary out there."

Anger bubbled in the back of my throat, but there was nowhere and no one to take it out on. The fact of the matter was, life was now scary now no matter how hard we tried to make it less so. No matter how hard we tried to forget.

I hugged him back, and that steely feeling swelled right through me. If you're a mum, or a parent, or hell, probably anyone with a dependent, you know that feeling well. The one that looks at the people you love in your life, especially the little ones, and is totally determined to make sure they have the best chance at life, the best chance at survival.

"Well, we're going to have to go and chat about the Magon." I could still hear it in the background, even from this distance. The occasional rumbles, the screeching, squawking roar of its voice off in the distance that sent all the hairs on the back of my neck rising when I caught wind of it.

Damn monsters.

"Mum, it got so close to us. So stupidly close. And it just ripped up so many of the monsters, grabbing them with its claws, pecking down to gobble up an entire Caneglobulous in one beak full. It's massive, and it's . . ." He looked up at me, not that he had far to look anymore. Damn time. "It could rip us apart without blinking."

His voice was steady, but still holding him in that hug, I could feel just how much his body shook. Probably the adrenaline wearing off or something. Damn. I tried to pour as much confidence into my voice as I could. "It could. But we're all going to figure out ways to survive this too, okay?"

It seemed to work, and he finally pulled away, blushing slightly as he realized he'd been hugging his mum for a good few minutes. "I'm hungry. Going to go inside and grab something to eat."

I watched him go before turning to Kyle and putting my hands on my hips. "What the fuck happened out there?"

My twin cringed. "Some of the scent traps we helped place this afternoon went off before they should have. That's what we get for trying to automate everything."

"Meaning the Magon caught the scent as well?" Seriously—that was so surreal. Did the scents rise or something?

Kyle nodded, and I noticed that Mason had passed out. Concern niggled at me, and I scanned him with my Mana Sense and Mana Purification again just to make sure we got all of the bits of poison out of his body.

He seemed fine, just completely wiped out. This new world wasn't ideal for him. I got the distinct feeling that he'd chosen Bard because he'd hoped it would leave him with his ability to perform music intact.

As well as I knew Mason, I was certain he'd envisaged giving grand performances in converted pubs all over the Gold Coast as a Bard extraordinaire. Maybe we'd have to sit down and talk about everything his Class did. I thought he might like that.

Except right now we had much bigger fish to fry, or a bird to fry, or whatever analogy would work for a massively mutated flying terror.

"Fine. Let's head in and see if we can get everyone up to speed and figure out what we're going to do."

Kyle nodded and I got the feeling this was going to be a very long night.

There were times when I really didn't want to be here. This was one of them.

Sienna pinched the bridge of her nose, glaring at Mike. "We're not stopping a perfectly good way of dealing with the monsters around us just because another monster decided to come and take part in the smorgasbord we created."

I could see Mike bristle under the implications. "We're also not sending people out to get slaughtered."

It was probably one of their first arguments. At least, the first one I'd ever seen. They'd always seemed to agree on everything.

I was about to step in when Hirish beat me to it, clearing his throat with a low rumble. "Listen. There is a way to use this to our advantage."

Well, that got the entire room's attention. The library was far more crowded than usual with about a dozen each of the Hakarta and Zarrie, Ginali and a contingent of his own Pharyleri crafters, not to mention the human heads of several of the patrol groups that went out and the usual suspects. It was starting to feel claustrophobic. Maybe we could get the System to expand this little area for us.

For the right number of Credits, of course.

With every eye on him, Hirish didn't even blink. Instead, he continued, making sure he projected his voice enough for all to hear. "If we intentionally lure all of the monsters into our main arena, but intentionally direct scent grenades toward the Magon's flight path and thus also entice it to the same area, we could even potentially take out the Magon itself."

Murmuring spread through the room like wildfire and my own thoughts ran rampant through my mind. Okay, this was a good twist. We could kill the Magon. Get rid of that flying menace that dogged our every step.

I remembered Zyrilian's warning about the System always needing to balance things out, so there'd probably be something big and nasty to take its place. But that was a problem for future Kira and the settlement.

Right now, present Kira had a mutant and creature wave, and a giant flying monster to deal with.

"How would you propose we do that?" I asked, trying to make myself sound less enthusiastic than the champagne popping enthusiastic that I felt.

Hirish grinned in that Hakarta way. The one where too many teeth showed and made you fully accept that he was in fact an alien that could probably pop our heads off with his bare hands—or teeth. Way too sharp teeth.

On the other hand, the fact he could unhinge his jaws a little more than a human made his eating overstuffed burgers a true sight to see.

"We study its flight path and figure out way to lob the scents directly in its path."

"There's no way we're going to take that thing down." Ray had his arms crossed, a scowl on his face.

Yeah, the Magon was fierce, but if Hirish was suggesting this, then there had to be a way to complete the task. The Hakarta worked for money, not for glory. Call mercenaries whatever name you wanted to, they rarely suggested plans with a shitty survival rate. Thus, his plan would be solid with the least amount of projected loss. I waited for the Pirra Clan leader to respond.

"We're not going to try and kill it ourselves." There was a hint of condescension in Hirish's voice, though I don't think it was intentional. He was just trying to explain his plan in the simplest possible way, and it dawned on me what he was thinking just moments before he spoke.

"If we lure the Magon into battle with multiple different species of mutations and alien monsters, then it will be fighting those first. Just like how we've been controlling the spawn overflowing lately.

"The Magon will focus on feasting and killing on the initial prey first, but it will take damage doing so. If we are prepared, and gather in strategic spots, we have a good chance of bringing it down once it's taken care of all of the other monsters plaguing us." He raised a hand, then cupped them together. "We allow our opponents to gather in the arena, trap the location beforehand. Make sure we get some heavy-duty explosives from the Shop. So, when it's time, we damage the monster with the traps and ground it—finish it off with explosives if necessary."

It sounded so simple when he put it that way. Yet also so dangerous.

If the Magon didn't come, if all the monsters decided to keep moving or broke away. . . . There were just so many moving parts to this that could go wrong. But . . . but what if it went right?

There was a lot of nodding at each other in the room, a mulling over his words, and more than a few looks of fear and greed. The lure of free experience and loot was huge, but the danger was just as great.

"That's going to take a hell of a lot of coordination," Kyle said thoughtfully. "Maybe we should check the Shop to see if we can buy any information on the creature? It could have flight plans right?"

"Definite possibility," Piola mused out loud.

"Then would they also have traps? Maybe something that could contain a creature that big?" Rin stepped forward, pushing the brown hair that had come free from her bun back behind her ears.

"Technically, doesn't the Shop have access to everything?" I turned and asked the Hakarta clan leader.

Hirish nodded. "For a price, there is nothing you cannot buy. A trap might be an excellent use of Credits, should you have them spare."

"Would it be possible to replicate one with our tech abilities?" Chris stepped forward, a thoughtful frown on her face. I could almost feel the excitement she was trying to hide. It glistened behind her eyes.

"Likely. Or at least, components of it, I would think." Ginali grinned, inserting himself into the conversation. "But I do know that there are definitely traps we could look at setting. It might be best if we start there."

"We can do that." Sarah piped up, her bright red ponytail already bobbing with some of her infectious excitement. "Take a look and see if we could replicate at least portions of it, give ourselves the best chances."

I watched as more people stepped forward, willing to help with the purchasing of viable Magon trapping devices from the Shop. It was a relief, since I wasn't sure our treasury would currently spread that thin.

It was pretty heartwarming to see this much teamwork and goodwill.

I glanced at Dor, who was watching me with a grin. We didn't even need to say anything to know what we were thinking.

The plan came together, better than I'd expected when Hirish brought it up initially. Sure, why not? Let's kill a dragonified magpie.

Just another Tuesday in the apocalypse, right?

"You're not saying much." Evelyn nudged me. "What are you thinking?"

"How surreal this is. That this is our lives now. That we could all die if even one aspect of this hair brained plan goes sideways." Yep. That's what I was thinking. Her face paled a little and I nudged her back. "You did ask. You should know better than that by now."

She shrugged. "Sometimes your thoughts can be a lot more inspirational, enlightening even."

I rolled my eyes, trying to stop myself from blushing. "I'll enlighten you in a minute."

"Promises." She smirked, but looked straight ahead, watching as the plans begin to unfold. "So, I guess we're going to fight a dragon?"

That was just it. Even if it was partially one, it wasn't all dragon. "No, we're going to fight a Magon. I do believe there's a difference."

"Pedantic much?"

"Yes. Yes, I am." And that was just it. The room was filled with a vibrancy to the Mana I hadn't seen often before. But there was something else. Something darker underlying everything. I couldn't help but think that killing the Magon was both a great, and at the same time, a very, very bad idea.

Chapter Thirty-Five:
Build Up

24 Weeks, 1 Day Post-System Onset
10 a.m.

I was counting down the time until we started Project Lure the Flying Rat Into the Trap. Okay, that wasn't what it was called, but brevity kept me from sane. I couldn't get over the sheer number of pressure plate traps the tech department had produced. I mean, I understood that we needed them, and that they were capable of it—but still. The sheer scope of what we were about to attempt was daunting.

Every type of mutated creature and monster out there that we could bait into the Thunderdome of doom, we were luring. We had so many scents it was dizzying to look at the array of different colored tags.

"Reinforcements done?" I muttered, knowing Kyle would hear me.

"Yep—the arena is as reinforced as it's going to get. Take a breath." He absentmindedly squeezed my shoulders.

I took in the spread of traps in front of me. That was a whole lot of luring right there. Dozens and dozens of trigger plate traps, as well as boxes full of scent grenades.

"These ones here," Sarah was explaining, her eagerness exuding waves of excitement, "when activated and thrown up toward the sky, they will bob in the air for about twenty seconds, including detonation. The scent should then float through the air and hopefully catch some updrafts. Should help to lure the Magon in."

"You're playing overseer?" Kyle teased from next to me.

"Of course. Got to see if everyone is doing things correctly," I quipped, not missing a beat, but somehow also wishing that I could do more than just watch.

"Don't worry, you know you and Dequasha have to help us all place the traps in the most strategic positions given Mana readings in the area, right?" He focused on me for a second, like he was willing me to answer the question.

"Technically." I smiled, but I didn't feel happy. Yes, it was exciting, but that was a lot of pressure. Mana could, in the event remote detonations failed, exert enough pressure to set the traps off too. We'd just have to be super precise. Tension played all through my back, giving me aches I hadn't had for a while. This was stressful. There was so much that could go wrong.

"It's okay, Kira." Kyle did that looking-me-in-the-eye thing to pass confidence onto me. Only today wasn't the right day for it.

"I'm fine. What I need to know is what about the trap?" Excellent change of subject if I do say so myself.

Kyle grimaced. "Yeah. We're lucky we took up donations for that. Cost a chunk of Credits. Like six hundred thousand."

Ouch. That was painful. "Did the treasury foot any of it?"

"A third." He sighed. "Like I said, it's lucky the people in the settlement are willing to work together."

"So. Flight path—check. Massive Magon-catching trap—check. Scent traps in place—check?" I asked, knowing I hadn't really forgotten anything, but still feeling like something was missing.

"Got it all. Stop stressing." My twin winked at me and walked over to talk to Mike.

Yeah. Good one. Telling me to stop stressing is like shoving me directly into stress.

Evelyn nudged me from the other side. "You're not sure this is a good idea, are you?"

I laughed. Poker face had never been my thing, and apparently the end of the world hadn't changed that. "No. I'm not. There's just so much up in the air. Pun not intended, and we don't know exactly why or how the Magon is going to react, or if this is even going to work. It's not like we can do a trial run with the Magon. Will the other creatures do the damage we need it to? Or are we just going to really piss it off? Call me stupid, but pissing off that thing doesn't sound like the greatest idea.

"I'm not trying to be a wet blanket, but we don't know anything about the damned creature except that it's really and truly strong." And could swallow any of us with one bite. But I didn't need to add that level of visceral horror to my concerns.

Evelyn squeezed my shoulders in a brief hug. "You're just being the mumma . . . bear. Since we already have a wombutt."

I laughed despite my current mood. She was good at that. "Yeah. I am." The thing was, even the laughter didn't assuage the fact that I was still completely certain this was not the wisest thing to do.

Watching the rest of our settlement get giddy about it, how they embraced this chance to take a win over the Magon, I could understand it. Kyle moved away, walking over toward Melody to talk to her. But not even that bit of bait bettered my mood. Evelyn left to join a large group of Archers and Ranger types who were likely discussing ranged strategies. I knew there had to be failsafe strategies for if the remote triggers to the traps and grenades didn't work.

Dequasha suddenly stood next to me, her calming floral influence doing nothing for my brain at that point in time. She had to know too, right?

"You know this isn't the best idea, right?" I muttered at her and her silence.

She didn't respond straight away, but her petal limbs rippled with some train of thought I wished I could have insight into.

"It is an idea. The idea has merit. In the end, it will all come down to execution."

I'd never thought of her as being able to scowl, but her expression right then definitely resembled one. She wasn't happy—I could feel that coming off her—and while her words weren't untrue, Diviner gave me this smoky overview of her mood.

"But tell me how you really feel," I snapped, because I was done with everyone being careful. "Spill it. What are you thinking?"

Dequasha cocked her head to one side and shrugged. "It's not as bad as you imagine. But we've been in the System a lot longer than you. There are things that it deals well with, and things that it reacts to. I am not yet certain how the System will react to this, should we succeed."

And yet again something I entirely hadn't taken into consideration. How had we gone almost six months and not really thought about how the System worked? Mana consumed my every thought as it was, and I still had so far to go to figure it out. But the System.

"The System funnels the Mana, right? I mean, even without it, the Mana would still be all around us." I gestured vaguely around.

Dequasha nodded. "Yes. And no. But yes."

Gee. Thanks for that clarification.

"Well, we're going to send everyone out on their usual patrols, I think." Because we were, and I knew that Dequasha knew it, except I wanted to say it out loud anyway.

"Of course. It makes the most sense. Placing the trigger plates manually has so far been much more successful than manually flying them in." Then she turned to me, and again, I couldn't read the expression in her eyes. "But we, we need to map out the best Mana flow lines."

"Say what now?"

"Mana flow. You've learned how to track it and identify it, to see what it's triggered with and exactly how that Mana might end up being used. You've become somewhat of an early warning system. Now you have to learn to apply it so that you can follow where it is that it goes." She sounded slightly impatient, but I had difficulty grasping her words.

"So the Mana flow does more than just show us what could be incoming?" Seriously, today was a day for headaches.

Dequasha nodded, her eyes back on the groups of people getting new devices from the tech team. "Mana, as you know, is in everything. Everything in this Dungeon World requires Mana to survive now. It is everywhere and in all places. Mana is just like oxygen in that it is a necessary currency now."

"Yes. Yes. I know that. Mana saturation is the whole reason we're in this Dungeon World mess to begin with." Yep, definitely a headache day. "This all relates to the Mana flow lines you just mentioned?"

"Mana is like scattered seeds on the wind that create a path. You can always follow its flow. I did think I'd already explained it clearly. I apologize that I didn't. You'll surpass my Mana reading abilities eventually, you know. Your field of expertise will end up far superior to mine."

I wasn't sure, but she sounded a little sad at that fact. "Right now, though, I'm still a clueless kid at this. So please, don't leave me to my own devices just yet."

"I think you'll surprise yourself," she said and patted me gently on my shoulder, like she was waiting for a response.

"Do you have time to go over some of this Mana flow detection?" I ventured to ask, because she hadn't left yet.

Dequasha smiled. "I think that is an excellent idea."

Stepping over to me, she placed one of her petal-like hands over my right one, lifting my arm to point at one of the walls that was still close to the center. "Can you detect the Mana flow that keeps that particular wall in place?"

Activating my ocular implants was second nature to me now. They were just another extension of my abilities, of my body. The crystalline overlay of the walls had a blue hue to it. Encased in Mana was more how I perceived it. An ever-present stabilization that represented our defenses.

"Yes. But it doesn't seem to be flowing, more rigidly bound into a form." Yeah, that was what it felt like for me.

"Only partially accurate," Dequasha murmured, pulling back her soft fingers. "Just because it isn't moving right now doesn't mean the Mana is not mobile."

She began to walk quickly toward it, and I rushed to follow after her. Reaching down, she picked up a small stone and hefted it in her hand. "Watch the wall directly in front of us."

I wanted to make a smart-arse comment, but I knew she was trying to help me understand my abilities, and that would be a dick move. The world would be a much better place if we all lived by the rule of *don't be a dick*. So I said nothing and waited.

When the stone impacted the wall, my sight picked up a definitive ripple. Even from that tiny point of impact, the Mana absorbed the shock and rippled outward like when you drop a stone in a lake. All within the confines of the casing. "Oh. I think I get it."

"The System allows us to use Mana more effectively. Sort of like a computer that directs the flow of power." The concept was eye opening, and I looked at my mentor for confirmation.

She frowned slightly. "Yes. Simplistically put and perhaps not as encompassing as the actuality. But I believe you've understood what I wanted to show you. Now you just need to apply that understanding to everything."

"Simplistically?" I asked, wishing I had more time to learn more right now.

Dequasha smiled. "There's a whole lot of System Mana conversion that could take years to understand fully. But for now, you have the basics. Work with those."

"We're done?" I asked, feeling a little disappointed.

"Oh, no. Now I want you to hunt down more System uses of Mana and understand how the Mana flow within those works too." Her chameleon eyes blinked at me, and I could tell she was excited.

To be honest, so was I. Understanding why and how the world had really changed? That made the scientist in me just giddy.

Nighttime fell, and I still didn't feel ready. T minus ten hours before we set this plan into action and my cold feet could have frozen the ocean. The house was too quiet. The kids and Kyle, Melody, Evelyn, and even a few more of our Archer friends were all out playing with Mumma and Wombie. I sat inside, with my hands clutched around a cup of warm kipatchya, watching the liquid inside like maybe it held all the answers I needed.

"You're not dealing well with this, are you?"

I looked up to find Mason standing in the kitchen doorway. He'd grown—at least I thought he had, a little. Human genome treatments for the win, apparently. His hair hung down into his left eye, but he didn't blink it away. Some things never changed. He'd always loved that artistic sort of look. Always enjoyed doing things just that bit differently.

"I'm just not feeling it." That was right, if a slight avoidance of the subject.

"Why?"

Typical Mason. Curious to a fault. "Shush. It's not like that."

"Then explain what it is."

Point. I got the sigh out of the way and turned to face him fully. "This . . . Mana ability I have. That everything in my Class plays off—it also gives me gut feelings. Like the stirring of the Mana all around us is sending me alarm bells. There's nothing definite, just this overwhelming feeling of *no*. So, you're right, I can't shake it. This sensation isn't about to bugger off."

"I see," he said in the tone that meant I knew he didn't actually see. But that was okay. He'd done what he'd set out to do, made me talk, made me put thoughts into words even if I hadn't been so inclined.

"Thanks, Mason." I meant it. I was kinda glad he was still here, still hanging on.

"Always." Then he paused just before leaving to join the others outside. "Thank you, for keeping them safe. I barely survived myself. I don't think I could have done it with them in tow. So . . . thanks, Kira."

And then he was gone. Leaving me with thoughts that didn't just hinge on the fact that the System probably wouldn't like us attacking its biggest predator this early in the game.

No, it left me to worry about mortality and leaving my kids without a parent. Because that was also the sort of guy Mason was. To make random comments that sent me spiraling. Not his fault, because my brain wasn't his.

But goddamn it.

Another sigh, but this time it involved stretching, letting the thoughts go, and trying to prepare myself for what I knew was about to come. I'd have to get to sleep, because tomorrow without sleep was going to be fucking woeful.

"Mum?" Jackson poked his head in, followed by the rest of him. "Can we chat?"

"Of course." Because talking to your teen wasn't something you ever rejected. There were precious few times in the last couple of weeks where he'd sought me out, so I wasn't about to let that go. "What's up?"

"Wisp. Turns nine in like . . . a week, right?"

I nodded, swallowing the lump in my throat. She was getting closer to System activation age. Weird how the world turned. "Yep. That she is."

"I think we should throw her a small birthday party. Give people rides on Mumma and maybe Wombie? Kind of let people realize that we can have some semblance of normalcy. You know?" His eyes were so bright, so full of hope.

Who was I to gainsay that? Who was I to give him that reality check that was *sure, we can have a party for her if we all survive the oncoming shitstorm*? I did what any good mother would do and pulled him in for a hug. "Of course. You just jot down whatever it is that you think would be best for her party, and I'll make it happen."

"Awesome! But it's a secret; you can't tell her. I want her to have the best day ever!" His entire body radiated excitement, positivity.

"Done," I said, feeling like maybe I had done something right in the world after all. I watched him go, wondering how I got so lucky to have such a good kid.

A kid who thought of others when everything else had a cloud hanging over it.

I wasn't sure he'd understand just what he'd done, but he'd lit that fire I needed under me. This trying to figure out why I felt disjointed wasn't enough. This wasn't the time to sit down and wonder if we *could* do something. This was the time to make sure that we *succeeded* in doing the thing.

In this case, killing that massive bloody pest in the sky. Sure, the System might spit something else out at us that could be ten times worse. But you know what? We'd take that on too.

Activate Mana Sense, Mana Purification, and Ecological Chain Specialist. We were so much more than a Class-7 Inhospitable ZFQ rating.

Go-go pissed-off Australians.

Chapter Thirty-Six:
Show Down

24 Weeks, 3 Days Post-System Onset

9 a.m.

We'd been up since sunrise setting up for the day. Trigger traps were all set, remote detonators ready. We'd run paths of them all the way through the Koala Bushlands, even through and down to the Daisy Hill area. Once we triggered them, there was no turning back.

Scents would waft up from behind rocks, underneath brush, in the sides of trees our Arborers had coaxed into helping us. I surveyed the expanded main arena from one of the stands disguised as brush at the base of the tree. There were stands up higher in several trees, but we'd decided that wasn't the best vantage point when we were, luring a flying beast into our midst.

If you didn't know that the area all around us wasn't natural, you wouldn't notice. The ground was a little smoother, cleared away by our Earthen Movers. The Landscapers had created all the hiding places for the scent traps both here in the Thunderdome, as Kyle insisted on calling it, and along the paths that led to and beyond all the nests we regularly patrolled.

The trees in the middle of it were placed strategically, as were any boulders. And the final crowning glory was the massive dragon trap we'd purchased from the Shop. Rin stood next to me, fidgeting with her hands as she looked out. She'd been in charge of placing the trap and I could tell how nervous that made her.

"It'll be okay." I tried to reassure her.

She shook her head. "That's not it. Even though we've been working on replicating it, and we likely can, I don't think we'll get a second chance at this. That creature isn't stupid. She's super smart. She will learn from this if we don't end it today."

"We will end it today." I hoped I managed to put more confidence into my voice than I felt in that moment. Rin's comments made me second guess the plan ever so briefly. We had to win. And we all knew it wasn't going to be easy.

The dragon trap had been painstakingly hidden between its four triggers and concealed under several layers of dirt. It would snap up with force when it activated, pushing through anything in its way. At least, it was supposed to.

Hirish's voice cracked over the walkie. We'd have to go silent after the triggers were set, couldn't afford to draw unwanted attention to where we hid observing the entire thing.

"Quiet down. We will be triggering the scent traps in five minutes."

Evelyn reached over from my other side and squeezed my hand. I wasn't sure if the shaking I felt run through her was adrenaline, fear, or perhaps just the breeze shaking the trees we were attached to.

I squeezed back.

Jackson was at home with Wisp, charged with keeping an eye on all the kids—helping Avery and Jana. At least they were safe.

And then Hirish triggered the remote detonations.

The scent bombs were triggered in the nests and beyond, slowly making their way back to the epicenter here, where we lured them all. It took a while, but I could tell when they were close, when puffs of Mana escaped into the air as the scents exploded from their hidden spots.

There was no turning back now.

It didn't take long for all of the creatures to converge on the arena, brought in via the many different paths toward the middle, the perfect epicenter for them all to clash. I could feel the vibrations traveling through the ground and up into my body as they trampled over the earth.

Their anger was palpable, and I could see how the Mana fueled each and every one of them. The sheer number of creatures blew my mind. There were Tetchrihorns, Trapickzyers, Caneglobulous, Emugators, Escridiums, and ones whose names simply escaped me.

They all gathered in the middle . . . and stopped, staring at each other as if they were statues.

That was unexpected. I squinted, watching the Mana flow, able to identify the scent differentiations ever so slightly. With just a small push, the Mana could send the stink toward the creatures who'd find it offensive.

Evelyn nocked an arrow with a small canister woven into the fletching. Even as she released it, I could see small wisps of Mana emanating from it, the scent contained within activated. It thunked right into the eye of one of the statue-like Emugators. It squealed, turned and tail lashed all around it, hitting one of the Caneglobulous in the process, and all hell broke loose.

"Nice shot," I whispered, hoping she heard me through all of the noise out there in the arena.

She nodded, and I could tell she'd been super nervous about loosing the shot. After all, we'd had no idea if it would set the monsters on each other, of if they'd all turn around and find us. Luckily, I think the scent contained within had masked ours. And now it was so loud as the creatures began to set upon one another, us humans may as well have been invisible.

We couldn't kill them, because we needed them to kill the Magon, but we could, in fact, help make them angrier at each other until Hirish had the time to lure the Magon down to do our work for us.

Slowly, we maneuvered our way out onto the edge of the battlefield we'd created. The sheer scope of mutated creatures, and System-imported and spawned monsters was intimidating.

They spread out before us like the stuff of nightmares. Tar creatures splattering bullets all around them. But the Caneglobulous contained the explosions within the bulbous flesh and spat out their own toxins in return.

Spiderwebs shot through to the trees, sticking one of the Caneglobulous to the trunk on the sideline with a sickening crunch as it expelled a mass of toxic goo from its mouth.

Multiple Trapickzyers appeared, making a chorus of chittering noises as they moved through the tree limbs. Maybe we should have stayed inside the enclosure for a little longer. Those spider-based creatures scared me more than the damned dragon we were trying to capture.

Thick and strong, the spiderwebs caught one of the Tetchrihorns in their traps, wrapping the spun web around the creature with lightning speed. This caused several of the other creatures to direct their attention toward the spiders.

We inched around the perimeter. I tagged several monsters with Mana Stone, seeking to keep our healers at least stocked in Mana. Mages, led by Ray and Eritia, fired strategically, making sure to send in their spells on a strict rotation so as not to pull the combatants away from each other.

Archers and Rangers followed the same pattern. They fired single shots into the midst, hitting their targets with slow burning damage over time that would stick with all the other damage they took. Not to mention strategically placing ice traps around the edges to make sure our bait didn't leave the prescribed area.

I'd never seen so many of us working together at once. Hundreds of us, all filled with adrenaline while we waited for the Magon.

We began to draw back, letting the monsters do our dirty work for us. That had, after all, been the entire plan. These creatures would only work together in the loosest senses possible, against the bigger threat.

Right now, they were intent on each other, fighting with abandon in such a swirled of limbs and abilities that I could barely distinguish how many of them there were.

I swallowed around a massive lump in my throat as we pulled back even more. Staying out of the direct line of fire was the smartest thing to do, even as I watched Gemma dart in and out as she set off a couple of the scent traps that hadn't triggered remotely.

The bigger the smell cloud, the better our chances of setting everything off in perfect order.

Koalzillas' claws raked through many of the tough spiderwebs, the sharp appendages making short work of the intricate designs. But the material stuck to them too, attaching them to the rest of the structure. The Koalzillas roared with anger, their irritation at the sticky substance all over their claws. Their cries reverberated through the surrounding trees and made me put my hands over my ears.

Claws encountered globby flesh, horns gashed into furry sides, and toxic goop ate through sticky webs. Slowly but surely, they were wearing each other down. I glanced around looking for Hirish and the Archer's he'd borrowed to send the airborne scent grenades up into the Magon's flight path.

I could barely see them where they stood, probably fifty or so meters from us, through the trees just beyond the arena. They were just lowering their rifles and bows, which meant they were done. Now we just had to hope this worked.

As we did, Kyle motioned for all of us to fan out, to the hiding places closer to the anchor points set up for the dragon trap. We could keep up intermittent ranged fire from there, and if all went to plan, we'd snap the trap closed and take down the Magon after it took care of all the other creatures.

Once it got here, that is.

Like I'd triggered it, a massive caw sounded over the entire battlefield.

That keening sound that was half roar, like a lion about to devour its prey. It signified that the magpie-dragon hybrid was about to divebomb near us, and there was nothing we could do about it. My blood ran cold.

"Take cover!" Hirish's voice bellowed across the battlefield.

We dove behind the viewing box closest to us, almost getting tangled in the brush that hid it. The last thing any of us wanted was for the Magon to see us humans before it focused on the prey it had descended to find.

We'd cleared enough of the area to make the arena that the Magon could set down, but considering flight gave it an aerial advantage, I wouldn't blame it for staying aloft as long as it could. There were still trees and boulders and ways for its prey to hide though, and that had been done very deliberately.

Couldn't make it too easy for it to kill its targets, or we were never going to whittle down its health. As it cawed again, every single one of the mobs turned to watch its descent. I could see them shaking where they stood.

The dirt and earth around us whipped up with the pressure from the Magon's wings as it buffeted the ground.

Koalzillas snarled; Caneglobulous hopped past the Trapickzyers they'd been puffing up against. Tetchrihorns pawed at the ground like bulls ready to go in for the fight. All of it, even as the Magon swooped down and snagged a Koalzilla straight from the ground. Just picked up that twelve-foot-tall creature and carried it up with it.

And then it let the monster go, falling all the way down to land on the ground in the middle of the clearing with an explosive thud that shook the very ground we stood on. There was a crunch as bones broke, but even as we watched the creature, it began to shake its head, growling in desperation. Yep, it's not like the System was going to let a fall from ten meters in the air kill a Koalzilla.

All the other creatures looked on in silence for one very loud moment, their eyes glued to that spot. The only sound was the descending wing flap as the Magon dropped back down toward us all.

And then three of the Emugators squawk-roared and took off in different directions as if their flight response had just got past their shock. The sheer terror in that sound acted like a catalyst for everything else. All at once the rest of the creatures broke into rabid fight mode.

Koalzillas began hurtling chunks of trees up at the Magon. Or earth. I couldn't tell; maybe it was their own feces. Most of the chunks flew wide, but some hit it dead center in the body. It cawed and turned to face them, angling itself down for what would have been a poised divebomb, except it never got that far.

Scaling the trees on the edges of the clearing, the Trapickzyers held themselves as high as possible, shooting their sticky webs directly at the creature's wings with a speed that belied the size and weight of the substance. Mana churned around every single monster, every single tree, every blade of grass trampled or otherwise.

It flooded the area, begging to be soaked in and scooped up, waiting its turn to be slowly refilled into the moving vats of Mana urns that were the monster bodies. The Magon cried out again, tugging at its wings, barely able to keep itself afloat with the massive, scaled feathers caught in those traps.

A few of the feathers drifted down, torn from their moorings, taking the webs that were sticking to them to the ground. The smell of sweat and adrenaline and musk and blood filled the air, clogging every breath I took— not that I was breathing much, as I waited in tense anticipation.

This had to work. It had to.

Caneglobulous shot their toxic slime up as far as they could, often falling short, but not seeming to care, their panic practically palpable. Only toads who got it into their heads to use tree stumps and trunks to jettison themselves off as they jumped managed to get their attacks to hit anywhere near parts of the Magon that could be damaged.

It cried out, struggling now, pumping its hefty wings up and down so forcefully that the trees the spider webs were attached to, began to bow and groan. Small tremors rocked all around us as roots began to pull from the earth.

The Magon's health was still ridiculously high, none of these attacks really denting it at all. It still sat around eighty-five percent when it snapped two of the six webs holding onto one of its wings and spun sideways with a lurch. One of the Trapickzyers on that tree was sent flying, landing amidst the monsters below.

I noticed a Koalzilla take an opportunistic swipe at the Trapickyzer before the monster scrambled back upwards, glaring at the Koalzilla but focused on clambering up another tree away from the thrashing Magon.

We couldn't afford to pull the complete ire of the Magon, so only our ranged were metering out damage in a very controlled manner. Enough to help chip away, but not enough to override the things sense of self-preservation against the other creatures. The majority of our attacks were DoTs, meant to tear down its massive regeneration, to chip away at the System-aided healing.

I tracked the Mana around us; my only contribution to the Magon portion of the fight was to maintain Mana Stone on her at all times. We didn't need crowd control, and we didn't require any sort of extra implosions that healed us. The less I took from it, the less it would notice us . . . or me, at least.

None of the creatures we'd lured into our trap seemed aware of us humans at all. Which was exactly what we'd been aiming for.

The Magon finally tore herself out of the second set of spider webs that attempted to trap her to those trees and shot up into the sky. For a few moments I wondered if maybe we'd chased her too far away, if perhaps she was done with today. That wasn't going to be good for any of us.

She proved my thoughts wrong a split second later when she banked in the air and dove straight back down toward the plethora of creatures still trying to hit her with their attacks. She raked through the arena, taking Tetchrihorns down, clearing out the Caneglobulous with piercing attacks, and ramming through the Koalzillas, sending them all sprawling from her wing attacks.

A small trail of blood followed her that was her own, having nothing to do with the creatures she demolished on the way. Her impact against the other creatures cost her as well, bringing her life down several percent more, even as she grabbed a Trapickyzer by one of its many legs and dragged it back up into the sky with her, keening all the while.

A part of me admired her ability to just pick shit up in her mouth and drop it to the ground. Those damned spider mobs had caused us all sorts of trouble when we fought them, but for the Magon? Not even a blink of her massive eyes.

Even if the damned System made it totally unrealistic for them to survive long falls.

Just a peck of the beak even while it flailed all of its appendages as she flew it through the air and executed what I thought might be her favorite trick.

She dropped the flailing spider, but unlike just dropping the Koalzilla, she pegged it. Deliberately reined back her head and shot it down as if she was throwing a ball with deliberate force at the ground. There was none of this light falling it had done with the Koalzilla earlier.

No, the poor Trapickyzer flew toward the earth ten times faster, attempting to shoot webs out to save itself, but nothing attached, only strands of sticky spider rope jettisoning out in desperation all around it, finding purchase nowhere until the monster finally hit the ground, right next to where the previous victim had managed to walk away.

It exploded into so many pieces of spider that it resembled a blood bomb. Bits and pieces, blood and viscera, splattered against all of the creatures in the vicinity. Some of those appendages even tore through a few of the closest creatures.

Another moment of silence followed again.

Several of the Caneglobulous hopped off in the other direction this time, with no rhyme or reason, totally panicked. Not that I could blame them. Being splattered all over the earth wasn't one of my priorities today either.

The Magon was not waiting, having flown back upwards and turning around to conduct a strafing run of its own, tired of getting torn apart. It opened its mouth, and fire exited.

A wall of fire shot past us all, barely missing the trees we hid behind, but the heat flowing off it made all of us sweat. When the flames cleared, all that was left of the fleeing toads were crisp piles of charcoal with the Magon perching atop several of them, her wings fanned back, cawing out a challenge.

Her health still sat at seventy-two percent, and I swear it regenerated noticeably even as we sat there stunned. But her Mana had plummeted when she used that firewall, and that gave me some measure of hope. Now we just needed to figure out how much more damage we had to do to kill her and outpace the System.

The Tetchrihorns reared up and rushed the massive dragon bird. I wished I had their sorts of guts. Mana pooled around the Magon; her ambient regeneration was off the charts. Even with the poisons, the chemicals, the electronic burrowing barbs and Mana damage, it kept rising.

Cold clarity hit as fear spread through me.

There was no way we could outmaneuver the Magon. Even with the copious amounts of mutations we had fighting technically with us, even with the amount of damage she was taking—we were still too little, still too weak.

Was the most we could hope out of this to not die, and maybe to clear all of the patrols for miles for a few days? Or was the trap really going to give us the small advantage we needed?

Damn it, the trap had to work. Or else all of this was in vain.

Even as the Magon launched itself at another of the Koalzillas, flapping its wings, grabbing at them with its legs like a cat when you try to stroke its stomach. Pecking with its beak and devastating accuracy. Drawing back to breathe fire on and roast its targets.

Hirish shot a message over the fight chat, raid chat, whatever you wanted to call it. To just reach all of us and not have to speak out loud and draw attention to ourselves.

Do as much damage to it as we can. Trigger the last wave of scent traps. Bring them down, clear the area. Do as much damage as possible. Stay out of it. Be subtle.

I could practically hear Gemma rolling her eyes. She was the least subtle rogue I knew. Nothing to do with how good her stealth capabilities were, and everything to do with her penchant for making mutations die in the most graphic ways possible.

I cracked my neck and pushed out my own command message since Hirish was on the opposite side of the clearing and I needed him to pay attention to my question.

Is our damage even noticeable?

I could practically feel Hirish bristling at the comment. There was a pause before he replied.

Every bit of damage helps prevent regeneration for that split second. It's the only way we can chip away.

That made sense. It did.

Got it.

I could tell Hirish wasn't going to be amused by my comment, but I'd had to make it. We had to know if this was already a lost cause. From his comment, I gathered that he didn't believe so. I'd have to have faith in his judgement for now.

Even as more monsters poured into the clearing, gathered there by the sheer amount of scent and battle, the sound of the rage in the clearing, I wouldn't let myself hope yet. We just had to work through it methodically and we would do this.

Drawn into the battle by baser instincts, the creatures were funneled through into the arena only to be met with fire and claws, beak and wings. All the while we attacked from the perimeter to from the outside take out the monsters that tried to slip into our sections of the twisting edge we'd created so they could flee. We couldn't risk them running, we needed their sacrifice.

Besides, the System would respawn their nests in a few days anyway.

Even with hundreds of us, we had to feel like tiny fleas biting her. Her damn feathers looked to be absorbing a chunk of the damage, offering her a high resistance to the vast majority of damage hitting her. The attacks that did get through barely budged her health.

I kept watching the Mana flows, trying to figure out what kind of damage types were the worse for her. If we could figure that out, we could do more damage, hurt her faster. From what I could tell, ice appeared to do the most damage, followed closely by earth, which was good news for me. At least once we got her grounded, anyway.

The rest of the day began to fracture, stretching out in front of us. Minutes like hours, hours like flashes in the pan.

Koalzillas, Emugators, Caneglobulous, Tetchrihorns, Trapickzyers, and just so many other creatures. They all went up against her, and were pecked, burnt, taloned and batted aside like so many ants.

Out of nowhere, another influx of creatures bombarded the very southern tip of our arena, plowing into the group of people we had waiting out the fight in that quadrant of the arena.

I wasn't sure where the creatures came from, but the screams to the south of us filled me with dread. Maybe there were scent traps we'd forgotten or something, but people were on fire, some people got impaled by Tetchrihorns who took them by surprise. And we had to redirect the creatures away from the survivors back to the Magon they were supposed to fight.

We suffered losses I didn't have the time to check up on.

Now that we weren't in the thick of things, unable to be in the center of it all, I felt like we were impossibly weak, sitting ducks, because those injuries hadn't even come from the Magon itself. No, they'd been from the regular daily monsters that we cleared all the damned time.

The sheer force of Mana that surrounded the Magon, that constantly flowed both into and out of her, blew my mind. She *was* Mana, made from it, a conduit for it. Except when she used her special abilities and drained a whopping chunk. We needed to make her use that Mana so we could even stand a chance.

Then there was a blur of movement right past us, faster than anything I'd expected, larger than anything I could place. Compact and quick, it sped right into the center of the arena, twirling around until it smashed straight into the unexpecting Magon, butt first. The impact could be heard through the arena, echoing through the trees as bones split and the creature keened.

When her attacker came to a halt, panting in all her glory, I gasped and stood up straight.

No. No. No.

Mumma Wombutt had come to our rescue with her armored butt and driven it straight into the Magon's side. The impact was still visible, even as the other creatures all dove in, ignoring the mutated wombat as they fell upon the Magon while she was stunned, taking advantage of the injuries.

It gave them precious moments to inflict unbridled damage on their flying nemesis. In a time where every percent of health brought us closer to victory.

I willed for Mumma to hear me, for her to understand that she needed to run. Our wombutt wasn't stupid, because she took one glance at me, and bolted straight back in the direction she came from.

And her brief presence might even have given us the advantage we needed.

❖

Even as the sun began to set, the blood of all the creatures marred the cracked earth beneath the Magon's talons, her health consistently dripping like the blood from the plethora of wounds encasing her body.

Her wings were shredded, so much that she couldn't fly consistently anymore, and I ached with guilt that I felt at harming her. Sure, she'd pick any of us off that she could and tear into us for her Sunday brunch, but that didn't mean she wasn't majestic and beautiful. Now . . . she was a bloody mess.

She was far stronger than we'd realized, and even hitting it with everything ranged that we had, even metering it out, we barely made a dent with our human abilities. All we could do was pile it on, so that over time that dent became a tear.

Most of the damage? It came from the creatures we'd lured into fighting for us. So, in a way, our plan worked, but in every way that it really counted—I felt like we were sort of cheating. But I guess we needed to cheat so we could survive. Right?

The Magon lifted herself about ten meters in the air, unsteady, one broken and featherless wing creaking and twisting in the wrong way. Only determination and anger seemed to help it rise, and even then, it only lasted a few flaps. With a keening cry of what sounded like impatience if you asked me, she plummeted to the ground, unable to support herself any longer.

She spun about, screaming in rage, batting monsters with her uninjured wing. Even as she got rid of one side, more monsters rushed her, as if sensing her death, the end of her existence, and hungry for her flesh and blood and experience. And fuck, did monsters get experience? I mean, I assumed they did, considering levels kept rising around us, but was that because *we* leveled or . . . I shook my head.

It'd been a long day, one filled with pain and blood and a throbbing headache. The Magon's ability to switch its resistances around to protect itself meant that every time I figured out which resistance was highest and which lowest and we switched attacks, it changed shortly thereafter too.

Always adapting. Eventually.

I had to keep watching; I had to give warning for when its fire attacks, now more intermittent than ever, lashed out. More and more of the creatures were torn down—by the Magon as it thrashed around. But the monsters made a mess of our arena themselves. Like the giant teethy earthworms that seemed to have taken apart one entire quadrant of our hiding brush where we'd had our hidden lookouts—forcing us into more exposed locations.

Which meant temporary solutions like force fields and my own Earthen

Walls were all that kept some of our people from getting swarmed by minor monsters who were attracted here but weren't dumb enough or big enough to take on the Magon.

"What *is* that?" Kyle's voice disturbed my concentration. He might not be my kid, but my twin meant as much to me. Damn it, why did he have to come? Even if he was head of the healers.

I focused on the Magon and noticed Mana pouring into it, which meant it must have a regeneration capability too. But the Mana inside it was concentrating, changing color. starting to shift towards it wings and I had a sudden sense of foreboding.

"DOWN!" I screamed over the battle net and out loud. I no longer cared if we were going to be seen or heard.

Hitting the ground behind the damned viewing room saved us. I never even saw the attack. I heard it go off, the ripping sound of hardened wings flying through the air at the speed of sound, the crack of the sound barrier being broken, the squelching as it impacted living bodies and hissing of the feathers flying overhead.

Then, the screams. So many screams. So many *types* of screams.

Earth mutants, alien monsters, humans, wood splintering and earth settling as the attack finished. The triumphant caw of the Magon as its attackers were felled. The smell, blunted so long ago after familiarity, exploding forth as I struggled away from the bottom of the earth. Blood, bones, viscera, and offal mixing in the hot Brisbane day, melting into the remnants of boulders, trees, and churned earth.

I gagged, even as I staggered upwards, Hirsh and Kyle and others shouting damage reports and orders, trying to get to those who still lived but were damaged from the attack. Only to stare at the Magon, now bereft of its feathers.

Still alive. Triumphant, even as the few remaining monsters around it scrambled upwards.

Fuck. What if it had damaged all dragon trap anchors?

Fear hit me, making me shiver. The creature still had over five or so percent of its health left. Tiny in percentage terms, huge in terms of actual numbers. And now, now that there was no one attacking it, it was going to regenerate.

"Attack! Kill it, kill it now, damn it!" Hirsh was screaming, as was Paola and Molly and everyone who had any sense.

"Trigger the trap!" I yelled. The Hakarta looked over at me and began the process to activate the prongs that should contain the creature long enough for us to whittle down those few remaining percent.

Except that wasn't going to work yet, I could tell from the look on his face.

"It's not in the right place," I whispered, looking at the spot in the map, that my vision showed me where it needed to be. The center of the X. But the Magon had kept moving, kept fighting and tearing down the anything it could lay its eyes on and now, it wasn't where we needed it to be. "We've got to lure it back."

Cold certainty ran through me. I knew what needed to be done. My hands were sweaty, my heart beating like a machine gun. Mason was here now; my kids would be fine should something happen. Not that I wanted it to, but right now thousands of lives were potentially on the line.

I put a hand on the slope of the earth, hating the idea but knowing if we didn't end it now; that intelligence, that rage . . . it would never let us live this down. If we didn't do this now, we were all dead.

I would do anything to keep my kids alive.

Anything at all.

So I acted.

Or I meant to. Because Evelyn was there, a second later. Pulling me down, snapping at me. "What the hell do you think you're doing?"

"We have to stop it, kill it! The trap, the explosive . . ." I repeated myself. Or did I say the other things in my mind? I wasn't sure, not with the adrenaline and headache pounding into me.

"Then we'll get it. But not you," Evelyn said.

Fear ran through me then, as I gripped her arm. Not her either.

Then, a cry. From all around. I twisted about, to see a trio of figures, running for it. Gary, Drake, and Gemma—all of them, running for the monster, taunting it close.

"NO!" I shouted, but my voice was drowned out. By the Magon's screams, its head tracking those three. It had no more Mana left, not enough to breathe fire anyway, so it followed after them, trying to chase them down, limping, beaten, taking hits from arrows and spells, only fractionally chipping away at its health.

"Don't hold back! Kill that thing. Distract it, but keep it moving," Hirsh roared over the channel. He and the unit commanders, they gave more specific orders. I couldn't help but feel impotent.

Support was useless. Even Water Siphon did little to the Magon, but every little bit counted. Making everyone else do more damage could only kill it faster.

Then Tanner appeared in the middle, right where the bloody magpie needed to be. He stood there, like a fucking hero, and taunted it, while Gary darted in, distracting it and keeping it in place.

Where X marked the spot, like sitting ducks with the mutated bird.

Hirish activated the trap, effectively scooping up the Magon . . . except only three of the prongs worked, and the portions that did made Gary lose his footing long enough to become a crunchy snack that echoed throughout the arena as the Magon chomped down, and then dropped his lifeless corpse when it realized it had been trapped.

My stomach rebelled, and it was only then that I noticed Rin sprinting across the clearing to the anchor that didn't trigger. Without it, the trap wasn't finished—the creature could still escape.

I hadn't known Rin could run so fast. She made it there, just in time to hit the anchor manually, just in time for it to snap up, just in time for a claw to rake forward and impale her through the chest where she stood before the trap finally closed into place, sealing her death.

Fuck.

No.

Later.

No time for grief now.

Right now.

There was just Tanner, holding his own inside the trap. He had to know right? Even so, grim determination rested on his features. No regrets. Sheer willpower.

It took seconds, I think? Perhaps minutes or hours, but I'd be able to play the scene back in my head, over and over again, every excruciating detail, for as long as I lived.

Gary's body bouncing lifelessly inside with the Magon, who screamed in frustration as it continued to trample him to a pulp, angry at being bereft of its regeneration thanks to the trap. The anchors held fast, even as Rin's body was stuck between the two seals, her arms flapping limply in death as the Magon continued to rage.

The explosive charges ticking up, the high-pitched squeal that threatened to shatter my eardrums. Tanner's determined resignation just before the bombs fully charged.

And the explosion that shattered everything inside that trap, making a crater below it in our now-decimated arena.

Dust and stone and dried blood rained down all around us, the explosives we'd attached to the trap having done their work, along with the fail-safes we'd buried in the ground beneath it rupturing upwards. The trap essentially left a bag of blood, feathers, and bone fragments, torn apart by the most powerful explosives we'd been able to muster. With all its System advantages stripped from it by the trap, the Magon died.

Hirish activated the release, dropping the massive trap down, even as I pushed away the rampant notifications trying to flash in my face.

It was a testament to how much the apocalypse had broken my sensitivity levels. The sight before me made me gag, but that was it.

The Magon's legs were broken, the fragile, hollow bones in its chest cracked and showing as the flesh itself was stripped from it as flame and acid ate away at its protection. It choked and keened, rolling half-blinded eyes towards us.

And it was still not enough.

What the hell? Even with Rin torn to shreds, with Gary an unrecognizable clump of bones and sinew mixed somewhere with the Magon's not yet remains . . . there was still a sliver of life left.

"Melee fighters, go!" Hirsh roared, raising himself up so he could aim his beam rifle too. Galvanized by his words, everyone ran in, screaming. I poured my Mana and anger into Water Siphons, into Mana Stones and Implosions, and I ran in as well, hefting my Warhammer.

This was it. Just half a percent with a creature that might as well be dead already.

The sounds of blades cutting into flesh, of the hard thump of blunt weapons like my Warhammer hitting flesh filled the clearing. The hiss of burning bones, noxious fumes choking the air as we struck and struck and struck again.

Every single blow, every single spell, was our revenge on it for taking so much from us. Maybe some of it was revenge on the System for Dungeon Worlding Earth.

Weak, struggling, its movements impeded by its injuries, by spells and Skills, it still struggled. It still managed to do some damage. Every time it managed to connect, someone fell, sometimes dead. Sometimes just injured badly.

Until, finally, it was done.

❖

"Fuck," I swore after watching the disgusting remains for at least ten seconds. Just to make sure it wasn't about to breathe again. I leaned against my Warhammer, my blood pounding in my ears, a few of the more crazed humans still stabbing or casting spells at it. Unwilling to believe it was dead.

Now that she was destroyed, defeated . . . I didn't feel the joy I'd expected to.

"Guess we bought ourselves a few days off patrol?" Evelyn piped up, her exhaustion showing.

"Yeah. Not sure what else we managed to buy with this, though." I couldn't get the crushed remains of Tanner, Gary, and Rin out of my head. Fuck. We'd only just got Gary back.

Kyle nudged me, his arms covered in blood spatter. "You know we have all the tools to keep this up now, right?

I nodded. "Yeah. We need to repair this arena and make some more though. Maybe we can build a tank so the next thing we get sent is easier to blow out of the sky."

"Not the worst idea." Zyrilian suddenly stood next to us, Piola at his side. "After all, the next thing is going to be harder to kill. Especially now the System has tuned in to what you can accomplish."

Ray scowled at him. "What the hell are you talking about? The whole plan was to get her out of the way. To just give ourselves a breather."

Zyrilian raised an eyebrow. "But we already told you. The System needs to fill the void. Your Mana levels are too high for low-Level monsters to contain it. There will always be an apex predator. And despite your sordid Earth history, I can assure you, the System does not view humans as that predator."

"Wait." Ray shook his head, like he was just trying to figure out what the Zarrie was saying. "Are you trying to tell us that since we killed her, we'll just get another in her place?"

Zyrilian shrugged. "Perhaps similar. Perhaps different. Perhaps worse."

"What do you mean perhaps?" The Ice Mage was doing the hot-headed thing again, not that I could blame him. It felt like Zyrilian was baiting him.

"What I mean"—and the Zarrie drew himself up to his full Anubis height and allowed his canine teeth to gleam through into his smile—"is since the Magon died, the System will seek to replace it as this area's apex predator. It could be something easier to deal with than the Magon—more suited to our Skills. It could be something significantly more dangerous. A baby dragon perhaps?" The Zarrie shrugged. "Though there are even worse things than dragons."

"What could be worse than a dragon?" I couldn't help but ask.

"We do not name them lightly. But their legends are known—the Hunger, the Titans, the Krakota—creatures without the control of a dragon." The aliens visibly shuddered at each name, making my eyes widen. I'm not even sure I wanted to know, not if it could make hardened Galactics look like the boogieman under the bed had crawled out.

"In the end, it does not matter. There will be more challenges to face. That's what the System does. Dungeon Worlds do not get to take it easy. Not for long. Not even established ones. And Earth hasn't even been fully integrated yet."

Fucking cuntnugget of a System.

Chapter Thirty-Seven:
Aftermath

24 Weeks, 5 Days Post-System Onset
10 a.m.

I watched as the kids ran around in the makeshift outside playground Kyle, Mason, and Jackson had set up for Wisp. They'd even taken Wombie's large girth into consideration so he could weave around the swing sets and slides with his exuberant passengers.

My daughter laughed, the expression natural and real, nothing forced about it. We even had cake for later.

If Garbo hadn't been ensconced inside a military-grade barrier for our protection from the mutated creatures beyond it, it would almost have felt like pre-apocalypse.

Maybe, if we pretended, we could believe that we hadn't lost forty people during that fight. Each of whom mattered. But especially the three I'd come to know better: Rin, Gary, and Tanner.

Damn it.

Mumma Wombutt rested behind me. She'd been sticking as close to me as possible since the Magon fight. I wasn't about to argue. I was pretty sure she'd saved our arses with her own.

Mason made his way over toward me, and it was like the System knew that I needed a distraction from reality, and promptly popped a notification up in my vision.

A Habitable Safe Zone

Part Four B: Just a few more!

Goals:

1 - Completed: 5,000 total inhabitants. This may include visiting species. Current population 5,001/5,000

2 - Completed: Expand your Township to the first extension point

3 - Completed: Utilize the Town's Quest-giving system more efficiently. Or. Use it at all! 280 Town quests handed out by Sienna, Dolores, Kira, Dale, Ginali.

4 - Survive 6 months as a township - Well, you're almost there!

Reward: 25,000 Credits for your city Treasury

That's it. Nothing else. It is just a bonus quest.

I raised an eyebrow, glancing back at the center where I knew Ray, Leena, hell, the lot of them were taking care of whatever newbies had just wandered into our domain. Maybe what we'd done here was good.

Even if we'd been ripped to shreds while killing the bloody magpie dragon. The final count of the dead had arrived, and now the mural had a lot more names and a lot more pictures. Someone had taken the time to get a galactic tablet and set in the wall, so that pictures—digital pictures—of the fallen would show.

In a never-ending loop.

I could still hear the crying, the screams of those left behind when we came back when I closed my eyes. The desperate looks of those searching for a loved one.

Especially since word of how bad things had gotten filtered back before we did.

Drake hadn't surfaced from his apartment in days. He was taking Gary's death hard. Most of us were.

Cuntwaffle. Shit. Damn. Fuck.

"You're in a bad mood," Mason so brilliantly observed as he took up a spot standing next to me.

Fine fucking observation, mate is what I wanted to say but didn't. After all, it's just how he was. Blatantly oblivious, sometimes endearingly so.

Just not today.

"Not bad, just irritated." Which was highly accurate in its own way. I brushed a strand of hair that refused to stay in my ponytail out of my eyes. "She gets to enjoy today, right? You're not leaving before tomorrow."

"How did you know?" But Mason shook his head, a small smile playing on his lips. "I wouldn't leave on her birthday. I'm not a total dick."

I laughed and punched him half-heartedly in the arm. "You're not a dick at all. You just have wanderlust, and we should always have known better than to try and tie you down with kids."

"Doesn't mean I don't love them," he said, somewhat defensively.

"I know. It shows. And they get that too."

He watched the kids playing—probably about fifty of them in that little makeshift playground. "Do you really think they do?"

"I know they do. In their own way—perhaps Wisp doesn't understand it quite as well as Jackson. But they get it. Although I can't say they'll be happy with you galivanting off now that the world has ended."

"We're trying to make contact with as many settlements as possible." He left the kid topic where it was. Typical of Mason. It made it easier for him to deal by just switching to the next topic. "We even sent people down Sydney's way. I volunteered to come up here knowing that I might see you guys."

There was a smile playing on his lips, part wistful, part knowing.

"It's good that you made it." And I meant it. The kids needed to see him, and I couldn't believe how lucky we were that he'd made it up here. So many of these kids were down one or more parents. Some were now with neighbors, relatives, teachers . . .

We'd been fucking lucky.

I still had nightmares it was Jackson who lured the Magon back into the trap area and got closed in with it and the explosives, by daring the Magon to eat him.

Some days, it wasn't Jackson, but Kyle. Wisp. Evelyn. Myself.

I waited a moment for him to speak, but he was intent on watching the kids. So I sighed, drawing his attention back to me. "You're telling them you're going. Not me. I will not be the bad guy."

Mason smiled. "Not the bad guy. Got it. Don't worry, I know better than that."

There was more he wasn't telling me, but I knew him well enough to know to just give him time. It didn't take as long as I thought it would.

"I'll be coming back through here on the way back down . . ." He paused, like he was gathering his thoughts. "Maybe by then you could come down and check out Pacific Fair. With the kids. The coast has been . . . unpredictable."

"Sure. Maybe in a few months when we have some more of this stuff figured out. As long as it doesn't put the kids in immediate danger." Wasn't about to commit to the idea because of people-eating monsters, but it had the potential to be good. I at least had to wait until I was strong enough to protect us all.

We stood in silence for a while, watching our kids like we had way back when Jackson played soccer. Companionable silence of two old-as-the-hills friends.

Suddenly, Mason chuckled. "What are you going to do about the Magon's replacement?"

I shuddered, having avoided precisely that thought for as long as I could now. "Level up and hope the System doesn't send a revenge replacement too quickly."

"Solid plan."

"Only plan."

Then there was a moment's hesitation. "Will Wisp be okay? You know, unable to choose a Class or anything yet?" He spoke the question in soft words, probably so they wouldn't carry to the kids.

"We'll make sure she's okay." It was the only answer I had for him, because it was the only answer I would give myself.

❖

26 Weeks Post-System Onset
8 a.m.

Welcome to the first six months of the rest of your life.

One side effect of the Magon fight strategy was that we had a far better hold on keeping monsters at bay. One that let us fight in patrols four or five days out of the week instead of seven. One that left us feeling more rested.

One that had me in a fucking holding pattern waiting on what the cunt of a System was going to send us next.

It allowed us to devise new arenas and send non-combatants with enough heavy protection that we could begin to branch out with multiple areas capable of holding funneled monsters.

Sure, it slowed the leveling even farther, but I was okay with that. With getting to see my kids grow up instead of the whirlwind of passing in the night over the first six months. With having time to actually organize the settlement.

"Mum?" Wisp yelled from the front door where she was waiting on me to get my arse into gear. "We're going to be late!"

It sounded so right. So easy. So . . . normal.

For just a moment, I had to remind myself that none of this was any of that.

Blinking to engage my Mana Sense, I watched the way the soft Mana bled into the streets, how it wound around us, around our wombutts in an even-keeled manner. That's what the Safe Zones did. They gave us a haven from the wild abandon that was Mana outside of them.

Sometimes I could glimpse it over the walls we'd so bravely erected, like it wished that it could somehow push inside and reach us, gobble us all up in the will of the Mana.

"Coming, Buttercup!" I called out, pulling my hair into a ponytail as I went.

Things might be in a lull, and we might have killed the Magon, but I was willing to bet something would come back. Bigger and badder than ever before and hellbent on proving the System's classification of us right.

In the meantime, Mana still flowed through our flora and fauna, mutating it in ways none of us expected. Not even the System, sometimes, I think.

All we could do was hang on for the ride.

I gave Wisp a quick hug as I caught up, smiling at her and her brother and the wombutts.

Hang on tight and keep our loved ones safe.

Authors' Note

Hi there! K.T. Hanna here.

I want to thank you for reading The System Apocalypse: Australia – Bloody Oath. I still miss my hometown of Brisbane, and am hoping to get to go back and visit in 2023. I hope you enjoyed the mutations as much as I loved writing them.

If you enjoyed the first two, then you're going to love the next books. Writing in Tao's world has been a fantastic experience and I can't wait to show everyone else just how amazing Kira can be. I will be taking a short break to work on some of my own worlds before diving back into SAAU – but there will be more!

If you enjoyed the book, I ask you, please take a moment to leave a review. **Reviews** are an author's lifesblood. Without them, our books sink into obscurity. With them, most algorithms allow well reviewed books to self-promote in some way.

Want to find out more about my books? Here is how you can keep in contact with me:

- Sign up for my Reader's Group and get a short story for free! http://login.somnia-online.c/
- If you'd like to contact me, my email is: kthannaauthor@gmail.com I'll do my very best to get back to you
- If you'd like to my books prior to publishin: previews of what I'm writing, or art I'm commissioning can be found on my Patreon! https://www.patreon.com/KTHanna
- I can be found in my FB reader group fairly often, and also on Twitter & Instagram.

-KT

❖

Thank you for continuing to read System Apocalypse: Australia! Continuing Kyra's story and working with KT has been amazing. I'm always amused by the insane monsters she creates. This brings the initial six months and the Magon part of the show to the end.

Now, there's going to be a slight break as KT writes a solo series, but she is committed to writing in the System Apocalypse universe (so long as it's financially viable). If you want to see her write in this world more, please, please, please leave a review and let others know. I want her to write more!

On another note, we've got the System Apocalypse second anthology being run for the end of August this year. If it works well, we'll probably make it a bi-annual event.

As always, if you're interested in what else I'm up to or the latest news on the System Apocalypse universe, check out my socials and website!

-Tao

About the Authors

KT Hanna

KT Hanna has such a love for words, a single one can spark entire worlds.

Born in Australia, she met her husband in a computer game, moved to the U.S.A. and went into culture shock. Bonus? Not as many creatures specifically designed to kill you.

KT creates science-fiction, fantasy, and LitRPG like it's going out of style, with a dash of horror for fun! She plays computer games, and ferries her daughter everywhere, all while looking after her cats, dogs, and her husband.

No, she doesn't sleep. She is entirely powered by caffeine, Chipotle, and sarcasm.

To find out more information about the author's other series, visit their website: https://www.kthanna.com/

Tao Wong

Tao Wong is an avid fantasy and sci-fi reader who spends his time working and writing in the North of Canada. He's spent way too many years doing martial arts of many forms, and having broken himself too often, he now spends his time writing about fantasy worlds.

For updates on the series and other books written by Tao Wong (and special one-shot stories), please visit the author's website: http://www.mylifemytao.com

Or visit his Facebook Page: https://www.facebook.com/taowongauthor/

Subscribe to Tao's mailing list to receive **exclusive access to short stories in the Thousand Li and System Apocalypse universes.**

Acknowledgements
from KT Hanna

I have a lot of people to thank. Even those who don't contribute directly through the writing craft keep me going and help me write my best stories.

Love of my life, Trevor, and my little Bria. It's his fault I found the genre, and her fault I never give up on writing.

I wouldn't be here without the following friends:

Amanda W.

Quinton Shyn

Dawn Chapman

Bonnie Price

Andrea Parseneau

M Evan Matyas

Eric Ugland

Dave Willmarth

Charles Dean

Daniel Schinhofen

Jay Boyce

Michael Chatfield

Luke Chmilenko

Tao Wong

PiousVenom

And of course my family:

Mumskin & Papilie, Tracey, Bev, & Robbie.

The entire Rainbow Room.

Kristen, Jess, Sylvia

And every one of my Patrons, not to mention my FB Group. You all help me maintain a level of sanity.

About the Publisher

Starlit Publishing is wholly owned and operated by Tao Wong. It is a science fiction and fantasy publisher focused on the LitRPG & cultivation genres. Their focus is on promoting new, upcoming authors in the genre whose writing challenges the existing stereotypes while giving a rip-roaring good read.

For more information about latest releases and new, exciting authors from Starlit Publishing, visit our website or sign up to our newsletter list: https://www.starlitpublishing.com/

For more great information about LitRPG series, check out these Facebook groups:

- GameLit Society

  https://www.facebook.com/groups/LitRPGsociety/
- LitRPG Books

  https://www.facebook.com/groups/LitRPG.books

The System Apocalypse:
System Finale

There's No Way Home

Not for John Lee. His search for answers for the System Quest has taken him deep into the Forbidden Zone, into the very arms of his enemies. He's betrayed family and friends and been betrayed in turn. The most powerful human in the System has come to the final leg of his journey.

And still, he has no idea if what he will find will fill the burning need within him. For the Redeemer of the Dead will not stop, until the cries of the lost and the sacrificed are answered.

No matter the cost - to the universe, to Earth, or to himself.

Complete series
Read the last book in the System Apocalypse series,
System Finale here: https://readerlinks.com/l/2453251

Somnia Online:

Initializing

Discover the class you were born to play.

Wren, a seasoned healer, is dismayed when Somnia Online automatically assigns her character, Murmur, to the Enchanter class. Determined to overcome the unexpected setback, she assembles her guild, intent on the coveted #1 spot. Twelve keys stand between her and victory, but finding them is only part of the puzzle.

Armed with telepathic abilities, Murmur rises to the challenge. However, old rivals have followed her to Somnia Online desperate for revenge. Intricate quest lines become more dangerous as NPCs absorb powerful artifacts, and Murmur begins to wonder just what sort of AI controls the world.

Murmur questions her sanity as the real and virtual worlds mesh together. Everyone is keeping secrets from her, even the AI, and Murmur's determined to uncover them.

Complete series
Read the first book in the Somnia Online series,
Initializing here: https://readerlinks.com/l/2453253

Glossary

Ecological Chain Specialist Skill Tree

Basic Class: Pest & Pathogens Unit: Microbiologist / Plant Pathologist / Entomologist / Hydrogeologist / Molecular Biologist - Abbreviated as: Ecological Chain Specialist

Earth Barricade		Seismic Awareness		Blood Transfer
Water Siphon	Mud Slide	Rock Slide		Mana Transfer
Treesong		Top Soil	Planted in Place	Impalantation
Vine Defense		Stone's Throw		Blood Dispersion
Cocoon		Ecological Outreach		Mana Dispersion

Ecological Chain Specialist Skills

Tier One (1-9)

Earth Barricade (Level 2)

Effect: Earth Barricade allows you to command the earth beneath your feet for the sole purpose of defending you and your allies. Size and strength of the barricade depends on level of spell and caster.

Mana Cost: 20

Mana Attunement (Level 2)

Effect: Using your affinity for the world around you, you can tap into the earth and coax it to warn you of any incoming threats. Radius and specific information increases with spell and caster level.

Range: 200 meters

Blood Transfer (Level 1)

Effect: Due to your devotion to understanding the world and mechanics of biological evolution, you are able to tap into the blood of your opponents and redirect that damage to heal yourself. Only usable on self. Caution: best used on enemies. Self heal only, damage and heal amount depended on level of spell and caster.

Mana Cost: 5 mana per second

Mana Stone (Level 1)

Effect: Taps into the Mana field of your opponent, sapping their Mana stores and distributing heightened Mana Regeneration to your entire target group. Level One redistribution equals 1mps for up to 8 people. 0.5mps if more to a maximum of 15.

Mana Cost: 135 per cast - 5-minute duration

Tier Two (10-19)

Water Siphon (Level 2)

Effect: Moisture is in almost everything, humans, intergalactic species. This ability allows you to siphon the water out of anything that contains it. Level of effectiveness dependent on caster and spell level.

Mana Cost: 60 Mana per Siphon. 25% water per application. Application duration—30 seconds.

Caution: Target will be immune to the effects of Water Siphon for 15 seconds after this application.

Rock Slide (Level 1)

Effect: Rocks are a strong part of the ecosystem around you. With the right level of encouragement you might even be able to use them to attack, or defend. The choice is yours. Strength and durability dependent on spell and caster level.

Mana Cost: 30

Mana Transfer (Level 2)

Effect: Due to your devotion to understanding the world around you and how to preserve and bolster it, you can tap into the mana saturation around you, bolstering your regeneration on a constant basis. Strength and capacity is dependent on spell and caster level.

Mana Cost: 20 Mana – 30 seconds of regen increase.

Tier Two Hybrid ability (20)

Mud Slide (Level 1)

Effect: Proficiency with Water Siphoning and coaxing the ground to do what you want, enables you to pull forth a mudslide. Usable twice per day. Usage, severity, and impact dependent on caster and spell level. Caution: Make sure you understand the lay of the land before engaging this ability.

Mana Cost: 65

Area of Effect: 3-meter radius from targeted casting. Damage minimum 2x caster Level per target.

Tier Three (21-29)

Treesong (Level 2)

Effect: Your affinity with nature and the life around you allows you to be at one with the trees. Sort of. The System and Mana have made vegetation come alive. Duration of Skill varies dependent upon strength of Mana Affinity.

Command Vegetation to attack your enemies, or just leave you and your friends alone. Assistance arrives with a price. The more time you spend in the clutches of Treesong, the more likely the voices will speak to you voluntarily.

Mana Cost: Commands: 12 per second

Requests: 60 per request.

Topsoil (Level 2)

Caution is advised. Too much power could go to their heads. Too little could shrivel what you hoped to help thrive. Practice makes perfect—Mana Sense lends understanding.

Effect: Supply nutrients to those plants around you and they will be more likely to come to your aid. Increases nutrition levels and ambient Mana levels by 15% on each use. Requires a period of 72 hours for nutrition levels and ambient Mana to collect. Repeated uses within the collection period will extend timeframe and provide a prorated fraction more level increase in effects.

Mana Cost: 10 Mana per second of Topsoil Treatment per plant.

Implantation (Level 3)

Duration: 10 seconds Effect: Implant a mana bomb into the chest of your enemy. The damage done to the enemy during the implantation phase will dictate the area of effect explosion of mana and health over your party once the detonation is complete as well as the damage inflicted by the bomb on your target. Should the target die before the bomb can complete its countdown, all benefits are forfeit. Use this wisely.

Damage: 25% of damage caused is inflicted on your target, 75% of damage caused is distributed as health and mana to your party/group. Higher levels of this ability will increase the impact levels and mana cost.

Recast: 240 earth seconds

Mana Cost: 25 mana

Tier Three Hybrid Ability (30)

Planted In Place (Level 1)

Exactly what it sounds like. Call on the roots and branches, vines or leaves, of the plants around you to aid in your adventures and root your enemies in place. Effect: Employs vegetation to grasp a single target with roots, branches and vines. Length of rooting dependent upon strength of vegetation used and ambient location.

Mana Cost: 30 mana per instance

Tier Four (31-39)

Vine Defense (Level 1)

Effect: Increase your Target's armor by 100% for 15 seconds by calling on the resilience of nature.

Note: Applying Topsoil and Treesong can boost the increase to 150%.

Caution: Fully effective only in vegetation-dense surroundings.

Mana Cost: 75 Mana (+cost of Topsoil and Treesong)

Stone's Throw (Level 1)

Similar to Rock Slide, this ability allows you to form any single type of earth, from dirt to pebbles, into a projectile to be thrown at your opponent. Must have requisite materials on-hand for Stone's Throw to be used.

Be wary of where you choose to use this.

Effect: The Stone's Throw will cause 180 damage. If the stone breaks on impact, it has the potential to cause another 25% falling damage to those it cascades over.

Mana Cost: 75

Blood Dispersion (Level 1)

Due to your devotion to understanding the world and mechanics of biological evolution, you are now able to corral the lifeblood of a target to aid your party. Damage done to the target is absorbed by this Skill and dispersed as health to you and your allies.

Effect: 5% of net damage done to target is returned as health to all members in the party within a 20 meter range.

Mana Cost: 95

Other Class Skills

Leadership (Level 5)

Mana Sense (Level 17)

Due to your natural affinity for, and your innate sense with Mana, you can see all Mana flows within your immediate vicinity. The more you access this ability, the more information it will give you, and the higher it will level. This is a passive Skill.

Shield of Power

This shield can be activated on a family member regardless of distance between them. It can absorb up to ten times the caster's hit points trading each hit point for ten shield points. Castable once per hour. While active the ally is locked inside and cannot disperse the shield before the caster allows it, or the caster dies.

Cost: 25 Mana + Hit Points traded for Shield

Note: Shield of Power is limited to a maximum of 200 Hit Points at current level of Skill

Blunt Weapons (Level 7)

Mana Purification (Level 2)

Analyze (Level 5)

Enables the ability to see another being's name, statistics, Class, and abilities to certain extents. May conflict with other Skills and abilities.

Note: Medium Perk may be used to allow Perk to be offered on a familial level.

Diviner (Level 2)

Permanent Passive ability. All Perception-based Skills increase 75% faster. Perception gains a 20-point boost, and you gain the Skill—Sense Motive—at Level 24. This will provide a contested chance (approximately a 50% chance using human subterfuge Skill-Level norms) to know when people are attempting to deceive you. Chance to divine increases with each Skill Level gained.

Mana Cloak (Level 6)

This is a passive ability that covers the body with a thin layer of ambient Mana, allowing the ability to sense surrounding Mana surges and mutations with greater accuracy. Works well in conjunction with Mana

Attunement. Can serve as a secondary Mana pool (100) if necessary. Full charge requires 2 hours of ambient Mana flow.

Note: This Cloak may be modified by the user and have a percentage of Mana regeneration from the user applied to it. The Cloak will upgrade accordingly.

Coocoon (Level 1)

Effect: Wraps your opponent in an earth cocoon for up to 42 seconds. This prevents them from moving, casting, or any combination of this. They will not regenerate Mana or Life while contained in the cocoon.

Mana Cost: 90 Mana

Equipments

Warhammer of the Orbtralon Chiefs

In order to access this item, an Orbtralon Chief, also known as Officer, must undergo several punishing trials which include besting his seven training officers in combat.

Weapon Stats Modifiers:

+10% of Strength

+5% of Constitution

+12% Mental Resistance

Weapon Requirements:

Strength: 26

Intelligence: 60

Perception: 50

Warhammer of the Orbtralon Chiefs' Ancestors

Weapon Ability

Note: Weapon must be actively equipped for this ability to be available.

Mana Forge

This hammer was forged in the Mana fires of the Orbtralon Ancestors longer ago than your piddly planet has existed. How a lowly Orbtralon Chief got a hold of it is a testament to how far they, as a species, have fallen.

This Warhammer blesses its wielder with the ability to take the Mana flow they can see and mold it directly into physical elements that this Warhammer will then utilize as it is wielded.

Warning: Be aware of the lure of Mana. It can grant you great power but demands a high cost in the process. Most Mana Forgers lose their minds.

Jacket of Reinforced Confidence

+ 5 Constitution

+ 20 Mana

Activate: Stealth Spelled

You must remain still for this stealth spell to work. Any movement other than breathing will reveal your location.

Duration: 30 seconds

Recharge: 90 minutes.

Dermal Underarmor

This thin layer of super-strong, under-skin protection can be enhanced and upgraded through Artisan-based Skills, providing a less bulky and always-present layer of added protection equal to 800 physical defense, 250 Mana defense. Can be damaged. Regenerates damage from ambient Mana within the vicinity over a period of 32 minutes.

Dermal Underarmor - Upgraded (Level 2)

This thin layer of super-strong, under-skin protection has been enhanced and upgraded through Artisan-based Skills up to Level 2. It provides a more refined and always-present layer of added protection equal to 950 physical defense, 300 Mana defense, and 50% stunning effect resistance.

Due to dermal sheathing disrupting external, unsafe Mana Flow and System-Assisted Skills along with a boost in confidence due to increased safety level, this upgrade increases Mental Resistance by 5%.

Can be damaged. Regenerates damage from ambient Mana over a period of 29 standard minutes.

To learn more about LitRPG, talk to authors including myself, and just have an awesome time, please join the LitRPG Group!

https://www.facebook.com/groups/LitRPGGroup/